THE BUTANE GOSPEL

Michael W. Hinkle

The Butane Gospel

Published by Wheatmark®
610 East Delano Street, Suite 104
Tucson, Arizona 85705 U.S.A.
www.wheatmark.com

International Standard Book Number: 978-1-60494-409-9
Library of Congress Control Number: 2009940458

TAPE 1

Okay. The red light's on, so that means this thing is recording, right? Okay. My name's Leon Butane. My friends call me Buzz. Today is Saturday, March 3, 2007, and I'm sitting in the backseat of this Dodge pickup cab heading south from Kansas City. I'm talking to this dictating gizmo because my time's running out and it's important for me to get my side of this out in case—you know—I'm not around after midnight tomorrow. You probably heard some stuff on TV or read about it in the papers and tabloids. But most of it's bullshit and I need to get everything straight, in my own words so the media freaks and religious freaks and whatnot don't have the final say. Let me just start by saying I never claimed to be a miracle worker or faith healer or prophet or nothing like that. I'm just a truck driver that drove into a shit storm that got out of control.

So I'm just going to settle in, take my time, pour myself a drink, and tell the whole story real methodical, to this red-eyed, dictating gizmo. Now I don't know who's going to be listening to all this, so I'm gonna apologize up front. It ain't my aim to offend or embarass anybody here, but the only way I know how to tell it is straight up. I guess they're going to feed these tapes into a voice recognizable deal, but they tell me it won't clean up my language none. So I'll try to tone it down. But you know how it is, once you get rolling, what comes out comes out. So here it goes.

The whole nightmare got started when my tanker jackknifed and my eyeball got knocked out again.

It was Tuesday, January 9, 2007. Just after dark, I was cruising east on Highway 9 headed for Tecumseh, Oklahoma, with a tanker load of fuel for

Love's Country Store. The opening riff of Steely Dan's "Do it Again" was playing on Nadine's sound system. That's what I called my rig—Nadine. Don't ask me why. It just seemed like that's what she ought to be called.

I was looking forward to offloading the fuel and getting home to my acreage just east of Jones, Oklahoma. I had it all figured how I was going to line up some John Wayne DVDs, lay in a supply of pizza, get a case of Coors in the icebox, and enjoy a laid-back weekend. Everything was pointing to an easy, gremlin-free mission. Nadine was purring like a well-fed puma, the road was clear, the music was good, and I was happy at the wheel. Nadine's got a damn fine pair of high beams and I didn't see any need to be anything but satisfied. Then it was like Mother Nature threw a giant monkey wrench in the program. This Angus cow and her calf just popped up like magic and stepped out in the middle of Nadine's headlights. They were just strolling my way in the eastbound lane, carefree as you please. I'd have probably been better off just plowing straight ahead and making chili meat out of both of them. But instead, I jammed on the air brakes and laid into Nadine's horn, hoping to scare those half-wit bovines off the damn road. Last I saw of mama cow, she was trotting north, relaxed as you please, with her calf close behind. I bet they got over on the north shoulder and stood there leaning on each other smiling with their cow faces and watching the Friday night fun. But believe me; I wasn't having any fun at all. No sir.

I felt like I was getting sucked into a slow-motion twilight zone watching the trailer lights on the tanker sweeping toward me out of the dark. The normal universe was unraveling in front of my eye, because the tanker took over being the driver and started steering the cab in a plumb out-of-control clockwise spin. It popped into my head: *This is probably what the end of the world will feel like. Your brakes fail. There goes your steering; your lane lines disappear; and all you see in your headlights is prairie grass, barbed wire, and stunted cedars. It'll end with you looking everywhere for a road that ain't there anymore.*

Anyone's who's ever been in a bad wreck probably knows how quick the world can get turned inside out. One minute you're a working man proud of your good health, happy disposition, and clean driving record. You blink your eye, the rules get all scrambled, and you're alone on a rodeo ride in the dark. There's not a goddamn thing you can do but waste your time holding onto the wheel. Steely Dan kept right on singing about wheels turning round and round, completely tuned out to the fact that I was in the middle of a disaster.

I didn't see the first fence post bust through the passenger side window, because that's the side my cryolite eyeball is on. It was no use really, but I couldn't help fighting the wheel. I was sure hoping the fuel wouldn't explode and cook me like a sausage patty. But that thought got crowded out when I found myself floating weightless, because Nadine started rolling over. Then there was a crash that sounded like it was coming from a far-off reverb chamber. Broken glass was floating around in the cab like sparkly confetti. Then, I wasn't weightless anymore. I crumpled onto the roof, because Nadine was upside down sliding. Woody splinters and grassy debris were crowding through the broken windows and lashing at my hands, arms, and face. It was like some part of Vietnam was just waiting for this minute so it could reach out and whip my ass like old times.

I turned weightless again, and Steely Dan's vocals got cut off. At that second, I stopped thinking of her as Nadine and started thinking of her as nothing but a gol' darn upside-down rig. The driver's side of the cab screeched against something real big and hard. There was a bright orange explosion, and that's when I thought my life was going to pass before my eye. It didn't.

Instead, real as I'm sitting here, I was in uniform, walking through a haze in the lobby of the Grande Coloniale Hotel in Saigon. I could smell flowers and strawberries. It was the only place in Saigon I ever found that didn't smell like the rest of the city. At first, I thought I saw an angel walking toward me across the lobby. But it wasn't. It was this real pretty Vietnamese lady. She floated past me with a fancy parasol on her shoulder. She glanced at me and smiled before she dropped the parasol to cover her face. Then she disappeared into a fading orange light. Before I had a chance to figure out what was going on, everything morphed back into that nightmare cab crashing through the dark.

The sound of grinding and growling poured over from the passenger side, and I tried to turn my head to see what was going on. I couldn't though, because there was a dull pressure on the right side of my face. That's when my cryolite eyeball came flying by me in slow motion. It looked like it was just circling in front of my face like something in orbit, just a sightless, orphan eyeball drifting away from me in the dark; an eyeball-looking moon sped up by time-lapse photography. Nothing was making sense, and I didn't care because the last lights in the world went out.

Everything was deep-cave dark, but I could hear music. It wasn't an angel choir or anything like that. I was thinking, *I hope this isn't what you hear if you're about to wake up in hell.* It took me a second, but I figured out it was the music from a movie called *Waking Ned Devine,* when Jackie was flying over the ocean, just before he wound up in a rowboat talking to Ned after Ned was already dead. I couldn't see anything, because there was fog hanging all over the universe. It started to blow away and stuff was getting visible. Then, there I was, floating and looking down at my own self stretched out on an operating table with medical people all over me like crawdads on bacon. I could hear a monitor beeping, and I knew it was keeping track of my heartbeat—or the heartbeat of the part of me down there on the table.

I really didn't feel like I had much of a stake in what was going on in that operating room. I mean, as far as I was concerned, the guy on the table could pull through or not and it wouldn't make any real difference to me. Then I saw this tunnel open up in the corner of the room. Sure enough, there was a golden light at the end of it that made me want to follow wherever it went. Everybody's heard about this is the kind of thing happening when you die. I knew I should get scared, you know, death and all. But I didn't. I just went along with the drift, feeling warm and happy about my prospects. I floated into the tunnel and left the medical team, their monitors, and their patient behind.

The last thing I heard as I drifted away from the operating room was a speed up in the monitor beeping and somebody saying something about "tacky cards." That didn't mean shit to me. I was ready to get to the end of the tunnel and step out into the bright lights of heaven above, because at that minute I was sure that's where I was headed. You couldn't feel so light and pleasant and be hell bound. You know what I thought? I thought heaven was going to be like Las Vegas on steroids, you know, nonstop fun and entertainment. But when I got to the tunnel's end, I didn't step out into glory like I expected. I got my ass dropped. Hard. And I didn't find anything like Vegas or even Disneyland. What I found was dirt.

I rolled to a stop and raised my head to look around. I knew right away where I was. I've been there a lot over the years. I was looking east across the lake on the southeast corner of the Oklahoma City Zoo. Over my left shoulder was a three-story wire cage with a big ass fisher eagle staring down at me from a great big nest he built high up in there. I didn't like the way that big, brown, predator bird was eyeballing me and not moving a feather. It was like he was a judge getting ready to pass out a sentence, with me being the defendant. I started looking around for a way out. I could see oaks and hackberries, and I knew by the colors it wasn't winter anymore. It was fall. The sun was up over my left shoulder, so that meant it was early afternoon. I didn't know what all this had to do with being dead. I knew that if I was dead, there wouldn't be any use in running, would there? But I was pretty sure that's what I was—dead.

Anyway, I ruled out heaven for two reasons. First, my right eye was still gone. From what I've heard, in heaven, I was supposed to get that back. No dice here. Then there was the smell. I don't remember anybody ever saying what heaven is supposed to smell like, but I was pretty damn sure it wasn't supposed to stink. I started looking around to see where the awful vapors were coming from. Turned out it was rhino shit. There was a big, old, gray rhino standing still as Mount Rushmore, except his lower jaw was moving back and forth, working and reworking a mouth full of hay. You don't expect to see or smell stuff like that if you're in heaven.

I sat up and dusted myself off. I was surprised to find I was wearing a pressed pair of blue jeans and a starched blue work shirt. No boots though. When I looked down at my hands, there wasn't a trace of grease under my nails. Somewhere along the way to the zoo, somebody must've buffed me up good and forgot to give me back my footwear.

I was thirsty though, real thirsty. In fact, I was so dang thirsty, I wanted to jump over the fence down by the lake and get me a drink. None of this was making any sense, and I was paging through the whole playbook trying to come up with an explanation that would give me some satisfaction. This had to be a LSD flashback, the whole gol' dang mind scramble. That's about the only answer I could dream up. I'll be honest here. I've enjoyed a flashback or two in my life. But usually when I get one, it just makes ice cubes in a glass of vodka turn purple or a bank teller turn into a cartoon clown. But your normal flashback doesn't take over the whole damn world like this, and it only lasts a minute or two. If that's what this was, if this was just a flashback, it was the grandmother of all gol' darn flashbacks, and I sure as hell was looking forward to it being over.

I staggered up to my feet and found that my legs were wobbly. That's when I saw those three sitting at the picnic table staring at me. The sight of them shook me up so bad that my poor feeble legs almost dropped my ass back into the dirt where I started. I blinked a few times and rubbed my eye, but they were still right there—Jack Benny, Ho Chi Minh, and Pinocchio. No part of them moved but their blinking eyelids. After I got used to the shock, I tried to speak up so I could ask somebody what the hell was going on, but that damned old dry throat of mine let me down and nothing came out.

That's when Jack stuck his hand out and offered me a snow cone, a cherry snow cone. Quite a coincidence, see, because that's my favorite flavor. Gradually, I started feeling myself getting encouraged even though my instincts were telling me to stay on my toes. I sort of crept forward on my unsteady legs and took the snow cone. Jack gave me a real kindly smile. Naturally, I gave him one back. Pinocchio's wooden eyelids moved up and down real slow. Ho was taking long drags off a cigarette and just sat there staring off across the lake. I took a sniff of the snow cone to see if there was any chemical or petroleum smell to it. But the only thing that drifted up was the cool smell of cherries. It was real refreshing to my nostrils. In fact, it was heavenly. That's the word that came dancing real happy-like into my head. Heavenly.

Still I didn't want to do anything hasty, being as I'm a conservative and all. So I barely touched the tip of my tongue to the top of that cone. I was relieved to find it was really cool and flavorful. I was about ready to dig right in, but then I thought I better take it nice and easy. I sniffed again. Still heavenly. I took a tiny little bite and I got washed all over by a wave of cherry-flavored pleasure. I gave Jack a big grin, and a croaking sound came out of my sandpaper throat. "Much obliged there, Jack." And I helped myself to a man-sized bite. Sure enough. Heavenly!

There were tasty little cherry explosions going off all over my mouth and sending cool relief down to my parched throat. *What would be wrong if it turned out that being in heaven meant finding three new chums at the Oklahoma City Zoo and enjoying the best damn snow cone in the universe for all eternity?* I reckoned if a fella had eternity to work on it, he'd get used to the rhino smell. I decided to keep an open mind.

I took another big old bite and since my throat was getting lubricated, I started to say something. Then, like a gol' darn lightning strike, the most crushing, cruelest, painful brain freeze you can imagine forced my jaws to clench and drove me right to my damn knees. I stayed down there with my eye closed until the pain eased up. It seemed like it took a long time; could have been years for all I know. When I could get my eye focused again, I started working myself back up on my feet.

You can bet your ass that I made a real close inspection of that damn snow cone. I touched it again with the tip of my tongue. It was good, but it wasn't heavenly anymore, because I was suspicious. I took a tiny nibble.

Sure enough, I got slammed back to my knees by another cruel-ass brain freeze.

Naturally that started me thinking about hell. *So this is what hell is; everlasting boredom with a bunch of speechless dummies surrounded by rhino gas and the mother of all deceitful damn snow cones teasing then betraying you for eternity. The worse you want some more of that cone, the harder it kicks your ass if you take it. What a bummer.*

There was a fifty-five gallon trash drum on the other side of the picnic table and I launched that good-for-nothing snow cone for a perfect two pointer. I adjusted the belt on my pressed britches and glared at all three of them with my one good eye. "Okay, boys. I need somebody to speak up and tell me what the hell's going on here." I was caught plumb off guard when it was Pinocchio who spoke up, and I'll be damned if he didn't sound like a full-grown college professor.

"I'm sorry about the snow cone, Mr. Butane. It was meant to be a friendly gesture. Honestly, I didn't know it would backfire like that. I hope it won't be a distraction, because I really need your close attention to what I'm going to say."

"Well I don't hear any apologies pouring out of Jack here, and he's the guy that handed me the infernal thing. How about it Jack? Did you know you were handing me a cone full of torments?" Jack just gave me a friendly smile and shrugged.

"He can't tell you anything, Mr. Butane. Neither can our other friend sitting here on my left. They're just here to help me make a point, which I'm going to explain later."

One thing that drives you crazy about carrying on a serious conversation with a puppet is they can't do much by way of expression. You can't read 'em. So when he was giving me the all-over eyeball, I couldn't tell diddly about what he was thinking.

After a minute or two of quiet, he said, "Would you like to sit down, Mr. Butane? You must be disoriented, and it might help you concentrate if you don't have to deal with so many—shall we say—confusing physical sensations."

I knew he was right about that—the sensations and stuff. The ones I'd been having there recently hadn't been any damn help at all. So I decided to take a seat and see if we could get down to business. After I got myself settled on that hard ass concrete bench, I decided to take the initiative about getting everybody's cards on the table. "You're Pinocchio, aren't you?"

"Very good, Mr. Butane. I am Pinocchio."

"Good. Okay, for openers where am I, Pinocchio? And don't give me any bullshit about the Oklahoma City Zoo. I can see that. But I mean, am I dreaming, or am I dead? Is this heaven or hell? Is this the gol' dang twilight zone or a flashback? Am I in a monster movie or what? I need some information so I can figure out what to do next."

"You're not dead, Mr. Butane. Right now you're on an operating table at the Metro Methodist Medical Center across town from here. Whether you live or die depends on the decision you make in the next few minutes."

When I heard those words, I would have bet serious money that in another reality somewhere there was a heart monitor hooked up to an unconscious guy named Leon Butane, and that monitor was pinging like crazy.

I wonder if there is a limit to how much off-the-wall, horse hockey bullshit a guy can choke down in a ten-minute period. There's got to be a point when the weird-shit-o-meter red lines and you just sit there blinking, sucking your thumb, and thinking about Lassie or something. I was getting close. I made a real focused effort not to sound discombobulated.

"Okay. You're saying my body is still alive someplace, back in the operating room."

"Yes."

"And the me that's sitting here in these nice pressed clothes dealing with killer brain freeze and a talking puppet, this here's my soul or what?"

"You're in danger of overthinking the situation, Mr. Butane. You're really not equipped to get involved in complex existentials right at this moment. For our purposes here, it's really very simple. I will offer you a choice. If you opt for door number one, so to speak, you survive your surgery. Door number two, you don't."

Well you can see how a fellow would smell a rat when he hears a proposition like that. If I chose door number one, would I have to agree to live the rest of my life as a humpback or a vegetable or an albino or something? What kind of choice would make a guy say "Naw, I think I'd be better off just going ahead and choosing door number two and being dead." I wasn't enjoying the suspense.

"Okay, I'm listening. Roll it out. What are my choices?"

"Your survival depends on your agreement to discover the identities of the men crucified with Jesus."

Naturally I thought my ears were playing tricks on me. "You mean Jesus Christ?"

"Please, Mr. Butane. How many Jesuses do you know of that were crucified? Of course I mean Jesus Christ."

"You're joking, right? This is a hairy goddamn joke to see how much of this goofiness I'll put up with before I start busting shit up, like puppets for instance. Give me a gol' darn break here!"

He wagged his wooden finger at me. "You're making a grave error if you think this is a joke. And I'm serious when I tell you it's none of my concern which way you decide. I'm only here to give you your choice and get your answer."

"Well hell, it's written right there in the Bible, ain't it? The names of the guys crucified with Jesus Christ? It's just a matter of looking it up, ain't it? What's the catch?"

"It's not so simple Mr. Butane. If you agree to do this, I'm sure you're going to find it's a difficult task."

"Suppose I say 'kiss my ass. I'm not making a choice.'"

"If you don't choose, then you are, in effect, making a choice not to accept the offer. I'm afraid you will be choosing either way."

I was starting to feel surrounded. I figured it wouldn't hurt to probe the perimeter. "Let's just say for the sake of argument I don't play ball. So I croak. Everybody dies sooner or later. Do I stay here, go to heaven, go to hell, what?" Ho gave me a little smile and blew a smoke ring. Jack didn't do anything except stare, and Pinocchio acted like he was sighing—which he wasn't because there aren't any working wooden lungs under his little painted overalls.

"I'm afraid you're just going to have to take your chances. I really have no information to give you on that score."

At that point, I sort of lost control. "Now wait just a goddamn minute here. You can't just jerk a fella out of the cab of his truck, slam him down on a operating table somewhere, spit his thinking self out in the middle of a goddamn zoo, tell him he's going to die if he don't agree to some harebrained snipe chase, and then just clam up and tell him he ain't entitled to any goddamn information. That's not fair, goddammit!"

The puppet heaved another fake sigh. "Please pay attention, this is not a debate. I'm not here to make explanations even if I wanted to. And do yourself a favor. Don't bother making appeals to fairness. You don't have and can't get the quantity of data you would need to make an informed judgment about what is and is not fair in your case even according to your myopic standards. If I may say, in light of the apathetic life you've lived, it's a little late for you to credibly raise the fairness issue. You must concentrate on the matter at hand, Mr. Butane. You don't have much time."

He was right you know. I outran any claim to fairness when I came out of Nam alive and walking. Something told me he was holding a lot more cards than he was showing. "Okay, buddy. Look, I don't understand any of this, but I'm going to play ball for now. I know I'm wasting my time asking this. But why does this have to be a Jesus deal? I don't know shit about religion. I'm not even sure I could find the names of these guys if they were written down in the Bible in block letters. Cut me some slack here. Ain't there some other puzzle that needs solving? Something that makes sense, for crying out loud."

"I'm sorry, Mr. Butane. This is, what you'd call, a take-it-or-leave-it proposition. There will be no negotiation. I really must have your answer. The surgeon is reaching the critical point in your operation."

"Hold on here now, can't you? Okay. What happens if I say 'Fine, I'll head out on this goose chase?' Suppose I make the deal now because I got no choice. Then later, when I wake up from this nightmare I decide to pull a double cross. What happens then?" The puppet nodded.

"That's a question I can answer for you. The vessels in your brain have been irreversibly compromised. One could rupture at any moment. If that happens, death will be sure and quick. No medical precautions and no treatments will save you. The moment you make the conscious decision to pull a double cross, as you say, your time will be up."

I got the picture. I didn't like it for shit, but I understood. Yep. If the puppet was shooting straight, I was boxed in and I knew it. I also knew being pissed off wouldn't get me a thing. But I couldn't help it.

"You sons of bitches knew exactly what I was going to do the second I got coughed out of that tunnel and into the dirt, didn't you? Choice my ass! You know goddamn well I got no choice. I got to make this deal. I can't run the risk that I might wind up in hell getting my ass scorched forever. Some gol' dang choice! Okay. Have it your way. I'll play your lame-ass game. Hell, that's all I can do, isn't it?"

All three of them nodded at the same time like their heads were on the same string. "You'll be happy to know you survived the surgery. You'll be in recovery soon. Now we have some housekeeping details to go over. First, your driving days are over. For the rest of your life—however long that may be—you will be subject to seizures. When that happens, you may lose consciousness. Obviously, you can't be driving when that occurs."

My controls got sucked into the spin cycle again. First, I was pissed. I mean really pissed. I wanted to grit my teeth and pound my fists on the table, the puppet, the commie, and maybe even the comedian. But then all the air went out of me and I could've started whining really easy.

"Now look you wooden prick. I'm a driver. I drive for a living. How am I supposed to put groceries on the table and pay the gol' dang light bill if I can't drive no more? Let me repeat! Goddammit, this is horseshit." When the puppet started talking again, it almost sounded like a threat.

"Do have a care, Mr. Butane. You must keep something in mind if you are to have any chance to come out of this with your life. First, you must know I'm not your problem. Indeed, you must consider the possibility that I may have information that might be of help to you. If you antagonize me, you may find it costly. So I must caution you. You would do well to mind your manners. Wooden prick indeed!"

"Sorry."

"Very good. I accept your apology. Now I must tell you if you are to have any chance of success, you must be alert and resourceful. You must not allow yourself to be taken off course by unproductive emotion. So listen. The neurosurgeon in charge of your care is a gifted physician. Feel free to tell him everything about this conversation. Tell anyone you choose. Your doctor will insist that nothing about this experience is real. He will attribute all this to the predictable after-effects of serious head trauma. He will urge you not to be concerned about our agreement. You will wish to be reassured. You will want to believe this is a dream or hallucination perhaps. But I must warn you in the strongest of terms. Don't yield to these persuasions. If you resign from this commitment, you will die." He sat there quiet, letting what he said sink in. It did.

"Okay? Now that's settled, you will have fourteen days to discover who was crucified with Jesus. The count will begin . . ."

I couldn't keep my mouth shut. "Now you just wait a minute you . . . you little . . . Pinocchio! You mean even if I do my dead level best to find out who these guys were and just can't do it, I'm going to die anyway? Jesus Christ! You might as well thunderbolt my ass right here, because I haven't got a prayer of coming out of this. Give me at least a month for crying out loud. Hell you guys know the answer to the question already. Right? What's the big gol' dang rush anyway?"

"Stop whining Mr. Butane . . ."

"I'm not whining. I'm just saying . . ."

"You're whining and it will do you no good. If you don't like the terms, reject the offer and take your chances. It's that simple."

"Okay. Go ahead with your song and dance. But just for the record I wasn't whining."

"The count will start on the morning after you wake up. Time will expire at midnight on the fourteenth day. No extensions, no appeals. Understand?"

"No, goddammit! I don't understand any of this horseshit. Somebody ought or be ashamed of himself for coming up with a cockeyed stunt like this."

"Come now Mr. Butane, you have no more business talking about shame than you did about fairness. To use the vernacular, you really don't want to go there." Of course, he was right again. I didn't need to be wading into any heart-to-hearts about shame and how to get out of it.

"Are we done here? Because I can't sit around jawboning with puppets and dummies all day. I've got to get busy wasting my time on a goose chase."

"You need to be sure you know everything I have to tell you before you charge off in all directions. You must find a way to compensate for your lack of education and training. You must find a way to make up for the shortcomings in your literacy. Frankly Mr. Butane, I have grave doubts about your prospects." I resisted the temptation to come back with a wise crack, but that's what he was expecting and I decided to start showing him how gol' dang smart I can be.

"Okay. I'm asking real nice. Do you have any help you can give me?"

"I'm glad you asked."

Smart ass.

"When you wake up, there will be a number of well intentioned bystanders who will offer to help you. They will propose an easy answer to your question. They will say 'We are all crucified with Christ.' This is not the answer you're looking for. You are searching for the names of actual men who suffered crucifixion in Jerusalem with Jesus of Nazareth. You must not allow yourself to be lured onto a sidetrack. Do you understand?"

"Okay, I got you. Real guys. Real dead. What else?"

"Now I'm going to provide you with some safeguards. These will come in handy at the outset of your endeavor." He jumped up like somebody gave his strings a yank. He clacked around in that jerky puppet walk until he was standing behind Jack. He put his little wooden hands up on the comedian's shoulders.

"You've been asking yourself what our two chatty friends have to do with all this. They're here to help you to this extent. You know this man as Jack Benny. But his real name is Benjamin Kubelsky." Now there was another shock. Not a big shock like some I had recently. But it was a shock. Of course I knew about stage names. I've known lots of strippers that had them. I just never thought about Jack having one.

"Kubelsky? That's his real name?"

"Right. Benjamin Kubelsky. Repeat it to be sure you have it."

So I repeated it. "Okay. Benjamin Kubelsky. I got it. I suppose our other pal here isn't Ho Chi Minh either."

"Right again Mr. Butane. But this will be a little more challenging." He made a clackety puppet walk over behind Ho and put his hands on the commie's shoulders just like he done with Jack or Kubelsky or whatever. "Let me introduce Nguyen Sinh Cung. Say it back to me a few times." He was right. That's harder. But he practiced me until I could spout it off the top of my head.

"Okay. Now I must tell you something about myself. You've seen the movie. You think the blue fairy transformed me into a real boy and I lived happily ever after. Unfortunately, however, I'm the original Pinocchio not the Disney version. And the original Pinocchio died a terrible death as punishment for his sins." He stood there for a minute looking at his little wooden feet. When I pictured the puppet kicking at the end of a rope, well, I couldn't help feeling sorry for the little guy. If it happened like he said, it's a pretty sad way for a little bitty puppet to wind up. When he looked up, I guess he was reading my face. "Don't waste time feeling sorry for me. You have problems of your own."

"Yeah. You're right. Thanks. Anything else?"

"Yes. I'm going to help you get started. You should begin your journey by paying a visit to your pastor cousin." It took me a minute.

"You mean cousin Augie?" Pinocchio covered his little wooden eyeballs with his little wooden hands.

"I'm afraid it's hopeless Mr. Butane. Maybe you should just give up right now. You have no chance if you don't think. Think Mr. Butane. It's your only hope. How many pastor cousins do you have? Of course I'm talking about your cousin Augie. Start with him."

You know I really did feel sort of stupid. Augie is the only pastor cousin

I know of. The puppet was just standing there shaking his head. Jack—or Kubelsky, or whatever—was looking at me like he was feeling sorry for me. Ho just sat there looking across the water and holding his cigarette in that weird way oriental commies do.

"Okay. Okay. I'll look the self-righteous son of a bitch up and talk with him. If there's anything else I need to know, I'm going to need a pencil and paper to write it all down. This shit's already getting complicated, and I'm not even started yet."

"Good idea. You don't strike me as a man who spent much time with pen and paper, but since you claim to be able to write, you should take notes. You might find it helpful."

"I'm warning you pine nuts. There's only so much abuse I can take from a puppet before I get the urge to make a wood pile. Are we winding up this interview or not?"

"Grow up Mr. Butane. You're wasting time. Remember this. It will be helpful. When your doctor is through explaining why none of this is real, and you start to feel like you want to believe him, say this, 'Izzy says he's sorry. Abraham was wrong.' Have you got it?"

"Say it again, pine turd."

"Izzy says he's sorry. Abraham was wrong."

"What the hell does that mean?"

"Never mind. Just remember it. Say it back to him just like I'm saying it to you. When you say those words, watch him closely. You will see what I mean. Say it back to me." I repeated it a couple of times, and he nodded.

"I'm going to say one more thing to you Mr. Butane. I really hope you make it." He made a jerky puppet gesture with his arms. "We all do." There was nothing about the way they were acting that made me think they were pulling for me. But it was his nightmare, so I just had to stand there and let him blab until he was through.

"Okay, it's time for you to go. Maybe I'll see you again later somewhere along the way. Goodbye, Mr. Butane, and good luck." They all bowed their heads and raised their right hands like they were going to wave. The whole thing disappeared in a flash of orange light and Ned Devine music.

TAPE 2

Okay I'm back. I'm supposed to be handing these tapes off one at a time so they can get labeled and kept in order so they'll be easier to translate when the time comes. So where was I? Oh yeah.

You've probably never woke up from a coma, but it isn't like other kinds of waking up. See, apart from sleeping, I've woke up from being knocked out, passed out, blown up, and anesthetized. But the coma deal isn't like any of them. First, you start hearing stuff, but it all sounds like gargling. Then you catch a word or two as people are changing your bed clothes and fluffing your pillow. Stuff like "Blah, blah, blah, changing, blah, blah yesterday." Then you start feeling things like your fingertips on the sheets. You can't open your eye, but you see a sort of deep-orange color on the inside of your eyelid. You really can't see anything yet, but you can tell by the voices that there are two or three nurses in there. You start to move your hands and feet a little bit. You're real thirsty, and you feel sort of like you want to roll over. But what really gets you to come around is when you find out you've got a tube snaked up your dick.

Now I'm sure they had a good reason for putting it in there. But when you've been through what I just went through—well, you're just not ready for that kind of invasion of privacy. You know what I mean?

Anyway, I was going to pull that puppy out of there, but I realized right quick that I wasn't qualified for the job. Who knows what might come out stuck to the other end of it?

When I was finally able to force my eye open I saw a nurse using a magic marker to make notes on a board thing hanging on the wall. I tried

15

to get her attention, but I couldn't because my throat was too dry. I wanted to swallow, but I couldn't find enough spit to do any good. So I just croaked over the dryness.

"Nurse? Hey nurse? Can you get me a glass of water and a Bible, and can you get this tube out of my—you know—my crank here?"

She stood there looking gut shot for a minute, and then went to flying around taking my pulse, my temperature, and blood pressure and stuff. Her name tag said she was Irene. Irene poured me some water, but my gol' dang neck was so rubbery she had to hold my head up so I could drink it. She checked my eye by making me watch her finger as she moved it back and forth in front of my face. I guess it's just automatic, but my right hand went up to check and see if my cryolite eyeball was in place. When I found out it wasn't, my hand stayed there to keep the hole covered up. After all these years, I'm still self-conscious about it.

One of the other nurses must have paged the doctor because the phone rang and it was him. Irene sounded real smart and professional when she gave him the run-down.

"Dr. Sugarman, this is Nurse Irene Grasso on L-TAC."

I found out later L-TAC means "Long-Term Acute Care."

"Mr. Butane woke up at 8:35 this morning. His vital signs are stable. He's afebrile and responsive. He's not completely oriented to time and place. He's requesting water, a Bible, and catheter removal." I guess the doctor was talking on the other end, because she got quiet.

She hung up the phone, and gave me some more water. "How are you feeling Mr. Butane? Can you move your arms and legs for me?" Hell, they all felt like they were made out of pig iron. I was able to move them a little bit, but I wasn't going to be dancing with no stars any time soon. The main thing was that my mind felt like it was hitting on all eight. I was glad to have that going for me.

"How long have I been in here Irene?" I was finally getting my eye to focus, so I could see that she was a tall, good looking woman with long brown hair. I figured her to be around forty-five. Her hands were smooth and cool, and the water she served up was the sweetest in the universe. I was really happy to wake up and find out she was my nurse.

"Dr. Sugarman is on his way. He'll answer all your questions. For now, though, do you think you can get up and get to the bathroom if I help you?

"Yeah, I think so."

"If you can do that, we can remove the catheter."

"Well in that case, the answer's sure as hell is yes, I can do it." She gave me a sweet smile and went to work fishing plastic out of my unit. It was sort of an intimate moment for me, but I got the idea it was just another chore in her work day. Story of my life. But she did it real professional like, and it was over before you could say *"Viva Las Vegas!"* Once our one second of romance was over with, I decided not to waste time being sentimental.

"Look here, Irene. I hate to start asking for favors so soon after we got introduced, but I really need your help on a couple of things. Is there someplace around here where you can get on a computer and look something up for me?" She straightened up and looked at me like I just switched languages to Filipino or something.

"Mr. Butane, you've been through a lot…"

"Call me Leon. I proposed to the first girl that touched me where you just did." She blushed a little bit.

"Well, Leon, in answer to your question. Yes, we have computer access. But it would really be better if you wait and get your information from Dr. Sugarman. He should be here very soon."

"What I need to know don't have anything to do with medicine. I'm tickled pink to get all the medical stuff from the doctor. I just need somebody to get on the computer and find out a couple of things for me. It's really important Irene. There's some stuff I need to know and I mean the sooner the better."

"Can't it wait until the doctor gets here?"

"Listen, Irene. I really need you to humor me here. I'm kinda touchy about time right now, and I'd feel a whole lot better if you'd agree to do this favor for me."

"Would you like me to raise the head of your bed?"

"No. I'd just like somebody to get on a computer someplace." She stood fiddling with a gold cross hanging around her neck.

"What do you need to know?"

"What was Jack Benny's real name? What was Ho Chi Minh's real name? What happened to Pinocchio? Not the Disney guy; I already know what happened to him. There might have been another Pinocchio before him, and I need to know what happened to that one. Come on Irene. I really need this as soon as I can find out. It ought to just take a few minutes on Google."

"Would you mind telling me what this is all about?"

"I will, I promise. Just not right now." I knew if I was to spill the whole can of beans right then, they'd probably wheel me straight to the psych ward. Her mouth opened like she was trying to get another question out. She looked at me. She looked at the clock on the wall. She looked at me again. Then her tender heart got the best of her.

"Okay, Leon. If it will help you relax. I'll be back in a few minutes. If I see the doctor coming, though, I'll have to stop what I'm doing because I need to be here while he's talking to you. Is that good enough for now?"

"You bet, Irene, and thanks. I'm falling deeper in love by the minute. I'll probably wind up asking you to go steady before I get out of here." She smiled her school teacher smile and headed for the door. "And don't forget the Bible Irene. I need to look some stuff up." She waved without looking back and disappeared into the hallway.

A few minutes later, she came back carrying a note pad and a Bible. I listened while Irene read off her notes. Sure enough, that part of what the puppet laid out was dead on. Jack Benny is Benjamin Kubelsky. Ho Chi Minh is Nguyen Sinh Cung and the original Pinocchio got strung up. While Irene was reading it off to me, I looked up and seen this fellow standing at the door. He was combed and polished like he just stepped off the page of a top-dollar vodka ad. He stood there polite like, listening to Irene telling me about comedians, commies, and puppets. She brought the Bible over and put it on the table by the bed. Then she reached over and patted my hand. That's when the fashion guy at the door did a phony cough to get her attention. It worked, because she jerked like she'd been hit with a cattle prod.

"Oh, Doctor Sugarman. I didn't see you there ... I was ..."

"I'll need the chart Nurse Grasso." The voice didn't go with the rest of him. He sounded like a kid.

"Of course, right away, Doctor." He stepped aside to let her out of the room. Then he came over and gave me a once-over like Irene done.

He took a seat there by the bed "Good morning, Mr. Butane. I'm Dr. Sugarman. I'm happy to see you so alert and responsive. No one really knew exactly what to expect. Tell me how you're feeling."

"Well, now that I've had some water and Irene's untethered me from that tube, I'm feeling better and more dignified."

Irene walked back and handed him a plastic clipboard. Everything got quiet in the room while Dr. Sugarman read over the chart like he was performing for an audience. Then he asked in his odd kid voice, "Tell me,

Mr. Butane. What's so important about Pinocchio that you would want to discuss him so soon after coming out of a forty-day coma?"

I laid there blinking for a second or two. "My ears must be playing tricks on me doc, because I thought I just heard you say I was in a coma for forty days. See, that's funny because I just saw you working on me in the operating room less than an hour ago."

"No Mr. Butane. You were brought here by Mediflight on January 9, and today is February 18. That's forty days by my count."

"Holy shit! You mean more than a month disappeared and I slept through the gol' darned Super Bowl?"

"It's true Mr. Butane. You've been here in L-TAC for over a month." While I was trying to fit everything together where it would make sense, he told me all about having bone fragments pushing on my brain. Those fragments caused swelling, and I was in danger of having a brain hernia, where everything inside my skull got pushed down to my Adam's apple. If they didn't release the pressure, I'd die or stay in the coma or wake up crippled or a brain-damaged vegetable for the rest of my life. I didn't hear all of it, because I was laying there mentally out of focus. I've had a night or two disappear on me. But this guy said I lost a whole forty damn days.

When I was able to get on beam again, I could see the doc was watching me real close. "Don't worry if you're feeling disoriented, Mr. Butane. Actually, considering what you've been through, I'm surprised you're functioning as normally as you seem to be."

So I said, "Oh yeah? Well how normal is this?" Then I unspun the whole Pinocchio deal starting with me watching the doc and his surgical crew working me over in the operating room. He sat there with a serious look on his face making notes in my chart. Irene stood behind him paying close attention to every word I said like I was a hypnotist or something, and all she was hearing was the sound of my voice.

Every so often, Dr. Sugarman would stop me and ask a question. Like did I notice any odd smells? Were there any colors that stood out? Was I tingling or numb? Was there pain? Stuff like that.

When I got through, he sat back with a real intelligent look on his Hollywood face and started spouting off like he was Doogie Howser.

"Mr. Butane, I'm going to call you Leon. Is that okay? Leon, the brain is a very mysterious organ. We know that consciousness and self-awareness are centered there; but we're only just beginning to get a handle on how everything works together. We know we can manipulate perception and emotion with electric stimulation and psychotropics. We know the brain can be altered by trauma. How one relates to external reality is a lot more plastic than you might think. We're making progress, but we're still unclear about how information is acquired, arranged, and retrieved. We do know that brain trauma, the kind of trauma that you experienced, can cause unpredictable mental effects. We've seen profound personality changes—short-term and permanent. We've had patients that experienced hallucinations—some quite bizarre—that were as real to the patient as the conversation you and I are having now. Completely imaginary. But if you administer a polygraph examination, there would be every indication that their experience was real."

"Okay, Doc. Yes or no. The puppet told me I'm going to have seizures for the rest of my life. Is that true? Are my truck driving days over?" His face got a little red.

He looked over at Irene and she shook her head like, "I swear I didn't say anything about it." He cleared his throat.

"We don't know, Leon. It's too early to say. But I'm afraid the most likely answer is yes. You're at risk for seizures for the rest of your life."

"So that part of what the puppet said was real, right? So how do you explain the fact that I got my first important medical advice from an imaginary puppet?"

"It's complicated Leon. I don't remember talking about that part of your prognosis in your presence during your coma. But I may have. It might have been mentioned in the operating room. There have been nurses and residents in and out of your room. Someone else may have made a casual comment. We really don't know what your brain did with incoming information while you were comatose. We know now that the brain can continue to process information even though a patient is in a permanent vegetative state. Someone must have said something, and at some level, your brain registered it."

"Okay. What about this information on Jack, Ho, and Pinocchio? I didn't know any of that before the accident. Where'd I get that from? Don't tell me some nurses and doctors was just standing around my bed and chatting about that off-the-wall shit and my unconscious brain decided to grab it and hang on. You heard Irene lay out the facts about Jack, Ho, and the puppet the same time I did. How do you explain the fact Pinocchio was right about that stuff too?"

"You must have had that information buried in a reservoir of discarded information that wouldn't be accessible under normal circumstances. Your injury caused these facts to bubble up to the surface. Believe me, Leon, we see this kind of thing all the time. I'm giving you my word. You don't need to have any anxiety about who was crucified with Jesus. You just need to worry about getting well and adjusting to the residual effects of your injuries."

"Like what effects?" He looked at his watch.

"There will be plenty of time talk about all of that when we have a clearer picture of your condition. Then we'll work with physical therapists, occupational therapists, and others if necessary to help you make the required adjustments."

Everything he was said made sense. I mean, if you got a choice between believing what you hear from a talking puppet while you're unconscious, and believing what you hear from a bona fide, high-powered Hollywood-looking brain doc who sees this kind of shit all the time—well you'd think your money would be on the doc.

I was starting to get happy thinking that the whole Oklahoma City Zoo deal was just an ultraweird, too-real, busted-brain mind scramble. None of that shit happened, and I came up with all this Trivial Pursuits information about Ho and whatnot because I had this mystery brain reservoir where I knew more stuff than I knew.

But then I got this creepy kind of chill. Didn't the puppet tell me my doctor would try to talk me out of believing the deal was on the level? Didn't he tell me if I bought it, I'd die? I almost forgot. So after the doc patted me on the shoulder and headed for the door, I stopped him.

"There's just one more thing doc. Pinocchio told me to give you a message." He turned back toward me in the doorway. But he wasn't looking my way. He was writing in the chart.

"Really? And what was the message?"

"He told me to tell you 'Izzy is sorry. Abraham was wrong.'" He froze solid. His eyes locked on me like a laser. His mouth started, coming unfrozen after a minute, but nothing came out at first. He sure enough looked bowled over. Irene acted like she was going to walk over and give him a hand or something but he shook his head and stayed locked on me. I was right back to believing that damn puppet again.

Words started coming out of Dr. Sugarman's mouth in a whispery sound. "Say that again, would you Leon?" So I repeated it. He looked a little unsteady when he walked back over and sat down real slow in the chair there at the bedside. His eyes were still zeroed in on me. "Why did you say that?"

"I told you. The puppet told me to give you that message if I started getting persuaded that it was all my imagination. Looks to me like he really hit a sore spot, huh? What does that Izzy and Abraham stuff mean?" He put the chart down and just sat there looking at his hands. He was using his finger to trace around the face of his watch. He started shaking his head real slow, and he was sort of mumbling.

"There's no way. There's just no way." Then he looked up at me with a real hard-to-read expression on his face. "My father gave me this watch, Leon. He got it as a graduation present from his father when he finished medical school. My father gave it to me for safe keeping on the day he left. I was just a child. I never saw him again. Have you ever heard of a place called Hizayon, Leon?"

"Never heard of it. Why?"

"Well, on October 8, 1973, my father died there. He left us to go join the Israeli army, and that's where he died. If we didn't have pictures, I wouldn't even remember what he looked like. You know what I remember? I remember him feeding me a load of poppycock about why he was leaving us. You know the Abraham story Leon?"

"You mean like in the *Ten Commandments* movie?"

"No. That was Moses. This is another story. God told Abraham to take his son up on a mountain. He was to take the boy up there and cut his throat, drain his blood, and burn his remains."

"Holy cow, doc! I'm no Bible expert or nothing, but surely that ain't in there—is it?"

"It is, Leon. In the Bible, God sends an angel to stop Abraham from killing the boy."

"Okay, now that's ringing a bell. Abraham didn't go through with the killing after all, right?"

"That's right, Leon. But for the rest of the boy's life, he could never forget the fact that his father was willing to put a knife to his own son's throat. How hard would that be to live with, do you think?"

"I don't know, Doc. Pretty tough, I guess. Still, I say all's well that ends well. But I'm not following how all this relates to the puppet's message."

"My father's name was Isadore, Leon. Everyone called him Izzy. I haven't mentioned him in years. There's no way you could have known."

I can't tell you what I saw in the doc's eyes as he sat there staring a hole in me and running his finger around and around his watch. All I can say is, it damn sure gave me chicken skin.

Dr. Sugarman was in a daze when he picked up the chart and wandered by the foot of my bed on his way out. He didn't pay any attention to Irene at all. But I did. She was standing there, white faced and frozen, watching the doc drift out of the room and down the hall. After he was gone, she looked over at me like I was pulling gold fish out of my ears with both hands. Then, like a reflex or something, she reached up and did that thing on her forehead and shoulders like Catholics do.

I decided to change the subject. "Irene. Irene, darlin'. Snap out of it. I need to ask you for some more help here." She blinked a few times and snapped out of it like I told her. "Can you tell me whether they rescued my eyeball from the wreck? I'm a little self-conscious about laying around in broad daylight with this hole in my face hanging out."

She smiled all sheepish like. "It's in the drawer there by the bedside along with the other things they brought in with you. Here, I'll get it for you." She hurried over to the table and took out a plastic bag that had my cryolite eyeball, my wallet, my Chisholm Oaks High School class ring, and what was left of my watch.

I held out my hand for the eyeball, but she wouldn't give it to me. She had to clean it first. She went to work scrubbing and disinfecting the hell out of it chattering away like she was nervous or something. She told me about the cards and flowers and stuff that folks kept sending to my room and about the people who dropped in to check on me. Mostly it was my little sister, Wanda, who came by every day on her way home from work.

Wanda. As soon as she mentioned Wanda's name, I started feeling guilty, because I hadn't thought about her one time since I woke up. I wasn't one bit surprised to find out Wanda showed up to look me over every day.

"What day of the week is it?"

"I guess you would be little out of touch after forty days in a coma. It's Sunday."

"When does Wanda usually come on Sundays?"

"It's usually about 5:00." I looked at the clock and it was a little after nine-thirty. I was glad there wasn't anything wrong with my memory, as I was able to call Wanda's home and cell numbers. No answer. Probably at church. I left messages at both numbers.

Irene asked if there was anything I needed right then. "I'd just like to know who got crucified with Jesus." I noticed as she was standing there looking at me, she kept touching that little gold cross around her neck. I figured I was wasting my time, but I just thought I'd ask. "You don't have any ideas who they were, I guess."

"It was two thieves, wasn't it?"

"Well, that's all I ever heard."

She shrugged. "I'm afraid that's all I know. If their names are in the Bible, I've never heard them mentioned."

"Okay. I guess I'll just dig around and see what I can find."

"Do you want me to turn off the TV?"

"No. Just turn off the sound." It was tuned to CNN, and there was something on the crawler about bombs going off in Iraq and Anna Nicole being dead.

Irene hung around the door a second or two looking at me with a puzzled look on her face. Then she disappeared to go do nursing stuff. I sat there with her Bible on my chest just looking at it. For the first time in my life, I got impressed by what a thick damn book it is. For a second there, I didn't have the first idea where to start looking. I knew the Bible was laid out in two parts—the Old Testament and the New Testament. I knew that the story of Jesus was in the New Testament. So I figured I'd start there. Soon as I opened it up, I remembered there were four Gospels—Matthew, Mark, Luke, and John, and I thought I remembered that the story of Jesus' life was mostly in those gospels.

Since Matthew was the first, that's where I started. Logical. Here's some more logic. Since the first part of Matthew is all about Jesus being born, the crucifixion part would be at the end. So that's where I turned. It was really pretty easy finding the right spot, because there were headings at the beginning of every story. I didn't have any problem finding the part that said "The Crucifixion." I guess I was sort of hoping that I'd get there and "Abracadabra!" there the names would be. No dice. But I damn sure wasn't ready for what I did find.

Right there at Matthew 27:38 it said that Jesus was crucified between two revolutionaries! No shit! Revolutionaries! Naturally I thought this was some kind of misprint or something. So then I turned to Mark, and sure enough, right there at 15:27 it says the same thing. They were revolutionaries. Now I'm no Bible expert, but to me, there's a big difference between being a thief and a revolutionary. Hell, the father of our dang country was a revolutionary, wasn't he? That sure as hell didn't make him a thief.

I figured something was wrong, but I didn't know how that was going to figure into my problem. There were still Luke and John. Well, all Luke says at 23:32 is that the other two guys were criminals. Meaning, I guess, that they could have been thieves or rebels or forgers or jaywalkers or any kind of damn outlaw. Big help there. But then, when I turned over to John, all he said at 19:18 was that there were two others. Hell, as far as John's concerned, these other two guys could have been as innocent as Jesus. Now I guess if you put all four of these gospels together, there's a way to make things add up. A revolutionary could be a thief too, and a thief is a criminal, and they were other men. So I figured, you know, a rose by another name, right?

Bottom line was, I had labels but no names. Maybe those names was buried someplace else in the New Testament, but before I could get my mind focused on it, I started building up a monster headache. I rang the nurse button, and Irene came in.

I told her about the headache, and she stuck a hypo into the gizmo attached to my IV. The headache started to back off, and a warm feeling started to wash all over me. I eased back on my pillow and just let it happen.

That's when a weird yellow light started shining on the TV. You're going to hear more about that light later. After you've heard the whole story, you may believe it was just a natural by-product of my head injury; you might think it's supernatural. I don't know. To be honest, at the time, I thought it was because of Irene's hypo.

Anyway, this light started shining on the TV, but not all of it, just the one word—*insurgents*. I was staring at it like I was hypnotized or something. Every time the word *insurgents* rolled across the bottom of the screen, it ran in slow motion and there was this soft gold spotlight on it. And it morphed right in front of my eye. It turned into *revolutionaries*. And I guess I drifted into a trance or something and an old familiar feeling started bubbling up from deep in my insides.

See, I went through a word-warp like this once before, when I was in Nam. When Woodrow and I got drafted—you're going to hear a lot more about Woodrow later—we was told we were going to Vietnam to fight the communists. They told us our reason for being there was to stand up for the rights of the Vietnamese people to decide for themselves what kind of government they wanted. According to what we was told, the people in South Vietnam wanted to be a democracy. The people in the North did too, for that matter. But the Russians and Chinese communists had a stranglehold on the North and were wanting to turn everybody in Asia into a communist. We had to stop them.

Well, I wasn't over there too long until I found out things was more complicated than that. There were some word games being played all over the place. First off, some of the people who turned out to be Viet Cong didn't know communism from cottage cheese. They just didn't like the idea that there were foreigners with guns running all over their country telling them what to do. When I thought about it, I had to admit I didn't blame them a bit for that. Hell, if the shoe was on the other foot and they were flying choppers and rolling tanks all over Oklahoma, I'd fight 'em. Bet your ass I would. Communism and democracy wouldn't have anything to do with it. So I could sort of see their point.

Now don't get me wrong. Some of them were communists for sure. But I couldn't tell the difference between those who were and those who weren't. So I couldn't get particular about why they were trying to waste my ass. In a firefight, it didn't matter whether they were communists or freedom fighters. Dead's dead no matter who is pulling the trigger or why they're pulling it.

From our way of thinking, the guys fighting on our side was the freedom fighters, because they were supposedly fighting to protect the freedom of the Vietnamese people. Know what the Viet Cong called our Vietnamese friends when they caught them? Traitors. Our freedom fighters were their traitors. So, when the chips was down, whether they were communists, freedom fighters, or choir boys, if it was going to be me or them, I was voting to elect them, and I didn't give a shit about the labels.

But just the same, we was calling them communists and they were calling themselves freedom fighters. As that crawler moved across the screen in slow motion with that soft gold light shining on it, my brain sort of opened up and I could see how, depending on your point of view, a freedom fighter could be a revolutionary. They could be the same damn thing. You start that hamster wheel turning, and no one can tell where revolutionary stops and insurgent starts, or where insurgent stops and freedom fighter starts. It just keeps rolling around and around. See what I mean?

I started feeling my heart beat faster because I was 90 percent sure this was important in some way, like a clue or something. I felt like I was blacking out and words kept circling around on the TV, the walls, the ceiling. Everywhere. *Thieves, revolutionaries, insurgents, freedom fighters.*

My teeth were clenched so hard that I was afraid my molars were going to bust. Then I felt a soft hand on my arm. It was Irene, and she had a real concerned look on her face.

"Are you all right?" She was checking my pulse and looking close into my eye. "You're pulse is rapid. Tell me how you're feeling."

I started to tell her I was fine when I saw this guy dressed in a priest suit looking over her shoulder. "I'm fine, Irene. I was just thinking about something. Who's your friend?"

"This is Father de Palma. He was on his way to see another patient and decided to stop in to have a word with you. Are you sure you're okay?"

"Yeah, I'm fine." I felt my heart slowing down, and I was glad to have somebody in there with me so I could stop chasing around word circles. Irene raised the head of the bed so I could get a better look at that priest fella. "So what can I do for you, Father de Palma? If you're in here to convert me, you'll have to check back later. I'm sort of in the middle of something."

He looked back and forth between me and Irene with a confused expression on his face. "No, no, Señor Butane. I am not here to convert you. I was hoping you could help me. But if this is not convenient, I can come back later." There were little sweat beads rolling out from under the bandages on my head, and I decided if I could get focused and keep talking, I could stay in control.

"No. Come on over and have a seat. I don't see how there's a thing I can do for you, but this might be a good time for some conversation."

Irene was keeping a concerned eye on me as she moved aside to make room for Father de Palma to sit down. He smiled when he saw Irene's Bible on the table there by the bed.

"You're a Catholic?"

"No. This here's Irene's." He looked over at her and I guess she thought she had to explain.

"Mr. Butane ... Leon ... asked for a Bible almost as soon as his eyes ... his eye ... was open. He was in a coma for over a month, Father."

His eyebrows went up. "This is true? After a month in a coma your first thoughts were of the Holy Book? This says much for the strength of your faith."

"No, no it wasn't like that at all. It's long and complicated. I'll tell you about it sometime. But you said you have something to ask me."

He pulled his chair up closer to the bed and lowered his voice. "Señor Butane, this may sound ... well, strange. But ..." He looked over his shoulder at Irene. She got the hint.

"If you're sure you're all right, Leon, I'll leave you two alone. Be sure to push the call button if you need me." There was that wonderful smile again, and she floated out like an angel. The priest pulled his chair up even closer.

"Señor Butane. Is there something you wish to tell me?"

"What? You mean like a confession or something?"

"No, no. I mean… a message perhaps." I just laid there blinking and chasing down some mental rabbit trails to see if there might be a message for a priest I was supposed to pass along. If there was, it was just going to have to stay undelivered.

"No. I can't think of a thing. But I have to ask, what made you think I might have a message for you?"

He studied my face real hard like he was hoping there might be a tiny message written across my forehead. While he was eyeballing me, I was checking him out. He was probably about forty, with a neat, trimmed goatee. A little overfed I'd say. Looked like a nice fella. But his eyes were all red looking with dark circles under them, like he needed a night's sleep. He took a deep breath and leaned back in the chair looking disappointed. He mumbled a little bit like he was talking to himself.

"I am sure this is where my dream was leading me. I'm sure it was to this room." When he said that remark about his dream leading him to this room, the hair stood up on my arms. I already had enough weird shit to deal with without getting involved in a Catholic priest's voodoo dream.

"No, I'm sure of it fella. You might check at the nurse's desk, because as far as I know, there are no messages for you in here." He sat there shaking his head like he didn't hear me. He just kept sitting there until he started making me uncomfortable.

Then, real sudden like, he acted like he got an electric shock or something. He jerked to the edge of his seat and started looking me real hard again.

"Perhaps if I tell you something you may be able to help me see what it means."

"Look. I feel funny calling you 'Father' … no disrespect or nothing. It's just that I'd prefer to call you something else. Okay? You got a first name?"

"Haysuse."

"Okay if I call you Haysuse?"

"Of course, if you prefer."

"Great. Now look Haysuse. I can see on your face that you got stuff you're trying to work out. I wish I could help you. But if I was to tell you all the crap I got on my plate right now, you'd think I was crazy. I'm afraid you're going to have to get your message someplace else."

"Señor Butane, please forgive me. But I am certain I am here this morning for a purpose. I had hoped that you might be able to help me. But is it possible I am here to help you. Perhaps we are searching for the same answers."

I guess I was looking at him sort of squint-eyed. "You haven't had any recent conversations with anybody strange have you? Like, oh, say a puppet or something like that?"

His bloodshot eyes got bigger and redder. "Yes, Señor Butane. Yes, I had a strange conversation last night in my dream. It's because of that conversation that I am here. If you would permit me Señor Butane, I wish to tell you about it."

You remember me telling you about that weird light that was shining on the TV a minute ago? Well, that light started shining on Haysuse there. It was like somebody else was talking through my voice box.

"Tell me about your dream, Haysuse."

"Last night in my dream I was standing on a rocky hillside in Mexico. The wind was blowing sand in my eyes so it was difficult to see. I thought I saw someone struggling up the hill toward me. As this person drew near, I could see it was a woman, and I felt I must go down to help her. But my feet would not move. So I stood waiting for her. I wanted to tell her I was sorry for not reaching out to help. I was going to explain that I couldn't move. But before I could speak, I saw that the woman was my mother." He reached out and put his hand on my arm. "My mother has been dead for three years, Señor Butane. There was doubt in her heart at the end. Not about her faith, but about me. She was afraid I would forsake my vows. You see, it is because of the abominations in the brotherhood. The betrayals. So much perversion." He stopped talking and real absent-minded like he took a string of beads out of his coat pocket. Then he took a deep breath and started talking again. "But I was in prayer, Señor Butane. Constantly. I admit I was tempted to leave the priesthood, but I believed my faith would prevail in the end. I tried to reassure my mother, but her doubt remained and burdened her heart at the end. There was so much I wanted to say to her." He stopped talking and kept fooling with his beads.

"In my dream there were tears in my eyes from the sand and from the sadness for my mother. She drew nearer, and I could see she was carrying a basket. And I had even more sorrow, because I was unable to help her carry it. When she finally reached the place where I was standing, I tried again to speak, but she smiled at me and put her fingers to my lips. She removed the cloth from her basket and you know what was there, Señor Butane?"

I wasn't expecting for him to ask me any question so I wasn't ready with any answers. Irene walked in about then, and I looked over to her for some help. She just shrugged. So I shrugged. Haysuse kept right on talking like he never even knew Irene was there.

"It was a record album. An old fashioned record album like we listened to when I was a child." He got sort of choked up for a second and reached into his pocket for a handkerchief. He used it to dab at his eyes a little bit.

When he started back up, he wasn't looking at beads. He was looking straight at my good eye like it was a crystal ball or something.

"She held the record up for me to see. She was smiling and turning it from side to side so I could see the writing on it. On one side was a word, a Russian word I think. I could not understand what it meant. On the other was a number. I was finally able to speak and I said 'Tell me what this means, mama.' And she said, 'This is to nourish you Chico. Read this and remember.' When I reached out to touch her, the dream ended and I was in my bed awake and weeping."

"All due respect, Haysuse, I'm all the way in the dark about what this has got to do with me."

"I think the writing on the record was sending me to you, Señor Butane. You see, I was thinking about the record as I was driving here to the hospital today. I was coming to visit Señora Suarez who will have surgery in the morning. She is in room 363. When I got on the elevator, I had the number on the record on my mind, and I pushed the button for the sixth floor. You see, the number on the record was 636."

"And?"

"That's your room number Señor Butane. This room is 636. I am certain my mother was guiding me to this room. I am certain you have something to tell me."

I was sure-as-hell certain that if I had some kind of magic message for Haysuse from his dead mom, nobody bothered to let me in on it. I guess I was laying there with my mouth open for a long time. But however long it was, Haysuse just kept sitting there waiting for his message, like the RCA dog.

"Look here, Haysuse. You got the wrong guy. I'm not any kind of preacher at all. Hell, I'm not even a church-going man. You must have got the number wrong or your mom was sending you to another hospital."

"That's not possible Señor Butane. I feel in my heart that my message is here in this room. Can you not feel the presence of the Holy Spirit?"

Well, it's true. I was shivering. But it was because I was getting the creeps. I looked over at Irene, and she was rubbing her arms like she was cold. She looked pale.

What's a guy supposed to say to something like that? So I said, "I don't know what to tell you Haysuse. I'm just a truck driver. I carry freight. I don't know shit about carrying messages from dead folks. Seems to me that if your mom or the Lord or somebody wanted to get you a message, they'd dang sure pick out a holier messenger."

He leaned forward and grabbed my arm. "No, no, Señor Butane. Any of us may become an instrument of God's will. He will often pick the humblest among us to use for his divine purpose. Here, let me show you."

He reached in his coat pocket and took out a pad and ball point. He wrote real fast and talked to himself in Mexican. He stood up and handed me the paper and took hold of my shoulder.

"Read this Señor Butane. I think you will see what I mean. But now I must go to see Señora Suarez. I will come again and we will speak further." I looked at the paper he gave me, and it made no sense. I was about to ask him what the hell this was supposed to mean, but Irene was already talking to him.

"You said there was a Russian word on the record Father de Palma. Maybe I can help. I took a Russian course in college. Do you remember what it was?"

He stopped at the door and looked at his shoes for a minute. When he got it recollected, he looked at Irene nodding. "Yes. It was *Petrushka*. The word was *Petrushka*. I'm sure of it." He was talking over his shoulder as he walked out. "Read, Señor Butane. You will see what I mean."

TAPE 3

So this here's the beginning of tape three, right? All right.

I ran my eye all over that paper trying to make sense out of what Haysuse wrote. What it said was "Numbers 22:28." You probably know what that means already. But at that minute, it didn't amount to apple butter as far as I was concerned. I was about to ask Irene if she had any idea, but when I looked at her, she looked like a woman fixing to faint. She was shivering so hard I could see it and her face was pale as my bed sheets. She was staring straight at me and her eyes were as big as hubcaps.

"Jesus Christ, Irene! What's wrong? You better sit down before you keel over." She stood for a second like she didn't hear me. When I started to get up so I could help her, she hurried over and put her right hand on my shoulder and covered her mouth with her other one. I could see a big smile through her fingers.

"Just a second, Leon. I need to tell you something important." She sort of skipped over to the door, peeked outside like she was expecting spies or something. Then she closed the door and hurried to the chair by my bedside. She sat on the edge with both hands on my right arm.

"Leon, I think there's something wonderful happening. I think Father de Palma is right. You've been chosen by God to fulfill a purpose."

"Come on now, Irene. You guys are about to push me over the edge here. If this shit keeps up, I'll start thinking I'm still in a gol' darn coma having a horror dream. What the hell are you talking about here?"

"Didn't you say that it was Pinocchio who spoke to you in your vision?"

"Well, yeah, if you want to call it a vision. It was Pinocchio, like I said."

"You heard Father de Palma say that the word on the record his mother showed him was Petrushka?"

"That's sure what it sounded like, yeah."

"Well, Petrushka is a kind of Russian version of Pinocchio. He's a puppet who is badly mistreated by everyone around him. Father de Palma's dream and your vision have to be related, Leon. It's just too freaky to be a meaningless coincidence. The Lord is working through you, Leon. I'm sure of it." She used her fingers to make that Catholic sign on her head and shoulders again.

"Now come on, Irene. This whole deal is nuts. Don't you think if God was going to give me a assignment, it would be something more practical than the hare-brained snipe chase to look for the names of a couple of guys who've been dead for a thousand years? You guys got to stop talking out of your hats and get hold of yourselves."

She went from being white to having a glow around her like a school girl in the middle of her first French kiss. "Let me see what Father de Palma gave you."

I was happy she changed the subject. I handed her the paper. "I sure hope you can explain what the heck this means, because if it isn't a hint about the lottery, it doesn't mean a dang thing to me."

She nodded and smiled real big. She explained that Numbers don't mean numbers like you count. It's one of the books of the Old Testament. Now if Irene hadn't been there, how the hell was I supposed to know that?

Anyway, Irene knows her way around the Bible, so she showed me what Haysuse wanted me to read. She went to the Numbers part, and you know what it says in the Bible there? An angel causes a jackass to open its mouth and talk to a guy! No shit! It's in there in black and white. You can look it up for your own self if you don't believe me. This guy named Balaam is riding this jackass, and an angel is in the way, so the donkey won't go near it. So Balaam commences to beating his ass with a stick to make it go. That's when the jackass speaks up and starts complaining about getting beat up.

Well, when Irene read that, the bulb came on in my brain, and I could see what Haysuse was trying to get across. If God can open up the mouth of a jackass to get a message to somebody, what's so far-fetched about opening up a trucker's mouth to get a message to a priest? Now that's what Haysuse was thinking, but I wasn't buying it. Before the jackass started talking, it had the advantage of seeing an angel. All I'd seen is a gol' dang puppet. That didn't stop Irene from staying all electrified. "Don't you see Leon? These connections have got to be important in a spiritual way. It wasn't just chance that you came out of your coma and spoke to Dr. Sugarman about 'Izzy.' As far as I know, no one around here knew what his Father's name was until you brought it up. There's no way you could know that. You didn't just happen to wake up on the morning after Father de Palma's dream, and it's not just happenstance that his mother gave him the number 636 and that's the very room where he found you." Her eyes started to sparkle, I guess because they were filling up. "All this is an answer to my prayers, Leon. I've been needing a sign, I've been so …" She got choked up and pulled a Kleenex out of her pocket. "I'm Catholic and I'm divorced and I … the church…."

Right then, Haysuse came charging back into the room and dropped to his knees right there by my bed and started praying real loud in Mexican. Irene jumped out of her chair and stood there with both hands covering her mouth. Haysuse was crying like a baby with an earache and praying so fast I couldn't understand him even if I did speak Mexican.

Then, that soft yellow light started shining on him, and I swear to God I heard music that sounded like a bunch of Catholic angels. I couldn't stand it.

"Knock it off Haysuse! Jesus Christ you guys are driving me crazy! Get off your dang knees and tell me what the hell's going on now."

He struggled to his feet and stood there wiping the tears off his face. Irene walked around the bed like she was on her tip toes. She reached out her hand like she was trying to calm a pony that was about to bolt.

Haysuse tried to say something, but got himself choked up again. Then he and Irene stood there holding hands and smiling at each other. They were both bawling like motherless calves. Hell, with all the hand holding, crying, smiling, and music, I almost tuned up and bawled myself.

"Would somebody please get a hold of themselves long enough to let me in on it? I'm getting tired of asking what the hell's going on here." The music and tears stopped and they both stood there blinking.

Finally, Haysuse spoke up. "It's a miracle Señor Butane, a miracle from Christ himself."

"Well I don't have any idea what kind of miracle you're talking about, so you need to take a deep breath and fill me in."

"It's Señora Suarez. She was blind from a tumor on her brain. They were going to operate tomorrow, but there was much danger. I was coming to pray with her and her family and receive her confession. But when she woke this morning, she thought she could see a faint light. The nurses were all amazed. They called the doctor to tell him. He said it was nothing— imagination only. But the light grew brighter and brighter. When I left you here and walked into her room, she could see me clearly the moment I came through the door. It was a miracle, Señor Butane.

"At first, she could count the fingers I held before her. Then, gradually, she was able to read. I called her doctor myself and told him what I saw with my own eyes. He still refused to believe. He is on his way to the hospital to see for himself. He will see Señor Butane. He will see as I have seen and he will believe. It is God's miracle."

I tried to process what Haysuse was saying. "I don't know Haysuse. I don't know if I believe in miracles." He let out a little giggle and patted his hands together like a kid getting ready for cake.

"It doesn't matter Señor Butane. Whether you believe or don't believe, Senora Suarez has her sight restored. Whether you believe or don't believe, I know I am a witness to the mercy of God and our sister Irena (that's how he says Irene) is uplifted in her faith. I can see it." I could tell that he and Irene were fixing to pray, when there was a real soft knock on the door. A tall, dark-complected fella stuck his head in. Haysuse ran over to the door and pulled him in by his arm.

"Señor Butane, this is Donato Suarez, He is here to thank you." Donato started creeping forward all sheepish-like, looking at me like I was the car of his dreams. That's when it started to sink in where this was headed. They were all serious about this miracle deal and they were thinking I had something to do with it.

Donato started to blubber something I couldn't understand, but I cut him off before he could get too wound up. "Now hold on. I'm red-lining here. I need everybody to clear out so I can figure out what's going on. There's only so much of this bullshit a fella can stand before his wiring starts to fuse."

Donato looked at Haysuse all puzzled-like, and Haysuse whispered something. Irene wiped her eyes and nose with a Kleenex and turned back into a nurse.

"Leon's right, Father. We really should let him rest now." Haysuse nodded like a bobble head.

"Of course, of course. You must be exhausted. So soon from the coma. All this excitement. You must rest." I guess he said the same thing to Donato, because he went to bobble-heading too, and they both started out of the room. Donato was walking backwards and Haysuse was walking along with him smiling over his shoulder. Irene the nurse herded them out. I was beat, I mean really tired, like I had just finished a twenty-hour haul. On top of that, an all-conference headache was starting up again.

After she got them two out of the room and closed the door, Irene fluffed up my pillow and adjusted the head of my bed until I told her I was comfortable. She asked if I wanted the TV sound turned on. I told her just to leave it off, as all I wanted to do was read the news crawling across the screen. She left for a minute and came back with some more pain medication for my IV, and I settled back to watch the news crawler as it drifted by.

I guess I dozed off, because I had one of those mini-jolts, like when you dream you're stepping up on a curb and you're really laying in bed. There was a tray full of food beside me and I didn't have no idea how it got there. For all I knew, this here was a miraculous lunch undelivered by human hands.

Then I saw this lady standing at the foot of my bed looking up at the TV. She was so still, she could have been a life-size cardboard cutout or one of those performers that stands out on the wharf in San Francisco and acts like a statue. With all the other crazy stuff that had happened lately, either of those deals would seem right normal.

Anyway, she was eyeballing the TV, and I was eyeballing her. I could see she wasn't a youngster, but she was real pretty in a Shirley MacLaine way. She had long brown hair with blond streaks, and she was wearing a green turtleneck under a trench coat with a red scarf around her neck. I was happy to appreciate a second or two of good looking calm after all the uncomfortable shit I'd been through in the last few hours. I started to say something, but I decided to just lay back and watch her as long as she was happy to watch that TV.

I glanced up to see what she was looking at. There was this televangelist doing his Sunday morning sheep shearing service. I'd seen this fella before, but at the time I couldn't have told you his name. You probably know him. He's got big white hair and always wears this white suit with a blue tie. He's a big guy, like a football player, big hands that show up on camera in close-ups all the time. When he gets worked up, he takes off his coat and he always has a real starched shirt with expensive looking leather suspenders holding his britches up. You know who it is, right? Ernest Bidding, *"Coming to you from the Tabernacle of the True Word in Mustang, Oklahoma—God's country."*

Well, anyway, this woman in my room was watching Ernest Bidding. He was all fired up like usual. His coat was already off and he was holding one of his big hands over his heart and he had the other one holding a Bible up over his head. The sound on the TV was still off. I couldn't hear him, but I knew he was saying something real smooth that involved the TV audience sending money in to his ministry.

I tried to figure out what was going through my lady caller's head. I couldn't read her expression. All I could say for sure was that she was paying real close attention. Then, she shook her head real slow like she was watching a fellow using snuff in a nursery.

She took a deep breath and mumbled something to herself. Then she looked over and saw that I was awake. I expected a smile or something, but her expression didn't change. So I smiled first. Couldn't help it. But she didn't send anything back. She gave me the feeling she was mad at me for some reason, but I'll be damned if I could tell you why. Hell, I usually get introduced to people before they come up with a reason to be pissed off at me.

She walked over to the bed and stuck her hand out, real business like. "Mr. Butane, I'm Kathleen Wister. May I sit down?" I knew she wasn't selling anything because she wasn't smiling.

"Sure. I'm between surgeries right at this minute, so you can be my guest." She didn't think it was funny.

"Thank you." Even in the few steps she took to the chair, I could tell she moved real graceful like a dancer or ice skater or something. She took her coat and scarf off and laid them on the foot of my bed. Then she took a seat and started pulling papers, recorders, and other stuff out of a Fifth-Avenue-looking brief case. "Mr. Butane, I'd like to ask you a few questions if you don't mind." She got herself all perched with a leather pad on her lap and a fancy ink pen at the ready. She looked at me like she was a pet groomer trying to figure out how to untangle a matted-up dog.

"Do you feel like talking, Mr. Butane?"

"Sure. I'm feeling fine right this minute. Go ahead."

"Before we get to Mrs. Suarez, I'd like to find out a little about your background."

"Whoa. Wait a minute. You're not a doctor, are you?"

"No."

"Are you part of my medical team or something?"

"No, I'm not, Mr. Butane."

"Do you work for the hospital?"

"No."

"You're not a lawyer or law enforcement or anything like that?"

"No Mr. Butane, I'm a journalist, and I'd like your version of what happened here this morning. But I'd like to know a little more about you first."

"Well, I'm sorry Miss... Wister, did you say it was? I'm sorry, Miss Wister, but I don't really know anything about it."

She looked at me out of the corner of her eye and smiled. "So modest, Mr. Butane. Unwilling to take credit. Unusual. Mysterious. Intriguing. This is the point where my curiosity is supposed to be overwhelming."

"Lady, it sounds to me like you're working from a script I ain't seen."

"I guess the last thing you expect is for me to take your word for it, thank you for your time, and simply walk out. That would surprise you wouldn't it? For me to just leave without letting you tell your amazing story."

"Oh! I got an amazing story all right, but I doubt if you know anything about it." Her smile got bigger and phonier. "Oh, let's be honest, Mr. Butane. If this modesty of yours gets out of hand, it won't do either of us any good. I won't get a story and you won't get any exposure. Tell me about Mrs. Suarez. We can come back and fill in the gaps later."

It was like she was talking to me in a foreign language. I was picking up bits and pieces, but I plumb lost the message. "Look, Miss Wister. All I know about Mrs. Suarez is what the priest Haysuse told me. She had a tumor and went blind. She came in this hospital to get operated on. They was going to do her surgery tomorrow. Something happened and her sight came back. I've never seen the woman. I met her husband for about fifteen seconds. Then I went to sleep. That's it."

"Father de Palma says her sight began to return about the time you awoke from your coma this morning. What do you say to that?"

"I don't say anything to it. I'm not sure exactly what time I woke up, and I damn sure don't know what time she started seeing stuff."

"Father de Palma says you had a vision while you were comatose. Is that true?"

"Tell you what is true. Father de Palma's got a big damn mouth. He should have asked me before he went to blabbing everything I told him."

"He says you delivered a message from his deceased mother. Any response to that?"

"It's bullshit." Now don't get the wrong idea here. Ordinarily I don't cuss in front of a woman I just met. But she was getting under my skin. She leaned back, took out a pair of glasses and looked me over real good.

"Really? So you're saying Father de Palma is being untruthful?"

"No. Dammit. Don't start putting words in my mouth. What I'm saying is Father de Palma is a blabbermouth that got his wires crossed. He may believe I delivered a message from his mom. But like I said, it's bullshit."

"So you insist you had nothing to do with the miraculous restoration of Mrs. Suarez's eyesight?"

"No. I didn't have a damn thing to do with it, Miss Wister. And I got zero interest in whether you get a story and less than zero interest in whether I get some exposure. What I need right now don't have anything to do with exposure. So, you're a pretty lady with lots of charm and all, but if you're wanting me to pretend I know something about what happened to Mrs. Suarez, you're barking up a empty tree."

She closed her pad and crossed her legs. I couldn't help but notice that she had some nice calves and ankles sticking out from under her skirt. I probably should be ashamed for being impressed that way, but I'm not. She tapped her tooth with her ink pen. I could tell she was thinking. She could probably tell I was thinking too.

"How long were you in the coma, Mr. Butane?"

I was glad she changed the subject. "Well, they tell me I was out for forty days. Doesn't seem like that long to me. I guess that's how a coma works."

"Do you belong to a church or any other religious groups?"

"What's this got to do with anything, Miss Wister?"

"Maybe nothing. Maybe something. I don't know. I'm just asking."

"For the last few years, about the only time I go to church is to attend somebody's funeral. I haven't been regular since I was a kid."

"Where were you born and raised?" I looked up at the TV and Reverend Bidding had one big hand raised over his head and he had a handkerchief in his other hand and he was using it to wipe sweat off his face.

"Tell you what, Miss Wister; I've got to say there's something about this visit we're having that's starting to give me an upset stomach. I'm sorry I couldn't help you with your story, but I need to get back to my nap. You can stay and watch the TV if you want, but I think I'm just going to lay back here and doze awhile."

She shrugged and stood up to put on her coat. While she was wrapping her scarf around her ears, she looked at me like she was trying to puzzle something out. "Would you mind if I come back later and ask you a few more questions?"

"You can come back any time you want, but I'm getting out of here tomorrow, so you better make it quick."

"You really think they'll let you leave tomorrow after waking up from a forty day coma today?" The way she asked the question made it sound like I was nuts for thinking I was leaving.

"Well, let's just put it like this, Miss Wister. I'm taking the rest of today to get my legs under me and I'm leaving tomorrow."

She looked like she was going to say something but changed her mind. She reached in her coat pocket and come out with a little red leather case. She took a card out and put it on the table by my bed. "Something tells me we might be able to help each other, Mr. Butane. Think it over and give me a call."

I was really sorry our conversation turned out to be so stuffy. I really would have liked to keep her around for awhile. There was something about her being there that made me feel good. But the truth is, I didn't have anything to offer her, and I didn't see how a journalist could help me a bit. So I didn't do nothing to keep her from leaving.

When she was gone, I looked at her card. There was websites, phone numbers, blog sites, radio letters, and program times all over it. Along with the information on that card, there was a real ladylike aroma. It smelled great, like wild flowers. I closed my eyes and imagined I was in field of daisies and clover listening to songbirds and having a picnic with Miss Wister. I was sure enjoying my daydream when I got the creepy feeling somebody was watching me. I looked around the room and there wasn't anybody there. But that soft yellow light was shining around the TV screen and Reverend Bidding was staring down at me.

Sunday, February 18, 2007, p.m.

You'd think after forty days in a coma, a fella would be all slept out. But I wasn't. Every time I stopped thinking for a second, I was in slumber land again. I was somewhere between being awake and being out when I heard

Wanda sob out my name. I managed to get my eye open just as she settled her big bosom over my face and started rocking back and forth and gushing all over me. "Oh Lordy, it's a miracle, Leon. I was afraid you'd never wake up. They told me you might not. Praise the Lord. Everything's going to be okay now."

I was getting smothered so I was pushing her back. "Wanda, darlin' I need some air or I'm going to relapse."

"Oh, I'm sorry Leon. It's just that I'm so ... I'm so happy, Leon." She was blubbering about how it was just the two of us now that mom and dad were gone, and her good-for-nothing ex-husband, Raymond, was living with a retired stripper, blah, blah, blah. She put her face down real close to mine with an *I-love-you-Leon* expression all over it. For a second there, I admit I got bowled over with emotion myself. It didn't surprise me one bit that she'd been coming up to that hospital day after day the whole time I was in that coma. She'd have kept coming too. If they had had to put me in a nursing home for the rest of my life, Wanda sure enough would be there every day, hell or high water. I was feeling ashamed of myself because if the shoe were on the other foot, I'm not sure I would be as faithful as she was.

It hit me then how narrow the gap was between where I was and where I might have been. If the dial was turned another degree or two, poor Wanda would have got stuck burying the last member of her family. Or she could have wound up spending the rest of her life taking care of an invalid, vegetable brother. Then it came back to mind that I wasn't out of the woods yet. Wanda might still find herself putting me in the ground if I couldn't get to the bottom of that Jesus deal. I was just on the verge of feeling sorry for both of us when I decided to grit my teeth and snap out of it. Wanda was crying, though, and I couldn't help letting a tear or two of my own leak out.

"How are you feeling Leon? Are you in any pain? Can I get anything for you?"

"Well, to tell you the truth, I wasn't hungry until this minute. What's on the lunch tray?" It was turkey and dressing with green beans, tea, and some melted orange sherbet.

Wanda was about to spoon some of the dressing into my mouth when she got real red in the face. "Oh my goodness, Leon!" She jumped up and carried the spoon over to the sink. The whole way over there, she was chattering nonstop. "For the life of me I don't know what I was thinking. I was about to put this spoon in your mouth without even washing my hands." She scrubbed her hands and the spoon real good.

When she was sure she wasn't feeding me any germs, she took up where she left off spooning me dressing still chattering away. "Now, Leon, I don't want you to worry about a thing. Me and Sonny down at the yard are seeing to it that all the worker's comp forms are getting filled out and I'm taking care of all the insurance stuff." See, Wanda's not only my sister; she's my insurance agent too. She's got coverage on Nadine, my house, my health policy, and the policy on the Mercury, everything.

"Pete, your neighbor, is looking after your place and I've been going over to get your bills. I've been putting off the ones that can wait, and I've been paying the others myself." She started cutting up the turkey and feeding it to me in tiny bites, like she thought being in a coma caused your mouth to shrink 'til it was baby size.

"There was a lawyer up here trying to serve you some papers, but me and Dr Sugarman ran him off and told him he should be ashamed of himself." I about choked on a tiny turkey bite.

"Wait a minute. Did you say a lawyer? What in the sam hill does a lawyer want to serve papers on me for?"

"Well, Leon, don't excite yourself until we find out from Dr. Sugarman if it's okay for you to get upset. I probably shouldn't even have mentioned it."

"Yeah, but you did mention it. So what the hell's this lawyer business all about?"

"Well I really don't know much about it, Leon. This lawyer fella says you crashed because you were negligent. Your tanker busted open in the accident and gasoline got spilled into this Farmer fella's well water. He says his wife and cattle got poisoned because of it, and now he says he's losing his hair and going deaf. I don't understand it all really. But he says you and Sonny owe him a gazillion dollars."

"Me and Sonny?" Sonny is the owner of Travertine Trucking. He's my boss. "Hell, I was the driver, not Sonny, and I didn't do diddly wrong. For crying out loud, it was probably the farmer's gol' dang jaywalking cow that caused the whole crack-up in the first place. How can them blood sucking lawyers sue Sonny over this deal, I'd like to know?"

"Please, Leon. You shouldn't be worked up. Just put it out of your mind for now. You really have more important things to think about."

She was right. "You're right, sis. I'll get around to straightening out this lawyer mess later. Right now I need to get my ass checked out of this hospital. I got important stuff to do."

She jerked herself up and stood with a Kleenex stuck to her nose. "What are you talking about Leon? If there's something that needs doing, let me know, and I'll take care of it."

"I'm sorry Wanda; I really can't explain everything right now. But you just got to trust me. I got to get out of here and I mean yesterday."

She was looking around like she needed an interpreter or something. "Have you talked this over with Dr. Sugarman?"

"Now look here Wanda, right now it don't make a shit what the doctor says. I've got to get out of here—tomorrow at the latest. Today would be better."

She frowned over her Kleenex. "You're scaring me Leon. You almost sound like you're talking out of your head. I can't help you unless you tell me what's going on."

I knew it was a mistake. I knew she'd never believe it. I knew she'd probably think I'd flipped my dang lid. But I needed her help. So I took a chance and spooled it out—just like I did for Dr. Sugarman. Except this time, I had the Suarez nonsense to add.

The whole time I was talking, Wanda's eyes kept getting bigger and bigger and her mouth was opening wider and wider and the Kleenex was dropping further and further under her nose. She walked over like a zombie and sat down. When I finished up the part about Haysuse and Mr. Suarez trying to give me the credit for Mrs. Suarez' miracle, she never changed her big-eyed, open-mouthed expression. She just sat there shaking her head real slow. When she started talking, she sounded like someone watching foam ooze out of a mirror.

"Oh, Leon, honey, you need rest now. Don't worry. Everything's going to be okay. You've just been hit real hard on the head and naturally, you'd expect some of your sense to get knocked out of you. It's just going to take some time." She started digging around in her purse for a dry Kleenex. I could tell she didn't believe a word of my Pinocchio story. She was just hoping there was a treatment where I could get my lost sense put back in. I decided to try to talk her out of it.

"Wanda, listen. I know this sounds crazy, but..."

As soon as I said "crazy" she started shaking her head real hard. "Now let's not be talking about crazy. Nobody's crazy. You've just got temporary insanity, that's all and the doctors can cure temporary insanity with electric shocks or something. They'll have your head screwed back on right in no time."

"Now come on Wanda. I don't have any kind of insanity, and I don't need no electric shocks. It all happened just like I told you. If you don't believe me, get the nurse in here. She'll back me up." Wanda hurried over to the bedside and pushed the nurse call button. While we were waiting for Irene, I tried to calm Wanda and get her to see how important it was for me to check out and how I needed her help, as I wasn't able to drive anymore.

When the nurse came in I was real disappointed. It wasn't Irene. The new gal's nametag said "Doris."

"Doris, would you ask Irene to come in here. I need her to tell my sister something."

Doris came over to check my pulse and look me over. "Irene's shift was over at three o'clock Mr. Butane. Is there anything I can do for you?"

My heart sunk some more. "Well, I really need Irene to explain to Wanda here what happened today. See, Wanda's thinking I got temporary insanity and I need Irene to explain about Mrs. Suarez' miracle and how it was an answer to Irene's prayer and all that stuff." Wanda and Doris gave each other that *poor-Leon-he's-so-out-of-it* look, and I knew I was outnumbered. Doris talked to me like I was a seven-year-old arguing about eating his turnips.

"Just relax now Mr. Butane. Irene will be back on at seven o'clock in the morning. But I really think Dr. Sugarman would be the most help if you need information." Doris went to writing stuff on the board—my pulse and blood pressure and other medical numbers. Wanda was sniffing and patting my shoulder with her pudgy little hand and dabbing her nose with her new Kleenex. I could see it wouldn't do me any good to try to get somewhere with these two.

"Doris, what time will Dr. Sugarman be here in the morning?"

"He'll be here before he goes to the clinic. He usually finishes rounds by eight- thirty. It should be somewhere around then."

"Okay Wanda. I hate to ask darlin', but could you come by about then so you and the doctor can get it worked out for me to be released?"

"Well of course I can be here Leon. But I just don't think you're ready to go home. I mean you're really in no condition to look after yourself, and there wouldn't be anyone who could stay with you while I'm at work. I think you ought to just stay put until the doctor says it's okay. We need some time to get things ready."

"Don't worry about a thing sis. Just come on up in the morning. I'm sure the doc and I will be seeing eye-to-eye before you know it."

Doris asked "Is there anything else I can do for you Mr. Butane?"

"Sure is. You can start calling me Leon."

"Fine, Leon. Just call if you need anything." I reached out and got hold of Wanda's hand.

She started whimpering. "Oh, Leon. I'm so happy you woke up. It's been terrible, and now that you're back, I'm just . . ." She pulled my hand up and kissed my knuckles. "Tell me everything's going to be okay Leon. You're all I've got left, and I need to know everything's going to come out right."

I thought the best thing I could do for her right then was give her a big old *"I-got-it-under-control"* smile. So that's what I did. "Hey, Sis. You just go on home and get a good night's sleep. Come on back up here in the morning, and you and Dr. Sugarman and I will have us a good chat. He'll tell you not to worry, and you'll feel a lot better. Wait and see."

"I feel like I ought to stay here with you tonight Leon. You might need me."

"No need for that sweetheart. Really, I'm fine. Anyway, I got nurses just chomping at the bit to charge in here every time somebody rings this bell. You go on home. I promise I'll call if I need you."

She smiled through her tears and leaned over to give me a sweet "I hate-to-leave-you" kiss on the cheek. "Okay, Leon. If you're sure you'll be okay. Remember, I'm just twenty-five minutes away. You hear?"

"I hear you sweetheart. Now you go on home. I'm going to rest now, and I'll see you in the morning."

She got up and gathered her coat and purse and started for the door. On the way out she stopped. "I love you, Leon."

I knew she meant it, and I knew it wouldn't do for me to get choked up. So I give her another big smile. "Who's the king of the world, Baby Sister?" We'd been doing this routine as long as I can remember.

"You're the king of the world, Leon." Then she was gone. I don't know whether she thought about it, but I did. That's what we said to each other when I left for Nam. Next time she saw me after that, I just had one eye.

TAPE 4

Let's see, this is number four, right? Okay.

I had this gnawing feeling that things was gearing up to get a lot more complicated. According to the puppet, my fifteen days would start the next morning. I couldn't afford to lay around in the hospital four or five days twiddling my thumbs while my time ran out hour by hour. But, hell, where would I start if I walked out of there at seven o'clock the next morning? I just had two clues to start with. The puppet mentioned Augie, my pastor cousin, and I had Irene's Bible that said the two men crucified with Jesus were revolutionaries. Not much to go on.

I spent the evening chewing over the problem and watching the crawler roll across the bottom of the TV. There was a story about a guy who died sitting in front of his TV. Nobody heard from him for over a year. He just sat there by himself with the TV on until he got mummified. There was a time when I'd have just scratched my head about it and then gone on down the road not thinking about it anymore. But I got this itch deep in my brain. This guy was sitting dead in front of a TV for over a year and nothing was getting through—because he was dead. And I was laying I front of a TV for over a month and nothing was getting through—because I was in a coma. I was wondering how many other mummies and comatose folks there were sitting in front of TVs around the world with nothing getting through.

I decided to think of something else. Sometime after supper, I rang for the nurse and told Doris my head was killing me. She put something in my IV, and I leaned back in bed and waited for my evening to get mellow. A few minutes later, there was a soft knock on the door. I didn't say anything, but the door eased open real slow and threatening like you see them do on monster movies. The longer it took to open, the straighter I sat up in my bed. The way things was going lately, I half-way expected something creepy to crawl into the room with me.

But it wasn't nothing creepy at all. It was a little fella dressed in a hospital get-up like I was. When he saw me looking at him, he put his hands together like he was praying and started bowing and taking tiny steps toward me saying "*Por favor, Señor Butane. Por favor.*"

I really didn't know what to say or do, so I just said the first thing that came into my mind. "How do you know my name, friend?"

"I have spoken with Señor Suarez and Father de Palma. They told me how you helped Señora Suarez, and I have come to ask you to pray for me, *por favor.*"

"Look, fella—what's your name anyway?"

"I am Francisco Ortiz."

"Well look here, Francisco, I know there're rumors going around, but you've got to take my word for it. I didn't do anything for Mrs. Suarez. And I'm not much of a praying man. So do yourself a favor and find somebody who's got more on the ball in the praying department than I do."

"Please, Señor Butane. I must speak with you. I have prayed to the Madonna, and I believe she is leading me to you."

I was getting plumb worn out talking to people who weren't listening to a damn word I said. Before I could say another thing, Francisco cut me off and started laying it on real thick.

"It's my heart, Señor Butane. The doctors tell me that I must have surgery tomorrow or my heart will fail. I have already had a warning. A heart attack. I am fortunate to be alive. I have been given another chance. I am a great sinner, Señor Butane." He made that Catholic sign on his shoulders and stuff and covered his face with both hands and cried.

I'm sure I must have groaned. It seemed like this shit was never going to end. "Francisco, I ..."

"*Por favor,* Señor Butane. I wish to change. I will become a more righteous man, a more humble man. I will never again be unfaithful. I will give up drinking and gambling. I will give tithes to the church. But I must have time, Señor Butane. If I die now, I fear for my soul."

"But I'm serious. I really can't help you man."

"Listen, Señor Butane. Do you know what they do when they operate on your heart? The doctors have told me. They use a sharp saw to cut open the bones of your chest. Then they use an instrument like a vise to spread the bones of your chest far apart. A vise, Señor Butane! I am told there is danger that my life will end on the operating table, that I might be put to sleep and never wake up."

He reached up with a bony little hand and took hold of my shoulder. "If they operate on me tomorrow, I will surely die. The Madonna has told me this."

"Well hell, Francisco, they can't make you have an operation if you don't want one. If it was me and I thought I was going to die if I let them operate, I'd skip it."

"But I can't, Señor Butane. The doctors tell me that if I leave without the operation, I will die. My daughters begged me to agree to the surgery, and from weakness, I promised. You see? If I leave and die, I die with a lie on my lips. If I die in the operation, I cannot make atonement for my sins."

He gripped my shoulder real hard. "You must pray for me, Señor Butane. I must have a miracle."

I heard myself talking, and I was sounding like a gol'darn busted record. "Believe me, I'd love to help you Francisco. But I haven't got any miracles, and I don't know any prayers except the Lord's Prayer, and I'm not so sure I can remember that one right at this minute."

Francisco whimpered, "Please. You must help me, Señor Butane. I have repented of my wickedness, and now I need time to make atonement. You are my only hope." He grabbed my hand and put it on top of his head. "Pray to God that I may be healed. Promise the Lord that if he will heal me, I will be a good servant for the rest of my life."

I tried to take my hand off his head, but he was holding it on there tight as super glue. Then he wailed loud enough that I thought the whole damn hospital could hear. "Please, Señor Butane. Have mercy on me!"

"Okay, okay Francisco. Jesus Christ quiet down will you. Just tell me this. If I go through with this and pray for you, will you go back to where you came from and leave me alone? Don't tell anybody about this, and don't blame me if this whole deal is a dud."

"I will do anything you ask, Señor Butane. I swear."

"This is nuts, Francisco. Even if I do this, it won't make a damn bit of difference."

"Please!"

I really wanted to help the old guy, but this was way out of bounds. The whole deal felt wrong. I didn't have any business putting on this kind of a show. But I didn't have the heart to chase the old bastard out without trying to do something for him. "Okay Francisco. Let go my hand."

"You will pray for me? You will pray that I am healed?"

"Yes, goddammit, I'm going to pray for you. But you've got to let go of my hand." He took his hands off me and dropped to the bedside like he was saying his good night prayers. I put my hand on his head, and I know for sure I was blushing all over, because I felt so ridiculous and sinful. I cleared my throat and got started with my blaspheming.

"Oh Lord, this here's Francisco, and he's got heart trouble . . . . For crying out loud. This is stupid."

"Go on, Señor Butane. I can feel the power of God in your touch."

"Right. Okay. Lord, like I was saying, this here's Francisco and they're fixing to operate on his heart tomorrow, but he's worried he won't make it through the surgery. I know you think this is out of line, Lord. Believe me, I do too, and I'm sorry. But Francisco wants me to pray that he gets cured. So that's what I'm doing. I'm praying that he gets cured. I guess that's all. Amen."

Well, Francisco started trembling all over like he was dropped in a deep freeze. Then there was that soft yellow light all around him, and I swear I heard that same Catholic angel music again. He looked up at me with tears all in his eyes and raised his hands up. I tried to take my hand off his head, but it was stuck there, and this time it wasn't because he was holding on.

At the time, I figured it was my imagination, but I thought I heard a camera clicking at the door. Anyway, Francisco kept on with his crying and hollered real joyful like, "I am cured, Señor Butane. I can feel it. There is no pain in my arm or my leg or my chest. It's a miracle. The Lord has answered your prayer! I am healed! I have been spared! *Muchas gracias,* Señor Butane! Bless you. Bless you."

The light faded, the music stopped, and my hand got unstuck from the top of his head.

Now this is embarrassing, but I'm supposed to lay out the whole story— even the parts that make me look bad. I don't like it a bit, but here goes.

See, a guy like me ain't got any business praying at all. I know, I know, everybody's supposed to have the right to pray. But I've abused the privilege. When I was in Nam, I was one full-time praying sombitch. I mean I was praying morning, noon, and night: *Lord, get me out of this firefight and I'll never swear or gamble again. Lord, let me survive this operation and I'll quit whorin' and start attending services with the chaplain. Lord let me get*

home alive and walking on my own two feet and I'll be a first class Christian.
But then, after every firefight, every operation, and every tour of duty, I'd
be back to whoring, drinking, gambling, doing drugs, swearing—every sin
in the book except faggotry and incest. By the time I got home, I figured
prayers was just words, and all my promises was nothing but hot air. For a
time, I got to suspecting there wasn't no God at all.

Well, I outgrew that, but I felt like I'd wrote so many hot checks to the
prayer department that there's no way God would cash another one. So, to
save me and the Lord any unnecessary embarrassment, I just quit. So see,
when Francisco wanted me to pray for him, I was really afraid I'd wind up
doing him more harm than good. So, if you can be sinful for praying, I was
damn sure committing a felony. I was laying there feeling ashamed when
Doris stepped into the room. It took her a second to take everything in. I
guess there's just a natural preference to not disturb somebody when they're
praying, so she stood there blinking. To tell the truth, I sort of felt like Doris
caught me scratching the wrong itch in public.

Anyway, she came over and put her hand on Francisco's shoulder. He
looked up at her all watery eyed. "It's a miracle from God. I am cured."

Doris gave me a stern look while she talked to Francisco. "Well, we
need to get you back to your room. What's your room number?"

"My things are in room 404. I need to get them and go home now. The
pain has ended. I am cured through the mercy of God and by the power of
Señor Butane's prayer."

Her eyebrows arched up. "Really? Did you cure this man Leon?"

"Hell no, Doris. He just came in here begging me to pray for him, and
I didn't have the heart to say no. That's all."

She helped Francisco struggle up to his feet. "Here, I'll help you back to
your room, and you need to tell your doctor all about it in the morning."

"But I'm cured. I don't need to stay tonight. I can go home."

"Well, we can't process anyone to leave tonight anyway. You'll just have
to wait until tomorrow in any case. For now, let's get you back to your
room."

I was feeling all rosy from the pain medicine, and it was making me
happy to see old Francisco happy, even though I was 100 percent sure his
heart was still toast. Before he left, he threw himself across my chest and
blubbered, "God bless you, Señor Butane. God bless you."

Doris eased him up off my chest and started herding him out the door.

She looked back over her shoulder with that same stern look. "You should get some sleep now, Leon. You've done enough entertaining for the night."

Well, as you can see, my first full day out of the coma was sure fun filled and action packed. But I was ready for things to get calm—so I could rest. So I could think. It was late when Doris came in to feed the goodnight juice into my IV. She turned off the light, but I asked her to leave the TV on. I don't want to say I was afraid of the dark, because that's a little kid deal. I'll just say there was something comfortable about having the TV on—even if it really didn't give you much light to see by.

I could feel myself getting rocked to sleep. You know how it is sometimes before you drift off you can see soft red images on the inside of your eyelids? Well there was a soft red word on the inside of my eyelids—both of them, which is strange all by itself, because I've just got the one eye. But there it was. "Field." It was kind of shimmery, watery looking, just hanging there. "Field."

I guess it was the medicine, because I tried to do something that I knew wouldn't work. My hand reached out to try to get hold of that word, like it was fruit hanging on a tree or something. My sleepy mind was telling me the word belonged someplace, and I needed to put it where it would fit. But it was on the inside of my eyelids, so I was wasting my time trying to get hold of it. Then it felt like the bed was rotating in a slow circle, and I was asleep.

Nadine and I were on a mountain road with my window rolled down. I was happy to be at the wheel, and it made me feel good to see Nadine all in one piece. I was in a low gear on a steep down grade, and Jesse Cook was playing "Toca Orilla" on the iPod. The whole cab smelled like pine trees. Everything was familiar. I've been on stretches of road like that a thousand times. But then there was something squirrelly about the highway. There weren't any lane lines, and the surface wasn't concrete. Hell, it looked like the paper the Declaration of Independence was written on. And it was unrolling like a scroll in front of me as Nadine headed down hill. There was some kind of writing all over it, but I was moving too fast to be able to read it. I was starting to get worried, because I was picking up speed even though I was in the lowest gear I could find. The faster I went, the faster that paper unrolled in front of me.

I could tell we were heavy loaded, because when I started trying to brake a little bit, Nadine didn't want to slow much. I knew if I worked the brakes too hard, they'd burn up, and I'd be at the wheel of a runaway for sure.

I must have been grinding my teeth hard, because my jaws were aching. Then I rounded a curve and started to think everything would be okay, because we were rolling onto an upgrade. In the ordinary world, that should have started slowing us down. It didn't happen. I kept picking up speed even though I was headed up hill with a full load. That's when I laid into the brakes with everything I had. No dice. There wasn't anything I could do to control the speed. All I could do was steer and hope that I was a good enough driver to keep the trailer behind me and the rubber side down.

I looked as far up the grade as I could; looking for an opportunity to slow down without going over the side. Then, up above me, I saw these three crosses, you know, like you see on Easter cards. Except there were question marks over two of them where the upright usually sticks out of the cross beams. If I was thinking that those crosses meant there was help on the way, I was wrong, because I wasn't slowing down a bit.

As that rig was breaking every common sense rule in the book and there wasn't anything I could do about it, I gave up hoping I could avoid a crack-up. I was just hoping I'd survive when it happened. I must have been doing ninety almost straight up when I passed them crosses at the top of the grade. That's when I heard whispering.

I didn't know whether I was moving out of one dream and stepping into another or whether there was somebody in the room with me. I opened my eye and tried to focus. There were three of them. At first, I thought those three crosses in my dream somehow transplanted themselves in my room and was whispering to each other. But they weren't crosses. They were people. When my eye adjusted, I could see it was a man, a woman, and a little girl with a cap on her head. The man was drifting around the room like he was on skates, setting poles up around my bed. The woman was standing in the glow of the TV, and the little girl was resting her head on the woman's shoulder watching me with real big, curious-looking eyes.

I still wasn't sure if it was a dream or not. So I decided to find out. "Hey. What's going on?" The man froze, and I was halfway expecting all three of them to disappear in a puff of smoke or something. But they didn't. The little girl just blinked her big eyes at me. After a second or two, the man spoke up as he was moving toward the bed.

"Evening, Leon." His voice was oily like a glad-handing used-car salesman. "I'm glad to see you awake. We were going to get you up once we got set up here, but it's probably better you woke up on your own."

He was back lit by the TV so I couldn't see his face, but he stuck his hand out for me to shake. "Do I know you, fella?"

"We haven't been introduced, Leon, but my name's Teddy." He stood there with his hand in front of my face. I didn't see any reason to be impolite—yet. So I shook it. He skated over to the woman and girl and put his arm around the woman's shoulder. "This is Tonya and this little angel here is Iris. Say hello to Mr. Butane, Iris." Iris put her left thumb in her mouth and waved at me with her other little hand.

Teddy started skating around again opening what looked like umbrellas on the tops of the poles around my bed. "We'll be through here in just a minute, Leon and then we'll finish up right quick and let you get back to sleep."

My lips and tongue weren't all the way awake, but they were working well enough for me to make myself understood. "What are y'all doing in here, Teddy?"

Teddy started talking in a sort of loud whisper. "Well, little Iris here wants to ask you a favor, but we need to be all set up and ready before she does. Tonya, close the door the rest of the way, would you?" Tonya closed the door real quiet like. I realized Teddy wasn't skating. He just had a sort of smooth walking way that made him look like he was on skates.

"Okay, Leon. Do you mind if we turn some lights on? We'll get better images." He didn't wait for me to answer. He just started switching on bulbs. It hurt my eye at first, but, to tell you the truth, I was glad to have some light so I could get a good look at this Teddy guy.

He was a good sized fella who looked to be about thirty. He had gold rings on all his fingers, a big gold watch on his wrist, and a couple of gold chains around his neck. He had some chewing gum in his mouth and he was really working it over.

"What do you mean 'images'?"

"Well, we're just going to get a few pictures of you with Iris while we have a little privacy. It'll just take a couple of seconds. We'll be out in a jiffy. Tonya, hand me that meter, will you?"

Tonya tried to balance Iris on her hip while she dug around in a duffel bag. She handed some type of gizmo to Teddy, and he moved over to where I was and took measurements up close to my face. I didn't like it.

"Great. Okay Tonya, bring Iris on over and sit her on the edge of the bed here." He was moving and talking real fast and my poor drugged up brain was having a hard time getting a hold. Tonya carried Iris over to the bed and set her there next to me. Iris never made a peep. She wasn't scared or anything. She just sat there with her big eyes looking at me and her thumb in her mouth. I reached up automatically to be sure my eyeball was in place because I didn't want the little girl to be upset.

I tried to shake the cobwebs out of my head when Teddy started taking pictures. "Now, just a minute here. What's this all about?" He never let up taking pictures.

"It would be better if we kept quiet Leon. We don't want to wake up any of the sick folks in these other rooms. They need their rest. Take your thumb out of your mouth, Iris, honey. Good."

He stopped taking pictures and came over to the bed. "Do you mind Leon?" He took Irene's Bible off the bedside table and put it on my chest. He picked up my right hand and started to put it on the Bible. Even in my dopey state, I didn't like being manhandled. So I jerked away. That's the first time I saw Iris change expression. She looked scared, like she might cry.

"It's okay, Leon. It'll just make a nice shot. And you don't want to upset Iris, do you? She's a real sick little girl and we all need to be sweet to her. It's okay, baby. Mr. Butane's a nice man. He's going to help us here. Aren't you Leon? Just put your hand on the Bible."

I couldn't stand to see little Iris looking scared, so I smiled at her. She pulled her chin down to her chest and put her thumb back in her mouth. I should have pushed the nurse call button, but I didn't.

"The Bible, Leon, if you don't mind. Good. That's great." More pictures. "You look fine Leon, but if you can, open your eyes a little wider. That would be great."

I really wanted to start putting up an argument, but I didn't want to scare Iris.

"Iris, honey, Mr. Butane hasn't had any candy in a long time. Would you like to give him some candy? Take your thumb out of your mouth, sweetheart." She looked at me for a second then nodded. "Tonya, start the video on cue, okay? Here sweetheart. Here's a jelly belly. They're Mr. Butane's favorites, aren't they, Leon? Okay Tonya, roll it."

Iris leaned forward and reached out with her thin little hand and put the jelly belly to my lower lip. I smiled and opened my mouth. She smiled and gave me the candy. "Great! You want to give him another one baby?"

She smiled and nodded. "Kill the video for a sec, Tonya." He gave Iris another jelly bean. "Okay. Let's go. You want some more candy Leon?"

Iris seemed pretty excited about putting candy in my mouth, so I let her do it again. "Okay. Now, you know what Iris? I bet it's been a long time since Mr. Butane's got a kiss from a little girl. I'll bet it would help him get well if you gave him a kiss. You want to give him a kiss? Okay Tonya."

Natural as can be, the little angel put her arms around my neck and kissed my left cheek. Having a sweet little girl sitting next to me so willing to help me get well sort of choked me up. "Outstanding! Give him one more kiss, so we'll be sure he gets well. Excellent. Okay now, Leon. I want you to reach up with your left hand and touch Iris's cheek. Would it be okay if Mr. Butane touches your cheek, sweetheart? Go ahead Leon. You don't want to hurt her feelings do you?"

So I smiled and reached up. She laid her little cheek in the palm of my hand and that soft yellow light started to shine all around her. "Unbelievable! Now put your hand on top of her head. Here, let me show you." He came over and positioned my hand. I could smell alcohol and tobacco on him. "Great. Right there. Now, Iris, you remember how I showed you to say your prayers? Remember? Okay, let me help you."

I was hearing music coming from somewhere over the clicks the camera was making. "Okay, hold it right there, Iris. Steady Leon. This is incredible. Just one or two more. Okay, Leon, raise your right hand. Great. Great. Okay, let's wrap it up. Iris, you just sit there with Mr. Butane while your mommy and I put our stuff up. Okay?" He started skating around the room closing up umbrellas and taking down poles.

Iris sat there watching me with her thumb in her mouth. While Tonya and Teddy were busy, Iris took a deep breath and laid her little head on my chest. I could see she was tired. I moved the Bible from under her head so she'd be more comfortable. I heard Teddy say, all excited like.

"Jesus Christ, look at that!" He jerked up the camera and started shooting pictures rapid fire again. "Jesus Christ, I hope the light's okay to get this." I laid the Bible on the table and got washed over by a feeling like I ought to do something to protect that little girl. So I put my arm around her to shield her from the camera flashes.

Tonya spoke for the first time. "We've got to go Teddy. I think somebody's coming."

"Sure baby. You finish up while I have a little talk with Leon." He picked Iris up. I didn't want to let her go. She still had that soft light around her, but the music was fading. Teddy put a clipboard on the bed. "Nicorette, Leon?"

"No thanks."

"I got some Johnny Walker in the duffel. Bet you could use a snort."

"Not right now."

"Suit yourself. Look, Leon. Here's the deal. You know what A-L-L is?

"Sure. It spells 'all.'"

He snickered. "Not this time. A-L-L is acute lymphoblastic leukemia. It's a kind of cancer, Leon, and that's why Iris is here. Anyway, she's been undergoing methotrexate treatments into her brain, and we're going to find out tomorrow whether they're doing any good."

"Look, I'm not altogether with it here. What's this little photo session got to do with Iris's treatments?"

He grinned. "We may be able to work a profit. See, if the test results in the morning are good, we give you credit for a miracle cure. We got spectacular pictures of a miracle while it's happening. All you have to do is help us sell the story. There's a way everybody can make out on this. If the test results are bad—well, we'll cross that bridge and see where we are. I need you to sign this form."

"I don't know what all this is about, buddy, but I smell a rat here, and I'm not signing anything in the dark."

There was something cold in his voice. "Iris wants you to sign this." Tonya came over and took Iris out of Teddy's arms. She laid her head on her mom's shoulder and never took her eyes off me.

I ignored Teddy and his clipboard. "Thanks for the candy and the kisses, Iris. They made me feel better."

She took her thumb out of her mouth and smiled. "You're welcome." Her voice sounded like little bells ringing.

"How old are you?" She held up three fingers. "You like music, Iris?"

She nodded. "I like the music in here."

"You can hear it?"

"A little bit I can."

"Do you want me to sign this paper?" She shrugged.

"Tell Mr. Butane you want him to sign the goddamn paper, Iris." She buried her face in her mom's hair. He barked at her, "Iris!" I took the paper off the clipboard.

"I see this form has your name and address on it, huh, Teddy? When I get out of here, I'm going to look you up and we're going to talk about what this is all about, and let me just tell you it'll be bad for you if I find out you've been mean to this little girl."

There was a kind of snickery laugh from the dark. "Don't worry, Leon, buddy. I'm the least of this little girl's problems, and for your information, I don't need your goddamn signature anyway. I got a witness that says all this was done with your permission. So you feel free to look me up any time. I got a license to carry. How does it look out there, Tonya?"

"It's okay." He hoisted the duffel onto his shoulder.

"I've decided to leave the Nicorette for you, Butane. I don't give a shit whether I quit smoking or not." Iris was waving her little hand as she took that soft yellow light and got carried out of my room.

Monday, February 19, 2007, a.m.

What woke me up the next morning was a hubbub outside my door. I mean, I don't have a lot of experience in what the usual hospital hubbub sounds like, but I found out right quick that what was going on out there wasn't normal.

When Irene came back in, she was trying to keep people out, and I saw a bunch of faces peeking in and getting a look at me. She was saying in a loud whisper, "You all run along now. Mr. Butane has been through a lot in the last few days and needs to rest so he can get well and go home."

When she finally managed to get the door closed, she smoothed herself out and tucked some renegade hair strands back where they belonged. She took a deep breath and got busy with her normal nursing stuff.

"What the hell's going on out there Irene? Sounds like a damn lynch mob or something."

"I don't know, Leon. If I didn't know better, I'd think there was a surveillance camera in here. Everything that happened yesterday and last night is all over the Internet, and people are lining up outside to get cured, or get autographs, or get pictures. Anyway, how are you feeling this morning?"

"I'm fine, Irene, but what exactly is all over the Internet?"

"On YouTube there are video interviews with Mr. and Mrs. Suarez and Father de Palma. There are photographs of you with an older gentleman here in your room. I gather they were taken last night after I went off duty. He says your prayers worked a miracle cure on his heart. Then, there's an absolutely incredible video, complete with background music, showing you curing a little girl with leukemia—or at least that's what they are saying.

It's all over the hospital this morning. She had an ALL diagnosis, but this morning's tests are negative. It looks like she's going to be well. It's all very inspiring, Leon."

It wasn't inspiring my ass a bit. It looked to me like shit was threatening to get out of hand, especially, since nobody was listening to a goddamn word I was saying about this miracle stuff.

"Look Irene. I really have to go. This is day one, and I know from experience my deadline's going to be crawling up on me before I know it. Can you get the doc in here so I can sign my discharge papers or bond papers or whatever?"

"Dr. Sugarman is making his rounds and should be here in a few minutes. He's down in intensive care now. He won't be long."

"Well, can we go ahead and start getting my stuff together so I won't waste no time when he does get through with intensive care and finds his way up here?" She checked me over again and acted like I hadn't said anything. "How about it, Irene?"

She smiled, but there was a kind of blush behind it. "I'm afraid you're going to be here for a few days, Leon. Dr. Sugarman is very enthusiastic about your case. He's planning an extensive work-up, the most extensive I've ever seen. I think you really threw him for a loop yesterday. Evidently there are some specialists coming in to do a battery of tests." Now I know what batteries are when you talk about flashlights, internal combustion engines, and military ordnance. But I don't have a damn clue what batteries are when you go to talking about medical tests.

"What, exactly, is a battery of tests, Irene?" You could tell she was uncomfortable about giving me any kind of medical information. "It depends on the situation. In your case, I really don't know. I'm afraid you'll have to get the specifics from Dr. Sugarman."

I knew for damn sure these hospital guys weren't on the same timetable I was. They were looking at my deadline like it was a symptom that could be slowed down or cancelled with the right therapies and medicines and shit. I was looking at my deadline like that's what it was. A deadline. On this side of it, Butane's alive. On that side of it, Butane's dead. I figured that no matter what I said, they wouldn't get as excited about the countdown as I was.

The commotion outside started fading. I heard deep cop-sounding voices telling people they needed to unclog the hallway so the nurses could get around to help sick people. "I guess that's hospital security?" Irene nodded just as the door opened and Dr. Sugarman stepped in. Wanda was with him. She hurried over to the bed and put her big arms around my neck. She touched my head like she was checking for fever. Then she stepped out of the way and Dr. Sugarman took over.

"How's our celebrity patient, Nurse Grasso? Has he been up?" I decided to get in the conversation.

"I'm not going to lie, doc. I've been better. But the truth is, I've had hangovers that were worse than what I feel right now. So I figure I'm a lot closer to being well than I am to being dead. I don't mean to step on any medical toes here, but I think I'm okay to go. What'd you say?" I was getting used to the routine he went through every time to check my pulse and stuff.

"You're a remarkable man, Leon. Your mind and body have endured a tremendous amount of stress, and, but for some noticeable muscular atrophy, you don't seem to be exhibiting any of the major classic sequelae we'd expect." I didn't know what that meant, but as far as I was concerned, good news or not, it was a side issue.

"Great! When can I go?" Wanda peeked around Dr. Sugarman while he looked in my eye and tested my tickle reflex.

"Now, Leon, let's not get in too big a hurry. After all, you've been in a coma and had brain surgery. And you just woke up a few hours ago for goodness sake."

Dr. Sugarman sounded right calm and professional. "I understand your anxiety, Leon. But we really can't risk a premature discharge. We have to let your brain function for a few days, then take a look at what's happening in your skull. I don't want to scare you, but you're not yet out of the woods. You're still at risk for a variety of problems. We need to know which ones are on the front burner and how we can go about offering you the best regimen for the most desirable outcome." It was like I was reading his mind. He was thinking, "And I'd like to look further into the question of how you knew about my father."

"I don't have time for that doc. I got two weeks from today..."

The doc and Wanda were talking at the same time. "Now, Leon..."

"I know, I know. You'll die in two weeks if you don't discover who was crucified with Jesus. I remember. But consider the probability you could slip back into a coma at any moment. You're still at risk for paralysis or death if we don't have an accurate picture." Wanda slipped into the chair like her legs turned to Silly Putty. Dr. Sugarman went on talking. "Let me suggest this, Leon. We can get you a laptop. We can arrange wireless access to use whenever you feel able and it's medically appropriate." Wanda wasn't listening.

"All due respect, doc. The only clue the puppet gave me was to talk to cousin Augie. He's somewhere in the hills of Missouri. He wouldn't drive across town to see me, much less across a whole damn state. I'm afraid the only shot I got is to get out of here and do some footwork."

That made Wanda look up. "Now Leon, you know that isn't so—necessarily. August might come to see you if you was to ask nice."

Dr. Sugarman had a couple more taters to throw in the pot. "Leon, you need to think about this logically. How do you expect to get to Missouri to talk to Augie? Legally, you can't drive. You'd be a danger to yourself and others. Suppose you're heading east on I-40 and lose consciousness. You could drift left of center and innocent people could be killed or injured. Not only would you be morally responsible, but you'd be legally liable as well. And maybe we would be too. It's just too dangerous." It sounded real final, and I didn't need any lawyer to explain what he was saying. If I was driving and blacked out and somebody got hurt, the blood-sucking lawyers would crawl out of the gol' darn woodwork and sue everybody in sight; me, the hospital, the doc, Irene, Steely Dan. Every damn body. I hated it, but I could see his point.

"Okay doc. How about this? Suppose I get Wanda here to drive me. She hasn't ever had an accident in her life. Hell, she's been driving forty years and she hasn't even had a speeding ticket. Suppose I give my word that for the next two weeks I won't drive a inch and two weeks from tomorrow if I'm still alive, I'll march right back in here and let you guys do all the guinea-piggin' you want to. Deal?"

Dr. Sugarman cocked one eyebrow and looked over at Wanda. "What do you say to that, Wanda? You think you'd be willing to go along with Leon's suggestion if it meant ignoring doctor's orders? Because we would certainly impress on you the risks you'd be taking."

I could see the wheels turning in Wanda's head. On the one hand, I'm her brother and blood's thicker than water. On the other hand, I'd had this lick on the head and was looking, acting, and talking a little loopy. Then, she was divorced, and Dr. Sugarman was a well-dressed, smooth-talking, sweet-smelling expert (ain't they all?) So I pretty much figured where she'd land before she said a word.

"Leon, honey, maybe we ought to do what the doctor says—at least for a day or two. We can talk about it some more later." She looked over at the doctor and batted her eyes. I thought I was going to be sick. If I left it up to Wanda and Dr. Sugarman, my ticket would get punched for sure. The only way out was ambush.

"You know what doc, you're right as rain. I'll just use your computer gizmo and solve the puzzle from right here in the hospital." He cocked his eyebrow again and looked me over good. You couldn't blame him for smelling a rat, because I was laying right there under his nose. Wanda didn't smell anything but the perfume on the doc's neck. She just sat there looking at him with calf eyes.

"What about your cousin Augie? I thought you were determined to go to Missouri to see him."

"Oh hell, doc. I'm surprised you didn't think of it. I'll just call the sombitch up on the phone. I'm sure Wanda's got his number. I'll just call him. He knows every damn thing there is to know about the Bible, doesn't he Wanda? Hell, he's probably got the answer off the top of his thick skull. Now that I think of it, I'll probably have the puzzle put together by this afternoon."

He tossed Wanda a *"game-set-match"* smile and patted my shoulder. "Good. And the truth is, Leon, I'm very hopeful we'll have you out of here in a week and, by then, we'll be sure we've done what we can to help you lead as normal a life as possible. And who knows, maybe the things we learn in working with you may give us some insight into matters of importance to the wider medical community."

My turn to hand out the big smile. "Obliged, doc. I aim to be the model patient in here. Nothing would please me more than being the model of medical importance." He smiled back.

"That's fine, Leon. Now we're going to move you out of L-TAC to another room and we need your help. You need to keep it quiet. We don't want a repeat of what happened here last night and this morning. Now I don't mean to be critical, but you really shouldn't encourage patients to ignore doctors' orders. See, your friend—Francisco was it?—told everybody you cured him. He said you assured him his heart was fine and he was free to cancel his surgery. He said you cleared him to go home no matter what his doctors might say. Unless we can convince him to come back, he's at extreme risk."

I was trying to explain that I never gave Francisco any medical advice when the transport people showed up to move me to another room. As they wheeled me out, I saw Irene watching me go. So I told them to hold on for a second. I called her over.

"I just want to say thanks for going out on a limb on that Google deal. I really appreciate your getting me that information. And thanks for loaning me your Bible too." I handed it back to her.

"Keep it Leon. I want you to have it. I think it'll be a help. And Leon, God bless and keep you." There was that sweet smile again. This time I figured it meant goodbye.

"Don't run off with another patient before I get back. If I get out of this, I'll come back and propose."

When they wheeled me out, Irene was touching her cross and Wanda and the doc were talking things over.

Tape 5

They deposited me in another room in another wing on the same floor. As soon as everybody was gone, I picked up the phone and started trying to call Woodrow Mulholland, by best buddy. I figured my only real chance was to bypass Wanda and the doc and go straight for some real honest-to-goodness redneck rescue.

Let me tell you about Woodrow. Me and him have been friends since we was little kids. We got drafted on the same day and took turns saving each other's bacon in Vietnam. He's a bona fide renegade outlaw and without a doubt the all time champion of thick-and-thin pals. I knew I could count on Woodrow no matter what—as long as I didn't screw up and give him too much information.

It took a while to figure out the hospital phone set-up, but my billfold was in the same plastic bag that my eye was in, and they put it on the table there by the bed. I did a quick go-over and seen that my cash and credit cards were all there. You know how it is. If you have a credit card that ain't maxed out, you're in business. I made the call and charged it to my Visa.

When Woodrow picked up the receiver, I was real relieved. He's such an oddball, there's no way of knowing whether he'll be home or off collecting roots and barks and stuff. If he is home, it all depends on his mood whether he'll answer the phone. "Hey Woodrow, it's me."

"Holy shit, Buzz! I thought you were still in a coma. Wanda told us they didn't know if you were ever going to wake up; and if you did, they weren't sure if you'd be right in your thinking." There was sort of a pause. "You're okay in your thinking, aren't you, Buzz?"

"Hell yes. I'm fine Woodrow. I'm a little behind on current events though. Slept plumb through the Stupid Bowl."

"Well man, I'm glad to hear your voice. When did you wake up?"

"I have been awake off and on since about eight-thirty yesterday morning."

"Great! That's great, Buzz. I guess you're still in the hospital, right? When they going to let you go home?"

"That's why I'm calling, Woodrow. I'm getting out today, but I need you to pick me up." There was another pause.

"Wouldn't Wanda want to pick you up? She's right there in town."

"See it's like this Woodrow. She doesn't get off work until this afternoon, and I don't feel like laying around up here for the rest of the day. I'm sick of this place. I figure if you was to leave now, you could be here..." I looked up at the wall clock. "... about twelve-twenty or twelve-thirty. What do you say Woodrow? You ain't busy, are you?"

I held my breath while he thought it over. It seemed like it took a long time for him to answer. "Well hell no, I'm not busy, and hell yeah, I'm walking out the door right now. I'll be there twelve-thirty at the latest." I love that guy. "What room you in?"

"Never mind that, Woodrow. Just pull up to the main entrance there on the north side of the Metro Methodist Hospital. I'll be waiting for you."

"Okay, Buzz. Be there in about three and a half hours."

"You're a true friend, Woodrow. I'll call your cell later to check on your progress. Be careful now, dammit. One wreck in the family is enough for now." He laughed that big old Woodrow laugh.

"I'll try to stay out of a coma until I can talk to you and find out if it's any fun. See you."

When I got off the phone and started checking around I discovered I didn't have any pants. No underwear neither. I don't know why it didn't occur to me before. All I had to wear was this hospital gown. You know how those things work. It's like an apron with arms. Even when it works right, it leaves your ass hanging out.

Well there was a nurse button there, so I pushed it. A couple of seconds later, this bony, Nurse-Ratchett-looking woman came charging in. The name on her tag said "Loretta." She flew in so fast and furious, I was thrown off guard for a minute and forgot what I was about to say. It didn't matter because she took the initiative. It was like frost was dripping off every word she said.

"Well, what is it, Mr. Butane?"

"I—uh. Well, I wonder if there's a pair of pants around here some-place."

"No there are no pants up here for you. The ones you were wearing in the wreck were ruined and nobody knew when you were going to wake up out of your coma. So, I repeat. There are no pants. Now, if you don't need anything other than pants, I have sick people up here on this floor who need nursing." Then she turned around mounted her broom and started toward the door. I wasn't satisfied.

"Before you get back to your other patients, ma'am, maybe you could get a hold of some of those paper britches like the doctors wear around here. I could put those on. I just feel kind of funny wearing this dress thing all the time. You can understand, can't you?"

She whirled around with fire in her squinty little eyes, rammed her fists into her skinny hips, and laid a real mean stare on me. "No, you can't have any paper pants and no, you don't need any pants. Here's what you do need. You need to get busy staying out of trouble. I heard about the com-motion you started over on L-TAC working your so-called miracles. On this floor, the only one allowed to work miracles is me. We don't have time for supernatural healings because we have sick people to take care of. Now I want you to forget about wearing pants until the doctor says it's appropriate for you to wear pants. And don't even think about working any miracles up here unless the doctor or I say it's okay. Now you stay there in your bed and think about getting well and don't be bothering the nurses up here caring for the sick." She "harrumphed" and started flying toward the door again. I should have kept my mouth shut.

"Pardon, ma'am. Just one more thing. If I can't have no pants, how about a pair of shoes?" Well then she really hit the ceiling.

"*Mister Butane,* the only reason a patient would need shoes is if he is going somewhere, and you aren't going anywhere until the doctor says so. Look here. These beds are equipped with restraints, and all I need is a doctor's orders and I'll hobble you right here in this bed. And be advised, Mr. Butane, I can easily fit you out with a diaper if that gown isn't good enough to suit you. Now are you going to behave?"

"Yes, ma'am." She was still grumbling when she finally zipped out the door. I took a deep breath and decided I was going to have to come up with a plan that didn't involve pants or shoes. I needed to pee.

I knew I was supposed to call for help before I got out of bed. But the idea of asking Loretta to come back in reminded me of an old joke. You know what the jack-rabbit said while he was making love to the skunk? I believe I've enjoyed about all this I can stand. So I decided to sneak into the bathroom and pee on my own.

Now I've got to set the stage for what happened next. I'm not bragging or nothing, but I'm a pretty good-looking hoss for a middle aged man. Did you see the movie *Gladiator*? Well, I've been told by more than one that I look like Russell Crowe in that movie. I hadn't seen my own face in forty-one days. The last time I remember looking at it, was the morning of the crack-up when I shaved it.

Well, there was a mirror in the bathroom and I wasn't ready for what I seen when I took a good look. It was awful. The face of disaster looking back at me from that mirror didn't look anything like a gol' darn gladiator, let me tell you. That poor shrunken sombitch staring back at me looked like the walking dead with bandages on his head.

I don't know what the hell they feed you when you're in a coma, but I'll tell you one thing. It's gangbusters for weight loss. And they didn't shave me, either. A gladiator may look okay with a beard. But a bearded skeleton looks like warmed-over shit. I stood there staring at myself until I was about to puke. It's probably ego, but for a minute there, I was thinking, *Hell, if I've got to walk around looking like this for the rest of my life, let's just call the whole thing off and let the gol' dang puppet punch my ticket right now.*

But, you know, that's sort of how I felt when I woke up in the field hospital and found out my eye was blown out. I got over that, and I knew I'd get over this deal. After all, if a fellow watches his diet, he can always find a way to gain weight.

There was shaving stuff there on the sink, so I decided I'd make myself feel better by taking a hot shower and mowing the whiskers off my bony old jaw. So I got the shower nice and hot, shed my hospital dress and stepped in. I've got to tell you that my legs were about to give out. There was a little seat they put in there for sick folks, and I had to sit on it until I was able to finish my shower. When the bandages on my head got wet, they peeled off real easy. I stepped out of the shower and made myself look in the mirror again. I was even more disgusted than I was when I was wearing my head gear. Know why? The sons o' bitches shaved half my head. No shit! Why in the cornbread hell would you shave just half a guy's head? I guess somebody likes playing jokes on unconscious, brain-damaged fellas.

I sat down a minute to rest and get over the shock, then I limbered up the razor and got to work. I started at the top and worked my way down. Now there was this big red horseshoe looking scar on the left side of my skull. Hell, it was big enough it looked like they could have pulled out my old brain and fitted a new one in.

I shaved my whole head. Shaved her clean. And when I was done with that, I started on my face. I'll tell you what. Being shaved and showered made me feel a lot better, but there damn sure wasn't much improvement in my looks. The whole exercise had me plumb tuckered out, so I decided to get some rest. I eased back into the bed and, before you could say "Bride of Frankenstein," I was snoozing.

I jerked awake when a nurse brought in some lunch. For a second there, I panicked. For all I knew, I slept several more days. I asked the lady with the food if it was still Monday. She laughed, "Yes it is Mr. Butane. It'll be Monday all day."

I looked at the clock and it was ten 'til twelve. Great! Woodrow should be getting close. When the nurse left, I called him. "Where are you, Woodrow?"

"Just getting off the Turner Turnpike. Be there at the hospital in twenty minutes."

"Great. Just pull up in front of the main entrance like I said. I'll be there."

"Okay, Buzz. See you in a few."

"Oh, Woodrow, keep the motor running."

He was saying, "Now wait a minute, Buzz..." when I hung up the phone.

I didn't have no time to waste. I had to get it in gear and decide how to make my getaway. As for my escape outfit, I didn't have but the one option. I was going to have to make a run for it barefoot and wearing nothing but that embarrassing, goddamn gown. Believe me, I knew how that was going to look. A skin-headed, skeleton-looking guy with a Frankenstein scar and a hospital gown casually strolling toward the front door on a February morning. Nothing odd about that is there? But under the circumstances, that's how it had to be.

There wasn't much of a pocket in my gown, but it was enough for my wallet and the folded up form I took off Teddy's clipboard. For a second, I thought about bringing Miss Wister's card. But I couldn't think of any advantage. So I left it on the table along with Teddy's Nicorette. I tucked Irene's Bible under my arm and headed for freedom.

I peeked out the door and my dad-burned old heart sunk. There was Dr. Sugarman and a couple of other doctor guys leaning over Loretta's bony shoulder looking back and forth from a chart to a computer screen. I figured their next stop was bound to be Butane's room. To get to the elevators, I'd have to walk right by them. No chance. But, to the right of my room a couple of doors down, was the stairway. If I made my move right then, I might reach those stairs before the doctors and Loretta caught on.

An Allman Brothers song was rolling around in my memory. As I stepped into the hall and headed for the stairway, I was singing to myself, *I'm not going to let them catch the Midnight Rider.*

Before I could get to the stairs, I almost bumped into a lady backing out of a room with a cart full of laundry. I gave her a smile and mumbled something about the men's room and hurried toward the exit sign.

When I got to the door leading to the stairway, I stopped long enough to size things up. The lady I passed was looking at me all puzzled-like. Dr. Sugarman and his crew were still bent over Loretta's shoulder, and the Midnight Rider slipped into the stairwell.

Almost half way down to the fifth floor, here's what the Midnight Rider discovered. After forty days in a coma, your legs and your wind ain't any match for a flight of stairs. So the Midnight Rider had to set his bare ass down on them cold steps to catch his breath.

It was pretty damn clear there was going to be an energy crisis somewhere on my way to meet Woodrow. In fact, I was only down one-half a floor, and I had five and a half to go. I'd never make it. There were only two options. It was the elevator or bed restraints. I took a minute to catch my breath, then hobbled the rest of the way down to the fifth floor.

When I opened the door, I got hit by a wave of discouragement. See, I didn't know what I was expecting, but for a second there, it looked like I'd just looped back to where I started. I had this terrible thought. Suppose this really was hell. Suppose no matter which floor you run to, it turns out to be the same one you just left, and Loretta was the boss of them all. I just couldn't stand it.

But when I could focus my eye on the nurse's station, I could see there was a different squad. I was real happy about that. Still, I didn't have any real hope that my wobbly legs would hold out.

Then I could see that fortune was on my side. I spied this wheel chair sitting outside the room a couple of doors down. I figured with some wheels to help me out, no one could stop the Midnight Rider.

I teetered over to the chair and took a seat. I aimed toward the elevators and like a flash I was on the move again. All but one of the nurses ignored me as I eased on by their desk. The only reason that one looked, I think, was because my driving was sort of erratic. I don't know if you've ever tried it, but just popping your ass into a wheelchair and taking off ain't as easy as it looks. You'd think a guy that can back a semi-trailer into a tiny parking space ought to be able to maneuver a damn wheelchair. But I had to use what was left of my legs to compensate for my lack of wheelchair driving skills.

There were a couple of ladies discussing Oprah or Dr. Phil or something when I rolled up to the elevator. I was huffing and puffing when I skidded to a stop to join up with their wait. They took turns glancing down at me, but they were too polite to make a production out of noticing the creepy guy that just rolled up. So they just kept up their conversation nonstop, being careful not to look at me too close. Can't say I blamed them.

When the elevator door opened, there wasn't anybody in there, so my two lady friends stepped to one side and let me zigzag to the back of the car. The elevator stopped on four. My internal alarm bells went wild when that gol' dang Haysuse got on with a couple of other priest-looking guys. They were so deep in their discussion that they didn't pay a bit of attention to the scarecrow hunkered down in the wheelchair at the back of the elevator. Fine with me. But it was hard to believe they weren't at all curious about me, because I felt like I was sticking out like the cricket in the ant farm.

Everybody on the elevator kept talking and I kept sitting, looking at my feet and acting like I wasn't even there. The elevator stopped on three. I guess that's where the cafeteria is 'cause I could smell fries when the door opened. Things got even more complicated. A couple of guys got on with cameras hanging all over their necks. Reporters. Everybody was talking to everybody, and I kept sitting there looking at my bare feet.

The elevator stopped on two. I tried not to groan out loud. Irene got on. She stood right in front of me. She and Haysuse hugged each other, and I'll bet you can guess what their topic of conversation was. Yep. Yours truly. They were talking about Señor Butane this and Señor Butane that while Señor Butane was hunkered down in the back of the car pretending he wasn't there. It took forever to get to that first floor. Irene stepped aside to let me off. As I rolled past her, she looked down and chirped, "Goodness, Leon, what are you doing down here?"

As soon as she said that, Haysuse hollered and reached out for my hand,

"Señor Butane! We've been looking everywhere for you!" You got to give it to them paparazzi guys. They got reflexes that would make a cobra proud. As soon as they heard my name, they almost pulled their camera lanyards through their own damn necks getting their gizmos up to start shooting pictures. That was the Midnight Rider's signal to fire up his wheeled cow pony and head for the revolving doors.

Right on cue, I saw Woodrow's pickup roll up outside. I made a bee line for the exit. I was a menace to every pedestrian in sight because I was weaving all over the damn place.

About that time, I heard Loretta shriek, "You hold it right there Mr. Butane! Don't make me have to run you down." That's when I really poured the coals to it. I was hollering, "One side!" and "Coming through!" Stuff like that. I could hear heavy thumping on top of a squish-squishy noise from Loretta's shoes and bat-like breathing. She was swooping toward me and closing in.

My odds was getting longer by the second as I could see there was a security guard sitting at the information table. When Loretta screeched, "Stop that man!" the guard watched me roll-walking as fast as I could toward the door, and because of his training, he figured I must be the guy he was supposed to be stop. But his reflexes was slow, so he didn't exactly spring into action. Instead, he sort of lumbered into action. Lucky for me.

I was about out of gas, and Loretta and the guard was gaining. I was almost to the revolving door when I realized that the chair was liable to get tangled up in there and I'd get nailed for sure. I didn't have any choice. I had to dismount and go the rest of the way barefoot and bare-assed.

I saw Woodrow's woolly head leaned over the wheel of his pickup watching what was going on. People was dodging out of the way as I left the chair behind and wobbled through the door. It was one of those automatic revolver deals and I couldn't tell if it was my imagination or if it was moving in slow motion. I could hear Loretta and the guard getting tangled up with the chair, and Loretta was yelling, "Where do you think you're going, Mr. Butane?" Woodrow opened the passenger door so I wouldn't have to slow down and I hollered back to answer Loretta's question.

"I'm going to get me a second opinion." I jumped into the truck, slammed the door and hollered, "Punch it Woodrow!"

He didn't waste any time trying to analyze the situation. He punched it like I told him. I looked out the back window and saw Loretta and the security guard tumbling out through revolving doors. The guard's glasses must have got knocked off because he started feeling around on the ground. I thought I saw clouds of steam coming off Loretta's tight, black hair-do as she stood there huffing and puffing with her feet wide apart and her fists pushed into her narrow hips. I blew the old sweetheart a kiss as we made the turn out of the hospital drive-way and headed for the turnpike.

Woodrow's chuckling was getting on my nerves, so I decided to change the subject. "Take me to my house Woodrow. I've got to get some pants on."

He threw his big old head back and gave out a loud "Haw, haw." I was probably blushing from my toe nails up.

"What the hell's so gol' dang funny?"

"Oh, nothing Buzz. There ain't anything funny about you driving that wheelchair like a maniac and making men, women, and old people jump for their dang lives. There ain't anything funny about you waiting until you have the attention of the whole cockeyed world, then jumping out of the chair so everybody could get a real good look at your bare, hairy ass. There ain't anything funny about your old head being peeled like an onion. But the most unfunny of all is seeing you in that damn dress. None of this is funny, Buzz. It's all pitiful and shameful."

"Goddammit Woodrow! You're the one ought to be ashamed here: making fun of a guy in my position who's only trying to pull off a heroic escape. And it ain't a dress goddammit! It's a gown." Well, that started him laughing again. Some pal.

So far as I could tell, nobody was on our tail. Woodrow finally got control of his damn self and slowed down enough to blend with traffic.

Now this is going to be important, so I've got to tell you about Woodrow's Dodge. On the outside, it's a green, piece-of-shit 1980 D150 custom one-half-ton club cab with the Macho Power Wagon package. On the inside, it's a by-God concert hall. Every couple of years, Woodrow upgrades the Dodge's sound system so she's always got the top-of-the-line speakers, receivers, amps—everything. And he's got her hooked up to an iPod that's got the damndest assortment of music you ever heard. See, I'm a classic rock, old-time country music kind of guy. I can take a little gospel in small doses.

But Woodrow likes everything. Blues, rock, jazz, opera, elevator music—everything. Stevie Wonder's "Superstitious" was playing when he looked over at me and said, "Okay, Buzz. Just what the hell's really going on here?"

So I gave it to him, the whole banana. The wreck, me floating over the operating table, the zoo, Pinocchio, Ho, Jack, the deadline, Dr. Sugarman, Ms. Suarez, old Francisco, little Iris, the revolutionaries, Kathleen, the bust-out. Everything right up to the minute he pulled up outside the hospital. He just sat there taking it all in and not saying a word as we motored down the highway.

My house was on an acreage in Jones, Oklahoma, about thirty minutes east of the hospital. When we turned off I-35 to go east on Britton road, we had about ten minutes to go and we went the rest of the way without either of us talking.

When we pulled off the county road and drove up my long gravelly driveway, I was glad to see that old Pete, my neighbor, was doing a good job of keeping my newspapers picked up. These days, if you live in the country, one thing you don't want is to advertise when you aren't home. There's a lot more mischief now than there used to be. When I'm on the road, Pete is real good about picking up my mail and stuff. I've never been gone for forty days, though. It didn't matter to Pete. No matter how long I was gone, he'd have just kept on looking after my place long as he was able.

When I went to get down out of the Dodge, I discovered that there weren't any bones left in my legs. I guess the exertion of the hospital getaway turned me into Gumby. So Woodrow had to give me a hand getting in the house. When we were inside, I wobbled into the bedroom to get some britches, and Woodrow took out the trash and checked the icebox.

I was never so happy to put on some Fruit-of-the-Looms and a pair of Levi's. There's just something about having on your own drawers that makes a fellow feel more like a man. Add a tee shirt, a work shirt, a good, broken-in pair of boots for good measure, and a guy can look forward to stuff getting back to normal some day.

Woodrow had us a couple of cold beers on the coffee table when I came back to the living room. I could tell he had a lot of stuff rolling around in his head, because Woodrow's a thinker. Me, I'm a driver.

We sat there drinking our beers trying to figure out what ought to be said next. Finally, Woodrow looked over at me all serious and said, "Do you know what tomorrow is, Buzz?" When I tried to think about it, the mule kick on the left side of my head started to get painful.

"Well, you know I've been in a coma for over a month. On top of that I've had an important thing or two on my mind today. If I forgot your birthday or something, I'm real damn sorry. I just didn't get around to checking my calendar. No Woodrow, I don't have a clue what tomorrow is."

He sat there in the beanbag looking at me with a sympathetic expression on his craggy face. Then he took a deep breath. "Well, for one thing, tomorrow's Mardi Gras, Buzz. And I was feeling a little bit depressed trying to figure out how to celebrate with you laid up in the hospital. Some of the guys and I was going to drop in to the hospital and say hi. But after that, we didn't know if we'd be able to get into things like normal." He clunked his empty bottle down on the table. "Tell you what. There's a smoked sausage and sauerkraut special over at the diner. What say we get over there, have us some pre-Mardi Gras kraut and let everybody get a look at what's left of you. They'll all be glad to see you finally woke up from your beauty sleep. They'll be disappointed to see you woke up before it had time to take. Maybe you should have given it another month or two."

The idea of seeing the diner gang and getting a big plate of Betsy's sauerkraut and sausage sounded great. It even put the bones back in my legs. I decided to overlook his childish insults. We piled back into the Dodge and headed for the Weloka Diner.

Let me tell you a little bit about the diner. It's a daytime hang-out for a lot of vets—mostly combat vets from Nam. We're a pretty close bunch and we do a passable job of looking after each other. Betsy's husband, Hank, was a friend of ours. After he got killed at Loc Ninh, we all rallied around to help her through. Turns out over the years she's been a lot more help to us guys than we was to her. She opened the diner in 1977 and, since then, it's sort of information central. Betsy's real good about keeping track of everybody in our group, and she makes a weekly run over to the Veteran's Hospital in Norman to look in on the guys there. If they need anything, she lets us know and we find a way to take care of it. Anyway, whenever we want to know what's going on with one of our buddies, somebody at the diner will know, or can find out.

Woodrow's real popular in there because he's the only guy in America with a mammoth ivory foot. He lost his left foot in the same firefight that got my right eye. He don't wear the government-issue replacement. He made his own foot, but I'll tell you more about that later.

Monday, February 19, 2007, p.m.

Weloka is the county seat of Shawnee County, just east of Oklahoma County, and it's about a half-hour from my house. So, by the time we got there, it was a little after two o'clock, and the lunch crowd was gone. There were still a few people drinking coffee and eating Betsy's pie.

Two of the guys in there, Stu and Billy, graduated from Chisolm Oaks High with me and Woodrow. They served in the 25th Infantry in Nam. You can usually find them in the diner in the afternoon, because they manage The Tolosa Gold Saloon, which means they work nights.

When we walked in, everybody went out of their way to not notice my shaved head and mule kick. Everybody said they was glad to see me awake and moving around with an appetite. A couple of them asked if I was going to make it to the Mardi Gras shindig at The Gold tomorrow. I was about to let myself get into a conversation about it, but Woodrow steered me away from Stu and Billy's table. I could tell there was something really bothering him, so we took a booth up front where we was away from everybody and could watch the traffic on main street Weloka. That's another good thing about our buddies. They can tell if you want to be left alone and they leave you alone.

After Betsy took our order, Woodrow took a deep breath, looked me in the eye and said, "Look Buzz. You're a guy that likes to hear it straight. So that's how I'm going to give it to you. There's a good chance this whole Pinocchio deal is a hallucination, just like your doctor says." I started to argue with him, but he interrupted.

"Just hear me out. Today's February 19. Tomorrow is February 20. That isn't just Mardi Gras. Think about it, Buzz."

Man it hit me like a RPG. February 20, 1970. We were in the armored unit of the 196th Light Infantry on patrol in Queson Valley. I'm not going into a lot of detail here because it's not important. But you need to know a couple of things. First, another name for the Queson Valley was the Death Valley, because a lot of people on all sides got wasted in there. Next, there weren't supposed to be any civilians in there. We'd swept the place several times resettling folks, so anybody in there was apt to be VC or NVA. Even if they weren't, anybody that slipped back after we swept the place was automatically under suspicion of being VC or a VC sympathizer. I'm not saying that was right or wrong. I'm just saying that's how it was.

Anyway, when we pulled out of Tam Ky that morning, we didn't have a clue that a fuse to a hell of a powder keg got lit in that valley the day before. See, on February 19, 1970, a five-man Marine patrol called a killer team went into a little village called Son Thang looking for VC. All the marines in there was real touchy because not long before that, a marine patrol got ambushed and almost all of them was wiped out. Anyway, this killer team didn't find any VC, but somehow they wound up opening fire on a bunch of civilians. Five women and eleven kids got killed. I guess when the press got hold of it, they called it the Marine My Lai.

Well, we didn't know about any massacre at Son Thang when we rolled out that morning. In fact we didn't know anything about it until a long time later. I don't know if it was revenge for the massacre, but the NVA knew we were on the way and had a dandy ambush set up. Woodrow and me and a black kid from Texas named Pittman—I think his first name was Everett, but everybody called him "Son"—anyway, Woodrow and me and Son was all in the cab of this M-151; it's a jeep we called a Mutt. Son was showing us a Valentine card he got from his sister when the world blew up around us. Something slammed into the Mutt and knocked us over. Woodrow was on the passenger seat so his window was on top when the Mutt rolled over. He pulled me and Son out. There was automatic and small arms fire from every direction. We was all sitting ducks unless we could find some cover, and the only chance we had was to jump into a muddy ditch across the cow path from where we was knocked over. A bunch of us was tumbling all over each other when we hit that ditch.

We were firing every which way, trying not to shoot up our own guys, when a grenade dropped in the ditch on top of us. Hell, it could've been one of our own for all I know. It landed right in the middle of the ditch with five or six of us and disappeared in the water pooled up in the bottom.

Everybody started hollering and scrambling to get out of there, but the first guy out got hit and fell right back in there with us. That's when everything went into slow motion. I was looking across the ditch at Son and he was looking at me and that grenade was getting ready to hatch between us. If you know anything about military ordnance, you know a grenade like that will kill every living thing that's exposed within ten meters of the blast—and there were at least five of us exposed—maybe more. I don't know. I could see in Son's eyes that he was thinking the same thing as me. If somebody didn't jump on that thing, everybody would die. Maybe everybody would die anyway.

So there we were, me and Son looking at each other both knowing one of us had to do it and both wishing it was the other guy. It seemed like an awful lot of time ticked off and I decided Son wasn't going so I just jumped praying like hell that grenade was a dud.

But Son decided a split second before I did because he landed on it first. I rolled off him and our eyes was locked on each other when that grenade went off. The last thing my right eye ever seen was the look on Son's face when he got blown up.

You don't want to know the whole story, but I should've been killed. My time was up when that grenade dropped into that ditch. If I'd done what I knew was right—without hesitating—I'd have been dead and chances are Son would be a middle-aged man living somewhere in Texas with battle scars of his own. But that ain't the way it worked out. That grenade killed Son and another guy—a Yankee kid named Burchall from New Jersey. It blinded my right eye and took Woodrow's left foot.

After we got evacuated and started healing up, Woodrow and I saw to it that word got up the chain of command how Son sacrificed himself for the rest of us. He got a medal. We sent letters to his mom and sister. We even went to see them once we got out of the army. For about eight or nine years after we got out, we called his folks and had some beers in Son's honor on February 20 every year. But we just kind of got out of the habit I guess. I'm sorry about that now, looking back.

When Woodrow reminded me about the next day being February 20, I got churned up in all kinds of emotions. First off, I was ashamed. How could you not remember the day when a guy died to save your ass? But then I started defending myself. For crying out loud! I was in a coma for over a gol' darn month. You couldn't expect me to hit the ground running with normal recall after a deal like that. But that wouldn't explain how I could forget it for the last few years. Then it started to sink in that Woodrow might be onto something. He waited until he could see the fog clearing off my brain, then he went on talking.

"I don't know how everything is supposed to hook up, but you know what they say, 'coincidence is the mother of suspicion.' And it just seems awful coincidental that you get sent on some kind of religious mission on the anniversary of the day a guy we called "Son" sacrificed his life for us. Maybe somewhere down deep you feel like you need to do something to make up for something. I don't know, Buzz. I'm just saying."

Well, holy shit! Of course, that had to be it! My scrambled up brain was pulling up all kinds of visions and making all kinds of connections that weren't any more real than a goddamn believable LSD trip.

If you've ever dropped acid, you know what I mean. The visions and hallucinations you have while you're tripping can sure as hell feel real at the time. The difference is, when you crash from LSD, you actually get suspicious of all the weird shit you think you saw. But I was finding out that you don't have any bearings at all when you snap out of a coma. Woodrow was right. My unconsciousness was wading through a mind swamp of guilt, regret, and stuff like that.

So I said, "You know what, Woodrow? You're right as rain. Hell, my brain got run through a damn blender, and I can't tell real from Shinola. This whole Pinocchio 'find-out-who-got-crucified-with-Jesus' deal is bullshit. I don't need to waste any more time on it. What I do need to worry about . . ." Then, it was like a bomb went off in my head, and I blacked out.

There I was, back at the zoo. This time, Jack and Ho were gone, and there was another guy sitting there with Pinocchio. This guy was a really scary, depressed-looking dude with a big damn scar on the left side of his neck. There was water dripping off of him like he just took a shower with all his fatigues on.

I was trying, again, to get a handle on exactly what the Sam Hill was going on when Pinocchio started clacking all around the picnic table in some kind of weird, slow motion, jerky puppet dance. When he started clacking his way up to where I was standing, I found out I was frozen stiffer than a two by four. Then he stopped and looked up at me, and I got shivers all over, because there were little blue tears running out of his painted eyeballs. He just stood there for a minute crying up at me. Then he said, really slow and mournful like.

"Mr. Butane. You see that man sitting there?" He pointed his tiny finger at the new guy. My vocals unfroze.

"Yeah. I see him."

"Your friend, Mr. Mulholland, would be very interested to know that Edward here was murdered in Manila and his body was disposed of in such a way that it will never be found."

I looked at the new guy—Edward. He nodded all slow and sad like. "I'm telling you this, Mr. Butane, because a moment ago you came within a breath of dropping dead in your plate of sauerkraut and sausage. I must warn you again, in the most positive terms, that the instant you resign from your efforts to carry out your assignment, your life will end. No questions asked. No appeals. No matter how compelling it may be to believe this is all imaginary; no matter how tempted you may be to seize a convenient and simple solution. No matter how frustrated you become in this endeavor. Unless you are fully prepared to face the great unknown, keep seeking, Mr. Butane. Keep seeking."

Give me a minute here to change tapes and get hold of myself. I'll be right back.

TAPE 6

So then, the next thing I knew, I was waking up stretched out on the floor of the diner. Woodrow was hollering at Betsy to call 911. I tried to talk, but it came out more like a squeak. "Hold on there. I'm okay. Just give me a little air here. I sure as hell don't need to be going to the hospital right now. I got too much to do."

I couldn't tell whether Woodrow was more scared or pissed. "Goddamn it Buzz! You scared the shit out of me. What do you mean you don't need a hospital? Your brain is fucked up man. I'm afraid you're going to croak on us or something."

"Table that for now Woodrow. Help me up. I got something important to tell you."

"Don't tell me to table it, you mule-headed prick! I knew this was going to happen. I never should have helped you bust out of that hospital. Betsy! Go ahead and call the goddamn ambulance." She ran to the phone and dialed 911. I thought I was going to puke. If they got me back in the hospital, they'd damn sure rope me in. I'd be in the soup for sure.

I reached up and grabbed Woodrow by the arm. "Listen, Woodrow, all that stuff you said about Son, all that stuff about me being guilty. I was believing it. Then, when I blacked out, I was back at the zoo with Pinocchio. Only this time there was this other guy with this long scar on the left side of his neck. The puppet said his name was Edward and you know him. He said he had a message for you, Woodrow."

Woodrow reared back like somebody put ice cubes down his shirt. "Wait a minute. What the hell is this? You've got to tell me what this message deal is about."

"Okay. I'm supposed to tell you this. Edward got killed in Manila and he's gone for good. Nobody's ever going to find his body. That's it."

Woodrow turned real red in the face. He took hold of my shirt collar and pulled my face real close to his and said sort of snarly-like. "Snap out of it Buzz. What kind of crazy hocus-pocus, voodoo horseshit are you getting me into? How did the fucking puppet know to tell you anything about me anyway? How did this puppet get a hold of any information about Uncle Ed?"

I felt really sorry for him, because it looked like he was getting spun around and chopped up in the salad master same as me. I was feeling like I might pass out again, but I couldn't, because the ambulance might be on its way. So I said to myself, *Butane, you need to calm down here, and you've got to calm Woodrow too. You've got to step careful here until you can come up with a plan."*

It was like Woodrow read my mind. "Okay, Buzz. We got to call off the ambulance and get some place where we can sort some of this shit out." Just as he said that, a police car and an ambulance came sliding up in front of the diner, lights flashing and sirens blaring. Woodrow said, "You okay to walk?"

"Yeah, I think so. Help me up." So he threw a couple of twenties on the table.

"Stand up straight as you can. Lean on me if you have to, but try to act natural." My legs were weak, but I was putting my jacket on and was stepping out the door and onto the sidewalk when the EMTs ran past.

Woodrow looked in the window at Betsy and the guys who was standing around looking worried. He put his fingers to his lips to signal for them to keep quiet. I crawled in the Dodge and Woodrow jumped under the wheel. We could see the ambulance guys looking at us as Woodrow backed out and drove west down Main Street.

On the way back to my house, Woodrow explained some stuff. "If this guy you saw in the zoo with Pinocchio was my uncle Eddie, you ought to know he was one scary dude. He got drafted in World War II and got sent to the Pacific Theater. I guess he was a hell of fighting man because he went ape-shit on the Japanese. I don't know how many decorations he got, but I guess he got every medal you can get for killing Japs. From what I heard, he liked the killing business. That scar on his neck came from a Japanese bayonet. It never even slowed him down. Tied the dirty sleeve of a Japanese uniform around his neck and kept right on fighting.

"When the war was over, Eddie mustered out, but he couldn't adjust. I don't know what all he did, but the only reason he didn't wind up in the pen was because he was a war hero. When the Korean War broke out, he reenlisted, went to Korea, and went ape-shit on the Koreans and Chinese. I guess he went too far, though. There are all kinds of stories about torture and murder. Hell, there were even rumors about cannibalism. They didn't want to court martial him, but they couldn't keep him around. So they threw him out. While he was waiting to get transported back to the states, he raped and killed a Korean girl. He disappeared before they could arrest him. The last anybody heard from him was a letter to my mom postmarked from the Philippines. That's it. We never wanted to hear from him again.

"All the kids in the family were afraid of him. We didn't need a bogeyman, because we had Uncle Eddie stalking around in our nightmares."

You can understand why all the hair on the back of my neck stood up as Woodrow as telling me all this. I've know Woodrow a long time, and he never mentioned a word to me about this Uncle Eddie guy.

There was one of those quiet times in the truck while we drove back home.

When we got to the house, there was a van parked out by my mailbox. I really didn't pay much attention to it. I had plenty of stuff to think about, and my head was killing me.

The first thing I did when we got in the house was look for some headache medicine. I found about a half dozen Advil and took three of them. The next thing I did was call Wanda. I figured she'd be going out of her head worrying when she found out about my escape from the hospital. Plus, I needed Augie's phone number.

I hadn't talked to Augie in fifteen years or more. Last I heard, he was preaching at a little church in Chittum, Missouri. I knew that Wanda kept up with everybody in the family so she'd know how to get in touch with him. When I got hold of her at the insurance agency, she was hot.

"Leon Butane what on earth are you thinking about? You get yourself right back to that hospital this minute. We've been worried sick about you! Where are you?"

"Look, sis…"

"Don't you 'sis' me Leon. You're about to cause me to have a heart attack, for heaven's sake."

"Okay, okay Wanda. I'll go back. But first, I need to talk to Augie. Do you have his number?"

For a second, I thought the line went dead. When she spoke up, she sounded like she was heading toward hysterical. "You're not serious about his Pinocchio nonsense. Sakes alive, Leon! I've got to be honest. That accident knocked the common sense right out of your silly head. You've got to get back so the doctors can take care of you. It's not safe for you to …"

"You're right, sis. What's the number? I really need to talk some things over with Augie."

"Just a minute." I heard her rummaging around in her purse. "Okay. Here it is. Are you ready?" I wrote it down. "Okay Leon. I'll meet you at the hospital."

"Now hold on a minute Wanda. I've got to do a couple of things first. I'll call you when I'm on my way back."

There was a kind of whiny sound in her voice. "But Leon, you said you were going back."

"And I am sis. As soon as I finish up what I'm doing. Now don't worry, Wanda. Everything's going to be fine. I'll call you in a little bit."

"Just tell me where you are."

"Bye bye, baby sister. Remember your big brother is the king of the world and he loves you."

"But, Leon …" I hated leaving her so tangled up on the inside. But she would never understand. And I had to focus.

I called the number Wanda gave me. Augie wasn't home. His wife, Naomi, told me he was out visiting the sick. I told her I needed to come up and visit. She said that would be fine and gave me the directions to their place in Chittum.

Woodrow was in the kitchen having a beer and looking out the window. He handed me one when I walked in. We sat down at the table and looked each other in the eye, each one waiting for the other to start. Since I was the one with the time limit, I kicked it off.

"Look here, Woodrow. You know I'd rather take an ass whupping than drag you into this nightmare."

"Well, looks like I'm in it now no matter what happens. I'm probably going to have bad dreams about Edward Mulholland tonight thanks to you and your puppet buddy. So, what does me being in this nightmare mean, exactly?"

"It's like this Woodrow. I've got a tall order to fill and two weeks to do it. Maybe it'll be easy. Maybe it won't. I wish somebody could tell me what I'm up against. But I'm in the dark. I don't know how much chasing around I'm going to have to do. But I damn sure can't drive myself, because with this seizure deal, I'd be a threat to the motoring public. Hell, you've seen it with your own eyes."

He took a long pull on his beer bottle and nodded.

"I hate to put you on the spot, Woodrow, but how about it? Can you be my wheels until this thing is settled? Two weeks, max."

He chewed on it for a minute. After a while he said, "Well, I've got to admit, I've seen a lot of weird shit in my life, but this here deal looks like it's going to wind up on the top of the weird index." Then he went back to his beer and sat there thinking some more. Then he asked, "You think you can come up with a plan to figure this out—I mean this who-got-crucified-with-Jesus stuff?"

"Well, first order of business is to talk to Augie and see where that leads. If that's a dry hole, I'll be expecting you to come up with something." That drew a snort out of him. "I'll just tell you this, Woodrow: I've got an idea there's going to be more to it than just looking it up in a book somewhere. We're just going to have to get lucky enough to scratch up something useful."

Woodrow nodded again and looked at me with that one arched eyebrow look of his. "What do you think this is really about, Buzz? What's so important about these two guys, and why now?"

That was easy. "I've got no idea, Woodrow, none at all. Believe me, buddy, I'd have sure picked out a different chore if it was up to me."

He nodded. "Well, amigo. Looks like you got yourself a chauffeur. So I guess I'll just come along for the ride—for now anyway. But I'd prefer if you don't dream up any more spooks out of my family's skeleton closet. That shit is probably going to give me indigestion for a month."

I slapped him on the shoulder "No promises, buddy."

After a second he said, "Now look. I'm not signing on to do the deal if you're planning on kicking the damn bucket in my Dodge. You've got to promise me if you feel a 'drop dead' spell coming on, you're going to warn me so I can hotfoot your ass to a hospital and drop you off. Okay?"

"Sure Woodrow. The minute I feel like I'm about to croak, I'll tell you."

He looked at me all squinty eyed and said, "To be honest, you look like you might go ahead and cash it in right here and now anyway."

"I'm not surprised. Right this minute I feel like the seven dwarfs are trying to carve their way out of my gol' dang skull."

"Not to worry, amigo. Old doctor Woodrow just might have the cure." He went out to his truck. When he came back, he stopped and looked out the window. "You know, that van is still sitting out there by your mail box. What do you make of it?" I looked out the window. There were a couple of ladies sitting in the van. Just sitting.

"All I can figure is somebody's lost and spending a lot of time looking at their maps." Woodrow shrugged and started putting marijuana in a mammoth ivory pot pipe. Once he had her all primed, he lit the pipe and passed it over to me. I heard the story before, but Woodrow tells it every time—like a ritual or something.

"I carved this pipe myself, carved it right off the tusk of an animal that lived and died in Siberia more that 15,000 years ago. I got a carbon-14 certificate to prove it." I handed the pipe back to him, and he took a big hit and sat back in the beanbag to give the pot a chance to start working. "It's spiritual, you know. When you draw marijuana through ancient animal remains, it picks up a sort of mystical power. It puts you in touch with something really primal and pure."

He handed the pipe back to me. I haven't smoked much marijuana in the last few years. Random drug tests. So I really wasn't ready for how strong this stuff was. And I was grateful, because my headache was no match for Woodrow's pot. The pain just kind of drifted off with the smoke. There didn't seem to be any need for conversation, so I just laid back and watched big smoky mammoths form up in front of me and lumber off into a world of disappearance.

Woodrow reached into the pocket of his overalls and took out his iPod so he could hook it up to my little old, antique stereo. To tell you the truth, if marijuana is good, it'll dress up the music coming out of any sort of system. So he hooked it up, and I settled back and listened to Sam Cooke singing "Trouble in Mind" while I was enjoying not having a headache. Sam was singing "I know the sun's going to shine in my back door someday." I was watching a whole herd of mammoths, big ones and little ones, all wispy and grazing on tall clumps of imaginary smoky grass. Everything was drifting off into sweet smelling space.

I heard Woodrow chuckle. "What's so funny?"

"I'm going to ask you something and I want you to tell me the truth. Don't put on a modest act or nothing. Okay?"

"You can ask, but I'm not making any promises."

"Do you feel smart right now? Now don't give me any horseshit. Think about it and tell me the truth."

So I asked myself. *How about it, Butane? Do you feel smart?* I busted out laughing because the truth was, I did feel smart, real smart.

"Me too. Right at this minute, you're the smartest you've been in forty days. So let's use some of that smartness. Tell me about puppets."

I took another hit off the magic pipe. "Well. Puppets have no life of their own. They fit over somebody's hand or somebody's got to pull their strings to make them dance and talk." Woodrow nodded and scratched his "Wild Bill" looking mustache.

"What makes us different from puppets, Buzz?"

"Because we think for ourselves and we decide for ourselves when we'll dance and when we'll sing."

"Do you think that's true all the time? Or do you think there's sometimes somebody's pulling our strings and we don't know it. Maybe sometimes we think we're doing what we want when we're really dancing to somebody else's tune. You think that's possible?"

Woodrow's an amazing guy. He hasn't had a minute of college. But he reads every damn thing. I mean he knows stuff about history, philosophy, politics, and religion. Everything. And he thinks about stuff, even when he isn't high. I'm not like that. I guess that's why he's the philosopher and I'm the driver—or was.

"Maybe I'm wrong, Woodrow, but I think I can tell the difference between doing something because I want to and doing it because I got no control."

He nodded. "I guess I can accept that—for now anyway. But let me just ask you this. When you were talking to the puppet, were you talking to the puppet or did you think you were talking to somebody else?"

A light came on, and I got his point. "You know Woodrow. At the time, I was taking everything at face value. I was talking to the puppet and wasn't even thinking about what a puppet really is."

He nodded. "Buzz, you remember who Ponce de Leon was?"

"I can't say I do, Woodrow."

"Well, he's the Spaniard that got famous for searching for the Fountain of Youth. Remember?"

"Oh yeah. Florida, right?"

"Yep. Somebody sold him on a crazy idea that if he could find this fountain, it was a magic way to get young and stay that way. Of course, it was all bogus. But if it wasn't for that, you and I probably never would have heard of Ponce de Leon." I waited for him to make a connection for me. He didn't.

"What the hell are you talking about, Woodrow? What does Ponce de Leon looking for the fountain of youth got to do with my problem?"

He winked. "I don't know Buzz. When I started talking, I thought I was making a point. I guess I forgot." My ass. He knew exactly what he was talking about, and I made up my mind to ask him about it when I got through enjoying my mammoth herd.

"Hey, Buzz, I got that nurse's Bible here. Can you show me that part about revolutionaries?" I showed it to him. "You got any other kinds of Bibles in here?"

"Yeah, I got the King James in a bedroom drawer." He went and got it.

"Okay. Show me that part about the jackass." I did. He looked at Irene's Bible and then at my Bible and back again. "Well, they both say it was an ass that talked to that guy Balaam. So they agree on that. But I'm with you Buzz. A revolutionary damn sure isn't necessarily the same thing as a robber or a thief."

We both sat back to try to think, but I couldn't stay focused on revolutionaries and jackasses. I was dreaming of go-go girls dancing through the clouds behind my mammoth herd. "Willie and the Poor Boys" was playing on Woodrow's iPod. Somebody knocked on the door, and Woodrow dropped his beer.

That knock was as unexpected as a lug nut in a yogurt carton. Woodrow was up quick. He put his hand on my shoulder. "Stay put, Buzz. I'll see who it is." He stuck the marijuana and mammoth tusk pipe back in his overalls and went to see who was at the front door. I was grateful for his initiative, because I didn't want to do nothing to rouse my headache again.

I heard women's voices, but I couldn't see who it was, because I couldn't get my eye to focus. After a minute of chit-chat, Woodrow and two ladies came walking over to where I was sitting. One of them was Miss Wister.

When Woodrow started the introduction, I interrupted him. "Yeah, Woodrow. I met Miss Wister yesterday at the hospital. It's Kathleen isn't it?"

She nodded. "I know how surprised you must be to see me here, Mr. Butane. I'm sorry to just show up like this. But there's someone I'd like you to meet. This is my friend, Denise Armando." The lady standing with her was really tall and well dressed. Rich looking. Could have been a model I guess. But her clothes was wrinkled, like she'd been sleeping in them. There were dark circles under her bloodshot eyes—like your eyes get when you've been crying a long time or you've got a bad hangover.

Woodrow, being the gentleman he is, offered the ladies their choice of beverage: beer, water, or RC Cola. We didn't know them well enough to offer them the hard stuff. They both wanted water, so Woodrow went looking for clean glasses. I invited them to have a seat, and they both perched on the edge of my couch with their knees together like they were school girls waiting for a home-ec lecture. Denise sat frozen like a statue, and Kathleen was fidgety and nervous acting.

"Miss Wister—Kathleen—it's really nice of you and Denise here to stop by like this to see how I'm getting on. But I've got to ask. How did y'all find me, and what are you two doing out here?" Kathleen looked back and forth between me and her frozen friend. I waited. Woodrow brought the ladies a glass of water each and he pulled up one of my kitchen chairs, sat back, crossed his legs and joined me in the wait.

Kathleen blushed. "Well, now that we're here, I'm really not sure how good an idea this is."

"Well, I can't have any opinion on it unless you spit it out." She took a deep breath, smoothed her hair and looked me in the eye.

"Mr. Butane—Leon, I mean, I don't know if you can help. But Denise is … believe me, I know how this sounds … we believe Denise is possessed by a demon." I heard Woodrow's boot hit the floor.

I felt like somebody opened a giant freezer door behind me. I got chilled plumb to the bone. Both ladies was staring a hole in me. I couldn't stop shivering, and the next thing I knew, I was laughing like a crazy man. I looked over at Woodrow and he was rubbing his jaw and frowning. I couldn't stop shivering and laughing. I reached up to wipe the tears out of my eye, and at the same time, Denise raised her hands to her face real slow and started to cry. Well, that put an end to my laughing fit. Everybody knows it's really bad manners for a fellow to be laughing when a lady is having herself a bona fide cry. I couldn't do anything about the shivering though. So I just grit my teeth and put up with it.

"Denise, I don't know what to say here. I'm not sure I believe there's such a thing as demon possession, and if there is, I don't know shit about how to cure it, pardon my French. I don't know what Kathleen told you, but no matter what your problem is, it's plumb out of my line." I was getting really tired of making that kind of speech.

Denise kept her hands up to her face crying without making a sound. Kathleen handed her a Kleenex and gave me a look that almost had me crying too.

"Would you at least do us the courtesy of hearing what we have to say? After that, if you can't or won't help, we'll thank you for your time, and we'll not bother you any further."

Well, hell. The way she asked so ladylike for me to just be courteous and listen made me feel about an inch tall. "I'm sorry ladies. Me and Woodrow here would be happy to hear about your demons, wouldn't we Woodrow?"

Woodrow *harrumphed*, crossed his legs again and took a long pull off his Coors tall-boy.

Kathleen patted Denise on the knee and said, "Do you want to? Or should I?" Denise sniffed and dried her eyes.

"No, I will."

Now the point here ain't whether I believe in demons. The point ain't whether you do. Hell, I'm not even sure Kathleen did. The point here is that Denise damn sure believed in them, and she was plumb convinced she had herself one.

Denise had one of the saddest stories I ever heard. It would be a downer for me even to repeat it all; so I won't. I'll just sort of hit the highlights. Seems Denise's demon was named Jules, and he got on her when she had a nervous bust-up. This Jules caused Denise to be terrified every time she looked in the mirror because of all the horrible stuff he was making her see. He was making her hear and say all sorts of foul stuff too. He wasn't letting her sleep, and he was making all her food look and taste like—well—road kill. She was getting close to the point where the only way she could get any relief was suicide. Now those are the high points. You can let your imagination fill in the gaps.

Now, Denise is rich. I mean crazy rich, as in hundreds of millions. Oil money, don't you know. Her parents are both dead; that's where she got her fortune. Her first husband's dead too: plane crash. Her son's dead: Iraq. Her daughter's dead: Suicide. She's got a second husband named Edgar, and he's a money-grubbing low-life who's been cheating on her for years. When she came down with this possession deal, Edgar jumped on it as an excuse to try to get appointed guardian so he could keep her from divorcing him. If he could get her declared incompetent, he could keep control of her money.

It turns out that Denise is a big supporter of Ernest Bidding. You remember him. He's that high-dollar, televangelist healer fellow that's got that big church in Mustang, Oklahoma. I told you about him. Anyway, Denise went to Bidding to get cured of her demon. He couldn't help her at all. So, naturally, he said she was suffering from a lack of faith, because he can handle demons if the victim's got faith. Denise quit making contributions to Bidding's Tabernacle and went looking for another televangelist.

Sure enough, the good-for-nothing Edgar saw an opportunity, so he and Bidding teamed up to see to it that Denise got ruled incompetent. Denise thinks Edgar promised Bidding a bunch of big contributions if the two of them could work together and get Denise out of the way.

So what the hell do you reckon all this had to do with me? Well, it's complicated. Denise is the money behind Kathleen's religious blog and the newsletter she publishes. When Kathleen told Denise about those supposed miracles that happened at the hospital, Denise told her to set up a meeting to see if I might be able to help with Jules, her demon. And I guess when you got money like Denise, if you holler "frog," lots of people are falling all over themselves looking for a place to jump.

Well Kathleen didn't have any trouble finding out where I lived. And it was easy to figure out this is where I'd run when I made my bust-out. So, here they were, sitting on my couch, all ladylike and me sunk deep into my furry bean-bag listening with my mouth open and Woodrow sitting in my kitchen chair rubbing his jaw and looking all squint eyed.

I started to say something, but I couldn't think of nothing that would sound right. So I looked over at Woodrow. He just gave me a *don't-look-at-me* shrug and started peeling the label off his beer bottle.

Have you ever been in a situation where the quiet is so heavy it feels like it could leave a mark on your skin? Well, that's how it was in my living room. Seemed like a long time. But it probably wasn't.

When it finally got where I couldn't stand the silence, I said, "Well, that's one heck of a sad story there Denise. I sure do wish I could think of a televangelist to recommend. But I don't use one myself. Sorry."

That made Kathleen speak up. "No, Mr. Butane. We're not here for you to help us find a televangelist. We know every major televangelist in America. We need something more in the nature of practical help."

"You need my help with what? Curing up your demon possession? Well I beg your pardon ma'am, but if you've seen *The Exorcist,* you know as much about dealing with demons as I do. And, to be honest Denise, you look *de*pressed, not *po*ssessed. I mean, have you been to a doctor or something?"

"Of course she has! Honestly, Mr. Butane, this lady has a half-dozen degrees from some of the finest universities in America. Of course she's been to doctors. She wouldn't be in this dump asking for help from someone like you if it wasn't a last resort! For heaven's sake, Denise, I told you this was a waste of time."

Ordinarily, I might get pissed off when an uninvited guest hauls off and calls my place a dump. But the truth is, it is a dump. It took me a long time to get this dump just like I like it. I feel at home in this dump. When I'm not home, I hang out in a dive which is a recreational dump. So I just let the "dump" comment roll right off my back. Woodrow couldn't keep his mouth shut though.

"For your information, me and Buzz—Mr. Butane—prefers dumps. We've never run into anybody living in a dump that had any problems with demons. Maybe you two ladies ought to take your pet Jules and go get help from somebody living in nicer quarters. We were real happy in our dump until you three showed up."

Denise had her hand up to her mouth. "Please, Mr. Butane. If you don't help me, I don't know what I'll do. I can't stand much more." There she was crying again. I would have cut off my fingers if that would help with her demon problem. But I didn't see how there was a gol' dang thing I could do.

"What do you want lady? Believe me, I want to help you. But I just don't have any ideas."

We were staring at each other. I tried to look away from those big, sad eyes of hers, but I couldn't. "Could I have some more water please?" Before I could get up, Woodrow was taking Denise's glass and headed for the kitchen. She kept up this steady quiet crying. I kept sitting there not knowing what to do. Kathleen was looking daggers at me, like I was doing something wrong. Finally, she spoke up again.

"I think we should go, Denise. There's no help for us here." Kathleen stood up and Denise stood up, still whimpering. Denise walked around the coffee table and stood over my bean bag with her hand out. It was like she was bringing the open freezer door with her. Then something came over me, I couldn't see nothing but the jewels around her neck, in her ears on her hands and in her eyes. It was like I didn't have any control over my own hand. I reached out to her. That soft yellow light shined all around her and everything started moving in slow motion again. When my hand touched hers, jewels started dropping out of her eyes and she took my hand in both of hers.

It was probably a quick move in real time, but it looked to me like she sank slow to her knees beside me and touched her forehead to my hand. I looked over at Woodrow for help and he was just standing there holding a glass of water. His eyes were like Frisbees. Kathleen come up with a camera from somewhere, and started taking pictures, like a machine gun. I looked down at Denise, and I'm going to tell you what I saw and heard. You can believe it or not. Up to you. Anyway she threw her head back like there weren't any bones in her neck. Then, her mouth opened wide—I mean scary wide—like a bull snake when it's swallowing a rabbit. Then there was three loud noises one after the other. The first was like a crack a big tree makes on the way down. Then there was a noise like you hear in your chest when you got the flu—sort of a wheezy rattle sound. And then there was this tearing—like a bed sheet getting ripped apart, but real, real loud.

Then it felt like an earthquake was rocking my house from side to side. Denise's eyes rolled back in her head and I realized all these sounds were coming out of her mouth. Honest to God, I thought she was going to die right there on my rug.

Then something grey and thorny started spilling out of her mouth and crawling toward my hand. It was oily and fast moving—the only fast moving thing in the whole nightmare. I tried to pull my hand away, but Denise had me in a kind of lock grip. I couldn't get free. I tried to holler, but nothing came out. I looked over at Woodrow and he was standing there like a statue. Kathleen was shooting pictures like a good journalist.

I automatically reached up with my free hand and did what I could to smack the shit out of that grey stuff that was spilling out of Denise's mouth and wrapping itself around both our hands. A broad horny-toad-looking head reared up and hissed like a snake and opened its mouth to show me all its shiny black teeth. I did the next thing that come natural. I took my finger and poked the little turd right in its little yellow eye as hard as I could. It squalled like a boar hog getting denutted, and some chicken-soup-looking stuff spilled out of its eye socket. I can't say what it was, but it smelled like four-day-old road kill on a July highway.

The thing was wagging its lizard-looking head back and forth over Denise's face, and I reared back and cracked it hard right across its ugly grey snout. Woodrow dropped the glass and ran across the floor and started trying to help Denise get to her feet. When he got there, the critter turned into a cloud of nasty smelling smoke and gusted over to the door. It piled up there rolling and stinking. That's when my voice came back to me. "Hell, Woodrow! Open the door and let that disgusting shit out of my house!" Woodrow started trying to get Denise to the door. "No Woodrow! I'm not talking about her. I'm talking about that thing. Open the damn door and let it out!" I was pointing at the place on the floor where that stinking smoke heap was piled up, and Woodrow was looking back and forth from me to the place I was pointing, and I could see he didn't have a clue what I was talking about. "Just open the gol' dang door, would you, Woodrow?"

When he opened the door, the stuff blew outside, and I was sure glad to see it go. The house stopped stinking and shaking. It warmed back up, and I stopped shivering. Then, the whole gol' dang world started to smelling like strawberries. Denise was laying on the floor shaking all over like a squirrel that got hit by a car.

Woodrow helped her to her feet, and Kathleen sat back down looking at me, like I'd just grown a pair of giraffe ears. Woodrow got Denise situated and asked if I was okay. I was. In fact, I was real relieved and happy, like my high was coming back.

Denise tried to say something to us but she wasn't able. She looked at me and gave me a glamour-mag smile. Kathleen asked her if she was okay.

"Yes. Fine. I'm fine."

Denise was starting to say thanks, but I interrupted her. "Listen, Kathleen. You better get your friend to a doctor to be sure she's not sick or hurt or something." Kathleen nodded. While she and Woodrow helped Denise out to the van, she kept looking back at me and whispering, "Thank you, thank you."

When the women were gone, Woodrow sunk back down into the couch. "Where were we before we were so rudely interrupted?" I was glad he didn't want to talk about what just happened, because it was too weird for me to process right that minute anyway.

He fired up the magic pipe, and while we were passing it back and forth, he winked at me. "Well, they were both pretty girls all right. But, to tell you the truth, I'm glad they took their rowdy friend and got themselves out of our dump." We passed the magic pipe back and forth to each other a few times more, and when we stopped, he looked me over real good. "Hey, Buzz. Do you mind telling me what the hell just happened?"

I didn't have any explanation. "I suppose you didn't see that smelly little grey fart that Denise burped up."

"I didn't smell anything Buzz, and I'm not sure exactly what I saw. But my money says it wasn't the same thing you saw. Suppose you tell me." So I told him just like I told you. He sat still for a second, and then shook his head like he was trying to get water out of his ear. "No. I didn't see nothing like that. Sure makes you wonder what's going to show up on Kathleen's camera?" Whatever was going through his head, he gave up.

The last thing I remember before I drifted off to sleep there in the bean bag was Steve Winwood singing "Spanish Dancer." Denise and Kathleen replaced the go-go dancers in my dream. They was dancing in a field of grass and wild flowers surrounded by mammoths pulling up prairie grass with their trunks and munching away with smiles on their big old ancient faces.

What I didn't know until later was that the good-for-nothing Edgar Armando, Denise's husband, got arrested that same night for possession of cocaine and taking indecent liberties with a couple of fifteen year old girls. I didn't have anything to do with his arrest neither.

Tuesday, February 20, 2007, a.m.

The next morning we got up, packed up Irene's Bible, and headed for Missouri to see cousin Augie. It's about a four hour drive up to Chittum. For February, it was a beautiful morning.

There wasn't much traffic and Ry Cooder was singing "Tamp 'em Up Solid" on Woodrow's iPod. So I settled back to enjoy the ride. I've got to admit, I was a little sad when I zeroed in on the fact that Woodrow was driving because I couldn't be trusted behind the wheel anymore. I could no more work in an office or a factory than a duck could kick a field goal. I guess Woodrow was reading my mind.

"Have you thought about what you're going to do with yourself if they won't ever let you drive again?"

"Of course I have. I can work in a radio station as a talk show host. I mean if they put a microphone in front of me, I reckon I could come up with an opinion on everything there is. What do you think about that?"

"Well, you'd probably be a better gas bag than driver, judging by the condition of the last truck you were driving."

We drove along quiet for a minute or two while I tried to think up a snappy comeback. By the time I did, it was too late, so I let it go.

"What are you going to tell Augie when we get there Buzz? He's going to think it's strange us driving all the way to Missouri to ask him a question like this."

"Well, I been thinking about that. No doubt Augie is important to us. After all, that's the only clue the puppet give me. The last time I did see him was years ago, and we didn't get along so good. We just got through burying Uncle Adolph, and Augie preached his funeral. Augie said something at the service. 'He that putteth his hand to the plow and looketh back is not worthy of the kingdom...blah, blah, blah.' He said it was a shame that Adolph died outside the church, because that meant there was no salvation for him. That comment was pointed at me too. See, I left the church when I got back from Nam."

Woodrow glance at me out the corner of his eye. "Your Uncle Adolph, ain't he the one who went alcoholic when his wife turned into a bingo addict and run off with the insurance salesman?"

"Yup, that's him. Anyway, Augie was trying to scare me back into church by threatening that I would wind up in eternal torment like Adolph. I just wasn't in the mood to get scared about such things right then. Maybe I was just being stubborn, but no matter what Augie said, I wasn't so sure Adolph was going to wind up in hell even if he wasn't a church-going man. He was a pretty 'good old boy.'

"I repeat, what were we going to tell Augie?"

"I guess we'll just have to do like we used to say in the 196th. Maneuver according to circumstance, Woodrow."

TAPE 7

Let's see, I left off when Woodrow and I went up to Augie's, right?

So there we were, Woodrow, Augie, and myself sitting on yellow vinyl kitchen chairs at a yellow Formica kitchen table, all three of us drinking coffee out of chipped cups that didn't match. There was a time when all this would look normal to me. Hell, this is the way I was raised up. But now that I've been out and around the world a little bit, I can see how backward this shit is.

But it just goes to prove the point I was making earlier. I wouldn't be happy living in Augie's dump and he wouldn't be happy living in mine, it's all a matter of taste.

Anyway, Augie and me are about the same age. He's a couple of months older, but if you ask me, he looks about seventy. It's probably all the tobacco the son of a bitch smokes. See, our branch of the Church of Christ don't allow a lot of stuff, like drinking, dancing, and fornicating. But, men can smoke as much as they want as long as they don't do it in the church house. Women ain't supposed to smoke, period. You probably know this already, but you don't need any education at all to be a Church of Christ preacher. Augie's got a high school diploma. Barely. But far as the brethren are concerned, he's qualified to be a preacher and spiritual trailblazer.

So cousin Augie sat there with his narrow, wrinkly, frowning face hanging out, squinting at the two sinners fidgeting at his kitchen table. We took up the first few minutes covering my accident, the coma, how Wanda was doing, stuff like that. I could tell by the way Augie was trying to keep the conversation light that he was hoping we could part company without me ever asking if I could borrow some money.

But his curiosity got the best of him. He couldn't stand it. "Well, what caused you to drive all the way up from Oklahoma to see me? Naomi said you didn't exactly say."

"Well, Augie, we came up here to try to borrow some money." Sure enough, his sour old face got a lot sourer and red too. Woodrow was rubbing the wrinkles on his forehead. "Relax cousin. I'm just having a little fun with you. We don't need any money at all. Woodrow here's loaded. No, I just came up here to see you because you're the Bible scholar in the family, and I need to ask you a Bible question." I guess I started him gulping when I said we wanted to borrow money, because he was still gulping and seemed like he couldn't stop for a minute.

Finally, he said, "Well there's lots of people in Oklahoma who know as much about the Holy Book as me. So why tack all the miles onto your question?"

"You're kin, Augie, and I just feel better asking stuff like this from kinfolk."

He looked at me real suspicious-like and then poked his thumb in Woodrow's direction, "What's your quiet friend here got to do with it?" I explained that because of my accident, I could have a seizure at any minute, and Woodrow agreed to drive me up here. Augie looked at me and looked at Woodrow then looked back at me and said, "Okay. What do you want to know?"

I asked him straight out, "Augie, who got crucified with Jesus?"

His eyebrows went up and his face looked like it was trying to change itself into a smile. "You came all the way up here to ask me that? Well, for mercy's sake, Leon. All you got to do is study the Word. It's right there for anybody to see. What a question! Read Galatians 2:20. Paul said 'I am crucified with Christ.' Then Romans 6:6 says 'Our old man is crucified with him.'"

I could see Woodrow chewing this over. He leaned over and whispered. "Did he say 'our old man'?" I shushed him off and let Augie roll along. I should've known Augie would be able to quote the wrong Scripture by heart. But Augie had the Spirit on him.

"We were all crucified with the Lord..."

"No, no Augie. I'm sorry to interrupt your fast moving train of righteous thought, here. But I mean who were the men that actually got executed with Jesus? I need their names."

His face got all solemn and suspicious again, "Listen, there are lots of questions you need to be asking. And there are lots of answers that I could give you that would make a difference between eternity in heaven and eternity in torment. What in the world does your question have to do with your soul's salvation?"

"Look, Augie, this is really important to me. I can't explain everything now. I just need you to tell me what you know about those guys."

"Something's telling me, Leon Butane, that you're up to some kind of nonsense. I can't quite get my finger on it, but all my instincts are telling me you're flirting with blasphemy here. You just need to look at your Bible and you'll know all about them the Lord wants you to know. They were thieves." Now you might expect that I was restraining the urge to strangle the self-righteous son of a bitch, and you'd be right. I was getting nowhere and, goddammit, I needed at least to get hold of a starting point.

So I decided to try a different direction while Woodrow helped himself to another cup of Augie's shitty coffee. I went out to the truck and got Irene's Bible, leaving Augie sitting there sulled up like a tree lizard. Woodrow was putting sugar in his coffee, and if I know Augie, he could tell you how much a teaspoon of sugar cost him.

When I got back into Augie's kitchen, I opened up to the right page in Matthew and showed him. "Look here. This copy of the Bible says the guys crucified with Jesus were revolutionaries." Then I flipped over to Mark and showed him that one too. He was frowning like a guy watching a bug eating his waffles. He grabbed the Bible out of my hands and looked at it real hard. The he looked at me. Then back to Irene's Bible. Then he slammed it shut and held it up and squinted at the spine.

"Aha! Catholics! This here's a Catholic Bible. See. Right here. '*New American Bible,* Catholic Book Publishing.'" He slammed it down hard on his yellow Formica table top.

"What the... what in the world do you mean bringing this here Catholic Bible in my house and pointing at it like that? You was raised better than that, Leon!" He shook his head real sad like. I've got to admit for a minute there, I felt sort of ashamed. I mean he was right. I did bring a Catholic Bible into his kitchen.

Woodrow came back to the table and sat down frowning and staring at the spoon he was using to stir his coffee. So then I said, "Come on August. I'm just confused here and thought you could help me clear things up. I didn't figure I'd get a straight answer from the Catholics. And Woodrow here's a Baptist. He says if I need answers to Bible questions, well I better ask me a Baptist preacher." Woodrow choked and coffee came out of his nose. Augie fixed him a mean, thin-eyed stare. I probably shouldn't have pitched Woodrow under the bus like that. Truth is, he don't have any religion at all that I know of. What I said about him being Baptist was crap. But I was moving fast trying to find a way to work on Augie. So I kept talking.

"You know what I said to that? I said 'No Woodrow. I don't care how far we have to drive; we've got to talk to my cousin August. After all, he's the only guy I know who can give us the real low-down on who these guys were.'" I had to stop long enough to take a break. "Listen, Augie. If we can get this right, it might persuade old Woodrow here to convert. Right, Woodrow?" Woodrow was wiping coffee off his nose with his sleeve.

Augie stroked his chin as he probably pictured Solomon doing just before he ordered that baby to get divvied up. Then he stood up. I forgot how tall and lanky the son of a bitch is. He walked out of the room. When Woodrow was sure Augie couldn't hear him, he spoke up. "What the hell is all that Baptist preacher and getting me converted horseshit about?"

"Just work with me here Woodrow. I'm only trying to maneuver according to circumstance."

Augie walked back in the room carrying a beat up old Bible that looked like it might have got brought over on the Mayflower. He plopped down in his chair and put it on the table in front of us. He laid his big hand on it real gentle, like it was a bottle of nitro. Then he closed his eyes and said, "God Almighty put everything needful for our salvation right here in his Holy Word. The King James Bible was good enough for the Apostle Paul, and it's good enough for me and you. The Lord commanded us not to add to nor take away anything from this book because if we do, we'll be struck with all the curses John wrote about in the book of Revelations."

I was thinking *Holy shit! We're going to have to sit here and listen to a whole gol' dang sermon.* Augie brayed on.

"It was God himself acting through the Holy Spirit that guided King James in translating his word from the original Latin into English so's each one of us could study the Scripture and find the truth of God's will for our life." Then he raised his hand and slammed it down on the King James Bible until it almost caused his old vinyl dinette to wobble off sideways. He leaned forward and put on a stare that made me want to get baptized. "Leon, if the good Lord didn't put it in here, it ain't important for you to know." Then he reared back in his chair looking all satisfied. "That's where your faith comes in, Leon. You've got to trust God. You can't be led astray by the Catholics, the Jews, the Presbyterians, the Episcopalians, nor the Communists...yea, not even by the Baptists!" He glared at Woodrow.

"Everybody wants to rewrite the Holy Bible. But in your heart, you know the truth. The Scripture tells us that the Lord was crucified between two thieves. They was thieves, Leon. Thieves!—not revolutionaries." Then he crossed his arms and said like he was putting the final *"Amen"* to it. "God said it, I believe it, and that settles it!"

So I sat there letting his words sort of evaporate like steam getting sucked into heaven itself. Well, I got to tell you, my heart was sinking. I didn't feel like I was getting anywhere, and this here Church of Christ preacher's mule-headedness was apt to be the death of me for sure. Why in hell would that puppet send me all the way to Missouri on a snipe hunt? Hell, if he was going to lure me into a dead end, why couldn't it be Vegas?

I decided not to give up. I tried another angle. "Okay Augie. I appreciate what you're saying. And you're right of course. But just suppose you was to have...like a revelation, say. And suppose the Lord was to say 'August Eli Butane, I got a test for you. In order to prove your faithfulness and stick-to-itiveness, I want you to do research and find out who got crucified with my son Jesus.' Where would you start?"

Well boy, that was the wrong octane for his motor, because he blew smooth up. He thundered "I knew it! Sure as you're born I knew you were up to the devil's work. After all the years of drinking and whoring and pot smoking, I knew in my bones you weren't coming to see me for Christian instruction. I knew you were surely coming up here to do mischief." He was so red in the face, I thought there could be a vessel eruption in his tiny brain any second. He stopped long enough to get his breath, and then he fired up again.

"Now I want you to have your iniquitous self out of my kitchen and take your Baptist friend and your Catholic Bible with you. Don't you know that the Lord don't need me or you or anybody else to tell him the names of them thieves crucified with Christ? God almighty knows everything from who laid the chunk!"

Well, I'd heard enough, so I was fixing to get out and get on with my wild goose chase someplace else. But that thick-skulled cousin of mine just couldn't find an end to it.

"Aren't you ashamed to come in my house knowing I'm a servant of God, and blaspheming right here in front of my very face?"

It looked to me like Woodrow was fixing to whip God's servant's ass. See, Woodrow believes it's bad manners to stay any place if you're asked real courteous to leave. But he'd rather take a bloody nose than get kicked out of a place without a fight. That's just part of Woodrow's code. And I'll tell you something else. Woodrow's a tough son of a bitch even if he does have a mammoth tusk stump for a left foot. Augie and Woodrow were both rolling up their sleeves, Woodrow was mumbling something about teaching Augie a thing or two about righteous humility, and Augie was fixing to smite Woodrow with the right hand of the Lord's fury. So I decided we'd better pull out before the angels and devils were forced to choose up sides.

"Okay, Augie. I'm sorry I blasphemed in your kitchen. I give you my word I didn't do it on purpose. It was an accident." And that was true. If I was blaspheming like Augie said, I didn't mean to do it. Of course, everybody knows that blaspheming is a sin. I've known that since I was a kid. But I've never been right clear on what you've got to do to be technically guilty of blaspheming. I mean I know what stealing is. I know what lying is. I know what whoring is. I'm just a little fuzzy on what exactly the blaspheming deal is.

They were still mumbling about the strength of one hundred cans of whup-ass when I packed up Irene's Catholic Bible. I got Woodrow by the arm and pulled him outside.

Woodrow stood in the yard making colorful threats about how he was going to use his stump on tender parts of Augie's body, and Augie stood on his porch shaking his fist raining *"woe untos"* all over Woodrow.

When I could tell they were running out of fearsome threats and it was about to get childish, I decided to save them from having to repeat themselves. So I pretended to get dizzy and acted like I was going to have a seizure out there in Augie's yard. That did the trick. Both of them came running over to catch me. Augie held me up while Woodrow opened the door of the Dodge and they were both trying to get me in the cab and mumbling how lucky the other was that I turned out to be so feeble right at that moment. Augie told Woodrow to follow him to the nearest hospital and Woodrow nodded and promised to be right on his bumper.

I was enjoying all the fuss they were making trying to get me into the pickup. When they started wrestling with each other trying to put my seatbelt on, I got tickled and started laughing. I couldn't stop. They both stood there blinking, looking at me and then looking at each other and then they started trying to pull me back out of the cab. Whatever differences they had, they were in full agreement this was no time for a joke. My laughing didn't keep me from getting the door closed. "Come on Woodrow. It's time to leave off playing with Augie. I'm hungry and need a burger."

Woodrow grumped around to the driver's side of the Dodge and got in flipping Augie the bird and firing off one last "Mule-headed Bible-thumper!"

Augie came back with a "Peg leg fornicator!" And with that, we were off.

Tuesday, February 20, 2007, p.m.

Woodrow had Scott Birum singing "Blood, Sweat, and Murder" on his iPod when we rolled into a burger joint in Joplin. We got all settled into a booth with our cheeseburgers, fries, and root beers. Woodrow took a long pull on his frosty mug and asked me, "Just what the hell was supposed to happen back there? The puppet sent us all the way to Missouri to see this guy. What the hell for?"

"I don't know, Woodrow. The puppet was real goddamn vague. All he said was to start with cousin Augie."

Woodrow shook his shaggy head. "I got to admit, I did hear something I never heard before. Nobody ever told me our old man was crucified with Jesus. Imagine that, our old man. Interesting. Still, I can't see it was worth driving all the way up here to get that." He looked like he was talking to his own self and said all sarcastic-like: "Our old man."

The place was jammed with kids playing all over the place, and there were adults trying to keep them all cornered. Woodrow watched them for awhile, stirring his root beer with a straw. "How many of these people do you reckon believe the same way as your cousin Augie?"

The way he said, *"your cousin Augie"* almost sounded like an accusation. "I can't say about people in Joplin. But in the church where I grew up, everybody believed pretty much like he does."

"Well, I sure as hell didn't grow up believing that stuff. Every once in a while, when I was a kid, my mom took me to church. But I hated every minute and didn't believe a word of it." He piled up his empty wrappers on our tray. "No, that isn't altogether true. I believe little David killed Goliath with a slingshot. I believe that because I want to believe it. No, that's not exactly true neither. I got to believe it. I got to believe the little guy can come up with an edge when he has to square off with a giant. There's probably some that would say that whatever gave David his edge in his fight with Goliath give the same edge to the VC and NVA when they squared off with us."

I wasn't sure I was following. "What the hell are you talking about here, Woodrow?"

He sat there for a minute all dreamy looking. Then he cleared his throat and asked me, "How many versions of the Scripture do you reckon there are?"

"I really don't have any idea, Woodrow."

"Well, I'll tell you something Buzz: If all we've got to work with are these two Bibles and Augie's brilliant insights, you're a goner for sure."

"I'm not sure what to do next. Find another preacher? Go to the library and look in some books? Drop down on my knees and pray? What?" Then a real creepy thought come over me. "Hey, Woodrow. You don't think this is all about the devil's work like Augie says?" I was glad he took the question serious.

"Well, first off, Buzz, I don't believe there is a devil. And if there is, he's got plenty of full-time preachers, politicians, and movie stars to work with. Why would he pick on you, and what's his interest in stirring up this crucifixion deal right at this minute? I don't claim to know what's going on here lately. But I can't see where the devil has any percentage."

"So you're saying it isn't the devil because that wouldn't make sense?"

"No, it wouldn't make any sense."

"Well great. I feel better. See because every other damn thing that's going on right now makes perfect sense, doesn't it? So something that doesn't make sense would stick out like a pimple on prom night, right? So thanks Woodrow. I can cross the devil off as a possible problem because, hell, that wouldn't make any sense."

"Okay, okay, Buzz. I see your point. We can't use the Bible, we can't use Augie. And we can't use common sense to help us out here. I guess we could use up the rest of our time—scratch that, your time—making up lists of stuff we can't use. So what is it we can use to get you out of this? And would it make a shit if it was the devil that was behind all this?"

I guess I could have swapped some more sarcasm with him. But I decided not to. "You know, Woodrow, the only bright spot so far in this whole fun house visit was the Catholic Bible saying Jesus was crucified between two revolutionaries. Deep in my bones I'm feeling this is the one good thing we've got to go on so far. Know what? I hope the Catholic Bible is right even if it means that most of the people I grew up with were wrong about King James and the Holy Spirit. And you know what else? If it turns out that getting to the bottom of this means that I'm somehow serving the devil, well, I'll just have to deal with it and square up with the Lord later."

Regular as clockwork when we headed back home, I started getting a headache. Woodrow's pipe and stash was in the Dodge cubbyhole, so we fired up. It was turning dusky, and my headache faded out on the turnpike between Joplin and Big Cabin. Woodrow had something on the iPod called "Enigma." Maybe it was the marijuana—probably was—but it seemed to me that Enigma was the perfect music for sunset on the turnpike.

Driving west into the sunset, I started seeing shapes in clouds that sometimes looked almost like Pinocchio. I knew there had to be strings attached somewhere. After all, he's a gol' dang puppet. But no matter how hard I looked, I couldn't see what was moving him.

I fell asleep in the Dodge and rested good until Woodrow pulled onto the bumpy-ass, gravel driveway that leads to his cabin up in the woods.

Wednesday, February 21, 2007, a.m.

I woke up wrapped in the real old fashioned quilts that cover the feather-bed in Woodrow's spare bedroom. For all I know, these was the same quilts that covered the James and Younger boys in the old days when Woodrow's family made mountain shine and furnished hideouts for outlaws and desert-ers on the run. That was back in Missouri before Indian Territory opened up for settlers and Woodrow's people slipped in to Oklahoma to stake their claims early. Sooners. There's a real strong strain of old-time bandit still running through Woodrow's veins. He'd probably still be making shine like his backwoods kinfolk if he liked the taste of the stuff. But he don't. So he grows pot.

Anyway, you probably figured out that Woodrow's got a lot of pecu-liarities. All he ever wears is overalls made at the Capitol Bo Dark Mill in Weloka. His furniture is all hand made by craftsmen in little towns around eastern Oklahoma and western Arkansas. All the honey in his pantry comes from bees that feed on flowers and clover growing within ten miles of his house. His peanut butter is made from Oklahoma grown goobers. He can make jelly and preserves from Chickasaw plums that grow in thickets on his own land, and he can make flour and tea from the damndest assortment of nuts, tree barks, and roots you ever saw.

It was his phone ringing that caught me in the middle of a great joint-popping stretch. I just laid there feeling good and smelling Hawaiian coffee brewing while Woodrow mumbled to somebody on the other end of the line. Since I didn't know I was going to be staying at Woodrow's, I didn't bring no clean underwear or nothing. So I was putting on the same stuff I wore yesterday when Woodrow came in bringing the phone. "It's that lady reporter." I was flummoxed.

"I wonder how the hell she got this number and how she knew I'd be here." He shrugged, scratched his beard and sat down in his rocking chair so he'd be comfortable while he eavesdropped on my conversation. "This is a real surprise Miss Wister. I sure hope you aren't calling for an encore demon removal job, because I haven't had breakfast yet. How'd you find me out here in the sticks?

"I'll explain it all later. But for now, I think I have some good news."

"I'm all ears here."

"I'll bet you haven't figured out who was crucified with Jesus yet."

"You're right."

"Well, I think maybe I can help you."

Just like a reflex I asked, "How?"

"I did some checking and I think I've found someone who may be able to point you in the right direction."

"Great. Who is it?"

"Not so fast. Before I tell you, there's something I need you to do for me."

Just like a reflex I said, "What is it?"

"This is going to sound odd, but I want to set up a meeting between you and Ernest Bidding. I want to videotape it."

Well, you might know that remark caught me plumb off guard. "What in the cornbread hell are you talking about? Why on earth would there be anything interesting about me and Ernest Bidding getting together and talking? I'd say 'Hello.' He'd say 'Hello.' He'd ask me if I want to make a contribution to his ministry. I'd say 'No. I gave at the office.' We'd shake hands, and that would be that. What kind of chucklehead would want to videotape something like that, and what kind of chucklehead would want to watch it if she did?"

"Okay, what do you have to lose then? You and Ernest Bidding have a nice chat. I get to videotape it. You get your answer to Pinocchio's question. Everybody's happy. Deal?"

My turn to say, "Not so fast here. I need to run this by Woodrow." So I did.

"Ask her what's the catch?"

"What's the catch?"

"There's no catch. It's a straight deal. I'll contact Bidding and see if he will agree to meet you. We'll pick a time and place. We'll show up, get the meeting on film, and that's that."

I told all this to Woodrow, and he said, "Keep her talking. There're still a lot of gaps to fill in."

"Come on Kathleen. You don't want to videotape this unless you think something's going to happen. What are you looking for here?"

"I'll be honest Leon. I don't know what will happen. Maybe nothing. Maybe something. I shoot hours of videotape every year that winds up in file thirteen. That means the trash can. Well, not really, because everything is digital now, so it's deleted. I'm just saying that I shoot hundreds more hours of video than I ever use. I don't even know if Ernest will agree to meet you anyway."

"Okay. Suppose I agree and Bidding says 'No thanks. I got better things to do than swap miracle stories with Leon Butane.'"

"In that case, it's not your fault there's no meeting. So I'll go ahead and tell you what I know."

"Hold on a minute, and let me talk to Woodrow."

I told him what she said and he said, "I smell a rat. She's up to something, but I don't know what it is."

"Do you see a downside to making this deal Woodrow? Hell, the upside is obvious."

"Okay. But don't sign anything and don't give her any money. It's probably worth the gamble." Then he gave me a big grin and said, "Hell, having spent the last couple of days with a snake-oil drummer like you, it might be interesting to sit down and have a heart-to-heart with a bona fide faith healer like Ernest Bidding."

"Okay Kathleen. We got a deal. But I won't sign nothin', and I won't give you no money."

She sounded a little whiny. "But you have to sign a release to allow me to use the video, Leon. It's just the way these things are done."

That grease ball Teddy and his clipboard came to mind. "Jesus Christ. Every time I turn around these days, somebody wants me to sign something. Why can't we wait until after the meeting to see if you get something you can use before we decide whether you need my permission to use it?"

"I just can't do that Leon. I need a release from you and Ernest Bidding both before I can start filming. If you're nervous about it, I'll give you a copy of my standard form so you can show it to your lawyer before you sign it."

That made me laugh my ass off. My lawyer! Give me a gol' darn break. I don't even have a German shepherd. What the hell would I do with a lawyer? So I told her to hang on a minute while I consulted with my lawyer, Woodrow.

"Ask her if you'd sign the same thing as this Bidding fella?"

She said, "Yes, of course." I told her to give me her number and I'd call her back.

"Okay, Leon. But there are a few more things I need to tell you. First, I need Woodrow's cell number in case I have to talk to you when you are out somewhere." I knew Woodrow hated it, but I just spun his number right off for her. "You need to be careful about going home. There are some people camped out in your yard. Some of them are waiting to get healed and some of them are just waiting to get a look at you. Off and on there are some media people wanting pictures and interviews. Oh, and there's a process server wanting to give you some papers."

Goddammit! I couldn't see how in the cockeyed world I could have wound up in the middle of a Chinese circle jerk like the one I was in. I could have kicked shit out of the whole flock of big mouthed yahoos that was spreading it around that I could cure people. And why in the Sam Hill couldn't the damn lawyer lay off for a couple of weeks and serve his gol' dang papers if I live through this deal? Didn't I have enough shit to worry about? "Great! Great news Miss Wister. If you know of any arrest warrants out there, keep it to yourself for now would you?"

"Sure. Just tell me when you're ready to hear about them."

"Hell, Kathleen. That ain't funny."

"Sorry."

"I'll call you back." I told everything to Woodrow. He thought everything was real damn funny. Especially the part about the arrest warrants.

"Serves you right for giving out my cell number without asking. Hell, it'll probably wind up on the goddamn Internet now. If it does, I might just have to turn you in for the reward."

"Kiss my ass, Woodrow. Let's go get something to eat."

The nearest town to where Woodrow lives is Onion, Oklahoma. I'm sure somebody knows why they named it Onion, but I don't. Anyway, Onion is on the way to Tishotaha, and The All American Café is right on the Onion bypass. We decided to grab some flapjacks to give us strength. Flapjacks'll do that.

When we got settled in a booth at The All American, Juanita brought us over some coffee. She's got a crush on Woodrow, so she stood there pouring real slow and looking at him with calf eyes.

"Where you been, Woodrow?"

"Just cleaning up after the ice storm. Juanita, what's on the news this morning?" She took that as an invite to sit down with us. So she did, right there, next to Woodrow.

"Well there's more stuff about that minister over in Arizona. Looks like he's turned out to be a real pervert. There're guy employees coming out of the woodwork saying he's taken liberties with them for years. There're lots of church leaders and politicians ducking for cover."

Woodrow was stirring sugar into his coffee. "Wasn't there some kind of problem with the parson over at your church sometime back?"

"Well yeah. But he wasn't a pervert. He just ran off with the deacon's wife is all."

Woodrow nodded. "You still go to church over there regular?"

"Sure, one of these days I'd like to get married in there." She gave Woodrow a wink and he came back with a weak smile. About then, our pancakes was up. Juanita got busy, so we finished up and got out before she could get back to gossiping with us. We were out in the parking lot when she stepped to the door and hollered. "Hurry back, Woodrow." He smiled and waved and we was gone.

We left Onion and drove over to Tishotaha, the county seat of Tishotaha County and dropped over to the County Library. Miss Evers is the spinster librarian that runs the place. She knows Woodrow, because he comes in sometimes to do research and acts like he can read. He's a celebrity in those parts, being an eccentric war hero, semi-environmentalist and all. Anyway, Woodrow went off to do something on his computer. I asked Miss Evers to help me find as many different versions of the Bible as they got there in the Tishotaha Library.

She said, "Well, you have certainly come to the right place. Because, in addition to being a librarian, I'm also something of a Bible scholar and Sunday school teacher." She peered up at me over her glasses like she was waiting for me to say something. So I did.

"Well I guess you're right Miss Evers. This must be my lucky day."

She beamed. "So then, what are you searching for? I'm sure I can help."

"Well, here's the thing Miss Evers. I'm trying to find out who were crucified with Jesus."

She stood there blinking for a minute and then said, "Well they were thieves of course."

"Yes, ma'am. That's what I was brought up believing. But I guess some people make out that they were revolutionaries or something and I'm just trying to find out as much about them as I can."

"Revolutionaries!" She said it all amazed and disbelieving. "Surely not. Surely that's a mistake! Are you sure there's a version of the Bible that says they're revolutionaries and not thieves?"

"Yes ma'am. I've seen it with my own eyes."

"Revolutionaries!" This time she said it more like a snort. "This must be a radical translation disapproved, no doubt, by the larger body of scholars. Come this way, young man. We have resources on hand that will answer your questions."

There's something about being called "young man" that makes a fella come along and do as he's told, no matter how old he is. She showed me a table and invited me to have a seat. I did. Then she swooshed herself into an office somewhere and came back carrying two books, some paper and a couple of pencils.

She plopped the two books down in front of me and said, "There," like just coming up with them proved her point. And you know what? They were Bibles. Both of them. But they weren't like any Bibles I had ever seen before. These looked more like textbooks. See, up to that point, the only Bibles I had ever seen was either leather or leather-looking stuff. I'd never seen a hardback Bible like this. And I'll tell you something else. They were both New Testaments. That's another thing I'd never seen before. A New Testament that was amputated from the Old Testament. But there they was, hardback New Testaments with nary a red letter in neither of them. I knew better, of course, but for a second there, I felt like I might have been doing something wrong just by handling those Bibles that were so all-fired different from what I grew up with. But I got over it pretty quick.

Miss Evers sat down beside me and slid some paper and a pencil over to me and said, "Let's get started," like we were doing surgery on somebody.

The first Bible she opened was *The Precise Parallel New Testament.* She turned right to Matthew 27:38 so we could start the operation. Maybe you know this already, but there are a lot of versions of the New Testament. Here's what they were: There was the Bible written in Greek; there was the King James version, naturally—they call it KJV for short; there's something called the *Rheims Bible*; there's the Amplified Bible; The New American Standard, or NASB; The New International Version, of NIV; Irene's Bible, which is the New American or NAB; and the New Revised Standard Version, or NRSV. All these versions were laid out side by side on the page so you could compare them real easy.

I couldn't read the Greek, of course. But almost all the others called our two guys 'thieves' or 'robbers.' Some of them said 'bandits.' When Miss Evers got to the NAB where it said "two revolutionaries," she sat there with her mouth open looking over the rim of her spectacles. "Well, I'll say." After she "hmmmed" to herself a little bit, she said, "Well this is the only one that says they were revolutionaries."

"Miss Evers, I don't know if it helps any, but I think this NAB deal is a Catholic Bible."

"Oh." She nodded her head like that explained everything.

Then she opened up the other Bible and I'll be a dang knuckle dragger if there ain't a shit load of other translations. This other Bible is *The Evangelical Parallel New Testament* and it's got a New King James Version, or NKJV; the English Standard, ESV; and the New Century which all call our guys "robbers." The New Living Translation calls them "criminals." So does the Holman Bible. But Miss Evers showed me a footnote where Holman gives another reading of that verse which is, sure enough, "revolutionaries."

And then, Today's New International, TNIV, calls them "rebels." That's a change because the original NIV called them "robbers." So I asked Miss Evers, "Are all these versions that make them out to be rebels or revolutionaries Catholic Bibles?" She sat there making notes and acting like she didn't hear me.

When she finally spoke up, she said, real sheepish like, "I don't know. I'm going to have to look into this. After all, it might make a world of difference if these poor men were something more than common thieves. There must be a simple explanation." She was talking to herself and looking from one version to another muttering, "Well, I'll say."

Every translation of Luke calls them "criminals" or "malefactors." In John, they was "others" or "other men."

"Is this all the Bible tells us about these guys Miss Evers?" She didn't talk, she just nodded. "Well, what do you make of it?"

"Well, I don't know. It does potentially cast quite a different light on them though doesn't it? I mean if they were something other than common thieves as we've always heard."

About that time, Woodrow came over and said, "We need to step outside so I can tell you something." I thanked Miss Evers and left her looking from page to page and book to book. I guess she forgot I was even there.

TAPE 8

We stepped outside. It was really warm for February, about sixty-five degrees, I'd say. It was clouding up though, like it might rain later on. Woodrow said, "Let me tell you what Miss Kathleen Wister is up to. She's a busy little bee, that one. I Googled her and found out that she's got a real popular blog. Some of her fans—and she's got a bunch of them—call her a neospiritual activist. Looks like she's got bulls' eyes drawn on a lot of the high profile church leaders. She spends a lot of time exposing their shenanigans—sexual, financial, and otherwise. She's got some critics too. Some Christians say when she airs the church's dirty laundry, she's really giving ammunition to the unbelievers. Then the unbelievers criticize her for being a cop-out. Since she's seen and exposed the corruption that's epidemic in the Christian religion, they say she ought to take the logical next step and give it up."

He shuffled through several pages he'd printed off and found what he was looking for. "She used to be active in a big evangelical church in Mesa, Arizona. The pastor over there got caught drilling a male prostitute and smoking meth. After that, she got herself off on this so-called neospiritual crusade. In this blog of hers, she really lays into these big time preachers that promise God's going to cough up golden blessings to people that send money to their ministries."

"Why's she interested in my deal, Woodrow?"

"I'm getting to that. There's pictures all over her blog which she says shows you exorcising Denise's demon. I've looked them over good, Buzz, but I don't see a trace of that horny toad deal you saw coming out of Denise's mouth. But you can tell from the pictures that there's something real strange going on with Denise. If I wasn't there, I'd think somebody doctored up the picture that shows how wide her mouth got opened. There's pictures and video of you supposedly curing up little Iris's leukemia. Then there's what this Wister woman calls first-hand testimonials about other miracles people say you've done." He gave me a big grin and slapped me on the shoulder. "Buzz, you're a by-God miracle-working celebrity."

"Holy shit, Woodrow. If this deal keeps snowballing like this, next thing you know, somebody will be nominating me to be the gol' dang pope."

"Hold on brother, there's more. She's got your whole story in there. Your military service, your decorations, your wreck, the operation, the coma, your chat with Pinocchio and company, this Jesus deal. Everything. She says at first she thought you were running some kind of con. But now, because of the people she's talked to and stuff she's seen with her own eyes, she's not sure. She figures the Lord wants her to find out just what all this is about. Maybe it's God. Maybe the devil. Maybe it's just some kind of weird, random, paranormal bullshit—my words, not hers. But whatever it is, she believes she's called to follow it, film it, write about it, put it in context, and again, my words not hers, see if she can turn a profit off it."

I couldn't think of anything to say, so he went on. "Did you know there was an Old Testament prophet named Amos? He was a fella who pruned sycamore trees. According to Kathleen, God picked this poor guy out and made him a prophet to come out of Israel and preach repentance to the people of Judah. She says there's no reason God wouldn't call a humble truck driver to bring a message to a sinful world. That's got to make you laugh, Buzz, but get this. There was another prophet named Hosea, and God commanded him to marry a prostitute named Gomer. Sounds like a beauty don't she? Anyway, marrying this prostitute was supposed to be some symbolic gesture to point the way to repentance."

"So what the hell does pruning sycamores and marrying harlots got to do with me?"

"I don't know, Buzz. She goes over that stuff in her blog. Do yourself a favor. Next time you talk to the puppet, ask if he'll let you swap chores and find yourself a harlot to marry. You're better equipped for that than you are chasing around trying to find out the answer to a Bible mystery."

"Okay, where does Ernest Bidding figure into all this?"

"Well, evidently Kathleen stirred up a hornet's nest by telling everybody that you were able to solve Denise's demon problem when Bidding couldn't do it. I didn't go to Bidding's website, but I guess he's accusing you and

Kathleen of cooking up some kind of conspiracy to give him a black eye—spiritually speaking. Judging by the back and forth, there's been bad blood between him and Kathleen for some time."

"With all the other headaches I've got to deal with right now, do I really need to get mixed up in a feud like this?"

Woodrow put his hand on my shoulder. "Let me ask you this. How confident are you that you'll drop dead like the puppet says if you don't find out who got crucified with Jesus? Give me a percentage."

"Well, based on everything that's happened so far, I'm about eighty-five percent sure the puppet laid it out straight."

He nodded. "Okay. How do you think your chances are without Kathleen's help?"

"I'd estimate about nil."

He nodded again. "Now, what do you think your chances are if she leads you by the hand?"

"I don't know, Woodrow. I don't know a goddamn thing about her except what you just told me and what I seen the other night. She says she thinks she can point me to the answers, but I don't know, really. I guess I'd say with her help, my chances are about ten percent."

He slapped me on the back and grinned. "There's your answer. You got no chance without her and a snowball's chance with her. I'd say the numbers don't lie." He gave me a wink. "Make the deal."

As you can see, it's hard to argue with Woodrow's logic. I love that guy. So I took Woodrow's phone, called Kathleen, and agreed to sign her release.

"Great. When will you two be back in Oklahoma City?"

"I'm on my way and should be there in about three hours. It's a little after ten now. We'll probably stop at Weloka for lunch so we ought to be there around two-thirty or three."

"Remember what I told you about not going home. The crowd around your house is getting bigger. I have to tell you, Leon, there are people claiming they're getting healed just from being near your mailbox."

My natural tendency was to accuse her of overstating things. But in this case, I didn't figure she was. All I could think to say was "Well, it's a good mailbox, but it ain't that talented. I guess I'll just have to avoid the house for now. I got a credit card with a $16,000 limit. Never been used. Me and Woodrow can live off of that for at least a couple of weeks. I'll worry about paying the bills if I'm still around."

"Good. Meet me at St. Knud's Catholic Church. It's on the Northwest Expressway west of MacArthur Blvd. You can sign the release there, and then we'll see who was crucified with Jesus."

Wednesday, February 21, 2007, p.m.

We got to St. Knud's a little after three o'clock. Kathleen's van was in the parking lot. I've only been in one Catholic Church in my whole life, and that was for a funeral. It was for a Vietnam war buddy of ours. There was too much kneeling and standing and chanting and razzmatazz for me. But I guess those kinds of ceremonies suit millions of people because there's Catholic churches all over the world. I was amazed how many Catholics there were in Nam.

Anyway, there was a little room on the right when you first walk in the door of St. Knud's. Kathleen and a heavy, gray-haired fellow were in there waiting for us. They both shook our hands, and Kathleen introduced Father Kelly. He had dirt all over his forehead. I figured somebody ought to tell him because it didn't look like he knew it.

"You got a little smudge up there on your face, Father Kelly."

He smiled. "Yes of course. It's Ash Wednesday." He said it like I must be dumb for not knowing.

Woodrow spoke up like he didn't care whether Father Kelly thought he was dumb or not. "Pardon my ignorance, Father Kelly, but what's the significance of having ashes on your face like that?"

"It's an ancient gesture of repentance. We begin Lent today and we prepare our hearts and minds to recall the suffering and death of our Lord."

"So this is a Catholic deal?"

"Many Christians of many denominations observe Ash Wednesday."

"Is it in the Bible?"

Father Kelly blinked at him for a minute. "No. It's a tradition handed down for generations from the church fathers."

"So you've got no idea who come up with it?"

Father Kelly frowned, and Kathleen decided to change the subject.

"Before we get started, Leon, I'd like you to go ahead and sign this release. She handed me this form and I read it over. To tell you the truth, I didn't understand a goddamn thing it said. Looked to me like I'd be agreeing to let her use photos and video in print and other media, blah, blah, blah.

So I asked, "Has Ernest Bidding signed this thing yet?"

"No, not yet."

"Well, I'll sign when he signs his, because I want to be sure I'm signing the same thing he is."

"Why is that so important to you, Leon?"

"Because he probably gets pictures and videos took of him all the time, and he probably knows all the ins and outs on this kind of stuff. He probably has lawyers look them over, and he might put stuff in a release I never thought of. I figure if he signs something, it's either going to be fair, or it'll favor him somehow. See what I mean? So, I believe I'll sign when he does."

"So, if you wait, you think you'll get the benefit of Bidding's lawyers without having to pay their fees."

"That's how mice survived in the days of the dinosaurs. They had to watch where the big guys were stepping."

"Tell you what. You sign this release, and if Bidding doesn't sign this one, we'll tear it up and you can sign whatever he does." I looked over at Woodrow, and he was looking out the window.

So I said, "Why don't we just wait to see if Bidding signs at all?"

"Look Leon, I trusted you. I brought you here and introduced you to Father Kelly. He's going to answer your question now whether you sign or not. If you want to stab me in the back, you can do it and get away with it. You can get the information you need, tell me goodbye, and we're through. But if you keep your word and sign this, I promise I'll be square with you. And I'll even do better than that. If you trust me, I'll do everything I possibly can to help you through this whole affair." She handed me a pen. "Let's be partners. It's good for both of us." I knew I was probably making a mistake. But then again, it's usually easier on my nerves when I trust people. It's just too damn hard going around being suspicious all the time. If you do, you're always in danger of outthinking your own damn self.

I took a deep breath and shrugged. "I guess I ought to be grateful I don't have to sign the damn thing in blood." I signed her release.

Then Father Kelly said, "Let me show you." He hauled himself up on a ladder and got a really big book down from a high shelf. Me and Kathleen got out our pencils and paper. Woodrow said there was a coffee shop down the street. He'd just take his laptop down there, and we could call him when we were done.

Father Kelly put his glasses down on his nose and said, "So you want to know who was crucified with our Lord?" He turned the big pages in the book like they were fragile and apt to crumble. I guess it was just out of respect, though, because the book looked sturdy and expensive and had nice gold edges on the pages. "There were, of course, two thieves crucified with him." I thought about stopping him right there. After all, so far as I could see, it was the Catholics who were saying they were revolutionaries. I made a note on my paper to ask him later.

"Ah, here it is." He moved the palm of his hand across the pages like he was smoothing wrinkles out of a baby's diaper. "Their names were Dismas and Gestas." My heart jumped until it nearly bumped my Adam's apple. I could have kissed Father Kelly and signed my house over to Kathleen. I was so happy, I was thinking about changing my whole life and becoming a Catholic. Problem solved. It's Miller time. Father Kelly kept on talking.

"Dismas was on the Lord's right hand and Gestas was on his left." He cleared his throat and adjusted his glasses. "You will recall in the Gospel of Luke we are told the pericope of the 'penitent thief.' It was this man who spoke the only kind words that Christ heard as he hung on the cross. This penitent thief was Dismas. He was canonized by Jesus himself. He is the patron saint of prisoners."

I wrote it all down and put an exclamation point at the end of it. Kathleen gave me a *"How-do-you-like-them-apples?"* look. I just sat there smiling and soaking up the warm glow. Dismas and Gestas. I got the spelling and wrote it down again using all capital letters. DISMAS AND GESTAS. No doubt the puppet didn't expect me to just happen to do an exorcism on the friend of the very person who knew the exact priest that had a copy of the book I needed to answer the question. Bet your ass! Dismas and Gestas.

So I thanked Father Kelly and shook his hand real energetic-like. "Thanks loads, Father Kelly! Far as I'm concerned, you're a damn fine Father. Finest Father I know. I'll never forget this, believe you me." I gathered up my stuff and was fixing to call Woodrow and tell him to pick me up and get ready for some good news.

Then a little itch developed in my skull. "Let me just clear up one thing Father Kelly. Probably nothing. I'm just curious. That book you're looking in says Dismas and Gestas were thieves. Right?"

"It's not just this book. The Bible itself says they were thieves."

"Yeah, I know. Except I got a Catholic Bible that says they were revolutionaries." Father Kelly gave me a Captain Kangaroo smile.

"Surely you misread. I have it right here." There was a Bible on the table and he found the verse in Matthew. "Thieves," he said pointing.

"Well, do you have the New American Bible here?"

"Yes, I think so. Would you like to see it?"

"If you don't mind. It's probably not important, but it sort of feels like a loose end that needs to be tied off." He got his copy of the Catholic Bible and found the verse. Kathleen was looking over his shoulder.

"It's as you say. 'Revolutionaries.'" He looked at me over the top of his glasses. Kathleen was frowning at the New American Bible. "Well, there's really no inconsistency when you think about it. It is, after all, possible to be a thief and a revolutionary at the same time. No doubt that is the case with these two men."

I really wanted to be satisfied, but I wasn't. I couldn't shake the feeling that the explanation wasn't as easy as Father Kelly was making out. Even if they were thieves but they were stealing for a cause, they might be more than plain vanilla crooks. It just seemed like there was something wrong with tagging them as thieves, if there was more to it.

"I'm sure you're right Father. I just need to nail it down. Were Dismas and Gestas revolutionaries or not?"

"Well, they were most assuredly thieves..."

"Okay, okay. I'll give you that. But were they revolutionaries?"

"It's hard to say without further study."

"So you're saying that I can't necessarily trust this here Catholic Bible when it says in black and white they were revolutionaries?"

"It may not be that simple." I could feel my ulcer index going up. So I turned to Kathleen.

"What do you say Kathleen? Were they or were they not revolutionaries?"

"Is this the only place they're called 'revolutionaries'? Just this one place?"

"No it isn't. They're called revolutionaries in Mark too. And they're called rebels in the TNIV Bible. And, so far as I can tell, that version isn't just for Catholics." She looked from the New American Bible to Father Kelly and then to me.

"I say we go with the majority. I say they were thieves."

"Okay. What about their names. Were they Dismas and Gestas or not?"

She turned to the priest. "Are there any other possibilities for their names?" He shook his head.

"The Church says they were Dismas and Gestas. These are the only names I am aware of." I borrowed Kathleen's phone and called Woodrow. He was at the coffee shop working on his laptop. I told him what we found out and asked him to check into it.

It was pretty quiet there in Father Kelly's library. I guess it got to him, because he started talking to fill up the space.

"You must not be distracted by trivialities. Whether they were or were not revolutionaries is of no import in the great scheme of salvation." Well that hit a nerve.

"Great scheme! I'm not here to learn shit about any great schemes. I'm here trying to get one straight answer to a simple question. If Jesus was crucified with Dismas and Gestas, great! I hope to hell he was. But if he wasn't, I got a wider field to plow and I don't have any choice but to start with what the Bible says—whatever that is."

I tried to calm myself and be logical. A second ago, I was the happiest guy on earth. Now, I was tied up in knots. Dismas and Gestas. I knew it was just too damn neat to be the right answer. There had to be a catch. I knew it wasn't Father Kelly's fault. And it damn sure wasn't Kathleen's. But I couldn't help taking it out on them anyway.

"Isn't this a fine can of worms? The last thing in the world I expected when I got thrown into this was that there were a hundred goddamn Bibles, and they couldn't make up their mind about something simple like this. I mean why should it be so complicated? Can somebody tell me?" There wasn't anybody falling over themselves to give me any answers. I apologized to Father Kelly and Kathleen. "I sure hope you're right about those names." He mumbled something without looking me in the eye. Kathleen walked out into the parking lot with me.

While we were standing there waiting for Woodrow, she said, "You know this is really surprising. I would've thought there would be more consensus on something so simple."

"To be honest, I never would have given a second thought to who those guys were if I didn't feel like my life depended on it."

"It's true that most Christians wouldn't think it's important." She stood quiet for a second watching the traffic roll up and down the Northwest Highway. "I'm getting the feeling there's something about this whole enterprise that's..." She dropped it.

I looked up at the clouds. It was going to storm for sure. "I wish to God I knew why any of this makes a difference."

"I don't know, Leon. Did Pinocchio give you any idea why it was important for you to carry out this search?"

"No. And it's getting more far-fetched and unfair by the gol' dang minute."

She looked up at the clouds and said like she was talking to herself. "Maybe." About then, the Dodge rolled into St. Knud's parking lot. Kathleen thanked me for signing the release and said she'd be in touch. She was walking to her van, and I told her to hold up a second. "What's your gut tell you, Kathleen? Is this Dismas deal the answer I'm looking for?"

There was sort of a regretful look on her face. "When we came here, I hoped it would be. But it's starting to look like you—we have more to do." She waved to Woodrow. He waved back. Then she got in her van and drove off.

As I climbed into the Dodge, Woodrow said, "Let's go back to the coffee shop. I got to show you something."

"I got a bad headache Woodrow."

"I know. And I got the cure buddy. But first you need to see this. It's important."

There's a Panera Bread Café down the highway a little bit. We went inside, and Woodrow fired up his laptop. In short order, he Googled Dismas, and pages started popping up. I followed along as he sailed through them.

"That name Dismas doesn't show up in any version of the Bible. But it does show up in the twelfth century in this bogus manuscript called *The Acts of Pilate*. This is supposed to be a record of Pilate's rule in Judea. You remember who he was. Right?"

"Sure I do. Pilate was the Roman boss that gave Jesus over to the Jews to get crucified."

"Right. Anyway, according to the *Acts of Pilate* and another bogus manuscript called *The Gospel of Nicodemus*, Dysmus, or Dismas, or Dumas— all of these spellings show up for the same guy—was the good thief. San Dimas, California, is named after him. And Gestas was the other one."

He was hitting the computer keys, and other sites were opening up. "Once you get on the trail, it's surprising what pops up. Look here." He highlighted another word.

"There's something called *The Arabic Infancy Gospel* from the fourth century. Experts say it's bogus too, just like *The Acts of Pilate*. And according to this deal, the guys crucified with Jesus were named Titus, who was the good thief, but this one calls the bad thief Dumachus which sort of looks like Dumas. See? This Arabic Gospel says Jesus met these guys when he was a baby fleeing to Egypt to get away from Herod. Supposedly, Titus kept Dumachus from robbing Jesus' mother and father on the road."

"Is any of this in the Bible?"

"Nope.

"So none of this is true?"

"Who knows? Some of this could have come from reliable documents that we don't have any more. But, hold on to your hat, because there's more. Here's an old Latin copy of the Bible that translates Matthew 27:38 to include the names Zoathan and Canna for the two guys who died with Jesus." Stuff was zipping across his computer so fast, I was having a hard time getting everything wrote down.

"Slow down here Woodrow. I can't keep up with all this." If he slowed down at all, it wasn't much.

"It's okay, Buzz. We can come back to it later for the details. I'm just trying to lay out the big picture for you now. There's another old Bible called the Codex Usserianus. If you look at Luke 23:32 on this Codex deal, it says their names was Joathas and Maggatras."

"Take a look at this. There is ..."

"Now hold on Woodrow, goddammit. How do you spell this *"use-your-anus"* or whatever?"

I was getting dizzy and my head was aching. "Stay with me Buzz. We're almost done. An old English Church guy named Bede got the name Matha for the good thief and Joca for the other one. Now if you really want to get out in left field, there was an Ethiopian tradition where these two were cannibals. Yeah, cannibals. These Ethiopians say the good thief was named Joctan—which looks a lot like the name of the bad thief according to Bede. To wind out our line-up, there was a seventh-century Latin source that calls them Lustin and Vissimus."

He waited for me to stop writing. "Even if the puppet lets you do a multiple choice answer, I'm not sure any of this shit's right."

We sat there looking at this screwy list of foreign looking names both knowing that we'd hit a dead end for today. I don't know what Woodrow was thinking, but I was thinking I had to come up with another plan, because I damn sure couldn't afford to go to the bank with what I had. It started raining, and we could hear thunder way off. Woodrow said, "Let's fix that headache, and then how do you feel about Chinese food?" I told him that sounded great.

"First to Go" by Leo Kottke was on the iPod, and there was a gentle rain falling on the Dodge. We passed the magic pipe back and forth and it was like my headache was getting temporarily cured by pot smoke and rainwater. You would have thought I'd be discouraged by spending the day mining fool's gold. But I didn't feel that way at all. There was something about the way things were coming together that had me expecting the good. See, it occurred to me that the dead end we hit today might be more like a bass-ackwards doorway. Putting names on these men—even if they was the wrong names—got me thinking about them like they were real guys. I mean flesh and blood people. Men with faces, height and weight; men who found pleasure in the world around them. Hell, they could have been men like me and Woodrow. I didn't feel that when I first started. They were more like movie characters—like Sinbad or Hercules. You know what I mean?

Maybe they were good guys who didn't deserve what they got. Maybe they've been getting a bum rap for hundreds of years. Could be that's what this whole deal was about. I tried to get a better look where this might be leading, but my headache shut me down.

After kung pao chicken and egg rolls, we checked into a Holiday Inn Express. *Rising Sun* was showing on the movie channel. Maybe you've seen it. Sean Connery plays a senior cop who knows his way around Japanese people. Wesley Snipes is a junior cop who's just learning his way around Japanese people. Sean and Wesley are working with a bunch of Japanese folks trying to solve a murder. Anyway, the last thing I remember before I drifted off to sleep was a scene where some lady was fooling around with a videotape. She was able to do this trick where she could move Snipes' head onto Connery's body and vice versa. So there was Snipes' head talking up a storm on Connery's shoulders. Snipes' hands kept making gestures along with a head and voice that was someplace else. I think I remember hearing it thunder a little bit and rain.

Thursday, February 22, 2007, a.m.

The next morning, Woodrow woke me up, knocking on the door. He had some Holiday Inn coffee for us. We turned on the news, and there was a story about people wearing Chinese dog fur thinking it was not real fur at all. There were pictures of these cute little puppies, raccoon dogs they call them, that had been made into clothes that got sold at Nordstrom's and other high-dollar places like that. There were sure a bunch of pissed off ladies when they found out they were going around town wearing puppy fur.

Woodrow's cell phone rang. It was Kathleen. Woodrow put her on speaker. "I need you to meet me back at St. Knud's. I think I may be able to get us back on track." I didn't hear a word she was saying, though, because I was watching a news lady doing a story. She was standing in front of my house. Demonstrators! For crying out loud there was demonstrators at my dang house. The news lady put a microphone in a guy's face and asked "What can you tell us about this Mr. Davenport?"

"Well it's just an outrage for a man to claim to work miracles and then try to charge people for it. He ought to be ashamed and people need to be wary of this deceiver." Deceiver my ass! I never claimed to be a healer and I damn sure didn't charge anybody for shit. Hell, I didn't get a dime for those miracles I didn't do. If you want to talk about deceivers, take a look at the sons of bitches selling puppy fur.

But then they interviewed a lady named Mrs. Bowlap, and she was telling my side. "It's unfair to condemn Mr. Butane out of hand. We should withhold judgment until we can hear his explanation. I've personally spoken to the families of some of those who experienced miracles as a result of some contact with this man. At this point, we really don't know what's going on. As far as we can tell, Mr. Butane has never asked for anything." Goddamn right! Woodrow sipped his hotel coffee and watched real quiet like.

Then the news people shifted over to Kathleen's blog where there were pictures of Mrs. Suarez, old Francisco, little Iris, and Denise and some people that I don't remember ever even seeing before. Then they interviewed another guy who said he doesn't know what's going on, but if I'm on the up and up, how come I'm ducking the process server?

I got so wrapped up in the news I plumb forgot about Kathleen. Woodrow gave me an elbow and I snapped out of it. "Say Kathleen. Did you know there were demonstrators outside my house?"

"Yes. They left last night when it started raining and came back this morning. I think Ernest Bidding is behind it."

"Why? What good does it do him to get everybody riled up about me being a deceiver?"

"He got a black eye because he wasn't able to help Denise Armando.

There's a lot of chatter about the fact an uneducated truck driver—no offense Leon—was able to work a miracle where Bidding failed. But really, this madness is taking on a life of its own. The exchanges being posted are approaching hysteria. It's a religious feeding frenzy. The video of your healing Iris is one of the top hits on YouTube. Some people are even saying you're a saint."

"Saint Leon? You've got to be kidding. Saint Leon? That's ridiculous. It's got to stop. You got to tell people to calm down about it. None of the wild stuff that's happening is really my fault. The only thing I done wrong was get busted up in the wrong truck crash."

"I understand, and there will be a time soon when you should come forward and tell your story. But now isn't the time. We need to concentrate on running down the answers you need, and that's why you need to meet me back at the church ASAP."

Ordinarily I know a wild goose chase when I'm on one. "I don't mean to be contrary here Kathleen. After all, Father Kelly is a nice enough old gent. But, all due respect, he's not as great a Father as I thought at first. I don't see where he can help us much."

"I know, I know. But we don't need him. Believe me, he's actually sorry he ever met us. He doesn't want anything more to do with us. We really fouled up his Ash Wednesday meditations. We're only going back to use the church library. That's where we should start looking again. Father Kelly won't be anywhere near us."

Woodrow shrugged. "It's as good a place as any to waste your time."

"Okay Kathleen, we'll see you at the church in an hour."

On the way back to St. Knud's, Woodrow said, "Say Buzz. I'm just asking. Is there anything else you ought to be telling me?"

"Like what, Woodrow?"

"I don't know. But if you got any idea what all this means big-picture-wise, I'd like to be in on it."

"I'm not following Woodrow."

"It's just that I'm thinking this chore the puppet assigned you looks like it's building up a lot of importance to more folks than just us."

I thought about it for a minute. "Hell, I don't know, Woodrow. I feel like I'm just rolling wherever the wind's blowing."

Then he asked me something that maybe I should have spent more time thinking about. "Tell me Buzz, do you trust Kathleen?" No hesitation.

"Sure I do. Why do you ask?"

"Well, she says now ain't the time for you to come out personally and put an end to this—right?"

"That's what she says."

"You agree with her?"

"Hell I don't know Woodrow. She's the media expert, not me. If she says now ain't the time, now ain't the time." I felt like he wanted to say something else. Argue maybe. But he kept his mouth shut and we drove on.

Kathleen was there when we pulled into St. Knud's parking lot. She met us at the front door. She couldn't wait to get it out. "Late last night, we received a post from Pinocchio."

I stopped in my tracks. "I don't get it."

"Pinocchio, or someone calling himself Pinocchio, posted an entry. I don't know what this means, but he said 'Pinpoint the rebellion. It's in there.'"

"In where and what rebellion?"

"I don't know in where, but I'm assuming the rebellion is the one that supposedly got those other men crucified."

I tried to process how this tied in to everything as I followed Kathleen into a room with bookshelves floor-to-ceiling. She opened her fancy brief case and pulled out a list of email messages. One was highlighted and it said just what she told us.

I stood there looking at it. Woodrow was looking over my shoulder. Kathleen was watching me.

"How about you Woodrow? Any ideas?" He took the paper from Kathleen's hand and studied the message.

He shook his head. "The whole damn world knows about Pinocchio showing up in your coma, Buzz. After all, Miss Wister here plastered it all over the Internet, didn't she?"

She stuck her chin out all defiant like. "As a matter of fact I did. It's part of the story, so I posted it."

Woodrow handed her back the paper. "Looks like somebody's jerking our chain."

"I don't know whether you're right or wrong Woodrow. But I do know this stuff about getting to the rebellion seems to match up with some of the stuff we're looking into. We ought to keep an open mind on this Pinocchio post."

Kathleen spoke up again. "That's why we're back here. We're going to try to bypass the translators and get to the truth of what the Bible really says about these men. I've been up most of the night looking things up, and I think I know where we go next."

She was right about Father Kelly. He wasn't anywhere around. Kathleen pulled a couple of books out of her briefcase. They were the same two books Miss Evers had at the Tishotaha County Library. *The Precise Parallel New Testament* and *The Evangelical Parallel New Testament*. Then she pulled a book off a shelf called the *Word Study Greek-English New Testament*. "Look here." She opened it up so we could all see it.

It's a pretty complicated book. On the outer edges of the pages, there's the Bible written in English. Most of the pages are taken up with Greek writing. On top of every Greek work, there's a number. Under every Greek word is the English word that goes along with that number.

"See these numbers?" She pointed to numbers on top of the Greek words. "Each one corresponds to a number in *Strong's Exhaustive Concordance.* If we look the number up in the concordance, it will give us all the English meanings of the word. This ought to help us get to the root word behind these various translations."

I thought I was following, but I wanted to make sure. "Show me what you mean Kathleen." She turned to Matthew 27:38 in the *Word Study* deal. There was a word written in Greek. Under it, in English, was the word "robbers." Above it was a number—3027.

Then she got another book called *The Complete Word Study Dictionary* for the New Testament and went to number 3027. "See. This is how it works. It shows that if you convert the Greek letters to English, the word you get is *lēstēs.*" I read the definition, and started to see the problem.

Woodrow saw it too. "It looks to me like *lēstēs* might have changed meanings over time. At first, it meant somebody who took somebody else's stuff by violence. But later, it came to mean "insurgent" or "zealot." Is that the way you see it, Buzz?" Naturally when I saw the word "insurgent," I remembered my little spell in the hospital and felt like there was another kind of connection being made.

Kathleen stopped writing and took a close look at the dictionary. "So it looks like the translators made a choice of which way to read *lēstēs.* Could be either way was okay."

Seemed to me there had to be a logical next question. "Okay. Why do you suppose some translators might choose to translate it one way and the others go a different way?"

"I don't know Leon. I'm starting to get some ideas. But we have other things to look at."

Kathleen pointed to another place in the *Word Study Dictionary.* "Look. This shows all the places number 3027 shows up in the New Testament. The one we're looking for is here at Mark 15:27. She turned to that verse in one of the *Parallel Bibles.*

I decided to save some time. "I've been through this drill with Miss Evers. There are a couple of these versions that call them revolutionaries." Woodrow took my word for it, but Kathleen checked it out.

Woodrow spoke up. "What do the other gospels call these guys?"

Kathleen turned to Luke 23:32. "Here's what we're looking for. In the Greek Bible, the English meaning is "workers of bad." The number is 2557. The English spelling for the Greek word is *kakourgos.*"

Kathleen turned back and forth in the dictionary looking at *lēstēs* and *kakourgos.* "Looks like the main difference between *lēstēs* and *kakourgos* is violence. *Lēstēs* necessarily involves an element of violence, while *kakourgos* does not."

"What do you say Woodrow? You're more of a scholar than I am." He didn't do anything but nod.

Kathleen was already looking at John 19:18. "Look here, the Greek word for these men is *allos*, which means "others." That's it. Just 'others.' Not violent. Not even law breakers. Just 'others.'"

Woodrow chuckled. "Hell, as far as John is concerned, these guys might just be innocent bystanders." He stood up and looked over Kathleen's shoulder. "Why do you suppose Luke and John choose softer words to describe these guys?"

Kathleen launched into an explanation that sounded like she was teaching Sunday school. "That's a question people have been asking for centuries. Why are there apparent inconsistencies in the Gospel accounts? Well, there are two reasons. First, some apparent inconsistencies aren't really inconsistent at all. It's just a different way of saying the same thing. Where there are real differences, it's no more than you'd expect. Any time you have different people witnessing the same event, you're likely to get differing perceptions and different recollections of what happened. What was important to one witness may not be important to another. That's why there are four gospels. So we have the benefit of four perspectives on the same events. Where these men are concerned, the Gospel writers are all correct. They were rebels. Rebels are wrongdoers, and they were, in fact, other men. I don't see any real inconsistency here."

Woodrow wasn't buying it. "It isn't that simple if you don't stop there Kathleen. I'm just not satisfied that explains it. Where else does *lēstēs* show up in the New Testament? Let's see what else the Bible has to say about it."

Kathleen ran her finger down a column while Woodrow and I watched. "Well, here's one at John 18:40. *Lēstēs* is used to describe Barabbas." I thought I knew who that was. "Remind me who Barabbas was."

Kathleen looked disgusted. "Oh really Leon. You don't remember Barabbas? He is the man Pilate released when Jesus was condemned." Of course, that rang a bell.

Woodrow was looking at it real close. "So John has no problem using the word *lēstēs* when he talks about Barabbas, but the men crucified with Jesus are just 'others.' Why?"

I shrugged and Kathleen acted like she didn't hear him. Woodrow pointed out Mark 15:7 in the *Parallel Bibles*. "Here it shows up again. What do you make of this? When *lēstēs* shows up in connection with Barabbas, they say here it means 'insurrection.' Why would the same word mean 'robbers' in one place and 'insurrection' here? Looks like some kind of linguistic razzle-dazzle is going on. I guess you've got to be an expert to get it. I damn sure know I'm not getting it."

Woodrow kept studying for a second then busted out laughing. "Are you ready for the confusing icing on the bullshit cake? Here's a translation called *The Message*. When it translates the *lēstēs* crucified with Jesus, they're 'criminals.' When it's Barabbas, guess what it is. 'Jewish freedom fighter.' How's that for a shell game? Same word—'Jewish freedom fighter' when it's Barabbas; Criminal when it's these other guys." He laughed again. "I smell something rotten in Denmark, kids."

I couldn't believe it. "Show me." He did. We looked at each other then at Kathleen and said at the same time. "What do you reckon this mean?" She didn't answer.

I couldn't let it go. "There has to be a reason Kathleen. If we're talking about the same word, how does it get to be that Barabbas is a Jewish freedom fighter and these men are just common thieves? How does that happen?"

She just shook her head. "I don't think I know enough to say anything right now."

Woodrow wasn't writing this shit down like Kathleen and me, but he was following the thread. "You know, I've got an idea. Somebody got nervous about Jesus being crucified with the rebels because that might give people the wrong idea, like maybe he was a *lēstēs* himself. So they play this word game to create some distance."

Kathleen shook her head "No one who heard the message of Christ or read his words could possibly believe that he was a violent revolutionary in the political sense. Anyway, the gospel writers and translators wouldn't dare intentionally mislead people. Why would they?"

Woodrow leaned forward and looked at her real stern and said, "I've been sitting here looking at this stuff just like you have Kathleen. Something isn't adding up. Somebody's trying to sidestep something."

She sat there for a minute looking from one of the books in front of her to the other and said, more to herself than to us, "There's got to be an explanation." So she kept looking at the Greek and going to the dictionary and looking at all those translations of the Bible. I was about to overdose.

Woodrow said, "Well, I'll tell you one thing. From what I'm seeing and hearing, Barabbas and the guys crucified with Jesus was guilty of the same offense—rebellion."

We waited for Kathleen to say something. She didn't.

I decided to push Kathleen off high center and get her moving. "Well, let's nail this down once and for all. Kathleen, who can give us the final word on what *lēstēs* means in the Greek when we're talking about these guys?"

She pulled herself away from the books and sat for a minute like she was letting a fog clear. "Professor Landreth at Oklahoma Baptist University is a highly respected expert in biblical Greek. He can give us the answer." She scrolled through the numbers on her cell phone and made a call. I guess Professor Landreth answered, because she explained what we wanted to know. She gave him some verses—Matthew 27:38, John 18:40, and so on. She told him about how the various translations were mixed up. She listened and hung up. "He'll call us back."

It was lunch time, and I was hungry. We decided to go eat. Kathleen came with us.

Okay. Be right back. I'm gunna change batteries in this thinamajig 'cause it looks like they're gettin' low.

TAPE 9

Thursday, February 22, 2007, p.m.

Over lunch at Red Lobster, we found out more about how Kathleen got so caught up in all this religious stuff. Her mom's name was Edna, and her dad, Leland Townsend, was a conservative Presbyterian pastor in Oklahoma City. Kathleen turned into an evangelical in college and married an up-and-coming pastor named Wendell Wister. Wendell got hired by Bidding's ministries as an associate pastor in one of the satellite churches. She was hired on as one of Bidding's assistants. She and Wendell were in on the ground floor when Bidding's megachurch went up in Dallas.

Bidding had a falling out with that church. I guess there were some questions about money, and he doesn't like to be questioned about how he handles things.

Somewhere along the way, Kathleen and her husband got divorced. They had been married more than twenty years, but never had kids. Her ex left the church and moved to San Diego. They don't have much contact now. After a while, something really unpleasant happened between her and Bidding. She wouldn't say what it was. But, she left Bidding's church and went to Arizona to join up with the Howard ministry. Bidding left Dallas and built himself a new megachurch in Mustang, Oklahoma.

Kathleen got turned upside down again when Reverend Howard got caught cornholing the gay guy. That's when she went on the dang warpath. I guess she's famous in the religious blogging world because thousands of people read her blog every day. Sounds like it's a kind of a religious tabloid. I shouldn't say much, though, because I only looked at it the one time.

Kathleen stopped right in the middle of her fried shrimp and hush puppies, "I need to ask you a question, Leon."

"Okay, shoot."

"Do you believe we're living in the end times?"

"You mean do I think we're getting near the end of the world? To be honest, the only time I think about it is when I hear some preacher talking about it. It's just not something I worry much about on a day-to-day basis."

"Do you think Christ will come back?"

"Well—yeah. I guess so."

"Do you think the earth will be destroyed by fire or do you think Christ will set up an earthly kingdom?"

My appetite was getting ruined. "I don't have any opinion on any of that stuff, Kathleen. I'm just a driver—or I was before my head got cracked open. I really am not qualified to have an opinion. I guess I believe in judgment day and all that. I just can't get myself in an emotional uproar over it. I'll probably spend more time thinking about it if I get out of this deal. So if you're thinking I'm a prophet or something that's got answers to your religious questions, you'd be as well off talking to a sea horse."

Woodrow never looked up from his clam chowder. "I think all that horseshit about judgment day and returning Messiahs is part of the mental toxins we've been building up for thousands of years."

I was hoping Woodrow's heathenism would get the focus off of me so I could eat. But Kathleen just looked at him and let it go. She wasn't finished with me.

"Leon, do you feel like you've been chosen by God to do something special?"

I about choked on my tea. "I'm sorry Kathleen, but nothing about this deal feels like God's doing."

She studied her hush puppies for a few seconds, then asked, "Does it feel like the devil? Bidding says there are only two powers in the universe capable of working miracles. If you're not in God's service, he says you're in the devil's service."

Now the truth is, I spent a lot of time thinking about the word "service." Not in the sense of God and the devil's squaring off and using people. So my thinking about it just sort of started tumbling out. "You probably won't understand this, because you've never been in war. But sometimes this is how service works. Technically, when I was in combat, I was serving the

United States Government. But when I was in a firefight, that didn't make a shit. I was in service to saving my ass. Period. Now if saving my ass turned out to be good for the U.S. of A., great! But that was bonus. It wasn't on my mind. That's how this deal feels. I'll do my best to figure this thing out even if the devil is behind it. That may be wicked and sinful and all. But I'll worry about getting it sorted out if I survive."

Kathleen was red in the face, and I could tell she wasn't liking what she was hearing. Then Woodrow spoke up. "Let me ask you something about the devil, Kathleen. Is he as smart as you are?"

"What a question! He was once with God in heaven. Of course he's smarter than I am."

"So he knows, just like you do, that God's going to kick his ass in the final show-down."

"There's no need to be trivial and sacrilegious, Woodrow."

"Sorry. But you do believe that Satan knows, just like you and all Christians know, that God will triumph in the end."

"Yes. It's no secret. So I suppose he knows."

"Well, if he's so damn smart and knows how this ends, why the hell wouldn't he repent?"

"Pride. He's too proud and vain to submit to God's sovereignty."

"Then all I can say is, he's dumber than a dog, because he knows how God's going to punish him for his pride. The devil's going to get humbled like nobody's business. He's going to get chained to a Bombay toilet for eternity. None of that really adds up, now, does it Kathleen? The truth is, there isn't any such thing as the devil."

Well, she really was riled up and I was starting to lose hope in ever enjoying my shrimp. So I stepped in.

"Look. I'm not interested in religious arguments right now. I'm just not up to it. I got to concentrate on getting an answer to a straightforward historical question. Who are these guys?"

About then Kathleen's telephone rang. It was Dr. Landreth, the Greek expert from OBU. She put him on speaker and asked what his conclusion was.

"The singular form of the word you're interested in is *lēstēs*. The plural is *lēstai*. I've looked at the verses you cited and the translations you referenced. I'm telling you there's only one legitimate way to translate the word in the context of the trial and crucifixion of Jesus. Rebellion. Rebellion against the Roman regime. *'Robber'* or *'criminal'* might be appropriate in another context. But the Romans didn't crucify people for simple robbery or theft. They crucified people for violent resistance to Roman authority. Those translations of the Bible that refer to those *lēstai* crucified with Jesus as rebels or revolutionaries are correct. Likewise, where Barabbas is described as a Jewish freedom fighter, that characterization is correct from the Jewish point of view. All of them were certainly regarded by the authorities as violent opponents of Rome. No question."

Sounded to me like that pretty much wrapped it up. Revolutionaries all right. I guess we forgot about the professor for a second.

"Hello?"

"We're here professor. If that's true, why are there so many inaccurate English translations?"

"Kathleen, I don't feel qualified to explain the long and frustrating line of historical distortions in the writing and translating of the New Testament. I can only tell you that these men were not simple thieves—no matter what the translators say." He sure sounded like a grumpy old codger. Kathleen thanked him and hung up without saying goodbye.

We sat there quiet for a minute. I imagine we were each running down our own private rabbit trail trying to figure out what to do next. The outline of the problem was getting clear in my mind. For hundreds of years, even up to today, Bible translators have been getting their facts out of whack. They're either doing it by accident because they're not very good translators, or they're fudging on purpose for some reason.

Woodrow was the first one to speak up. "So now we know they were rebels. And whoever the Pinocchio is that's sending love letters to Kathleen says we need to pinpoint the rebellion. That's what he said, right Kathleen?"

She pulled the paper out of her purse and looked at it again. "Pinpoint the rebellion. It's in there."

Woodrow nodded. I'm guessing this Pinocchio thinks it's important to know which rebellion these guys were part of. And when he says 'it's in there,' he probably means it's in the Bible. Right?"

Kathleen didn't answer. She just stood up real quick like.

"I may know where to go from here. I have to go home and get some information. I'll call you later." She grabbed the check. Woodrow and I were grumbling about it, because we've never had a girl pick up the tab for us before. She ignored us, paid the bill, and was gone.

Woodrow watched her pilot her van onto the Northwest Highway and drive east. "You know, Buzz, that girl may be having as bumpy a ride on this trip as you are."

"Maybe. But you better believe I'd trade places with her in a heartbeat. Her damn life ain't at stake here."

He looked at me all wide-eyed. Fake surprise. "You mean you'd trade places and become a woman if it would save your life?"

"Cut it out, Woodrow. You know what I mean."

"Well I'm glad. No doubt you'd turn out to be a piss-poor excuse for a woman. Now that's settled, what do you want to do next?"

"Hell, let's take a look at Ernest Bidding's blog. From what Kathleen says, I'm the current star of his show."

"You know, Buzz, that's a good idea. Let's find some place that's got Wi-Fi and take a look." He stumped out of the Red Lobster, and I followed him.

Now let me tell you about Woodrow's foot. He could wear a government-issue replacement if he wanted. But he prefers to make his own. He buys mammoth ivory from somewhere and makes his foot out of that stuff. You'd think 15,000 year old ivory would be brittle. I guess it is sometimes. But some of it is really hard.

Woodrow has two or three mammoth ivory feet that he treated after he got them made up. I don't know how he does it, but he says he can wear them for another thousand years and they won't wear out.

He even made me an eyeball out of mammoth ivory. I don't wear it, though, because it doesn't look real like my government-issue peeper. No, they keep my ivory eyeball in a place of honor at The Tolosa Gold Saloon. My buddies down there bring it out for me to wear on special occasions.

So far as I know, Woodrow and I are the only two guys in the world that got mammoth ivory decorations to go along with our purple hearts.

Anyway, we carried the laptop back to the Panera Café, and Woodrow Googled Bidding. A whole shit load of stuff turned up. Some of it we already knew from Kathleen. But a lot of it was new.

To start with, he was a football star at the University of Alabama back in the eighties: played linebacker. He went to the pros and played for Dallas a couple of years, then got hurt and went back to school at North Texas Theological. When he got out of there in the nineties, he got into the ministry working for that big Pineway Baptist Church in Dallas. He left there and started his own church called the Great Light Tabernacle. He was there until 2002 when he came up to Mustang, Oklahoma, and started up the

Tabernacle of Revealed Truth. He's been preaching in Mustang for the last five years.

He wrote some books about "the inbreaking of the Spirit." I guess all these Evangelicals are preaching and writing about it these days. His theory is that God is drawing together a lot of different threads. Some of them we see and some we don't. The Lord's fixing to establish a new spiritual reality on earth, and the chosen ones are going to enjoy the everlasting fruits of this new deal.

There were newspaper and magazine articles about him and other big-time preachers working together on charities and stuff. He hangs out with some high-powered politicians too: senators, governors, presidential candidates, people like that. Apparently, Bidding's been involved in several scandals. Nothing sexual. But a lot of people have complained about his financial wheeling and dealing. Three rich widows set him up with his first church. They all chose up sides and had some kind of falling out over money, and he left Dallas. One of those widows moved to Oklahoma to help him start up his Mustang tabernacle.

It looked like the widow's family filed lawsuits to stop her from pouring all her money into Bidding's church. There were a lot of back-and-forths about whether the case ought to be tried in Texas or Oklahoma. Big mess. Bidding won. So the widow and her money wound up in Oklahoma.

Then there was stuff about him buying planes and condos with church funds. I guess his contract says he can do it, so all his critics can do is belly-ache. Seems his followers are ready to overlook his high-on-the-hog lifestyle because they keep coming, watching, praying, and contributing. The IRS didn't like it though, and I guess he's always litigating with the tax guys over something. He must be charmed, though, because it looks like he always turns up on top of that stuff.

One of his books is called *The Devil's Rising Power*. The idea there is that Satan is gathering his forces for an end-time free-for-all, and the devil's on a campaign to drain off the faith of God's people. This is supposed to weaken the forces of good.

I elbowed Woodrow in the ribs. "You're right Woodrow. Looks like the devil is a dumbass. He still thinks he can win."

"Well, maybe he figures that since he's got such a powerful recruit as Leon Butane, the tide has turned."

"Laugh if you want to buddy, but if anybody at this table is working for the devil, it's the atheist."

"You got me wrong, Buzz. I'm no atheist. I just am not a dualist." I would have asked what dueling has to do with atheism, but Bidding's blog popped up on the computer. Kathleen was telling it straight. I was all over it.

Bidding was saying that the only power able to work miracles, if it ain't God, is Satan himself. He said I should come forward now and declare whether I'm a worker for God or a worker for the devil. He quotes a verse in the Bible where it says if a guy is working miracles in Jesus' name, he ought to be left alone. If I'm a worker for God, he wanted to offer me his hand in friendship, love, and cooperation. If I'm a worker for the devil, then he planned to come against me in the name of God Almighty, the Lord of Hosts.

Well, that pissed me off. I didn't set out to do miracles, and I didn't ask for a fight with Ernest Bidding, and I damn sure didn't ask to get called on the carpet in front of God Almighty, the Lord of Hosts.

So I said to Woodrow, "Give me your phone."

He looked at me sideways. "Who are you aiming to call, Buzz?"

"I'll tell you who I'm aiming to call. I aim to call the goddamn reverend on the goddamn phone and tell him to find somebody else to rake over his holy coals, because he's got the wrong sinner here."

"Now calm down. It won't do a bit of good for you to call him. He probably won't take your call, and if he does, he'll just tell you to fuck off in some churchy way. He'll get a laugh out of it, and you won't get anything but steamed. No doubt he'd plaster it all over his blog how you called up and admitted as to how you're a devil worshiper and it would be his holy word against the word of Butane, the false prophet deceiver. How do you think that would come out?"

I was about to argue out of pure stubbornness when Woodrow's phone rang. Naturally it was Kathleen. "I've got good news and bad news. The good news is that one of the world's great experts on the historical facts surrounding the crucifixion is a retired scholar in Kansas City named Dr. Broward Ryland. He wrote two volumes on it called *The Crucifixion of the Christ*. The bad news is, he is in really bad health and can only give us an hour tomorrow. I tried to set it up for us to talk with him over the phone. But he wouldn't do it. For some reason, he wants to see you, Leon."

"What in the world does a retired Bible scholar in bad health want to see me for? He doesn't expect for me to work a miracle and cure him or something, does he?"

"He wouldn't say much over the phone, Leon. He just said he'd see us at one o'clock, so we need to leave at seven in the morning."

Since Woodrow and I didn't have any alternate plan, we agreed we'd be up and raring to go. Just as we were about to sign off, Kathleen remembered something.

"Oh, by the way, Dr. Ryland said something strange at the end of our conversation. He asked me if I knew who St. Matthias is. I said 'I'm sorry. I don't. I'm not a Catholic.' He said, 'Neither am I now, but you don't need to be Catholic to know who St. Matthias is.' He told me to look into it. It might be important to what we are looking for. I asked him what he knew about our problem. He just mumbled that he knew enough, and he'd see us tomorrow."

Woodrow asked, "Did he sound senile?"

"No. He sounded eccentric."

"Well, about this Saint Matthias deal. What's up with that?"

"I'll check and have something for you tomorrow."

Kathleen promised to come by the hotel a little early and have some tea for the road. Then she hung up.

Naturally, the next thing we did was look on the computer to see who this Dr. Ryland is. Wikipedia gave us a run-down. Over the years, he has written tons of stuff about the gospels, mostly Mark and John. In 1988, he left the priesthood and published *The Crucifixion of the Christ*.

So it looked like maybe this guy knew his stuff even if he might be a kook. It took us a while to get the right spelling, but when we were finally able to Google Matthias, we found out his feast day, according to the Catholics, was sure enough coming up on February 24. He's supposed to be the patron of reformed drunks. That couldn't have anything to do with me and Woodrow because we're not reformed. Anyway, Matthias doesn't show up in the Bible until after the resurrection. But the Wikipedia article says he was one of Jesus' disciples a long time before that. He was the guy that got picked to take Judas' place after Judas turned Jesus in to the authorities for the reward. It figures that if the disciples needed a replacement, they wouldn't pick a guy off the street. They probably knew Matthias pretty good before he got picked.

We figured we'd about worked that angle as much as it could be worked for the moment. So we packed up our stuff and headed out to the Dodge.

When we stepped out of the coffee shop, the wind was blowing so hard Woodrow had to hold his ball cap on with both hands and was mumbling as he was sideways walking toward the Dodge.

On the way back to the motel, though, I couldn't help but kick the Matthias deal around some more. "Okay, it's interesting. But what the hell do you suppose Matthias has to do with who got crucified with Jesus?"

"Well, for one thing, he could probably answer your question for you if you could talk to him."

"How do you figure?"

"Doesn't it stand to reason that Jesus' disciples would want to know who it was getting crucified with their boss or master or whatever they called him?"

"Yeah. I see what you mean. That's something they'd probably want to know all right."

"It isn't likely they'd say, 'whatever you do, people, don't tell us who those other guys are who are being executed with Jesus, because we've got no curiosity about it at all.'"

"Okay, so what? So Matthias knew who they were. Lots of people must have known who they were. That does me no good if somebody didn't write it down someplace where we can get hold of it in the next few days."

Right on schedule, I started getting my regular late day headache, and I wasn't able to think with my usual laser sharpness. "Let's call it a day, Woodrow. What say we do a headache treatment and get some barbeque over to the County Line before we go back to the motel for a movie?"

"Deal."

While we were driving down the highway, the winds caused the Dodge to rock so hard it would be risky for us to pass the pipe. It was still too light to park somewhere, and Woodrow didn't want to smoke in the room, because somebody might get suspicious. Woodrow's got great antennas, and his feelings about what's safe and not safe have kept us out of a lot of trouble—especially in Nam. So if Woodrow says, "It ain't safe," then it ain't safe.

We decided to go through the car wash at 63rd and the Broadway Extension. That would give us a few minutes to take down a hit or two. When we pulled up, there was a couple of cars ahead of us. That was okay because you can sit still and have a smoke while you're in line and nobody thinks a thing about it.

Just as we pulled the Dodge into the wash, Woodrow's phone rang. It was Kathleen. We couldn't hear a thing she was saying because of the mechanical sprayers and wipers and stuff. So we had to call her back after we were high and the Dodge was clean.

Woodrow put her on speaker. She was upset. "I really don't know what to say. Things are spinning out of control. Some of the people logging onto the blog are threatening violence. Some of Bidding's followers are so whipped up, they're not rational. I mean they're scary. Some of them say there's proof you're a devil worshiper."

"Proof my ass! How can there be proof of something that ain't even true? Can't somebody get a hold of these crackpots and tell them I got nothing to do with the devil or devil worship? All I'm trying to do is keep the puppet from punching my gol' darned ticket."

Kathleen sounded like she was about to cry. "I've been in touch with Bidding and he says he is warning his followers to cut out all this violent talk and leave the correction of this problem in God's hands. But he says this is partly your fault, Leon. If you would just come out and say that what you're doing, you're doing in God's name, that would help to diffuse the situation."

"Well tell him I can't say anything like that, goddammit, because that would be pure bullshit. I'm not doing anything, and what I am doing, I'm just doing to save my own ass."

"I really don't know what to do right now, Leon. I've never been in the middle of something like this. Let me think about it, and I'll try to come up with something." She didn't sound like a happy gal when she got off the phone.

All this upset had me in danger of losing the bonus from Woodrow's pot. So we decided the Dodge wasn't clean enough and we had to go back through the car wash again.

When we got back to the motel, we found *Little Big Man* on the movie channel. The last thing I remember before I slipped off into sleep was Chief Dan George shaking somebody's scalp in front of Dustin Hoffman's face and asking, "Do you see this fine thing? Do you admire the humanity of it?" I've seen that movie a bunch of times, and I've always felt a little guilty, because I never really got the chief's point about the humanity of that scalp. I guess there's not enough Indian blood in me to catch his drift. Just as I was nodding off, I was thinking if I could just stay awake for a few more minutes, I'd finally get it. No use. I was in dreamland.

So there I was, back at the zoo with Ho, Jack, and the puppet. Jack looked at me and smiled. Ho was smoking that same cigarette and still holding it like all the Commies do in the movies. Pinocchio came clacking over in that jerky, bouncy puppet walk, and he came right up to me.

I searched real close to see if I could find the strings that were making him move. I couldn't see a thing. He just stood there for a minute looking up at me. Then real smooth and quick like, he reached his little wooden hand up and got hold of my thumb. Not hard. Gentle. Like a little boy would. I really don't know how to describe how his hand felt. It wasn't like skin or wood. It was really smooth and soft, like concentrated air I guess. It's hard to explain. Anyway, he was looking up at me, and when his lower jaw moved words came out of his mouth. But it was like they were coming from somewhere else—all around, like stereo.

"Mr. Butane, I'd like to show you something." He started clacking off toward the lake, and I just let him lead me—same as I would a little boy. When we got to the lake, he let go of my thumb, jumped up on the rail, and stood there swaying like he was trying to keep his balance. It's bullshit, of course, because puppets don't have any balance of their own. But just the same, he stood there swaying and acting like he was looking at something out in the water.

"I'm following your progress Mr. Butane. Your friends Woodrow and Kathleen think your search has implications for a larger constituency. What do you think?"

"I think you know what I think without asking. I will tell you that you guys got my curiosity up. For the last couple of days, I've spent more time fretting about those two fellas than I spent worrying about Jesus in my whole life. I'm starting to get pissed off that people have been making them out to be plain vanilla thieves—or even cannibals—when I don't think that's what they were at all. It's bad enough that the Jews tortured and executed them, but it looks like the Christians have robbed them of their good name."

"Romans, Mr. Butane. It was the Romans who crucified them. Not Jews."

"Whatever."

His head swiveled on a dowel rod, and he was looking at me eye-to-eye this time. For some reason, at that second, I got real curious about the water out in the lake. "Is this what you brought me out here to see?" I started looking around on the ground. There were some little pieces of gravel down there by my foot. I picked one up. I reared back and threw it as hard as I could. It plunked into the water with a little splash and disappeared in ripples just like it's supposed to.

I must have been under a spell or something, because words just started pouring out of me. "You know I've sort of been here before. When I was in

Nam, I knew I ought to be spending more time thinking about how to be more of a righteous guy. But it was all too confusing under those circumstances. So I just concentrated on saving my ass. Same deal now. I'm sure every time you dig below the surface of anything or anybody, you're likely to start turning up worms. So I'm just going to put off worrying about wider implications and theology and stuff until I can figure a way out of the jam you've got me in."

"I didn't say anything about theology." He turned his head back to where he was facing the water. "Why didn't you follow up, Mr. Butane?"

"Huh?"

"You said when you were in Vietnam, you put off thinking about the subject of righteousness until you were safely out of the war zone. So you escaped with your life. But you never gave a serious thought to the core question of how your life related to the concept of righteousness. Now you say you'll think about it later, once you escape this crisis—if you escape this crisis. What makes you think you won't slip right back into your morally apathetic life once the danger is past?"

My first reaction was to tell the little knothead to wait just a goddamn minute. That he'd better be careful who he was calling morally apathetic. I wasn't sure what he meant, but I was pretty sure it was meant to be a kick in the nuts. But I didn't say anything about it, because he was right to ask the question. I mean, somehow, I guess it was his business. Way down deep, I knew the odds were that I'd forget all about these big religious questions if I got out of this hornets' nest alive. I don't know. Maybe this would break a chain or something. I mean, my life was going to turn into a sort of hell if my driving days were over. There was a part of me that was saying, *They'll find a cure. They'll heal up these seizures, and I'll be driving again before you know it.* But the hard core part of me was saying, *"It's bullshit. You've got to face these tough old facts. You're driving days are over buddy. Give it up and figure out something else."*

You know, I've seen guys turn religious when they start getting old and think about dying. To tell you the truth, I always sort of thought those guys were some species of hypocrite. They pat themselves on the back for giving up fornicating about the time their testosterone drops, and they're starting to lose interest anyway. But I'd have an ironclad excuse for converting, wouldn't I? I mean I could say that you only get so many brushes with the Grim Reaper before you get the message: you've got to change. I could say that the end of my driving days was God's way of saying "The table you're on is cold, Butane. You need to find another game." I could say that. Hell, I might even persuade myself it was true. I've seen people persuade themselves of a lot more squirrelly things than that. Maybe it would come to that. But I wasn't ready yet. Right then, I felt like I had a fight on my hands, and I didn't know how to do anything but fight back. So the puppet was waiting for an answer.

"I don't know. Maybe it's laziness. Maybe I don't like to work that hard at figuring things out when I know it's no use. It's all Greek to me anyway."

"Typical, the reason you can't answer the question is the same reason you can't face the problem. It's really a form of cowardice you know." Well that chapped my ass royally. I can stand a lot of shit, but I can't bear to have a gol' dang puppet call me a coward. But when I tried to fetch the little pile of sawdust shit a smart rap right on his painted little skull, I found I was frozen. Not cold frozen, but frozen up like an engine that's thrown a rod. The puppet rolled his wooden eyes sideways and looked at me without turning his head.

"In a way, I admire that, Mr. Butane. On the one hand, you can ignore references to your laziness and your ignorance. You can even admit the facts in this regard. On the other hand, you set such store by your courage. If it's questioned, you're ready to fight. Of course, in this case, your behavior speaks against your claim to courage, don't you think? After all, you're prepared to pick on someone who is not nearly your size. But you were right in thinking this would not be a fair fight. You were wrong in your assessment of who has the advantage. But really, Mr. Butane. What I said, I said for your good. For the next few days, you have the opportunity not only to solve a mystery that will save your life. Temporarily. But, at the same time, you might discover something about yourself that will open new vistas on what it means to be Butane—whoever that is."

I could feel myself coming unstuck. I was tingling all over and wondering what in the cornbread hell he was talking about. I could tell he was right about something though. If he wanted to, he could have used his magic puppet powers to stomp my ass right there. I wouldn't be able to lift a glove to stop him. So again, there it is. Maybe the truth hurts. Maybe you can be a coward on the inside and still act all brave on the outside. If the outside you is the only one you know, you could live your whole life being a kind of coward and never know it. Now that would be an upside-down deal, wouldn't it? I've seen myself as a war hero and all-around tough guy, and convinced everybody else to see me that way. But maybe this whole time I've been sort of a closet coward.

I decided to spend more time thinking about it later. For now, I had some questions for the puppet. "Look here, Pinocchio. I've got to know something. You know there are miracles going on all around me and people think I'm doing it. There're people back there claiming I'm really working for the devil. I don't know who's behind your operation here, but it isn't the devil is it?" I could hear Jack snickering behind me, like I was a kid that misspelled "cat" in front of the whole class. The puppet's shoulders moved up and down like he was taking a deep breath. I could see it coming and decided to head it off.

"Now come on here. Don't give me any mumbo-jumbo confusing horse-shit. Just tell me straight out: am I working for the devil on this deal?"

"You'll process any answer I give you as mumbo-jumbo, Mr. Butane. Were you working for the devil in Vietnam? You killed people. You saved lives. You did terrible things. You performed acts of wonderful courage and kindness. Who was in charge of that 'operation'?"

"I knew it. I knew I wouldn't get a straight answer. If you're so goddamn smart, you'd know I've been asking myself that same thing for thirty-fuck-ing years—just what was I doing in Nam? I told you before, I'm not a deep thinker, and I can't figure out two heavyweight calculus problems at once! Shit! Thanks a lot. Thanks for the help brother." He jumped off the rail and started clacking back toward the picnic table.

"Yes, quite typical. The very picture of ignorant, whiny vulgarity. A shallow example of a spiritual vacuum with an assembly-line, one-size-fits-all, western-male, macho self-image. Anyone can see you're the right man for this job. This 'operation.'"

You got to give it to the little wooden squirt. He sure knows how to lay out a string of highbrow insults. The only response that came to mind was, *Oh yeah? Well same to you, buddy.* But I knew that wasn't exactly what I wanted to say, so I didn't say anything.

When he got back to the table, he turned around. "Whatever you think, Mr. Butane, I'm here to highlight one of the more important discoveries that might be in danger of being overlooked. Don't forget what Dr. Ryland said to your friend. Matthias was chosen to replace Judas among the twelve. The events surrounding that decision are more important than they seem at first glance. Take a close look. I repeat. It's more important than you know. Now get some sleep. You have a busy day tomorrow."

"Well, before we part company, you're not sending Kathleen emails on her computer are you? I mean, because if you are, we can skip these charming visits you like so much and you can just insult me electronically, the easy way."

"Be sure to take something to write with."

"Ok, Mom. Thanks for the help."

TAPE 10

Friday, February 23, 2007, a.m.

I slept okay, but woke up feeling unsettled.

It was Friday morning, and I listened to the news while I shaved. The weather lady said some of the wind gusts that was blowing me and Woodrow around yesterday were up to sixty miles per hour. There were tornadoes in Arkansas and blizzards in the Midwest.

A truck bomb went off in Iraq and killed at least thirty-five people—worshippers—coming out of a Sunni mosque. I suppose the dimwit killers think they're doing this to please Allah. If Ernest Bidding wants to see the devil's work, let him take a look at that shit. It beats me why these Muslims are killing each other by the thousands because they've got differences of opinion on how to worship God. I guess years ago Catholics and Protestants killed each other by the thousands for the same reason. Hell, I'm a killer myself, and the reason I did it was good enough for me at the time. But all of us shit our diapers until we learn better.

The weather lady said it looked like it was going to get up to about sixty-two degrees, so we would have good roads and a fair day for our drive to Kansas City.

Kathleen showed up right on time.

I explained about the dream and how we needed to take a closer look at Matthias. Woodrow said "Well, I hope somebody's keeping track of all these helpful tidbits. What are we up to, three now? Pinpoint the rebellion, talk to Augie, and what was it he told you last night, Leon?"

"Take a closer look at Matthias."

"Yeah Matthias. Well you guys have fun chasing these ghosts. I'll be consulting Freud to see if I can find a way to deal with your sexual repressions and craziness."

Kathleen wanted to take her van to Kansas City, because it's part of her business and she can deduct it. Not a chance, though. We needed Woodrow's sound system if we were going to be trucking.

The Stones were doing *Start Me Up* when we hit I-35 and headed north. If everything worked out okay, we'd be in KC in time for lunch. I know a first-class barbecue place called "Randall's." Kathleen had Map Quest directions to Dr. Ryland's house. He wasn't far from Randall's, so the timing looked like it was going to work out fine. Kathleen settled into the backseat of Woodrow's Dodge with her laptop and some books.

"What's going on in the war? Anything big happen while I was napping?"

"There was a marine corporal named Dunham who threw himself on a grenade back in April. Gave his life to save some of his buddies. Sound familiar? Anyway, the president just awarded him the Medal of Honor. First one awarded since Nam. It got some of us thinking about Son's family again. We sent a letter to his mom, but it came back. I guess she died." I decided to change the subject. "Have the Republicans decided who they're going to run against Hillary?"

Kathleen spoke up. "Looks like Hillary's not a sure thing for the Democrats."

I wasn't surprised. "You know, I was wondering whether the country was ready for a woman President. When I got knocked into my coma, it was looking like she was a sure thing. But I figured somebody would show up to give her a run for her money. Who's the challenger?"

Kathleen sounded real proud. "Barack Obama."

I was stunned. "Who the heck is Barack Obama?"

This time Woodrow spoke up. "He's a black Senator from Chicago."

"You're shittin' me! I've never heard of him. You're not serious about him being a threat to Hillary."

Kathleen's turn again. "He made a speech at the last Democratic convention."

"Is that it? Is that all he's done? Does that qualify him to be president?"

"The country is ready for change. That all by itself gives him a chance no matter what he's done. No matter who gets the nomination—whether it's Hillary or Obama—the Democratic candidate's probably going to win."

"You agree with that Woodrow? Are these the choices? Is the next President going to be a woman or a black guy?"

He nodded. "That's how it looks buddy. Hell, it may wind up that we have a woman as President and a black Vice President. You think the country's ready for that?"

"Well, that'll teach me to let myself get put in a coma. I'm asleep for a few lousy days and wake up to find out the country is going to hell in a hand basket."

Kathleen mumbled something about me being a chauvinist racist. I ignored her.

The rib joint was already almost full when we walked in about 11:30. We enjoyed some truly dynamite barbecue, some good old-fashioned home-brewed iced tea, fresh hot rolls with lots of butter and honey, and we were right on time for our meeting with Dr. Ryland.

We walked up to his door at one o'clock sharp. Kathleen rang the bell a couple of times and nobody came. I heard a dog barking inside. After a minute or two, Woodrow knocked. There was a little glass window at the top of the door and Woodrow was looking in since he was the tallest of us. He said, "Here he comes." A little old man pulled at the door a couple of times before it opened. I say he was a little old man, but really, he's just real bent over. He was probably a pretty good-sized fella when he was young and able to stand up straight.

He spoke up in a clear professor-sounding voice. "Come in, please." He stood aside and let us walk by him into his living room. "I've been looking forward to your visit. I do hope you had a pleasant drive. The weather is so unpredictable this time of year."

There was a fat, blonde cur wagging his tail and smiling like he missed us and was glad we were home. He just looked up and grinned as we filed past him one by one.

Dr. Ryland started pushing on that heavy door trying to close it. I stepped over and closed it for him. He patted my arm and tottered past us toward the inside of his house chattering something about a cup of coffee or Diet Sprite. He showed us into a dusty little study all full up with books, magazines, and knickknacks.

Kathleen was the first of us to speak up. "Thank you, Dr. Ryland. The drive was fine. I'd like some water, please." Woodrow and I got coffee. It was awful. There was a table in his study and we sat down while he puttered around talking in circles about St. Matthias Day. Every once in a while, he stopped in the middle of putting things in drawers and on shelves and shot me a sly glance.

Then he went right on chattering, "Mr. Butane, I've been following your story on Miss Wister's blog. Choppy waters, eh? This new technology is marvelous. Even a dusty old book worm like me can step into a stream of dynamic discussion without being drawn fully into the world of modern marvels. A tremendous amount of vulgarity and nonsense, of course. But then, there are treasures to be discovered in the unlikeliest places. You agree, Mr. Butane?"

"I really don't know about computer treasures, Dr. Ryland. I don't own one."

He nodded and chuckled. "Indeed? My compliments. A man who doesn't feel the need to be integrated into the Boolean tribe. A man who, according to Miss Wister's blog, has no schooling in theology or Bible history; no schooling in medicine. And yet Mr. Butane is able to work wonder cures and feels driven to solve an ancient biblical mystery. What put you on the trail of St. Matthias, Mr. Butane?"

"I don't remember ever hearing anything about St. Matthias until you brought him up to Kathleen here."

The smile never left his face. He chuckled and took a seat next to Kathleen and sat real quiet sipping hot tea and looking like he was having the time of his gol' dang life. Kathleen came out with a nervous cough and started talking. "Dr. Ryland, if you've read the blog, you know..."

He interrupted her. "If you don't mind, Miss Wister, I'd like to hear from Mr. Butane."

Sounded like my cue. "Dr. Ryland, I'd like to know why St. Matthias has something to do with the solution to my problem."

He stroked his little white goatee and rolled his blue eyes from one of our faces to the other, like a cop studying guys in a line-up. "Mr. Butane, I think I may have some understanding about your need for this information. I could do you more harm than good if I tell you what I think at this point. You might find yourself charging up the wrong battlement entirely." He leaned over Kathleen's shoulder and poured some more water in her glass. His shaky hand spilled drops over his tabletop. He reached into the pocket of his wrinkled old suit and came out with a handkerchief. He got real focused on wiping up those drops. Then, out of nowhere he asked, "Do you know what today is?"

I said "Is this a trick question? Because we all have calendars."

"This is the anniversary of Spinoza's death. You know who he was?" I heaved a sigh and decided I'd just have to ride along with him for awhile until he came back into orbit.

"I'm sorry doc. The only Spinoza I ever heard of was some South American dictator, and I don't have any idea what the anniversary of his death has to do with anything."

The old man slapped his knee and gave out with a loud, cackly laugh. "Marvelous! Marvelous! You really are a remarkable vessel Mr. Butane. Wonderfully uncut. No, I believe you're thinking of Somoza, the former ruler of Nicaragua. No, I'm speaking of Baruch Spinoza, the philosopher whose theories concerning the nature of God caused the Jewish community to issue a writ of *cheren*—an excommunication from their fellowship."

He gave us that cackly laugh again. "You really must excuse me. There are so many connections." He waved his hand over his head. "So many. And without deep study and clear thinking, they will be overlooked. Don't you agree?"

Of course we were wasting our time with this poor demented old guy. Looked to me like he was a mental goner. I was feeling sorry for him. The way all this was going, I figured the best thing to do was just ease on out the door after we finished our coffee and try to find somebody else who could tell us something helpful for a change. This Kansas City deal was turning into a total water haul.

Then, just like that, he got real focused and looked me right in the eye. "Of course I know why you and your friends are here. I knew you were coming and I can help you."

I took this as my chance to try to finally get somewhere. "Please tell us why St. Matthias is such a big deal."

"Very well. Enough fishing." He winked. "Now tell me if any of this sounds familiar. Judas Iscariot, who betrayed Jesus, died a violent death. Yes? After the crucifixion, the remaining disciples decided there must be a full complement of twelve, So Judas had to be replaced. Yes? There were two candidates, Matthias and Barsabbas. Any of this familiar?"

"To be honest, Dr. Ryland, before yesterday, I don't remember hearing about any of this."

Woodrow looked bored. Kathleen looked embarrassed. She squirmed in her seat a little bit. "Dr. Ryland, I've read the story in Acts like everybody else—except for Leon and Woodrow—but I never gave a thought to who they really were. I've never heard any preachers say much about then."

The old man went on. "Then you know nothing of their precrucifixion involvement in the Jesus movement, and you know nothing of their subsequent activities?" We all sat there shaking our heads. "Well, we will leave that for now. Tell me what you have learned so far concerning these cocrucifieds."

I summed it up. "They were revolutionaries."

"This is all you have to go on?"

"Hell yes. Dr. Ryland, right now, this is all we've got."

"You're going to have to do better. The Bible tells us these men spoke to Jesus while they were on the cross. Have you studied these accounts? No? This will never do. You must study every single word the gospels say about these men. And you must study every word the Bible says about the crucifixion. After all, as I understand it, your life depends on it, and you have nothing else to go on at this moment."

Kathleen leaned forward and put her hand on Dr. Ryland's shoulder. "Dr. Ryland, our time is extremely short. We can't commit months or even weeks to this. If you can't give us the answer we need, can you at least point us in the right direction?"

He winked at me again. "Mr. Butane, you believe your life depends on this. Yes? You must plunge into unfamiliar scholastic and investigative waters. Yes? I think I can furnish a good foundation to work from. Now pay attention. I don't have the strength or patience to repeat myself."

I hoped maybe we were finally getting somewhere.

"I'll divide my remarks into two parts. In the first part, I'll give you some facts you will need. In the second part, I'll give you the methodology you need to use in arranging and analyzing those facts."

I was never for shit in school and when he started talking about this "methodology" crap, my heart sank by the second. I was hoping Kathleen could follow what he was saying so she could explain it to me later.

Dr. Ryland took a drink of Diet Sprite and launched. "None of the Gospels as we have them today were written by eyewitnesses to the events of Jesus' life." Soon as he said that, I was stunned and didn't believe it. My whole life I thought the guys who wrote the Bible were disciples who were talking first-hand stuff. If this guy wasn't such a hot shot expert who wrote books, I'd have thought he was off his rocker. Kathleen was frowning like she didn't agree with him. But she was writing down what the old man said anyway.

"I can see this is somewhat of a surprise. You were probably taught that the Gospels represent four different accounts of the events witnessed first-hand by those writers. Here's another surprise you should keep in mind as you try to unravel this knot. The apprehension, trial, and crucifixion of Jesus were probably the first part of the Gospels written. Everything else was likely added later. So how do we know this is true? You don't have enough time, and I don't have enough energy to summarize the scholarly proof in support of everything I'm saying. If you like, I can provide you with an excellent bibliography."

I was thinking *Glad you said that, because I was just fixing to ask for an excellent bibliography.*

"For now, allow me to summarize. You can check me out later if you like. Mark was the first of the four accepted Gospels to be written. There's nothing in the Gospel itself to indicate it was written by Mark. This is merely a traditional attribution. Matthew is the first book in the New Testament order because Matthew was a favorite of those who assembled the Canon. So if Mark was not an eyewitness to the events he relates, where did he get his information? First, there were oral traditions about the life, deeds, and death of Jesus—Yeshua as he was known in his time. Eyewitnesses related what they saw to others who, in turn, related it to others and so on. It is possible that Mark drew some of his material from accounts of people who actually claimed to have witnessed the events. There may also have been written gospels prior to Mark. Possibly in Greek and/or Aramaic, and he may have had these to draw on. Some scholars think this is probable. And then, Mark may have created some material from his own imagination."

Kathleen dropped her glasses on her notebook and dropped her ball-point beside them. "Are you suggesting that part of the Bible is just made up?"

"That's precisely what I'm suggesting, young lady. There's a long and highly esteemed tradition of injecting things into the various parts of the Bible that were not there when the documents were originally written. There's also every indication that the oral versions of the events were undergoing transformation the instant they left the lips of the witnesses."

She shook her head. "I'm sorry Dr. Ryland. I believe the Bible is the divinely inspired word of God and those who wrote it were guided by the Holy Spirit and every word in the Bible is true."

That comment floated out there like a challenge. Dr. Ryland opened a desk drawer and came up with a dog treat. He dropped it in the cur's mouth.

He sat there massaging his dog's ears, and I was getting antsy. Finally, he took a deep breath like he was tired. "Miss. Wister, you recall in Luke the beautiful description of Jesus' prayer before he died? 'Father, forgive them, for they know not what they do.' A sublime sentiment I'm sure you'll agree."

"Of course I do, but what has that to do with the issue at hand?"

"You believe Jesus said that from the cross?"

"Of course I do."

"Very good. Now I'll tell you, as a fact, that some of the earliest surviving copies of Luke's Gospel don't have that wonderful prayer in them. Now what are the possible explanations?"

She had a defiant look on her face, "One explanation I can think of is it was there in the original, got dropped by somebody who made a mistake copying it, and the omission got carried forward in some copies after the original was lost or destroyed."

"Very good. What else?"

"I don't know Dr. Ryland. I can't think of anything else right now."

"Of course you can. How about this? These earlier documents are intentional plants by the devil himself to create doubt in the minds of scholars and students concerning the inerrancy of the Bible. That would explain it. Right?"

"I suppose that could happen."

"Yes and how about this? Jesus didn't say it, and that's why it's absent from those early documents. Well intentioned Christians copying the gospel of Luke were convinced that such a prayer is precisely what Jesus would say if someone was near enough to hear him, and so they put it there as if he really did say it. That could happen. Yes?"

"Yes."

"Someone could experience a revelation and actually believe they are present at the crucifixion and actually hear Jesus say it. He or she might believe they are actually correcting an omission. Yes?"

"Yes."

"You can't think of any credible reason that beautiful prayer, if it was there, would be intentionally dropped can you?"

"No."

"Now, Miss Wister, I'm telling you as a fact that prayer is not in our earliest versions of Luke. If you are to have any hope of uncovering the truth, you must have an open mind. You must entertain the possibility that the texts have been manipulated and corrupted. You may, after careful study, decide to reject this as an explanation. But if you won't allow yourself to consider the possibilities as the facts unfold before you, you will be hopelessly handicapped."

I figured I had to interrupt here. "Look. I'm not going to get a fair chance to die of old age if this goes on too long. Dr. Ryland, I need you to get back to your facts and methodology. As far as I'm concerned, I've already seen enough to make me wonder what the hell's going on with all these Bible versions. So, no matter how Miss Wister feels about it, I want to hear your advice."

The old man asked Kathleen if she needed some more water. The way she said yes made it sound like it was the saddest decision she ever made.

Dr. Ryland patted Kathleen on the shoulder like he was saying *I'm sorry.* Then he went on with his facts. "When Matthew and Luke wrote their gospels, both of them had Mark in front of them, and to a large extent, they simply copied what Mark had to say. But sometimes, they didn't. Just look at the way they handle the crucifixion. Mark says 'revolutionaries.' When Matthew copies Mark, he repeats 'revolutionaries.' But when Luke copies it, he changes the description to 'wrongdoers.' Mark wrote nearer in time to the actual events. So, he has a good chance of being closer to the truth. That's somewhat of an oversimplification, but not bad as a rule of thumb. If Matthew or Luke alter the wording as it appears in Mark, you need to ask yourself why. Maybe it's just an effort to make the text read better. This is, in fact, the case in some instances. But if they change the facts as represented in Mark, there must be a reason.

"So where does the Gospel of John come in? Matthew, Mark, and Luke are called the *Synoptic* gospels. This is because in Greek, Synoptic means viewing something with the same eye. John, in its current form, is the last gospel written, but it may come from earlier eyewitnesses and gospels that go back to the time of Jesus. For our purposes, John is most helpful when it corroborates events reported in the other gospels. As in most cases, where the witnesses agree, their testimony on those facts is more persuasive. But as for who was crucified with Jesus, John tells us less than anybody.

"These are the core facts we're working with. Now for the methodology. You need to study. Read carefully all the facts from Jesus' arrival in Bethany before the fatal Passover. Pay close attention to every event leading up to the empty tomb event. You've got to look closely at everything that's related, but not one gospel at a time. This is absolutely critical. You must look at them all at the same time keeping in mind what I just told you. And you must consult the original Greek. There are study aids that will help you."

He took a magic marker and stood up by a big easel he had set up in his study. He started carrying on like he was teaching a class. "I'm going to cut years off your study. First, I'm going to give you a list of names. Don't just take the Bible's discussion of these men at face value. There are important clues between the lines Look at the texts very, very closely and apply your common sense."

He wrote in big clear letters and said each name aloud as he wrote. There was no trace of the clumsiness and confusion we saw when we first got there. "Lazarus, Simon the leper, Simon the Cyrene and his sons Rufus and Alexander, Simon Iscariot and his son Judas Iscariot, Simon the Zealot, Barabbas, Barsabbas, we've mentioned Matthias, Joseph of Arimathea. Make a folder for each of these men. Assemble and compare everything the separate gospels say about them." Kathleen and I were both trying to write fast enough to keep up.

He turned the page and started on another sheet. "Look closely at every violent death mentioned in Jerusalem at that time." As he reeled them off, we wrote them and put numbers beside them. "Jesus, the two crucified with him, Judas Iscariot, the murder victim mentioned in connection with the violence that involved Barabbas." He turned to another page.

"Look at every instance of violence mentioned and cross check to look for overlap. The Barabbas revolt, Jesus' disturbance at the temple, the bloodshed at Jesus' arrest. There are riddles here that will, if you can solve them, bring you close to a solution to your problem. Remember, we are looking at real events involving full-blooded human beings reacting to overpowering emotions—desire, fear, anger, hatred, sorrow. We are viewing this all through the distorting lenses of time and bias." He turned pale and started to sweat a little. He tottered away from his easel and sat down stiff and feeble. His yellow cur waddled over and put its head on Dr. Ryland's knee.

"Remember this. Paul knew and associated with people who were, in Jerusalem in April, 30 CE, which is the most probable date for the crucifixion."

I got a shiver. "You suppose Paul knew the names of the men I'm looking for?"

A thin smile showed up on Dr. Ryland's face. He sounded almost happy. "Most certainly. Their names were doubtless well known to the early followers of Jesus. Why would the gospel writers omit their names? Some reasons are benign. But if their names were actively suppressed, the explanation could be more problematic."

Kathleen spoke up again. "Do you seriously believe the names could have been withheld intentionally?"

"There's certainly precedent for it in the New Testament."

She was close to being plumb aggressive. "If I were to call you on that, Dr. Ryland, how hard would it be to prove it right now?"

"So simple." He reached behind him and pulled a Bible off the shelf and opened it to Mark. "See here at 15:21. 'Simon from Cyrene, the father of Alexander and Rufus.' Now look at Matthew 27:32. All references to Simon's sons are dropped. Same in Luke. John doesn't mention Simon or his sons."

"Well, there could be ...."

"Of course there could be benign explanations, as I said. But before you hurry to embrace the benign, be sure you have a legitimate plausible reason to reject the alternatives. It is possible Rufus and Alexander were well known and important to the early church. It could be as a complicated Christology was being crafted, these men and those who knew them were, for some reason, intentionally marginalized. There could also be benign reasons why translators for 2,000 years have failed to inform the reader that Barabbas's name was Jesus." Kathleen was on full stun. "Yes, Miss Wister, I can prove it in less than a minute." He started to get up. Instead, he sat back down and pointed to a book on one of his shelves and asked me to get it for him. I did.

"This is the latest and best copy of the Greek New Testament. It is the 27th Edition of the Nestle-Aland *Novum Testamentum Graece.* In light of current scholarship, this is our best estimate concerning what the autographs—the original writings—looked like. Here at Matthew 27:16, you see this word?" He leaned over and set the book down in front of Kathleen. He pointed to a verse with his crooked old index finger. "This is Greek for Jesus. If you like I can show you where it appears in reference to Jesus of Nazareth." He turned a few pages and pointed to another verse. "But here, it is in reference to this word. You see? This is Barabbas. You don't need to take my word for it." He pulled a new looking Bible out of a desk drawer. "Here's *Today's New International Version.* Here is the same verse. See for yourself. Jesus Barabbas."

She looked at it for a few minutes then looked at Dr. Ryland like she was about to cry. He leaned over and patted her arm. "I think I know what you're going through. I've been through it myself. Many times. So you see. The answer to your question is certainly yes. The names of these men could be intentionally withheld, just as other names were omitted or withheld."

Just like that, he stood up and hobbled over to the door. "I hope you'll excuse me, but I'm afraid I've overextended. I hope I've been of some service." I was about to boil over with questions. But I was afraid if I asked him anything else, either he or Kathleen would keel over. We all got up and started for the door. The doc's fat yellow cur led the way. Before we could get out, Dr. Ryland stopped and put that crooked old finger against his nose.

"You know what else today is?"

I was thinking, *Holy shit. Here we go again.*

He grinned and said, "This is the anniversary of the day Watson and Crick discovered the structure of the DNA molecule. Do you believe that discovery was the beginning of the end of our belief in free will? Do you suppose that science will ultimately prove that all of us are mere servants obeying the demands of our DNA?"

Woodrow was pulling me toward the door. "We'll just have to get back to you on that, Dr. Ryland," The tired old professor stood at his door and waved. We were still in the driveway when Kathleen's phone rang.

She listened for a minute. "Thank you, Dr. Ryland." She hung up. "He told us to drive carefully and to be sure and call if we run into a dead end."

Friday, February 23, 2007, p.m.

It was getting cold as we headed back to Oklahoma City. As usual, I was getting a headache. I was wishing we could put Kathleen on a bus or plane or something because I didn't feel like firing up a bowl with her in the Dodge.

Woodrow had "Old Black Betty" playing on his iPod as we made our way back to I-35 and headed south. There are lots of versions of that great old blues song and everybody that records it puts their own touch to it. I like them all.

On the way back to Oklahoma, Woodrow and I tried to cheer Kathleen up, but she was all wrapped up in her thoughts. Maybe this is just the male chauvinist pig coming out of me, but I can't stand to see a lady unhappy. See, it's different with guys. You can sympathize with guys. And usually, that's enough to make them feel better. But with women, even if you're going through the exact same miseries, there's ways they suffer that guys don't know anything about. See, my folks are both dead. Cancer. And I miss them for sure. But Wanda hurts about it in a whole different way. I'm not going to lie. I cried at both funerals, mom's and dad's. But when it was over, I wiped my eyes and that was that. I didn't cry about it anymore. It's not that I didn't love them and miss them. I just don't cry about it.

But Wanda can up and cry without warning. We can be talking about things right along and she'll be fine. You know. Stuff we remember. We can go along for months talking about it off and on. Then, just like that, the faucets turn on and there she goes. I try to help, but it's no good. She's just got to cry it out. And I just got to let her. I don't get it.

Well, something like that was eating Kathleen on our way to Oklahoma City. I guess there was something about it that made Woodrow feel like he had to get to the bottom of it. He was looking at her in his rear view mirror off and on.

"Kathleen, you know who Marco Polo was?"

She answered him but she never took her eyes off the country rolling past her window. "Sure. He was the Italian traveler who visited the court of the Mongols in China. Thirteenth or fourteenth century I think. Why?"

"Well, I was just wondering. Am I right about this? Did he write a book that people still use to learn about the customs and stuff in the lands he visited on his travels? I mean I read somewhere that a lot of what we know about the set-up at Kublai Khan's court, we know because of the stuff Marco Polo wrote. Is that right?"

"I don't know. I guess so. Why?"

"Well, I just read somewhere that it's still a useful book after all these centuries. That's all."

"I suppose you're leading up to some kind of comparison between Marco Polo's book and the Bible"

"What I'm leading up to is a question. But you have to let me lay the foundation first. See, Polo's book not only tells us about the operation of Kublai Khan's court, he also tells us about giant birds that are called rocs and these birds are so big they're able to carry elephants off to feed their big ass chicks."

"Nice. So what's your question?"

"Do you think we have to throw out everything Polo says just because he was wrong about these monster birds?"

"If you're trying to make a point, let's talk apples to apples."

"Hold on. We'll get to the Bible in a minute. I'm just talking about Polo now."

"Okay. No. We don't have to throw the whole book out just because he was wrong about the birds."

Woodrow glanced at her in his mirror and drove on without saying a word. Nobody said anything for a long time. I guess Kathleen couldn't stand it.

"The difference, Woodrow, is that Marco Polo's book is not the inspired word of God. The Bible is. We're not qualified to pick and choose what parts we'll believe and what we won't"

"Do you believe what Dr. Ryland said about Barabbas's name being Jesus?"

"I don't know."

"Well, that's a start. If you're leaving open the possibility that somebody made an intentional change to the inspired word and that change found its way into the Bible that people read for hundreds of years, you might open some important door for yourself."

"Great! Open doors to what? Atheism?"

Woodrow laughed. "Why are you being so chatty, Buzz? Why don't you weigh in on some of this?"

"I just got to say I never read Polo. But no matter what he says, there ain't any birds big enough to carry off elephants. Maybe there were in dinosaur days. But if they were around today, somebody would've made a movie about them."

"What do you think about this Bible question? You think the English translations you've looked at are the infallible word of God?"

"I believe in the Bible, if that's what you're asking."

"Do you believe that Barabbas's name was Jesus?"

"Whether it was or wasn't, I don't think it makes a shit."

He laughed again. "Well, I disagree with you, Buzz. I think it's important. I don't know if it's important to the answer to your question. But it's important to the bigger picture. Kathleen agrees with me. She thinks it's important. Don't you Kathleen?"

She just kept looking out the window. As we got close to Oklahoma City, she got her computer out of her bag and we could hear her typing like a fury. I was feeling sorry for those keys, because it sounded like she was really beating hell out of them.

When we got back to the Holiday Inn parking lot, me and Woodrow checked out Kathleen's van to make sure no vagrants had busted in to put up for the night. Before she could drive off, I put my hand on her shoulder. She looked up at me all surprised and jerked away. I guess she gets uneasy when a man touches her like that.

"Look, Kathleen. This probably ain't going to mean a thing to you, but I want to say something. I'm not up with you and Woodrow on how all this stuff fits together, big picture-wise. I just hate to see you get all worked up over these oddball questions about Bible translations. You don't have to be an atheist to know that people can be tricky and underhanded. That goes for people who translate the Bible just like anybody else. And if there's tricky and underhanded Bible translators, that ain't God's fault. So don't worry about it. We just got to figure out what's important and not get distracted by the other."

That last part sounded like something Father Kelly or that goddamn Augie would say. Anyway, she sat there sort of sniffling in the dark inside of her van. Then, out of nowhere, she reached up and squeezed my hand. I felt like somebody turned a heat-lamp on me or something. I don't know what she meant by touching me that way, but it made me want to pull her out of that van and hold her 'til she got it all cried out. It made me want to—I don't know—do something. But all I could do was step back and let her roll up the window. I got all over washed by this lonely feeling when she drove across the dark parking lot toward the street. I don't know how long I would have stood there if Woodrow hadn't spoken up.

"Come on Buzz. You need some rest."

We walked toward the stairs, Woodrow stopped and watched as Kathleen's van pulled out onto the Northwest Expressway.

"What is it Woodrow?"

"I don't know. Probably nothing. Just the same, maybe we should follow her home. You need some medicine anyway." I was glad he was being careful to watch out for her, and I was happy to get some relief from my headache. It was dark enough we could pass the pipe back and forth in the Dodge and nobody would notice. We followed her all the way to Nichols Hills where she lived. In case you don't know, Nichols Hills is the part of Oklahoma City where lots of old money lives. I wasn't surprised. Kathleen just looks and acts like a woman who ought to live in Nichols Hills. Not the old money thing. It's just that she's got class, if you know what I mean.

Anyway, after we were sure she got into her house okay, we drove back to the Holiday Inn.

We went to our rooms and I fell asleep pretty quick.

Okay, I have to turn this thing off for a minute. Be right back.

TAPE 11

Sorry about that, but I had to make a pit stop. Let's see, we just got home from our first trip to Kansas City. Right?

When I woke up on Saturday morning, I noticed that there was a little peach fuzz growing on my head. I guess it had been growing out a little bit ever since I'd left the hospital and I just didn't notice it until that morning. I was looking forward to my hair growing all the way out so I wouldn't look like such a freak. I was just hoping it would grow out enough to cover that horseshoe-looking scar carved on the left side of my head.

Anyway, the news that morning said Al Sharpton and Strom Thurmond were related, and Al Gore was up for an Oscar. I was thinking, *There's really no end to the total craziness in the universe, is there?*

Woodrow and I met up for coffee in the lobby. If we were going to do like Dr. Ryland said and look at all the Gospels side-by-side, we needed Bibles—lots of Bibles. One of the versions we needed would be that Greek deal if that was the closest thing to the original. Neither of us could read Greek, so we'd need a dictionary like the one Kathleen had at St. Knud's. We needed space where we could spread out. We'd need privacy so we could talk without calling attention to ourselves and worrying about anybody eavesdropping and bugging us with questions. And we needed coffee. I damn sure am not that good at book study, and if I've got to do it, I've got to have some hot joe to help keep me focused.

We didn't expect to hear from Kathleen for awhile. We figured she was probably beating the bushes trying to get settled about whether Barabbas's name was Jesus. Anyway, as we was leaving the motel, the lady behind the desk said, "Hey. You're Leon Butane aren't you?" I wasn't surprised, because my name's written right there on the register.

So I just said, "Sure."

Then she said, "You're the fellow that's been working miracles aren't you?"

Woodrow grabbed my arm and said, "Let's go, Buzz."

"How come?"

"Because this little gal is liable to start crowing about the celebrity she's got holed up here and demonstrators and news people might turn up. Then the process servers won't be far behind. I just think it'd be better if we stayed out of sight for now." Soon as he said that, I knew he was right on the money. Like I said before, I don't know anybody with better instincts than Woodrow.

We scampered back to our rooms, loaded our shit together and checked out. Sure enough, as we was wheeling the Dodge out of the motel parking lot, a Channel 9 news truck was pulling in. And you'll never guess what was playing on the iPod as we pulled into traffic heading on west on Northwest Highway. Yep. *Midnight Rider.*

Mardel's Christian Bookstore isn't far from the motel, and we was almost there when Woodrow's phone rang. It was Kathleen. Woodrow put her on speaker. "Have you seen the news this morning?"

"Just the part about Sharpton and Thurmond being kin. But what's more important is, we just dodged a Channel 9 news truck."

"Well, they're in a hurry to see you because you're headlining again today. Your house burned." At first, I thought she was joking, and I was dreaming up a snappy comeback. I knew she was serious when I could hear tears in her voice. "I'm so sorry, Leon."

Woodrow gave a left turn signal so he could pull a 'U' and head out to my place. I was on full stun, but Woodrow could still talk.

"How did it get started?"

"The fire and police departments are on the scene. They're reporting Leon Butane hasn't been seen since he left the hospital. There's news footage of the demonstrators who've been out at the house off and on. At first, the authorities said someone might still be in the house. But now that the fire department has been able to get inside, they're letting everyone know there doesn't seem to be anybody in there. There's no official statement about what started it, but an anonymous post on my blog says it was divine retribution."

Woodrow had the pedal down headed toward Jones. Kathleen kept talking. "Leon, you need to call your sister. The news people found her and she's worried sick about you."

"Okay. I'll call her. We've got to go."

"Just a minute, Leon. I know your first reaction will be to rush out there. But don't. The police are very interested in talking to you and I think we should discuss it before you talk to them."

Woodrow eased off the gas. "What are you thinking Kathleen?"

"Well, we really don't know much about the situation, and I'm starting to worry about you two getting deeply involved in a criminal investigation—if this is arson."

"Surely they can't think I did this."

"Well, let's listen to her, Buzz. No need for us to rush into a situation. If the house is burned up, you can't do no good out there right now anyway. Let's let the smoke clear and give ourselves time to size things up a little bit."

You already know how I feel about Woodrow's instincts. If he says we ought to lay low, then by God we're laying low. Then he said, "Until we get a better handle on where the traps might be, let's just stick to the plan we laid out this morning."

"Okay. You guys are right. I'll call Wanda and let her know I'm okay. Then we'll try to concentrate on Dr. Ryland's facts and methods and stuff." Woodrow turned his left hand blinker on again and headed back toward Mardel's.

Kathleen was still on the line. "Where are you going and what are you going to do right now?"

"We're going to get some books, find us a hideout, start digging, and try not to think about my gol' dang house getting burned up."

"Where are you now? I'll meet you."

"No thanks. We'll take it from here."

"You can't do this alone. You need me. I know my way around the books and I have contacts." The phone was quiet. I guess everybody was thinking about who needed who and what for.

Woodrow spoke up. "One thing you have to do is lay off the blog thing."

"I can't. Somebody has to defuse this. Right now Ernest Bidding and some other out-of-control radicals are fanning the flames. People are saying that any believing Christian that sees you should come against you in the name of the Lord."

"I don't know what the hell that's supposed to mean. 'Come against me!'"

"Well, one thing it means is that believers are supposed to confront you and command you to submit to the power of God in Jesus' name. And they're supposed to drive out the demon possessors that are allegedly giving you this unholy power."

"Well, hell, maybe I ought to turn myself in to the evangelicals and let them do their voodoo. Believe me nobody wants me to be rid of this unholy power more than I do."

Kathleen said, "Leon, I don't know for sure yet, but I might know a way to get things back under control."

"Does getting it under control include getting rid of the process servers and lawyers?"

"I'm afraid I can't help you there." I guess that figured. "So really, tell me where you are and what you're planning to do. Exactly."

"Well, first thing is, if we're going to do what Dr. Ryland suggests, we're headed to Mardel's to buy four copies of the New Testament, that *Interlinear Greek Bible*, and a Greek dictionary. Then we'll probably go hide out at Woodrow's place since somebody burned my gol' dang house down and the gol' dang motel clerks are on the lookout for me, and everybody's probably on the lookout for Woodrow's Dodge now."

"I've got a better idea. Why don't you use my place? It has a library with a nice conference table and some comfortable chairs. I probably have most of the books you need. There's plenty of room for you to stay and everybody would have his own bathroom, so there's lots of privacy. Woodrow, you can park your truck in the garage so it would be out of sight."

Sounded good to me but there was an ingredient missing. "You got coffee?"

"I'm not a coffee drinker. But I'll stop at Neighbor's gourmet coffee and see to it that there's plenty."

I could tell Woodrow was worried about something. "Look, Kathleen, you have to be careful. You have to keep all this under your hat. We don't need a bunch of paparazzi types and wing nut demonstrators circling around your house trying to get hold of us for pictures, miracles, interviews, lawsuits, and stuff."

"Don't worry. I don't need my house burned down on your account. See you at Mardel's."

Next thing I did was call Wanda at the agency. "Wanda? It's me. I'm okay." I heard the phone fall off her shoulder and get muffled all over her big bosom as she chased it around trying to regain her grip.

"Oh, mercy. Oh, mercy, Leon. Did you know your house is burning? We were terrified you were still in there. But you're all right. Right?"

"Yeah, I'm fine, sweetheart. I'm just trying to stay out of the cameras until I can get stuff sorted out."

"Leon, please go back to the hospital and let the doctors look after you. I'm worried sick, and every time I turn around, there's a reporter or photographer or somebody wanting pictures and wanting to ask me questions about you, about how we were raised and about your religion and your military service, what you been doing. They've been pestering me to death."

"You haven't told them anything, have you?"

She sounded sheepish. "Well, at first I didn't want to be rude, so I answered all the questions they were asking. Then, when I saw myself on TV and heard what they were saying…"

"Wait a minute, Wanda. You've been on TV?"

"Yeah, two channels. But anyway, I started saying 'no comment' when I saw how they were trying to make things look."

I felt my stomach doing somersaults. "How are they trying to make it look, Wanda?"

"Well, that one fella, that guy living with the little girl's mom, you know, the little girl you cured of leukemia…" I started to interrupt her and say again that I didn't cure anybody, goddammit. But what's the use? I just let her talk.

"Anyway, he says you cured her by praying to the devil."

"Teddy said that? The piece of shit. He said I was praying to the devil? Wanda, that's a goddamn lie! I never prayed to the devil!"

"I know, Leon. That's what I was telling the news people at first. But they kept twisting stuff, so now I'm just saying, 'no comment.'"

"So now, when they ask if you know whether your brother is a devil worshiper, you say, 'no comment?'"

"Yes, Leon, because I don't have no comment about that."

"Yes you do, Wanda. You damn sure have a comment. Here's your comment. 'No! Leon Butane ain't no goddamn devil worshipper!' See, there's your comment! Holy cow, Wanda!"

"Now, Leon. You got to be calm. You don't want to blow up nothing in your skull."

"Be calm? How can I be calm when my gol' dang house is burning down and my sister ain't got a comment about whether I'm a dadburned devil worshiper?"

"Leon, please go back to the hospital." I could tell she was crying. I was sorry I yelled at her.

"Listen, sis. I'm sorry I yelled at you. But from now on, if anybody asks whether I'm a devil worshiper, tell them 'Hell no!' Other than that, no comment. Okay?"

"What if I don't say anything, Leon? I'm afraid everything I say is wrong." I felt like I was getting smothered.

"Okay, Wanda. Just don't say anything. I'm going to find a way to get all this straightened out. I can't go back to the hospital just now. But I will when I can. Okay?"

"Please, Leon."

"About the house. Do I have enough insurance to cover everything?"

I could hear her sniffling. "Of course you do Leon. You're my favorite customer. I've made sure you got every kind of coverage there is. But you got forms to fill out."

"You know all the answers to all the questions on them forms Wanda. Fill them out for me, would you? You can go ahead and sign my name too. You've done it before."

"But Leon, we'll need to set up a meeting with an adjuster. Do you have a phone number where I can reach you?"

"I don't know for sure where I'll be, Wanda. I'll be in touch."

"Be sure to keep receipts. You got a living allowance under your policy."

I had to laugh. "I can't explain it right now, Wanda, but that's funny. I don't think there's a policy in the world that could offer me enough of a living allowance to satisfy me right now." She started to sputter about full coverage, and I just laughed again. "Never mind Wanda. I'll call you later."

"But listen, Leon. You remember that old man that said you cured up his heart attack?"

"You mean old Francisco. Yeah I remember him."

"Well he's dead."

I was sick for all the wrong reasons. "Please tell me his heart didn't give out. Everybody will be saying me and the damn devil did it."

"No Leon. He was driving drunk and got killed in a car wreck."

I couldn't think of anything to say for a minute. I just sat there remembering how he was promising the Lord he'd get righteous if he could dodge the surgery. Isn't that what me and the puppet just got through discussing? You'll promise any damn thing when you're under the gun, and once you get out, you forget all those promises about being a better man. Well I felt sorry for old Francisco and his family. I was feeling a little bit sorry for me too.

"Are you there Leon?"

"Sure I'm fine. I'll talk to you later sis."

"Leon I…" I hung up.

We went to Mardel's, and Kathleen met us there to help us pick the books we needed. She had a couple of versions of the Bible and an interlinear Greek Bible at home so all we needed was a dictionary and a couple more Bibles.

Saturday, February 24, 2007, p.m.

We followed Kathleen to her house in Nichols Hills. She told us how she inherited the place from her folks when they died in the Oklahoma City bombing back in '95. The house is on one of those lots with big trees and ivies all over it. It's made out of brick and stone with four chimneys. She showed us our bedrooms and, hell, this was a lot nicer than any motel I ever stayed at.

"Are you two hungry?"

I said "No," but Woodrow grinned and said: "You know, I could do with a sandwich. Something exotic if you got it." She went to make a sandwich out of low-fat pastrami, cheddar cheese, and zesty zinger pickles and left Woodrow and me in her library. It looked like something out of *The Thomas Crown Affair*. We stood there for a minute with our arms full of holy books. There was something about being in high-dollar surroundings that made me feel like I'd be getting out of line if I just hauled off and sat down without being asked. Woodrow got over it before I did. After he took a seat, I did too. Kathleen came in with Woodrow's sandwich, a pot of coffee, and some fancy mugs. We arranged our stuff on the conference table, took a deep breath, and dug in.

The first thing we did was try to get a handle on whether the Bible gives any clues about what revolution these guys were involved in. I opened up the NIV at Mark 11. Kathleen had Matthew at chapter 21, and Woodrow was looking at Luke 19. We were starting with Mark because Dr. Ryland said that was the first Gospel written.

The first case of violence I found in Jerusalem before Jesus got crucified happened when he went to the temple. I had my finger on Mark 11:15. "Okay, kids. It says here Jesus went into the temple. And it doesn't say anything about the disciples being with him. So I guess they were some-place else or they were just standing around, because this says the only one doing anything was Jesus."

Kathleen was looking at Matthew 21:12. "Same here. He was with a crowd when he entered Jerusalem. But it looks like he was alone in the temple."

Woodrow shook his head. "It really doesn't add up though, does it? Luke says the same thing at 19:45. It makes it look like what Jesus did in the temple, he did by himself. But I don't buy it."

I could see Woodrow's point, but I wanted him to spell it out. "So what do you think happened?"

"I'm not sure. But I do know this. It makes no sense for him to slip away from his disciples and go to the temple by himself after he made such a big public deal coming into Jerusalem. No matter what the Bible says, I'd bet my ass the disciples were with him. And probably others too."

Kathleen sounded a little defensive. "So what if the disciples were there? Jesus still could have acted alone. He probably told them to stay out of it."

"Possible. But the Bible doesn't say that, does it? I may be wrong here, but it's hard for me to believe that once he started the ball rolling, everybody just stood around like cattle. Somebody probably tried to stop him and somebody tried to defend him and there had to be more people involved. My common sense tells me there was more to it."

Kathleen said, "Well excuse me, Woodrow. But if I have to choose between your common sense and what the Bible says, I'll side with the Bible, thank you."

"Suit yourself. I'm just saying ..."

That's when I interrupted to try to get us back on track. "Well, let's not argue about what the Bible doesn't say. Let's be really careful and methodical about what it does say. That's what Dr. Ryland said to do. Right? So let's see what happened. Okay. Mark says when Jesus got to the temple, there were five parts to it what he did. Here they are. Number one, he drove out the people buying. Number two, he drove out the people selling. Number three, he turned over the tables of the moneychangers. Number four, he turned over the benches of people selling doves; and number five, he wouldn't let anybody carry any merchandise through the temple courts. How does that match up with what you've got in Matthew, Kathleen?"

She kept studying and writing for a minute. Then she said. "Matthew only has the first four. He doesn't say anything about Jesus interfering with people carrying merchandise." I checked it out and she was right. Matthew sure enough dropped that last part.

Woodrow said, "Look here. In the back of this Bible, there's a map of what the temple was supposed to look like in Jesus' time. Looks like a pretty big place, and it's got several courts. There's a real big one called the Court of the Gentiles. Then there's the Court of Women and the Court of Men. But those two look like they're really combined into one big court. Then there's the inner court. So if Jesus stopped people from carrying stuff through those courts, like Mark says, what did he do exactly?" We both looked at Kathleen and it seemed like she didn't hear us. She was looking back and forth between Mark and Matthew.

So I spoke up. "Well, if Mark is right, he couldn't do it by himself. I'm guessing Passover back then was a big deal and them courts would be full of visitors. If Jesus was going to stop that many people from moving around in that much space, he had to have help."

Woodrow added. "There would have to be a pretty good dust up too. It wouldn't have been one-sided. There would have been brawlers on both sides. If Dr. Ryland is right, Matthew had Mark's Gospel in front of him and decided to drop the part about Jesus interfering with people carrying stuff through the temple. That's one way to head off some of the embarrassing questions about exactly how Jesus stopped all these people from carrying stuff."

I agreed. "What do you think Kathleen?"

"Well I don't know yet. What does Luke say?"

Woodrow said, "Luke sanitizes the hell out of it. All he says is Jesus drove out the people selling stuff. Nothing about the people buying. Nothing about turning over the furniture, and nothing about stopping people from moving around in the temple. He admits there was some violence, but he paints a lot tamer picture than Matthew and Matthew is tamer than Mark." He scratched his jaw. "Okay. Let's assume what Dr. Ryland told us is right. Mark came first. Matthew softens the way Mark puts it, and Luke drops almost all of it. Matthew and Luke were toning it down to make it look less and less like rebellion."

Kathleen shook her head. "I'm not sure I accept Dr. Ryland's thesis. We could still be dealing with four different eyewitnesses, in which case, we'd expect different viewpoints."

I was getting worn out trying to keep everybody focused. "Check it out when you want to, Kathleen. It should be easy to do. For now, let's just agree that the Bible tells us there was some kind of violence in the temple and Jesus was in the middle of it. We can't tell by looking at this how serious it was. Mark damn sure makes it sound serious, though."

Kathleen turned some pages. "Let's see what John says." We all turned our Bibles to John and looked.

I said, "Hell, Kathleen. Looks to me like John left out the whole dang episode. I don't see where he says a word about it. Do you see anything, Woodrow?"

"If it's here, I can't see it. What about it, Kathleen?"

"No. It isn't here."

"If it happened, why would John just drop it?"

She answered me in a kind of whisper. "I just don't know yet."

Woodrow gave her a real stern look. "Well, let's cut to the chase. There was violence at the temple. No matter how anybody soft pedals it, these gospel writers wouldn't make up something like that. Hell, it looks like they're trying to paper over the whole deal. Looks like there was enough trouble there for the authorities to call it rebellion if they wanted to. If that's so, then our revolutionary guys sure could have been at the temple and joined in the fracas. Kathleen, is there anything in the Bible that you know of that would eliminate that as a possibility?"

"I don't know."

I could tell Kathleen wanted to get off of it. I decided to do her a favor and move along. "Okay. Let's say that's a possibility. Now the next place where it looks like there was violence was when the authorities came to make the arrest. Here at Mark 14:32, it says an armed crowd showed up in Gethsemane where Jesus was found. One of the guys standing near drew his sword and took a swing at the servant of the high priest. Looks like he delivered a head blow and cut off the servant's dang ear. According to Mark, Jesus didn't say a word about it. He just makes an argument about not being a rebel or a criminal—depending on your translation. Then everybody runs off. One guy got grabbed by the authorities and took out leaving his clothes behind him. How does that compare with Matthew?"

Again, Kathleen was flipping back and forth from Mark to her place in

Matthew. "Yes, there was an armed crowd that came to arrest Jesus. And yes one of his followers used a sword to strike the servant of the high priest. But in Matthew, Jesus disapproves of the violence. Okay. I know what you're thinking. This is a pattern. Matthew softens the temple episode and at the arrest makes an effort to weaken the impression that Jesus was somehow tolerant if not supportive of the violence. But there are too many instances in other places where he disapproves of returning violence for violence. It was understood."

Woodrow said, "Well, no matter what he said, I'm looking at Luke here, and John and everybody agree that there was bloodshed when the arresting party came to take him in. Bottom line here is this: if you're looking at this from the viewpoint of the authorities, you've got two situations that might qualify as violent rebellion. Something violent damn sure happened at the temple, and then there was bloodshed when they came to make their arrest."

I was feeling sorry for Kathleen, but I could see Woodrow was onto something. "Well, what do you say Kathleen? We've got two places here that could have enough behind them to qualify as revolt, whether you call it that or not. Is there any place else."

She was flipping through Mark real quick like until she got to the end. "I don't see anything."

Woodrow pointed at something. "Take a look at Mark 15:6. According to this Bible here, Barabbas was being held because he was with some guys that were guilty of murder in the insurrection."

Kathleen took a long look at the verse he was talking about. "Yes, I see. That means there must have been another event in Jerusalem that constituted an uprising and someone was killed. That's probably the rebellion we're looking for."

Woodrow wasn't satisfied. "Look how he says it: 'in the insurrection,' like we're supposed to know which one he's talking about."

"No doubt he didn't need to spell it out, because the early Christians knew which one he meant."

"Or he didn't need to spell it out because it's already spelled out. I think when he says 'the insurrection' he means the one he's already talked about. I think there was an all-out riot when Jesus got arrested. I think people got killed. And I think Barabbas was there and got caught. These other two fellows too."

"You're stretching, Woodrow."

"Okay. Maybe. But let's work from the facts. Yes or no. Did Matthew tone down the level of violence that happened at the temple?"

"Well, that was an entirely separate incident."

"Just stay with me for a minute. Yes or no." I could tell she didn't want to play along. But she couldn't get stubborn under the circumstances.

"Assuming Dr. Ryland is right, and Matthew had the same version of Mark we do, then, yes, he toned it down. But...."

"All right, and Luke toned it down even more. Right?"

"Yes."

"Now we could argue all day about why they might do that. But would you agree that one reason they might change the story is to whitewash the level of violence that happened?"

"I don't like the word 'whitewash.'"

"Downplay, then. They might want to downplay just how much violence took place when Jesus started things rolling at the temple." Kathleen sat staring at the Bible and running her fingers over the words.

"Come on, Kathleen. It's like Dr. Ryland said, we won't get anywhere unless we at least consider the possibilities."

She took a deep breath. "All right. I see what you're driving at. I'll grant as a possibility that the disturbance in the temple might have been more serious than we usually think."

"Why couldn't the same thing happen with the arrest? I mean they admit there were armed men on both sides. They all admit there was bloodshed. Why is it so hard to believe men died and then there were several arrests?"

"That's going too far Woodrow. The Bible doesn't say any of that." I could tell Woodrow was getting frustrated.

"Okay. Let's do it your way. Mark says they all ran off. Right?"

"Yes."

"Who was chasing them?"

"I don't know. The Bible doesn't say. I'm assuming the authorities."

"Exactly. You don't need the Bible to tell you what your own common sense tells you."

That's when I stepped in again. "Well it says here at Mark 14:51 that there was a fellow they tried to catch, but all they got was his clothes and he ran off naked. Looks like they aimed to arrest him too."

"Looks to me like they aimed to arrest as many of them as they could catch. How many got away Kathleen?"

"All of them."

"Now who's stretching? Where does it say that?"

"It doesn't say any of them were caught, either."

"Hell, Kathleen. That's my point. The Bible doesn't say. There are giant holes here that we have to fill in with our common sense. We know the guys crucified with Jesus got caught somewhere."

Kathleen sat back in her chair and crossed her arms. "For purposes of argument, Woodrow, suppose you tell me how your common sense is linking everything up."

He gave her a big smile. "Do you think you can hear the whole song and dance and resist the urge to argue or black my eye?"

"I'll try."

"There was a full blown riot at the temple. There was another full blown riot at the arrest. That's what the authorities were afraid of all along anyway. There was armed resistance. People got killed. At least one of them was in the arresting party. Jesus and at least two other guys got arrested. They got tried together. They got condemned together. They got crucified together. That's the best explanation for the facts we have."

Hell. I was convinced. Kathleen wasn't.

"If you're right, Woodrow, why hasn't anybody ever come up with this idea before?"

"Somebody had to Kathleen. You can't look at this real close and fair-minded and not see this as a possibility."

"Surely I would have heard."

"Well, the truth is, Kathleen, you didn't know until we met Dr. Ryland that Barabbas' first name was Jesus. How do you explain that?" She blushed. He looked over at me. "Buzz, I don't know how far down the field this moves the ball, but before they were crucified together, Jesus knew these guys. He was there at the rebellion that got them arrested."

Kathleen said she needed some air so she got up and walked out. Woodrow looked like he wanted to call her. But he didn't. We sat there for a minute looking at the books like they was a pitiful pile of mildewed pillow cases. Woodrow heaved a big sigh. "You better go talk to her Buzz." Funny, 'cause I was thinking the same thing.

I found her sitting in a glider, looking at her shoes, just swinging back and forth. I was drinking coffee watching her out the kitchen window.

A gust of sadness blew over me. That warm, yellow light was shining on her and she changed. She turned into a little girl wearing blue checkered dress with white socks and black shoes. The glider was gone and she was swinging on a kid's play set—you know, the kind that has a slide hooked up to it. She was swinging really high, and when she was on her way up, her long brown hair trailed out behind her like a thoroughbred's tail on race day. What made me sad was that she was making that little girl giggle every time she went higher. I wasn't sad because she was having fun. I was sad because it hit me that I spent some time lately with a grown up woman named Kathleen, and I had never heard her laugh—not once.

I could have watched that little girl that used to be Kathleen all day long. But she changed back into the sad grown up Kathleen sitting on the glider swinging by herself.

Ordinarily, I don't bother folks when they're thinking. And I could tell she was thinking. But I got overtook by this strong feeling that I ought to go talk to her. When I stepped out into the back yard, she looked up in my direction, but, for all I could tell, she didn't even see me.

There was a fancy looking bench catty-cornered from her glider, so I took a seat and looked around her yard at the statues of pixies and angels peeking out here and there. I figured if she wanted to talk, she would. If not, we'd just sit there and soak up what was left of the afternoon looking at pansies.

I really don't know how long we sat there quiet, but she finally stopped swinging and said. "Thank you."

It was like I was reading her mind. I knew she was thanking me for sitting there with my mouth shut until she was ready. She had her hands in her lap and was still looking at her shoes. When she spoke up again, I felt like she was talking—I mean really talking to me—for the first time.

"Leon, you were married weren't you?"

I didn't know where the hell that question came from. But I decided to just go with it. "Yeah, a couple of times."

"Do you mind if I ask what happened? If it's too personal, you don't have to tell me, of course."

"Well, my first wife found another fella while I was in Nam. My second wife ran off with a bowling pro and lives in Phoenix. I guess the price I pay for being so much fun when I'm around is that I'm real easy to forget when I'm out of town."

That made her smile a little bit. It wasn't a full grown smile. It was just a baby. But it was a smile anyway. I figured the door was opening. So I put my foot in.

"How about you? How'd your marriage end? If it's too personal … well, you know." Another baby smile.

"Divorce. It ended in divorce."

"You or him?"

"Does it matter?"

"No. It really doesn't matter at all, Kathleen. But I was just thinking. You're beautiful. You're smart. I don't know you too good, but you seem like a real nice person. Maybe a little quirky, but who ain't? There're lots of reasons a woman like you would get fed up with a guy. But I can't imagine why a fella would let you go unless there's some craziness about you I can't see."

"He was gay, Leon. He was homosexual."

How's that for an out-of-nowhere stun grenade? "Holy shit, Kathleen! I'm sorry. I mean, for crying out loud how'd that happen?"

"When we met in college, there was nothing to suggest that he had that tendency. He was handsome and charming. He was very involved in my church. Very involved in volunteer work. He swept me off my feet. My parents loved him. Everyone did. I couldn't imagine being married to a finer man. When he proposed, I was the happiest woman in the world.

"He had a job as the associate pastor at Ernest Bidding's church in Dallas. We waited until I got my master's, and then we got married. Ernest officiated. It was a beautiful wedding. Everyone said it was one of Dallas's 1978 social highlights."

"You couldn't tell he was a fag?" She shot me a frown.

"He wasn't a fag, Leon. He was a homosexual."

"Okay, if you say there's a difference. When did you find out he was a fag—er, a homosexual or whatever."

"It was years later."

"How many years?"

"When we divorced in 2004, we'd been married for twenty-six years."

"You mean you was married to the guy that long and didn't have any idea? You couldn't tell?"

"No I couldn't Leon. I didn't have anything to judge by. The way I was raised … the way he was …. You wouldn't understand."

"Well, I don't, to be honest. But I'd try if you'd explain it."

She started to say something, then shook her head. "Maybe later." She looked at her watch. "I have to call Bidding's office in an hour. They're very interested in meeting you. They don't like our timetable, though. They want at least a month to set things up."

I really didn't like the way the conversation swung away from her and her husband and got centered on Bidding and his timetable. But I made my mind up to bring her back around later. "Well, I guess you'll tell them I ain't got a month. I got a little over a week. If they want to talk to a live Leon, they better get on the ball."

"Don't say that, Leon." She stood up and brushed her fingers across her eyes. "I don't know how all this back and forth is going to wind up. But in my heart, I know you're going to be fine."

I'm such a pig. I tried not to notice what a great looking woman she is as she walked back into her house. But I couldn't help it.

My headache started firing up so I went looking for Woodrow. He was right where I left him, in Kathleen's library working over his computer. When I came in, he sat back and stared at the screen.

"You know, there're some people that say none of this stuff about the crucifixion even happened. No temple deal, no triumphal entry, no other crucified guys, no disciples. None of it. Here's a guy that's got a website that says the whole deal is a myth that's patterned on other myths that were current when the Christian Church was getting formed."

"Break it down for me and tell me what you're talking about, Woodrow."

"Well, take the communion, for example. Christians say the bread is Jesus' body. Right? And the juice or wine or whatever is his blood. Well evidently there were other religions in the Middle East hundreds of years before the Christians showed up that had rituals where they'd symbolically eat the flesh and drink the blood of their god."

That took me plumb off guard. "You're kidding. So other religions had communion before the Christians took it up?"

"Yep. And this fella says the twelve apostles are really just myths that are supposed to represent the twelve signs of the Zodiac. He says it's all symbolic; the number twelve, their names everything. Then there's this religious guy—hell, he's a bishop in some Christian denomination. He says the whole New Testament was written to fit a liturgical calendar, and none of the early Christians believed the facts written in the New Testament were true at all."

"I'm fighting my afternoon headache, Woodrow. So my thinking's fuzzy. Give me the bottom line, will you?"

"Okay. If these guys are right, you're fucked, buddy. The puppet sent you on a mission to find out facts that don't exist."

I had to sit down. My brain started to race, and a sort of panic went to creeping up on me. But then I got hold of myself. *This is just talk. No need to get my panties in a bunch until I take a closer look.* I took a deep breath, and that breath, all by itself, made me feel better.

"So what do you think, Woodrow?"

He looked up at me and scratched his jaw. "Well, I think it's roughly half and half on this stuff. Some parts of the New Testament were made up to promote a new religion.

"So I'll cut to the chase. I think Jesus was crucified in Jerusalem. I think the names of those other guys who died with him were in the story the way it was originally told. And I think those names are buried in the New Testament somewhere, and I think it's just a matter of digging them out. There must be a way to separate the ore from the overburden. But I can't see how to do it right now."

"What does your gut tell you, Woodrow? Are we going to get this figured out in time?"

He slapped me on the shoulder. "My gut tells me the odds are against us. But that's when we do our best work."

Well, I figured he was right.

TAPE 12

Me and Woodrow figured that, since we were guests, it would be rude to invite ourselves to pull out the magic pipe in Kathleen's house. She, for sure, would disapprove of us getting high on illegal herbs. So I told her we had us an errand to run. She said that was fine, as she was waiting on the call from Bidding's bunch, and she needed to get current on her blog.

We piled into the Dodge and drove from Nichols Hills over to Byron's, our favorite liquor store in the whole world. Byron stocks every kind of intoxicating spirit you can legally buy in the State of Oklahoma. We needed to pick up some Chivas for my neighbor, Pete, and some Wild Turkey for Woodrow and me. Then we stopped at the mall and bought a copy of *The Big Lebowski,* our favorite movie.

On the way back to Kathleen's, we were in Saturday evening traffic, so we didn't have to worry about driving during rush hour.

My headache was so bad, it was making me blind, so, since the car wash is on the way to Kathleen's, we stopped off to clean the Dodge and give the pipe a workout. Chris Cross was singing *Sailing* on the iPod. I was amazed how quick Woodrow's pot could heal me up. I couldn't help but wonder, though, whether I was going to have to put up with these gol' dang head busters for the rest of my life. That would be bad. But not as bad as being dead—I think.

While we were waiting to get the truck washed, I asked Woodrow what he thought about Kathleen. "Well, she's a nice lady, but she's wound too damn tight. She's too used to fooling around with people living in a world that isn't real. It's made for thinking flabby"

"You mean all the religious stuff?"

"Yeah. That and the money. It isn't her fault, really. Because of all that mission work she told us she did in Mexico and Haiti and wherever. She probably thinks she knows something about poverty and generosity. But it's really like theater in the round. It's a show that's got an admission price. After your ten days or two weeks in the show, you go home to your house in Nichols Hills. Nine times out of ten, nothing important really happens except people write more and bigger checks."

"Pardon me, Woodrow, but what the hell does mission work got to do with anything. I'm not following."

He chuckled. "She's a nice lady, Buzz and she'd go crazy if she heard me say this, but I feel sorry for her. Before she knows it, she's going to be an old lady and she won't know what it was like to be a full-blooded human being. She won't have any way to measure her life by anything real. She's lived her whole life in a box somebody else built for her. If something doesn't change she'll die there."

I started to tell him about her being married to a fag and all. But I figured I owed it to her to keep my mouth shut. You just don't go blabbing stuff people tell you in confidence. The only reason I'm spilling it to this machine is because she told me to. She told me to spool every detail out there no matter how embarrassing it be.

Anyway, me and Woodrow picked up enough Chinese food for everybody and cruised on back to Kathleen's house. She'd never seen *The Big Lebowski*, so we talked her into watching it with us. Woodrow and I mixed some Wild Turkey with RC cola where Kathleen couldn't tell and we all had a great time watching the movie.

I looked over at Kathleen and the light from the TV was covering her face with a soft blue color. Maybe it was the combination of pot and Wild Turkey, but when I heard her laugh for the first time, I got ... well. I ... Well, it was a real pleasant evening.

I slept good in a big bed in one of Kathleen's guest rooms. I dreamed about her swinging in her glider and laughing.

Sunday, February 25, 2007, a.m.

I made breakfast for everybody that morning. I didn't mention it before, but I'm a pretty damn good cook. I whipped up a cheddar cheese and hamburger omelet with jalapeños for Woodrow. He was drinking coffee and reading a newspaper. When Kathleen came in, everybody said "good morning" but I was the only one that sounded cheerful. Kathleen looked like she hadn't slept a wink. I poured Woodrow and myself some orange juice.

I was asking her what kind of omelet she liked when her phone rang. I started putting a cheese, tomato, and mushroom omelet together while she went into another room to talk. You never know whether a good vegetarian omelet might help her get over her faith crisis.

Somebody on the TV news was talking about some sensational tomb of Jesus deal. There was going to be a TV special about it Wednesday night. Then there was an interview with a fella that was the first Episcopal bishop to be an outright fag. At first, I thought they were interviewing the fag about the mystery tomb. But they weren't. I guess he was saying that the churches ought to do more to accept gays because, *"Doesn't Jesus challenge the greater whole to sacrifice itself for those on the margins?"* I don't know. That's a hard one.

Kathleen came back in. "That call was from one of Bidding's people. They say the great man himself wants to discuss things with you in person. He is willing to agree to have a taped meeting, but he wants his people to do the taping. He wants ownership of the tapes and he won't agree to sign the release.

I said, "Right this minute, I don't give a shit about any of it."

"Think about it Leon. This may be a way to get Bidding's followers to lay off. We could negotiate an agreement that would involve Bidding calling off the hype. I will agree to stop criticizing him on the blog. This thing's got to be defused. It's way out of control. I think Bidding is worried about your house being burned. Everybody suspects one of his crazy followers did it. No doubt his legal advisers are considering the possibility you might file a lawsuit. He could probably beat the case in court, but he'd rather avoid that kind of publicity at this point in his life."

"Okay. So what's supposed to happen at this meeting?"

"Bidding's been saying you're possessed. He claims he can cast out your demon. He says this would be one of the most dramatic confrontations in the history of Christian television."

Of course, I said "That's horseshit. I don't have a demon."

"What do you have to lose then? If you agree to the meeting, you get Bidding off your back and you might make some money."

"You're kidding. Money? Really? How much money?"

"That's hard to say right now. It's obvious why Bidding wants the tapes. He needs control in case something happens that makes him look bad. But he's so arrogant that, in his mind, that's not a realistic possibility. The way he sees it, he's too good to be made to look bad. Since he's the only divinely anointed prophet alive today, how could an uneducated sinner like Leon Butane make him look bad?"

"Well, I can see his point, I guess. Okay. What about me? What am I going to look like when this super slick TV preacher gets hold of me in front of the whole damn world? I'm the one that's going to look like a doofus. Tell me about the money."

"I think the real reason he wants to do this is because he sees the financial potential. I don't know what he's thinking, but there is a lot of room for negotiation, and if you give me the okay, I'll see what we can put together."

"What about the release I already signed?"

"Let's tear it up. That was our agreement, wasn't it? I'll go get it right now. If we can't come up with a release everybody can sign, then there won't be any deal at all."

She brought her briefcase into the kitchen and pulled out the release I signed; she stood right in front of me and tore that paper to shreds. I've got to say that her tearing up the agreement almost put a lump in my throat. I got a whole new confidence in her. It means a lot to me when somebody can be trusted to keep their word. "Okay. But let's be clear. I don't have to do anything if I don't sign something. Right?"

"Right." She stuck her hand out for me to shake. And we did. I used the handshake as a excuse to hold onto her. I guess I was sitting there looking calf-eyed, because I heard Woodrow chuckle.

"What's so dang funny Woodrow?"

"Maybe nothing. But I just got to ask Kathleen a question here. Are you saying you'd make a deal with Bidding to keep quiet about him from now on? You'll overlook anything he may do, no matter how out-of-bounds, if he'll lay off Leon here?"

She blushed. "I'd have plenty to write about if I never said another word about Ernest Bidding."

"I'm sure that's true. I was just wondering if this kind of agreement is in the religious crusades playbook. *I'll overlook your shenanigans if there's something in it for me.*"

Kathleen stood there looking at the tore up paper in her hands. I couldn't stand it. "Come on Woodrow. Kathleen's only trying to use the tools at hand to get me out of a jam."

Woodrow was staring a hole in her but she kept looking at that ripped up agreement. "Well, you're right Buzz. She's just using her tools. And I got the feeling she knows what she's doing."

There was a kind of smelly quiet there in the kitchen for a second or two. Kathleen changed the subject.

"Would you agree to come to Dallas with me and talk to a man down there?"

"Who?" She reached into her briefcase and came out with a book called *Rescuing the Word* by Dr. Emmet Ayers at the North Texas Theological Seminary.

"He's one of the world's foremost evangelical scholars and he should be able to clear up a lot of the apparent troubling inconsistencies we turned up in the last few of days."

"Well, I don't mind going down there if you think he can get me closer to the answer I'm looking for."

"He has a Doctorate in Theology and is an internationally known expert on the historical Jesus. Talking to him surely wouldn't hurt anything."

"Okay. Set it up and we'll go talk to him."

"Where will you and Woodrow be today?"

"Well, I'm not sure you want to hear this, but we're going to deliver some liquor to a friend of mine so I can get my mail. Then we're going to take a look at my burned up house."

She looked a little hurt. "You've misjudged me Leon. All I want you to do is be safe and stay out of trouble. I may be getting close to calming things down. If you should show up on the news for DUI or devil worship, things would get complicated again."

Woodrow grinned. "Oh, don't worry about a thing. We always do our devil worship in the dark where nobody can see us, don't we, Buzz?" She didn't think that was funny. It must have been too early for her to get our jokes.

She didn't eat the omelet I made for her, so Woodrow and I took care of it. Then we went one way and Kathleen went another to do whatever she was doing. Me and Woodrow headed for Jones where I used to live.

We could see what was left of my house when we turned off Spencer Road onto the county line. I'm trying to think of a way to tell you how pissed off I was.

See, I bought this house here in Jones just to get away from everything when Treena, that's my ex, ran off with her bowling pro boyfriend. I kind of wrapped myself up like a cocoon in my truck and my house. Now they were both gone.

I sure could have used something to chew on—not because of the pain, but because of a major overflowing case of *pure-dee-old-let-me-get-my-hands-on-the-pig-fucker-that-did-this-and-I'll-kick-his-mother-fucking-ass-from-here-to*…. Well, let's just say I was real pissed off.

Woodrow stopped the Dodge and sat there looking at the remains of chez Buzz like he was studying a two headed collie. Then he pulled out his phone and banged in Kathleen's number—real hard. When she answered, Woodrow surprised me by how calm and cool he sounded, "Kathleen, do you have any idea who done this to Buzz's house?" She hem-hawed around a little bit, and Woodrow got real specific. "Did anybody say anything on that blog of yours that might give us a clue who done it?"

"I've reported what I know to the police. They're looking into it. They want to talk to Leon, too. I told them I'd be sure he got the message to him."

"So who—exactly—are the police looking into? You might as well say it because we're going to check the blog ourselves."

"Okay. There's a man named Elmer Tollifson who calls himself the Lord's Sergeant at Arms. He's a religious fanatic that started his own church in Edmond. He requires his followers to believe and confess that every word in the Bible is literally true. He's always agitating for the teaching of creationism in schools. He organizes demonstrations at school board meetings and generally causes low-level disturbances whenever he thinks he can stir up some media attention. He's picketed churches that offer fellowship to homosexuals. He's picketed hospitals and doctors that perform abortions. He enjoys being arrested. He thrives on going to trial. He's never been caught advocating or doing anything violent, except one case when a nurse's husband got roughed up at one of his antiabortion demonstrations. The witnesses were all Tollifson partisans, and they all testified he was just defending himself. He got off.

"There is always mischief and vandalism somewhere around his activities. Slashed tires, broken windows, and anonymous threats. Things like that. Anyway, Tollifson prophesied that God was going to rain fire down on Leon Butane and all his house. So far, the authorities are saying that the most likely cause of the fire is a propane leak. They're not 100 percent convinced, but that is the most they'll say so far. But they're questioning Tollifson, because it's just too coincidental that he predicted your house would burn. And it did."

Woodrow asked, "Where can we find this Lord's buck private?"

"Calm down Woodrow. You can't prove anything and you can't do anybody any good by starting a lot of trouble. Leave this to the police. Anyway, we have an appointment in Dallas tomorrow at the North Dallas Theological Seminary. Dr. Ayres is having lunch in his office from noon to one o'clock and he can see us then." Woodrow said we'd see her at the house later.

We walked around my yard looking at the mess. Everything but the foundation was an ash pile. The burned-out corpse of my Mercury looked like it put up a fight and went down swinging. It made me proud. That's an American-made car for you. Any moron could see this here was no propane leak. Propane isn't smart enough to blow up the house then come outside looking for a car to burn. I guess the official story was going to be that there was a gas leak in the Mercury and the propane and gas teamed up to gut my house and car and piss me off.

Well, there was nothing we could do, so we decided to go get the mail.

My neighbor's name is Pete. He's a disabled Korean War vet. He's got back problems, diabetes, emphysema, and he's an alcoholic. But he's a pretty good old boy. He picks up my mail and keeps an eye on my place while I'm on the road. I always bring him a bottle of Chivas when I come back. I take it off my taxes as a business expense. He thinks that's a hoot. Me too.

Anyway, Pete was happy to see me and the Chivas. He poured us a snort in plastic OU go-cups and set a trash bag full of mail down at my feet. He don't have any teeth so it's creepy when he grins. "Hey Buzz. I'm real sorry about what happened to your house." He took a long hard pull right out of the bottle which caused another grin. "When people started showing up over there with picket signs and stuff, I called the dang po-lice. They came out and got the squatters out of your driveway and made 'em stay up on the road. There was TV people too, with cameras and everything. Reporter folks talked to all five of us neighbors here on the section line. They was real interested in finding out if we knew anything about you doing miracles. I don't know what the others told them, but I said 'Hell yes, Buzz done a lot of miracles for me.' I told them my well water wasn't fit to drink and you came over and cured it."

I said, "Hell, Pete. That wasn't any miracle. Don't you remember? You and me installed a water softener. It wasn't that your water wasn't fit to drink. It was just hard. All the well water around here's hard. You know that."

He winked and said, "Sure Buzz. I know that. But since I didn't know what your play was, I decided to string along."

I could feel my stomach getting upset again, just like it did awhile ago when I heard how Wanda was helping me. "What else did you tell them?"

"Well, I told them how Mrs. Dickens, before she died, was blind for seven or eight years and you fixed it where she could see her TV and read *The Enquirer.*"

"For crying out loud, Pete! I didn't do anything but take the old lady over to the mall and get her eyes checked and get her some glasses from LensCrafters. She'd turn over in her grave if she heard you say I'd done a miracle. Surely you didn't tell them anything else." He winked again and took another snort.

"Yep. I told them I had emphysema, and you freed me up from the oxygen bottle."

"Well hell Pete. That's a goddamn lie. You're hooked up to it right now."

Pete used his old brown fingers to work some tobacco from behind his lower lip. "Yep. I told them you were one miracle-working son of a bitch!" I could see that talking to Pete must have been loads of fun for the reporters, but it wasn't doing me any good. So I just gave up and took a deep breath.

"Thanks for taking care of the mail, partner. You need anything?"

He just raised the Chivas bottle up over his head, and waved. "Don't think so, Buzz. I believe I got it all." I told him thanks for keeping an eye on the place even though it did get burned up.

As we walked out the door, he said, "Don't worry about nothing, Buzz. It's under control. But listen here, when you decide to use one of your magic miracle powers to rebuild your house, let me know, because I damn sure need to be there to see it." We could hear him cackling the whole time we were walking back to the Dodge.

Sunday, February 25, 2007, p.m.

The Weloka diner is set up for wireless Internet access now, so we decided that's where we'd have lunch.

Betsy was pouring coffee for a couple of retirees when we walked in with Woodrow's laptop. She came over to our table and sat down, "Well, hello. Glad to see you boys back after the way you hightailed it out of here the other day. We been following youir exploits on the news. It isn't every day we get a couple of famous healers here in the Weloka Diner."

I said, "Come on, Betsy. Lay off that healer stuff. I'm trying to get it all straightened out."

"Sure, sure kid. But at least tell me what the hell's going on and how all this got started."

"Never mind right now, Betsy. You wouldn't believe it if I told you anyway."

"Well, you're going to have to spill it sooner or later. That's all everybody's talking about around here ever since you nose-dived in here your first day out of the hospital. We're all dying to know."

"You got my word, Betsy. Once the situation gets cleared up, I'll come in here and tell you the whole megillah. But just trust me for now. I really can't say much."

She patted me on the shoulder. "Okay. I just want you to know, we're all real sorry about your house getting burned down. If you and Woodrow need a place to stay, you can put up at my house." While she was walking away with her coffee pot, she said over her shoulder where everybody could hear. "You two will have to arm wrestle over which one of you gets to sleep with me though. The other one has to sleep in one of the guest rooms." That got a chuckle from everybody there. I'll tell you, there's nothing like a friend in need.

By then, Woodrow had located the Lord's Sergeant at Arms on the Internet. He's a busy boy. He shows up at the Capitol. He shows up at schools. He shows up at churches. He shows up at press conferences. Hell, looks like the son of a bitch is everywhere. He writes books. He writes articles. He writes editorials. Seems like he's a guy who believes we're in the last days and we're coming up fast on Judgment Day.

Anyway, he's got a squad of hardcore believers that keep things stirred up wherever they go. I guess these are some of the people who turned up to picket my house. They're always on the lookout for signs that Satan is bringing his forces around to lead the weak astray and cause the faithful to get slack.

He's got this blog of his own, and it made out that I was part of some huge 'choosing-up-sides' deal. God and his bunch on one side and the devil and me on the other. This was such bullshit!

We could see that the Lord's Sergeant at Arms had a church in Edmond, and they had regular prayer meeting every Sunday evening. That would be coming up in about four hours. That was real convenient, as Woodrow and I had the same idea. We could use a little churchification. So we decided we'd just drop in and hear what this holy hot shot had to say for himself. I won't say we plumb forgot what Kathleen told us about staying out of trouble. I'll just say we didn't reflect too hard on her meaning.

Since we had four hours to kill, I had in mind another errand we could run. The form I took off Teddy's clipboard was in my pocket. I gave Woodrow the address and asked him to drive me over there.

"This the guy who said he saw you praying to the devil?"

"So Wanda says."

"Well, let's go see him."

Since Midwest City was on the way to Edmond, it was no problem stopping off on the way. The house was a little plain white place that looked a lot like mine before it got burned up. There was a little beat up Toyota pickup in the drive. Didn't look like the vehicle a guy wearing gold chains would drive. Woodrow was standing behind me when I rang the bell.

When Tonya opened the door, you would have thought she was looking at Ed McMahon. "Oh, Mr. Butane! Is it really you? Oh my goodness! Iris, guess who's here. It's Mr. Butane. Please come in. Don't mind the mess. We're trying to get things together to move."

Iris came running out of a back room somewhere and skidded to a halt when she saw me. She grinned and blushed and popped her thumb in her mouth. I was glad to see her. Tonya was busy fussing with her hair and stuff. She gathered up a bunch of stuffed animals off a solid old couch. "I know the place is a mess. Please have a seat. Can I get you two a coke or something?" She handed Iris a chewed up looking monkey and disappeared. Woodrow fished around in the pocket of his overalls and came up with a key chain that had a crystal on it. He's always got a pocketful of Arkansas crystal to give away to folks who look like they need some luck. He held it up for Iris to see.

"Would you like to have this?" She had a big smile behind her thumb. She nodded. He put it on the coffee table and sat back. Iris picked it up real bashful-like and ran to the other room to be with her mom.

Tonya came back in with two Cokes. She started gushing about what I did for Iris. I cut her off.

"Is Teddy around Tonya?" Her smile disappeared.

"No Mr. Butane. He's gone. For good. I'm really sorry about what he tried to do. He sure thought he was going to turn his pictures and video into big money. He still thinks he will. But he's really mad because Iris and I won't help him."

"What does he want you to do?"

"He just wants us to back him up in whatever he says, and it wouldn't be right. Mr. Butane, I don't believe it was the chemo either. I think God saved Iris, and I think he used you to do it. I don't know how. I'm just grateful you and the doctor were willing to let God use you." Iris crawled up in her mom's lap still clutching her little crystal keychain. I couldn't think of a thing to say.

Tonya went on. "I tried to straighten out what Teddy said—you know—about you praying to Satan and all. I told everybody that was just a lie. I think a lot of people believed me, but some didn't. They had their minds made up no matter what I said."

"Well, I appreciate you trying to help me, Tonya. Do you know where I can find Teddy now?"

She hoisted Iris onto her hip and went to her purse which was sitting on her TV. She rummaged around a bit and came up with a card.

"He's out of town today, but he'll be here tomorrow afternoon." She put the card in my hand.

"Blanche's Nirvana Massage?"

"It's his sister. He's staying there 'til he can get a place of his own."

"Thanks Tonya. Listen, I got a score of my own to settle with Teddy, but I gotta ask: Was he ever mean to Iris?"

"Well, he never hit her. He'd scare her and talk mean. She'd cry sometimes. But he never hit her."

I looked over at Woodrow and saw the muscles in his jaw working. Iris was holding the crystal up to the light.

"Was he ever mean to you Tonya?"

Her mouth was still smiling but her eyes was watering. "Mr. Butane you need to be careful with Teddy. He's always got a gun on him and he has some really dangerous friends."

"Hey Iris, can I look at your crystal?" She slid down her mom's hip and carried her crystal and her monkey over to where I was sitting. She held the crystal toward my face. "It's real pretty Iris. Take care of it and it'll bring you good luck. Thanks for talking with us Tonya. We got to go now." I touched Iris' nose with my little finger, and me and Woodrow started for the door.

"Mr. Butane. Thanks again for everything. Thank you and God bless you. Please be careful." We waved, and Iris waved her crystal at us. Toby Keith's *Time for Me to Ride* was playing on the iPod when we got in the Dodge.

We showed up at the Church of Unyielding Faith about fifteen until six, and a Marine-recruiter-looking guy met us at the front door. Only real die-hards show up for Sunday prayer meeting. You could tell the usual church routine is to shake hands with everybody who comes in, because that's what the recruiter done. His voice said "Welcome, I'm Jim Turpin," but his eyes said "I'm Jim Turpin, and I wish you guys would crawl back to the rock you dug out from under." I guess we stuck out like grizzlies at a petting zoo, with shaggy old Woodrow and me all skin-headed and carved up. You could tell Jim thought he might recognize me but couldn't quite place it. So we shook his hand without telling him who we was and brushed on in to take a seat on one of those old-fashioned, hard-assed pews near the back of the sanctuary.

A few minutes later, old Jim Turpin came hustling up with another guy, a big dockworker looking guy who put his hand out and said, "Hi. I'm Ed Guffman, and I want to welcome you to the Church of Unyielding Faith. Can I get your names for our fellowship roster?"

I told him, "Sure. My name's Leon Butane and this here's my apostle Woodrow Mulholland." Jim, Ed, and Woodrow all snorted at the same time and I just gave them a big old grin and said, "We were in the neighborhood and were on our way home from looking at the ash pile that used to be my house and decided to stop by and get an earful of what the Sergeant has to say." Jim and Ed looked at each other, "harrumphed," and headed off to tattle on us.

Woodrow asked "What the hell is this 'Apostle Woodrow' shit?"

"Okay, I admit that was maybe out of line. I was thinking they probably get a lot of husbands, wives, uncles, brothers, and stuff like that in here. But I bet they never get an apostle. Hell, I'll bet you're the first one they've ever seen."

He looked real thoughtful for a second, then said, "Well, when you put it that way, I guess I see your point." There was a smile starting across his face when he thought about it some more. "Apostle Woodrow. It does have a sort of a holier-than-thou ring to it. Maybe I'll try it on for a while and see how it fits. We'll have to come up with something good for you."

"Why can't we both be apostles? You be apostle Woodrow and I'll be apostle Buzz."

We was getting a kick out of being a couple of outlaw apostles in church on Sunday night while the other outlaws was out misbehavin' and drinking beer.

About that time, Jim and Ed came rolling down the aisle from the back of the church with the Sergeant himself in the lead. You wouldn't know it by the way he spouts off, but the Sergeant's a little bitty fella. He came storming over like a whirlpool in a shitter and said, "May I ask what you two want in here?"

I said, "Apostle Woodrow and I were out shopping for a place to get baptized, and we thought we'd check out this here Church of Unyielding Faith, and we have to say that Jim and Ed here were near the top of the list of handshaking fellers. Wouldn't you say so, Apostle Woodrow?"

He nodded "I'd say amen to that."

The Sergeant made a face like he was licking a dip stick. "I don't believe you. I think you two came in here to make mischief and I think you should leave."

I said, "Mischief? Mischief? Hell, mischief is something kids do. Me and Apostle Woodrow here don't believe in making mischief anymore. We graduated a long time ago to the category of advanced hell-raising. Oh, no. We certainly didn't come here to cause no mischief."

He stood there blinking for a minute and then said, "Well, whatever. You and this, Woodrow, have to go right now. Services are about to start."

Then, in a deep, rumbly growl, Woodrow said, "That's Apostle Woodrow to you. And we'll leave after we've said our prayers. But first, we just wanted to ask if you all have any idea about the identity of the shrimpy, cowardly, chickenshit, firebug that burned Apostle Buzz's house down?"

Then Ed moved the tiny Sergeant aside and said, "You been asked politely to leave. This here is the house of the Lord and you two ought to be ashamed for making light of it." He started rolling up his sleeves. "Now, you two can leave because you've been asked. Or you can leave because you've been made to do it."

There weren't many people in the church, but they were all turned around watching, and some of them were on their feet. Woodrow said, "Apostle Buzz here's got brain damage, so I reckon I'll just take him out of here. But if it wasn't for that, I'd sweep the sanctuary aisles with your unyielding, hypocritical asses."

Of course Woodrow was right. I didn't know how much damage would get done if I took a lick to my already dented up skull. So neither of us liked it, but we got up to leave. Honest. That's what we intended to do. Then one of them, Jim or Ed, I don't know which, just had to make a crack. "You boys just consider yourselves lucky that it was just the house that burned. But maybe you won't think you're so lucky when the rest of you is burning in eternal hellfire later." So Woodrow fired off a cannon-ball-sounding fart and hollered "Amen!" And the fight was on.

Jim, Ed, and the Sergeant were no match for me and Apostle Woodrow. We was juggling them like ping-pong balls. Two more worshipers jumped in, and we was thumping them pretty good too. But we could see some of the others hitching up their britches and headed into the scrap, so we figured it was time to start fighting our way to the door. By the time we got there, they had six or seven Christians fighting on their side. Me and Apostle Woodrow might have been getting the worst of it. But there were some folding chairs there by the door. We picked up a couple of them chairs and started using them to turn the tide again. Well the Unyielding Faith bunch backed off huffing and puffing and bleeding.

I decided to be polite. "Apostle Woodrow and I would like to thank you all for your hospitality. I can't remember when I enjoyed a church meeting so much. Just the same, we've decided not to get baptized here tonight, but we'll try to round up some more sinners and apostles and fetch them in for your next Sunday morning services." We dropped our chairs, slammed the doors, and made for the Dodge. Apostle Woodrow and I both had bloody noses and fat lips. We figured there'd be bumps and bruises shared out among the Unyielding brethren, and we figured the Sergeant himself would wind up with a shiner.

Don't get the wrong idea. It wasn't me or Woodrow that popped the little fella. It was one of his own disciples. I picked him up and was using him for a shield and one of his own guys was aiming to bust me in the nose. Well, he missed his aim and clobbered the Sergeant instead. I guess I should have dropped him after that, but I figured I might need his other cheek for something, so I held onto him as long as I could. He's a pretty good little wiggler, though, and I finally had to drop him.

All in all, considering the numbers, I'd say it was a draw.

"Gimme Shelter" by the Stones was playing on the iPod as we headed back to Kathleen's place.

TAPE 13

The next morning, we headed for Dallas to meet this evangelical scholar that Kathleen set us up with. She hardly said a word to us. She was furious about us getting in a ruckus at the Unyielding church. We kept trying to explain that we didn't start the scrap and were only trying to defend ourselves. "You shouldn't have been there in the first place. Do you know Tollifson's blog is claiming that you two marched into his church to proclaim the power of the devil?" Woodrow chuckled but I didn't think it was funny.

"Well that's just hog wash Kathleen. Me and Woodrow wasn't proclaiming nobody's power. We just wanted to ask if anybody there knew anything about my house."

"Did you two call yourselves Apostles?"

"Woodrow did."

"Well, according to Tollifson, you two announced that you were the devil's apostles and he and some of the faithful members of the congregation overpowered you with the Lord's help and drove you out."

"You mean the little son of a bitch is claiming they kicked our ass? You know, I've got to say I sort of admired the Unyielding bunch for putting up their dukes and all. But it really chaps me that they can't own up to the fact that we were holding our own even when they were ganging up on us."

I was starting to get worked up about it when Woodrow said, "Cool down now, Buzz. Remember what they say, 'sticks and stones ... blah, blah, blah.' Okay. We got our licks in, and if they want to be crybabies about it, that's their problem."

Kathleen said "You know, they're probably going to press charges. Then

191

you can add local police and sheriff's deputies to the list of people trying to catch up with us." We decided not to mention that we had plans to visit Teddy sometime in the next couple of days. She'll probably think that was a bad idea.

On the way to Dallas, Woodrow switched on his radio. There was a news story about a twenty-nine-year-old guy posing as a twelve year old so he could enroll in school. Evidently he was a sex offender who just wanted to be near kids so he could pick off targets he figured was easiest. I was stumped.

"How do you figure a deal like this could happen Woodrow? Can you just enroll in school with no parents, no birth certificate, no medical records or nothing?"

"I guess you can. That's what this guy did."

Kathleen spoke up from the backseat. "That happened in Arizona didn't it?"

Woodrow must have been paying closer attention than I was. "That's where he got arrested. But this guy had a record of propositioning minors in Oklahoma before he pulled up stakes and moved to greener pastures in Arizona."

I didn't mean to hit a nerve. But I guess I did. "You spent some time working for a church in Arizona didn't you Kathleen?" She sounded real bitter.

"Yes. Yes I did Leon. Here's how such a thing can happen. People saw a twelve-year-old boy because that's what he said he was. They might have seen the truth if they'd looked behind the mask. But they didn't. Believe me, now that he's been exposed for the predator he is, outsiders can't imagine how anyone would be taken in. That's how people can be so easily deceived. They're so willing to accept things at face value. Sometimes, even when you put the truth right in front of them in a form that can't be reasonably contradicted, they won't give up on their treasured misconceptions. They won't. They won't. I ..." She just left it hanging there.

"What are we talking about here Kathleen? Are we talking about this transplanted Oklahoma pervert or do you have something else in mind?"

She sat for a minute looking out her window. "I don't know, Leon. I really don't know what we're talking about. I'm having a hard time telling where one question stops and another one picks up. What they all have in common is that I'm not getting any satisfactory answers."

Woodrow switched off the news. "You guys are depressing me. Look at it this way. The guy was a skillful deceiver. It worked for a while. Some people got hurt. He got caught. Today we're having a nice Monday drive on a clean highway and the only thing stopping us from making the most of it is my choice in radio stations. I'm doing my part to correct my error right now."

He switched on his iPod, and Leon Russell was singing *It's a Hard Rain Gonna Fall*. He came out with a belly laugh. Kathleen ignored it. I shrugged, scratched my horse shoe looking scar, and sat back to enjoy the music and the road.

We got to Dallas about noon; Kathleen guided us to the North Texas Theological Seminary. When we got to Dr. Ayers' office, he wasn't there. There was a cartoon on his door showing a guy shoveling snow, and there was one of those cartoon bubbles over his head showing he was thinking of a guy mowing grass. Then there was a cartoon bubble over the grass mower's head showing the guy shoveling snow. Then there was another grass mower bubble and so forth until you couldn't see bubbles anymore, because they were so tiny.

So I asked, "Woodrow, what the hell do you suppose that means?"

He shrugged. "I don't know for sure, Buzz. I need to think about it."

Kathleen said, "It's a humorous representation of the fact that people are basically unsatisfied no matter what they're doing. They wish they were doing something else, even when what they're doing is something they thought they wanted to do before."

I said, "Well hell, that ain't funny. Cartoons are supposed to be funny." Kathleen tried to explain how sometimes cartoons exaggerate a difficult reality and put it in a way that helps us smile, while at the same time giving us a different look at the bigger picture. All I could think to say to that is, "Bullshit. It still ain't funny."

Woodrow put his hand on my shoulder. "Picture this, Buzz. Suppose you put a bubble over the head of every Christian on earth, and they were thinking about being angels in heaven, sitting on clouds, with wings and playing harps. Then you put a bubble over every angel's head and they're dreaming about being back on earth doing common earthly stuff like cooking or driving or bowling. Would that be funny?"

Kathleen and I both said at the same time, "No it wouldn't." He sure thought it was by the way he laughed.

About that time, Dr. Ayers came in carrying a Taco Bell bag. He's one of those guys that grows hair all over his face to compensate for the fact that he ain't got any on his head. His beard was mostly gray. But he had a dark stripe that started under his lip and spread out like a funnel that covered his chin and ended where his beard stopped in a neat cut line on his neck. It put me in mind of a skunk.

While he was unlocking his office door, he was talking fast. "I'm so sorry I'm late. Staff meetings ran a little over this morning. You know how long-winded some administrators can be." He laughed and Kathleen laughed, but Woodrow and I didn't think it was funny. I guess I was the only one that couldn't get anybody's jokes that day. Dr. Ayers and Kathleen were chatting about some people they both knew, and she asked about his next book. "It's coming out in June. It's another book about the theology of Paul" I couldn't wait. I was about to run out of reading material on the theology of Paul.

There were only two chairs in his office, so Dr. Ayers called his secretary, Adele, and told her to bring one up for Woodrow. He dug into his burrito while we waited for Adele to bring Woodrow's chair.

Between bites, he looked us up and down and said, "Let me say again how sorry I am that we have to rush through this meeting. I wish I had more time to get to know you, Mr. Butane. You've started quite a firestorm haven't you?"

I started to answer him about that firestorm remark, but he kept talking nonstop, so I couldn't get a word in.

"I really thought I was going to have more time this afternoon, but they're airing a special on the so-called tomb of Jesus this week, and I've been asked to tape a response. The film crew is setting up in the auditorium as we speak. Be sure to tune in. I think you'll find it interesting."

Kathleen thanked him for making time for us. He kept talking while he worked on his burrito. "So, what exactly is it that I can do for you?"

"First off Dr. Ayers, were the men crucified with Jesus revolutionaries?"

"Yes."

"Was Barabbas's name Jesus?"

"The weight of authority says 'yes' but I disagree. I could explain why, but that would take too much time."

"Why did Luke simply call the cocrucified 'wrongdoers' and John call them 'others'?"

"Luke and John wrote their gospels at a time when use of the term *lēstēs* might distract from the core message. The catastrophic revolution that culminated in the destruction of the temple in 70 CE was still fresh on the minds of the Roman public. So Luke and John chose less provocative words while still being careful to be accurate. Nothing sinister about it I assure you."

"So why did John think it was okay to call Barabbas a revolutionary but not the men crucified with Christ?"

He gulped down some burrito, cleared his throat, and said, "I don't know. I suspect John felt there was little risk of misunderstanding because Barabbas was not so closely associated with Jesus. He was a step further removed than these other men. Distortion is more likely if there is confusion concerning those who shared Jesus' fate." You know the word that came to my mind? Spin. You know, the kind of verbal razzle-dazzle that comes out of somebody's mouth when the truth hurts. Adele brought in a chair and Woodrow was squirming ten seconds after he sat down.

Kathleen asked, "What insurrection was being referred to in Mark when he talks about the event that led to Barabbas' arrest?"

"I don't know. So much of what happened back then is lost to us forever. There's really no way to know anything about the insurrection he's referring to. It must not have been much of an insurrection, though. Josephus would have mentioned it."

I elbowed Woodrow and whispered, "Who in tarnation is Josephus, and why do we give a shit what he says or doesn't say?" He shushed me because he was zeroed in on Dr. Ayers. I figured I'd ask later. Everybody but me was real focused.

"Might the insurrection Mark refers to be to the disturbance in the temple?"

"No. There's no indication anyone other than Jesus was involved. We're not even sure the disciples were there. They're not mentioned."

That's when I piped in. "Doc, does it make sense for Jesus to come into Jerusalem looking like a king of the Jews and then go to the temple and start a ruckus all by himself? I mean, he really couldn't have stopped people from tagging along even if he wanted to, could he?"

"Of course, the Bible tells us there was a tumultuous reception when Jesus entered Jerusalem. And of course the crowd was acutely interested in Jesus' movements. But I'm sure if others were involved in the so-called cleansing incident, that's an important fact that would have been mentioned."

I didn't want to be contrary, but I wasn't sold. I was one hundred percent sure this commotion at the temple was a big deal to Jesus and his followers, and I was one hundred percent sure some of his followers went there with him, and I was one hundred percent sure when Jesus started raising hell, his followers weren't just standing around like potted plants.

So I asked, "Well, how about this Doc? Were the gospels right when they described what happened in there?"

He smiled, "If it's in the Scriptures, it happened."

"Well, then, tell me why Matthew and Luke tone the whole deal down from the way it comes out in Mark. And, if Mark's right, tell me how Jesus went about stopping people from carrying things through the temple? It looks to me like he or somebody had to use some force or threats or something."

Dr. Ayers was looking at me all narrow-eyed while he took a long pull on his Coke straw. Then he said, "As for the 'toning down' as you call it, the essence of the event is what we are meant to focus on, not necessarily the details. And as for the suggestion that force was used to interfere with temple operation, not necessarily. The force of Jesus' personality was powerful enough to cause people to stop what they were doing without the need for physical involvement. After all, according to John, that's what happened to the members of the arresting party in the garden. Look at John 18:6."

Then Woodrow said, "Well if that's what happened, if he just used his personality to put a stop to people coming and going, how come Matthew and Luke dropped it? Seems like they'd want to use it. Wouldn't that be more support for the idea Jesus was the son of God?"

Dr. Ayers looked at his watch. "This is another of the mysteries and I really don't know the answer." He wadded up his taco and burrito wrappers and dropped them and his Coke cup into a waste basket. He put the palms of his hands on his desk and said, "Listen. You're not the first to try to dig for some truth in a world beyond what the Scriptures say. Every single time that happens, those who are seeking get distracted from the message. You need to let go of these worldly concerns and have faith that God provided all the information you need for your salvation." He put his hand on a Bible there on his desk and looked at all of us one by one real slow and said, "Right here."

I told him, "Look. I've already heard this speech from my cousin Augie, and he ain't a doctor of theology like you are. He's barely got a high school diploma. I don't have time to get all wrapped up in the message right now. I'm not looking behind the words because it's a hobby or something. I'm looking behind the words because my fucking life depends on it—pardon my French."

He still had that *"I'm-smarter-than-you"* half-smile on his slightly red face. "Now, now, Mr. Butane. Did it ever occur to you that this might be the very moment in your life when you are being tested? Perhaps the moment when all your instincts tell you to bypass the message and delve into the extraneous matters is the very moment when you should throw your trust onto the word of God? Let me pose a question to you, Mr. Butane. Suppose the price you pay for acquiring the answer to your question is to spend the rest of eternity in torment. Would you still want to know the answer?"

I thought about that for a minute while I was scratching my scarred up head. I said, "I don't get your drift."

"What I'm suggesting is this. Put your faith in God. Surrender to the word. Confess Jesus as your Savior. Trust in the Lord. Then, even if you lose your life, you'll gain something much greater. You'll gain life eternal and union with the Father. But, to be honest, I don't think anything will happen if you give up your search."

I felt something creepy and cold like a snake in my throat. I'd felt it before. In Vietnam, on patrol, when somebody told me Charlie's eyes were all over us. The VC were waiting for us and hoping we would make the wrong move. Let me tell you something about that feeling. I loved it. I hated it. I only felt it when the danger of bleeding and dying was nearby. I loved it, because I always took that feeling as my cue to ramp up my *"careful"* index. It gave me the edge I needed to save my bacon many a time.

Something was wrong here. I could feel it.

Then the professor started talking again. "I can see you're torn. I know that God is speaking to you right now. You'll feel better, you'll feel peace if you answer him right now. He's already suffered death for you. He came back to tell us that death is not the end. It's nothing to be feared. Take his hand. He'll be with you."

When he mentioned Jesus' death, something slammed into my brain. If I learned anything in the last few days, it was that there was a 2000-year-old confusion that was keeping us from knowing what the facts really were. Maybe this confusion was an accident. Maybe it was on purpose. Maybe it was the devil's work. I don't know. But for damn sure, there was a cover-up of some kind. And this bird wanted me to risk my life without having a gol' dang clue what the odds were. As far as I was concerned, we weren't getting anything useful out of this guy.

Kathleen broke in on the quiet that settled over our little group while Professor Ayers waited for me to come to the Lord. "Doctor Ayers. Matthew and Mark tell us that the men crucified with Jesus joined with the others in verbally abusing him. Luke says it was only one of them and the other actually spoke in Jesus' defense. Are these accounts reconcilable?"

His *"I'm-so-smart"* smile got *"I'm-so-smarter"* "Of course. Putting the accounts together, we see that the so-called penitent thief experienced an on-the-cross conversion. No doubt he had some prior knowledge of Jesus' teaching and was impressed by Jesus' behavior during the crucifixion process."

Woodrow piped in again. "If that's true, if this 'good thief' guy came to the Lord before he died, how come Mark and Matthew overlooked that little detail? Seems like something they'd want to talk about."

Professor Ayers cleared his throat again. "Perhaps the witnesses who failed to mention the conversion left the scene before it took place. Perhaps they were aware of it, but didn't deem it important enough to relate. This is another question that will be answered in due course."

I was thinking, *Perhaps somebody just made that shit up.* I could tell that Woodrow was thinking the same thing. We were both ready to go, but Kathleen had another question.

"So, at least in the beginning, they were both abusing Jesus?"

Professor Ayers nodded his bald head like he was getting tired and said, "Yes."

"Why would they do that? Why would two men who hated Rome to the extent that they took up arms and risked crucifixion be abusive to Jesus? If they were going to strike out at anyone with their dying efforts, why wouldn't it be the Romans whose regime they hated, who tyrannized their country, tortured them, and now inflicted the cruelest of executions on them? Why turn their hatred on an innocent man who was also a victim of Roman cruelty and injustice. I don't understand."

His expression never changed. His face might have got some more red in it. Maybe because his burrito was turning on him. Maybe because he was tired and put off by these questions. Anyway, he was starting to his feet.

"It's really quite simple. These were men of violence. They were committed to the liberation of Israel through hatred and bloodshed. Jesus was preaching liberation through love and tolerance. Obviously these men believed that Jesus' methods would result in a prolongation of Roman rule.

They viewed him as a quisling, and therefore, in their view, he was as guilty as the Romans. There is historical support for the proposition that these rebels were very capable of turning their violent attentions against their countrymen who disagreed with them. Now I hate to rush you off, but I have a lot to do before the spurious 'lost tomb' program airs."

Woodrow and Kathleen were talking at the same time, but I outtalked both of them. "What in Sam Hill is a quisling?" Dr. Ayers smiled like I was his pet dog. But he didn't answer me.

Kathleen was saying, "I'm sorry, Dr. Ayers. I just can't believe they were abusing him on the cross just because of a difference of opinion regarding methods!"

He was shoving us out of his office. "These are excellent questions and I want you to make another appointment some other time and we will delve into them to a greater depth. But I'm afraid I'm out of time for now. Thank you for coming. I look forward to our next visit. Good luck, Mr. Butane. Think about what I said. You'll see I'm right."

As we were being hustled out, Kathleen spoke up one more time. "Just tell me this Professor Ayers. Couldn't it be that they were abusing Jesus because they somehow blamed him for their predicament?"

"Of course not." And the door closed behind us. She sat down on one of the chairs in the reception area and started writing so fast and so hard I thought her pages might catch on fire. I don't know about Woodrow, but I was feeling like I'd just been to a magic show where you can see all the strings and levers. Some trick.

When we got back in the Dodge and headed north to Oklahoma City, there was music playing on the iPod that sounded familiar, but I couldn't put a name to it. Woodrow asked Kathleen if she knew what it was, but she was busy typing on her laptop. Without looking up, she said, "The theme from Pee Wee's Playhouse."

"Right, but do you know the name of the song?"

"No."

So I put in my two cents worth. "I didn't even know Pee Wee had a damn playhouse."

"The song is called 'Quiet Village' and *Pee Wee's Playhouse* was a TV show that came on Saturday mornings starring Pee Wee Herman. See there was a grown man that looked and acted like a kid and made a million dollars at it."

Okay. I saw a couple of movies on cable while I was on the road that starred that Pee Wee guy. They were funny, but I didn't know anything about his TV show. So I asked, "What's that got to do with anything?"

"Nothing. It's just what happened to be playing while we're leaving that Ayers flake behind. One of these days we'll get it figured out that we're not going to get shit that's helpful out of Texas." Of course, I had to agree with him. On the other hand, they do have a hell of a football team and some damn fine cheerleaders.

Monday, February 26, 2007, p.m.

Once we were out of Dallas and had a straight shot to Oklahoma City I asked Woodrow to put everything together and roll it out for me.

"Okay. Here's how I see it. Jesus and his disciples show up at the temple determined to stir up some kind of trouble. They start turning over tables, chairs, roughing people up, and just generally raising hell.

"There had to be some kind of security or police or somebody responsible for crowd control. The authorities wouldn't just stand around and let somebody get away with starting that kind of disturbance—especially if Mark is telling it straight. No doubt some people got beat up. It's possible somebody even got killed. If you ask me, this whole temple free-for-all could have been the reason for the arrest."

"Well, just to play devil's advocate, Woodrow, if you're right, how come they weren't arrested at the temple. There's a lot of preaching and stuff in the temple before the authorities catch up with Jesus and his disciples. What do you think about that?"

"Okay, Mr. Devil's Advocate. Now that you're admitted your true occupation, consider this. Could be somebody did get arrested there. Maybe our two guys?"

"Adds up for me. What do you say, Kathleen?"

"If that's where they were arrested, why wouldn't the Bible just come out and say so? Why would there be such a big secret about when they were arrested?"

Woodrow glanced in his rearview mirror. "I'm starting to develop a conspiratorial mind-set here. And my ESP tells me everybody's trying to put as much space as possible between Jesus and these other fellows. Even Dr. Ayers says Luke and John might have been careful in their word selection so they wouldn't rile up the Roman public reading their work. If Jesus started a ruckus that got these men arrested and executed, that could be embarrassing for early Christians trying to distance Jesus from the rebels, couldn't it, Kathleen?"

"It might be embarrassing for some."

"Okay. How embarrassing is it that there was bloodshed at the arrest? That's got to be a problem for people who say Jesus was the prince of peace."

"Not at all. Jesus didn't participate in the violence and he clearly disapproved of it."

"Not according to Mark he didn't. Not according to the earliest gospel we have."

"I'm not arguing with you Woodrow." Maybe she wasn't arguing because she was tired of it. Maybe she wasn't arguing because it was a losing point and she knew it.

Woodrow decided to get me in on the action. "Okay. Leon, what do you say? Is it plausible there was a riot when Jesus started the ball rolling at the temple?"

"Sure."

"Bloodshed?"

"Possible."

"Fatalities?"

"Maybe."

"Arrests?"

"If it was bad enough there probably was."

"You see any flaws in the scenario Kathleen?"

"I'll grant you it's one of a number of possibilities."

Woodrow didn't rub it in. We drove along quiet for a few minutes.

There was some real good highway music coming through the Dodge's sound system. "Who's this on the iPod, Woodrow?"

"This is 'Ghost Train' by a guy named Mark Cohn. Pretty good stuff, huh?"

"Yeah, it's pretty good." More silence. I decided to pitch Kathleen a slow one over the plate. "Hey Kathleen, what's a quisling, anyway?"

"It's a man's name. He was a Nazi puppet in Norway. After the war, he was executed. Some people use 'quisling' as a synonym for 'traitor'"

"So he would be the opposite of a freedom fighter."

"Yes."

"So Dr. Ayers thinks Jesus was a quisling?"

"No. His point was that the men crucified with Jesus might have seen him that way. That would explain why they were abusing him on the cross."

"You buy that Kathleen? Does it add up that these guys who were being put to death by Rome would pick on a guy being tortured and executed just like they were?"

She thought about it for a minute. "That does seem a little hard doesn't it? It isn't a very satisfying explanation, I'll admit. But I suppose it would be one explanation."

Woodrow spoke up again. "Maybe there is a better one. Maybe it's like you said, Kathleen. Maybe they blamed Jesus for getting them all in that jam in the first place."

She sounded just this side of fed-up. "How could that possibly be, Woodrow? How could anyone blame Jesus for the execution of these men?"

"Well, here's one scenario for you. Suppose these guys are in Jerusalem looking for a fight anyway. Suppose the word's out that a new guy is here to overthrow the Romans. Suppose there's a rumor that when this Jesus guy starts the ball rolling, the Jewish people will rise up, and God will step in on their side. The Romans will be defeated, and there'll be a new Jewish King on the throne. So, Jesus lights the fuse, and these guys jump in on his side. But it doesn't happen like they expect. There's no uprising. The fuse fizzles. God doesn't show up. Some insurgents get arrested and the others get scattered. Instead of being on the winning side, these poor sons-o'-bitches wind up crucified. Couldn't they blame Jesus for letting them believe he was the Messiah and then leading them to execution? Makes sense doesn't it?"

"I don't know, Woodrow. I'll have to think about it."

Woodrow eyeballed her in the rearview mirror. "You've already been thinking about it Kathleen. That's why you asked Dr. Ayers that question. Hell, your question is what got me started thinking about it. If the men on the cross were directing their hatred to Jesus, it had to be because they were blaming him. That's the best explanation I ever heard. And, like it or not, someday you're going to have to make up your mind about some of this stuff. In the meantime, everybody agrees that the Bible gives us two cases of violence leading up to the crucifixion: the temple and the arrest; those are the only two we know about."

For me, trying to figure out what really happened was like trying to see mud cats at the bottom of a mossed-over farm tank. I had to stop thinking about it for awhile. So we just drove on listening to music. Woodrow put on three versions back-to-back of *I Heard it through the Grapevine.* Marvin Gaye, Gladys Knight and the Pips and Credence Clearwater Revival. I like the Credence version best.

Anyway, my head was about to burst open, so Woodrow pulled over at the rest stop down by Davis, Oklahoma. Kathleen thought we was just going to get some natural relief, which we did. And she about pitched a hissy when Woodrow broke out the magic pipe.

At first she was just irritated because she thought it was for tobacco. But she isn't dumb. When Woodrow unrolled his baggie, she figured it out.

"You're not serious. That's marijuana isn't it?"

Woodrow gave her a wink as he was packing the bowl. "Yep."

"Well, you just stop it right now. That's illegal and I just won't be any part of that kind of activity."

I felt a little sheepish, but Woodrow just went right on with what he was doing.

"I'll tell you, Kathleen. There's no real fundamental difference between taking a toke or two and having a cold beer or a cocktail or a glass of wine. Except pot's better. To take a line from your friend Dr. Ayers, I could explain it all, but it would take too much time."

"For your information, Woodrow, there's nothing you could say that would get me to approve of the use of illicit drugs."

Believe me, I was in need of headache relief. But I thought maybe we should wait until we could drop Kathleen off at home and run to the car wash. I believed I could stand the pain that long. Woodrow stopped and sat looking at Kathleen over his head-rest. "I'll bet you never had a drink of alcohol in your whole life?"

"Never."

"Not even in college?"

"Never means never, Woodrow." He sat there real still just looking at her. After a second or two, she blushed and looked out her window.

"I bet you're the only one you know who can say that. I mean the only one you know over forty."

"I'm sure there are others."

"Bet you've never said a cuss word neither, have you?"

She didn't answer. "Just drive me home, then you two can do whatever you want. If you're going to go on with this pot party, let me out here, and I'll walk home."

Woodrow explained to her real patient like, "Look Kathleen, this here is purely for medicinal purposes. After all, if Buzz didn't have to bust out of the hospital like he done, he could've had a prescription for some stuff a lot stronger and more habit forming than pot."

He pulled a copy of a magazine article out of the Dodge's cubby hole and handed it to her. "Take a look at this. It's the findings of a bunch of bona fide scientific research fellas proving that pot is a for real pain treatment with fewer side effects than other stuff that some doctors prescribe." Woodrow sounded like a lawyer making a jury pitch, "Now, Miss Wister, if you're cold enough to come between an injured man and his badly needed pain relief, then by God you can just start walking."

She chewed on her lower lip for a second. "Well, if legitimate researchers say it has beneficial effects and if it's truly for medicinal purposes, maybe it's okay for now. Just this one time. I really don't want to see Leon in pain. But you better get to a doctor and get some legal medicine." As Woodrow put a match to the bowl and was taking a big hit she said, "Hey, wait a minute. Maybe it's okay for Leon to take some. For medicinal purposes. But that doesn't give you a license to smoke an illegal drug."

Woodrow peered over at her while he was holding in his toke to be sure he was getting all the weed had to offer. Then he let it out real slow. Smiling. "Kathleen, let me ask you something. You believe in the Golden Rule?"

"Of course."

He nodded. "Say it for me."

She said, real huffy like, "Do unto others as you would have them do unto you."

He passed me the pipe, I got over my guilty feeling and took it. "There you go. I'm just doing by Buzz here as I'd want him to do by me. See, if I was the one with brain damage and needed some sweet weed to ease the pain, I damn sure wouldn't want to get high alone. I'd want somebody tender hearted to share these mellow moments with me." He took the pipe back from me and took another hit. Without letting it out, he said, "Hell Kathleen. I'm just doing my Christian duty here."

Kathleen started saying something about the sin of sacrilege when Woodrow cut her off. "I got a proverb for you Kathleen. Are you ready? You listen too Buzz, because it's real profound and it's right up your alley. Are you ready? It's an Arab proverb, and it goes like this: 'The beauty of the basil leaf is not the least disturbed despite the filthy beetle bug that crawls across its face."

I just had to say, "Well holy cow, Woodrow! That was deep. I don't have any idea what the hell that means. But it sure is deep. What does it mean, anyway?"

"I don't know, Buzz. It's probably over both our heads. I guess the Arabs get it. I'm thinking if you say it over and over again and think about it long enough, maybe you can reach Nirvana. I come closer to believing it when I'm high. What do you say Kathleen?"

Kathleen just rolled her eyes. "Give me a break."

We put the pipe away and headed the Dodge north again. Something by Duke Ellington called *The Mooch* was playing on the iPod. When I looked in the backseat to tell Kathleen something, I was surprised to see her crying real soft like. I wanted to ask what was wrong, but I was pretty sure I knew what it was.

Kathleen had been a good girl her whole life. She got raised up believing the Bible and looking up to all these hotshot preacher guys. She probably had some notion that she was going to meet somebody who was faithful like she was, and she and her husband would be in some kind of—I don't know—holy matrimony or something. Now here she was: no kids; divorced; wondering whether she was wrong about everything; motoring north on I-35 in a Dodge with a couple of potheads. No wonder she was crying to herself. I developed a half-ass heartache being ashamed that Woodrow and I was adding to the load she had to carry.

I tried to think of something that might cheer her up when a idea came shining through my window. "Well look here, Woodrow. The moon's getting full. What d'ya say? Weloka is just a little bit off the highway. Let's drive over to the Knob." Nehi Knob is on the highest rise of ground in Shawnee County. You can see the lights of Weloka and Oklahoma City from there, and when the full moon's rising, you can see it reflecting off Weloka Lake. It's about as pretty a spot to think about bugs and basil leaves as any place I know.

Kathleen wasn't interested. "Listen. I really don't have time for any side trips. I need to get home. There's a lot that needs to go in tomorrow's blog." So I guess technically we kidnapped her, because we drove her over to Nehi Knob whether she wanted to go or not.

When we got to "The Knob," the temperature, according to the Dodge thermometer, was twenty-nine degrees—Fahrenheit that is. We don't believe in that Celsius, metric horseshit.

We all bundled up and stepped out into the cold. All three of us climbed up on the hood of the Dodge. I was glad to see Kathleen being such a good sport about being kidnapped like she was.

She looked at me all sad eyed and asked, "Are you getting scared, Leon?"

I didn't answer. Not right then anyway. It's hard to be scared when you're sitting out in the moonlight high with a beautiful woman and your best friend. Then I realized that maybe I was a little bit scared.

"You know what's going to happen here this summer Kathleen? I mean right here where we're sitting? There's going to be whippoorwills singing all around this spot. There's going to be lightning bugs. You'll be able to see ripples on the lake where fish are coming up to the surface. What scares me is the idea that everything may be going on without me ever hearing or seeing it again. I mean, summer's going to be here whether I'm alive or not. I know it's selfish, but the thought that everything will just keep rolling and all you people will just go on living your lives without me well ... well that's what scares me."

Little clouds of frost came off her lips when she talked. "You think maybe you might be in a place even more beautiful than this?"

When I laughed, my breath blew out like a big steam leak. "Kathleen, there isn't any place more beautiful than this—at least not as far as Leon Butane is concerned."

Kathleen wasn't satisfied. "No really Leon. Do you believe in heaven? Are you afraid of hell? What do you think happens when we die?"

I shivered a little bit when she asked me that probably 'cause I was cold. I don't know.

"Well, the Bible says there's a heaven and hell. I guess I believe in 'em. I suppose the best of us get to heaven and the rest of us have to take what comes. Whatever hell is, I just hope it ain't as bad as everybody says. I mean if it is a lake of fire, I sure hope you get numb after awhile 'cause I hate getting burned and I'm afraid that's where I'll wind up if I can't figure out how to get righteous." I sat there for a minute being surprised that me and Woodrow never talked about this before as close as we was. I should know what he thought about, you know, the afterlife. "What about it, Woodrow? What do you think happens?"

"I think everything in the universe tries to hold itself together as long as it can. A frog thinks the most important thing in the world is being a frog. Raindrops tend to stay raindrops 'til they fall into the ocean. Then they blend in with everything else that used to be a raindrop. Whatever it is next, that's the most important thing."

"Are you talking about reincarnation Woodrow? Are you saying raindrops come back as frogs and frogs might come back as people? Is that what you're saying?"

He laughed out a couple of frosty clouds. "I don't know how it works, Buzz. I suppose we could be a couple of recycled frogs or raindrops of crucified thieves or sponges. Whatever. Hell, I suppose we could turn into angels when we die. Truth is, nobody knows for sure and any preacher who says he does is full of shit. All I can say for sure is there's some kind of logic to it and none of us has enough information to know how the pieces fit together. All I can say for sure is that whatever happens when you die it's bound to make sense on some level. Everything does."

Kathleen pulled her collar up around her ears. "I feel sorry for you, Woodrow. It must be lonely to think like that."

"Nope. In the first place, I believe I'm in good company. We're in good company. We're all headed to the same place—wherever that may be. On top of that, I don't have any subconscious suspicion that I'm holding on to a helium balloon with a smiley face drawn on it. Whatever happens, I'll just tag along with Buzz here."

Kathleen started shivering, so we figured we better put her in the Dodge so she could get warm.

We didn't talk much the rest of the way home. Funny. I was calling Kathleen's house *home*. As we pulled into the driveway, we were listening to some music that sort of got me all choked up because it was real beautiful. I asked Woodrow what was playing on the iPod.

"It's called *My Wife with Champagne Shoulders*."

Tuesday, February 27, 2007, a.m.

At first, I didn't know where I was. I thought it was in Mexico, because there were lots of people leading donkeys around and there were goats and women carrying baskets full of bread and produce and stuff on their heads. I was standing on a rocky hillside trying to get my bearings. After a second or two, I knew I wasn't in Mexico, because lots of the men were wearing turbans or shawl things on their heads and they all had beards. Everybody was walking uphill to a walled up city, and as I looked closer, I thought maybe I was on a movie set, 'cause there was a couple of guys on horses that looked like they was playing a part in a Spartacus epic.

I could tell by the way everybody's clothes were blowing that it was really windy. But I couldn't feel anything. I thought I'd go take a look inside the city, but I was in a kind of invisible bubble or something and couldn't get it to go nowhere. That's when I started suspecting I was dreaming or having another vision or a flashback or something. Whatever it was, I was looking at Jerusalem in the time of Jesus. I started straining real hard to see what was going on up closer to the gates. I could see a group of people— maybe twenty or thirty of them—waving tree branches in the air. There were three or four women with tambourines. I could see a fella sitting on a donkey in the middle of them. I couldn't see his face as they were moving away from me into the city. I was thinking *Holy Shit! That's Jesus H. Christ himself over there riding on that jackass.* I sure wanted to run up and take a look. How many chances are you going to get to see the real Jesus? But I couldn't move, because I was trapped. I was thinking, *goddamn this bubble.* Then an explosion woke me up.

It was a brick crashing through Kathleen's front room window. There it was, laying on her carpet surrounded by sharp pieces of busted glass, a white-looking brick. Somebody had written *"repent"* on it in big black letters with a magic marker. Kathleen was standing there in her robe looking at that brick with her mouth open. Once we made sure she was okay, Woodrow and I charged outside to see if we could get a bead on whoever had done it. They were long gone, the chickenshits.

We came back inside and stood in Kathleen's living room feeling useless as goats at a baby shower. She was sitting on her couch crying to herself.

She reached in the pocket of her robe and come out with a Kleenex and put it up to her nose. "I've tried to keep this house just like it was when Mother and Dad were here. It was just so …." She choked up.

I took a good look around for the first time trying to see it like she did. There weren't a lot of knickknacks around, mostly pictures and trophies Kathleen won when she was growing up; softball, track, basketball, cheer-leading. Stuff like that.

Seeing her sitting there crying on the couch in front of that broken window was almost too much for me. I'd be the first to tell you that I'm no expert in the way women think, but nobody likes to have their house targeted by some cowardly jerk aiming to do something damaging and hurtful. I was pretty broke up when my house burned down. But I wasn't quite as sentimental about my digs as Kathleen was about this place.

I tried to think of something helpful to say. "Hell, darlin', it's only glass. Woodrow and I can get that fixed up for you in nothing flat. You'll never even know it happened."

She looked up at me all red-eyed and said, "It's not just glass. It's a window."

Well, that caught me plumb off guard. Soon as she said it I could see she was right. There can be a hell of a lot of difference between a plain old piece of glass and a window. She kept talking—more to herself than me.

"I used to watch this window when I was playing outside to see if my parents were watching me. Dad would be standing here with his arm around Mom's shoulders. Even today, when I pull up in the driveway, I expect to see Mother and Dad there. Mom and I stood at this window and watched cardinals build a nest in the tree across the street."

I just sat there feeling bad and being helpless. She said, "I know it's silly, but when I was a little girl, I believed there was a kind of memory in this glass, a kind of magic that could soak up the glances and smiles that passed through it." That made me really sorry about that *"It's only glass"* remark.

I wanted to put my arms around her and try to make everything all right. But I wasn't sure how she'd take it. So I just kept sitting there feeling useless. I decided the only constructive thing I could do was get pissed off. I picked up the brick and looked it over real good. I've never thought of a brick as being something that ought to be ashamed of itself. But this one should. There it was all hard and stupid with that word *repent* wrote on it.

Of course the window could be replaced with new glass. But the replacement wouldn't have anything to do with Kathleen's childhood and wouldn't have any connection to her mother and dad. I was having a hard time putting this busted window somewhere on the "bad" scale. Of course it was bad. But in Nam, I'd seen whole villages rounded up and told to leave their huts, fields, animals, and cemeteries. Just get out. *Dee dee mau.* They carried whatever they could and left homes that maybe their families had lived in hundreds of years. That shit's pretty high on the "bad" scale. But when we made them do it, we thought we was helping 'em. We was trying to keep them from getting caught in a shit storm. We figured "homeless" was lower than "dead" or "crippled up" on the "bad" scale. At the time, it made sense. So part of me was looking at the bright side of Kathleen's busted window. I mean, hell, look at me. The sons of bitches burned my whole gol' dang house down. I'd have been happy if they'd just busted out my window.

But just the same, and I know it isn't logical, I felt worse watching Kathleen sitting there crying over those glass slivers than I did watching those Vietnamese folks getting kicked out of their homes. Anybody who tried to put up some kind of fight to stop us from doing it—well, we just couldn't allow it. So we moved them. There's got to be something wrong with thinking like that. I knew there was something wrong with it. There's probably something racist about it if you get right down to it. But you know what they say. You can't help your feelings.

Anyway, you can't stand around crying all day. Somebody had to clean up the busted pieces. So I told Kathleen, "Listen, I know you feel awful, but you got to get yourself together and go pack some stuff." She sat there blinking at me. "Kathleen, it's going to get down in the twenties tonight and it'll be real cold in here. We could probably bundle up and build fires in some of these fireplaces. But it would be better if we go someplace where we can stay warm." I didn't figure we could get a measurement and a piece of glass cut to fit in one day. We'd be lucky to get it done in two days or three. So we'd just have to change our headquarters for now.

Woodrow was already on the phone arranging for somebody to come out and start the job. Kathleen finally snapped out of it and went to get herself ready to go. I told her to pack for a week. "I suppose you better call and report this to the police."

She was moving real slow and sad down the hall to her room. She spoke without turning around to look at me. "I'll call from my room."

We decided to drive over to Jimmy's Egg for breakfast. One reason we love Jimmy's Egg is because you can decide for yourself where you want to sit. If it's full, you just wait your turn and take your place when somebody leaves. If it ain't full, you sit where you want. And here's a bonus. They make a damn fine omelet. Not as good as mine, of course, but pretty good just the same.

TAPE 14

We got all set up with coffee for Woodrow and me and hot tea for Kathleen. I asked, "What do you reckon you're supposed to repent of, Kathleen?"

"I don't know, Leon. Seems like the only thing I'm doing these days is repent. I'm repenting for drifting away from God. And I'm repenting for getting involved with you two and all the craziness you're involved in."

Really, I'm not the thin-skinned sort, but that last comment hurt my feelings. I probably sounded flustered. "Well I'm sorry as hell for all the trouble we caused you. But you just keep one thing in mind sister. It was you that came looking for us."

It got real quiet at the table. She didn't act like she heard a word I said. I started to say something else, but Woodrow gave me the sign to keep quiet.

Then he started talking. "Look Kathleen. I can't say one way or the other whether you're doing some legitimate soul searching or just feeling sorry for yourself. I can't say whether you've been as bad a gal as you seem to think you've been. Maybe you don't either. What we do know is that for some reason, you've been pitched into the same boat we're in. Could be you volunteered. Could be you were drafted. I'll be honest. If we've made any progress, it's because of you. Now I don't know what's going to happen from here on out, but you need to snap out of this funk you're in and help us solve this problem. However, it turns out, you can go on your way when it's over. That's just my opinion."

She never even looked up from her teacup. She just took a deep breath. "I guess I should try to look at the bright side. Surely there is one here somewhere." She shivered and looked at her watch. "I need to get someplace that has wireless access so I can see what's going on with the blog." Looked to us like the subject was closed for that minute. I figured a way we could kill two birds with one stone. We could get her to some wireless access and see an old friend at the same time.

We have a buddy named Le. He's a Vietnamese guy who opened a coffee shop over in Edmond. We figured his place wasn't too far out of the way, so we took her there.

She got right to work on her laptop. Me and Woodrow had some designer coffee and got busy shooting the bull with Le. Let me tell you a thing or two about Le. He was just a kid when the communists overran South Vietnam. He had kinfolks that fought on our side, so his family was somewhere on the Communists' shit list. He and his family had to sneak out of Vietnam on a boat. I guess the boat was supposed to be big enough for sixty folks and more than a hundred showed up to escape. They were at sea for more than twenty days. The last four, they didn't have any food or water. There was another boat that had some more of his kinfolks on it. They got lost. Nobody knows what happened to them.

Anyway, a cool thing about Le is how much he loves this country. Me and Woodrow and some of the guys from the Tolosa Gold were at the federal courthouse in Oklahoma City when Le took the oath to be a citizen. He's sort of a religious half-breed. He was raised up Buddhist but converted to be a Catholic so he could marry his sweetheart. Her family's Catholic, and she wouldn't marry Le unless he changed over.

Le says he gets up every morning and thanks God he's got water running in his house. I guess there was a time he had to haul up the family's drinking water in buckets. He thanks God he's got a car that will start and carry him over to his shop. At work, he thanks God for all his customers. He feels like most of them are his friends. He thanks God he's making a good living. He thanks God for his health, for his family's health and so on. Le is the God-thankingest guy I know. He's probably the happiest too. Sometimes he makes me wish I was a Buddhist/Christian half-breed.

Le filled our cups again and took a seat at our table. He must have ESP or something, because he said right away, "You three look like travelers on a hard path."

"And a hard path it is, Le. Looks like I might be lining up to kick the bucket here in a few days."

"Kick the bucket? This means trouble of some kind?" For a second there, Woodrow and I were at a loss. Then we laughed. We could see how Le wasn't following. What the hell does bucket kicking have to do with dying anyway? So I explained the whole thing.

Le looked real thoughtful and said, "Approach thy grave as one who wraps the drapery of his couch about him and lies down to pleasant dreams."

I was knocked back for a second. "Holy smokes, Le, that was beautiful. Did you read that in the Bible or something?"

"No. It's something I memorized from a class I took when I got to America. It's from a poem." It sure made my *kick the bucket* crack sound crude.

I meant what I said, though. What Le said about that drapery deal was beautiful no matter where it came from. But it sure as hell isn't practical. Most of the people I've seen die were killed in war. And I didn't see any of them looking like they were headed for pleasant dreams. Of course, I didn't see any of them working on a for-sure two-week deadline neither. To tell the truth, no matter what I might say to Kathleen, I was a little scared. But way down deep, I just couldn't make myself believe I was getting close to the end. I expected to find a way out. Naturally I know everybody's time runs out someday. I just couldn't see mine running out like this.

About that time, Kathleen took a real sharp breath and took her fingers off her computer.

Woodrow raised an eyebrow. "What's up?"

"It looks like Ernest Bidding has come up with a proposal that might work. He wants us to form a corporation that would own all the rights to our meeting. He'd own 75% of the stock and you would own 25%. We'll have a 'get acquainted' sit down to make sure all the loose ends get worked out.

So I asked Kathleen, "If I get twenty-five percent and he gets seventy-five, what's your cut?"

She got this real cold look on her face. "I'm not expecting a cut." Then she said sarcastic like. "I'm going to do this because I gave you my word I'd help you through to the end."

There I was getting my feelings hurt again. She was helping me just because she gave her word. Nothing more to it. No feelings or nothing. What the hell was I thinking, anyway. I decided I probably wouldn't see any cash either.

Kathleen said, "Your televised meeting with Ernest Bidding will be next

Sunday, March 4. We'll have the 'get-acquainted' session on Saturday. He says you shouldn't worry about a thing. He says the Holy Spirit is going to free you from the grip of this evil puppet. When you're released, he wants you to be ready to give your testimony to the whole world about the saving power of Christ Jesus." The way she said it made me think she didn't believe a word of it.

"Great! I'm looking forward to it. Then you can go your way and we can put this whole snafu behind us." That was bullshit. I wasn't looking forward to it at all, and I don't know anything about giving testimony to the world.

She sat there frowning into her teacup. She was just getting ready to turn her computer off when a message popped up on her email. Her eyes brightened as she read. "Well, this is good news. Dr. Barry Soames of Claremont University is a noted authority on the history of the Holy Land during the Roman rule. If there's anybody who has a handle on any historical documents that would help us, he does. He is going to talk to us by speakerphone tomorrow noon. That's ten o'clock his time."

"So what exactly can Dr Soames do for us?"

"I don't know. Maybe nothing. But there are some documents that help shed light on some of the events that occurred in Judea during Jesus' life."

"You mean there are papers that mention Jesus that aren't part of the Bible?"

"Yes. There is an ancient Jewish historian named Josephus who covers a lot of the political goings on throughout Jewish history."

I remembered Dr. Ayers said something about him. "So who is this Josephus fella?"

"He was a Jewish commander during the anti-Roman rebellion of AD 66. He switched sides, and after Jerusalem fell, he moved to Rome where he wrote about the history of the Jewish people and the events leading up to and during the revolt. He makes a passing reference to Jesus. I really don't know what else he wrote that might be helpful. Then there are the Dead Sea Scrolls. I don't think they mention Jesus, but there might be something useful there. There may be other documents that I haven't heard about. Anyway, Dr. Soames will be able to tell us if there's anything extrabiblical that sheds light on our problem."

After explaining all that, Kathleen turned off her computer, and we packed up and headed back to the Dodge.

When we left Le's, there was a piece of shit green '99 Camaro with a couple of people in it sitting in the parking lot a few spaces down from the Dodge. I couldn't see their faces, but the driver stuck an arm full of tattoos out the window and flipped ashes off his cigarette. I thought I'd seen that same car a couple of times in the last few days. Once driving down Kathleen's street and then again behind us in traffic this morning.

Sure enough, when we pulled out of the parking lot, the Camaro waited for us to get through the light, then he pulled out onto Santa Fe and followed.

Woodrow and Kathleen were discussing how important it was for us to stick together until everything got cleaned up. I was keeping my eye on that Camaro. After a few minutes, I lost sight of it. But when we got on I-35, there it was, about a half dozen car lengths behind us. I pointed it out to Woodrow.

"Have you seen that car before?"

He eyeballed it in his rearview mirror and shook his wooly head. "Nope."

"Well, I've seen it in Kathleen's neighborhood. It didn't look like it belonged, but, hell how would I know for sure. But it's been following us since we left Le's." Woodrow took another real close look in his rearview mirror.

"You don't reckon these are the people that heaved that brick through Kathleen's window do you?"

I was about to say, "I don't know," when Kathleen's phone rang. It was the Oklahoma City police wanting to talk to her about the vandalism at her house. They wanted to send somebody out to get a statement. She said she was on her way out of town. They were kind of pushy about seeing the house and damage. She said okay. Since all three of us were in the Dodge together, Woodrow and I didn't have any choice but to go along. She said the police wanted her at the house at one o'clock. We could drop her off and use the time to go to the bookstore and get Dr. Soames' book for a preview of what he had to say.

Tuesday, February 27, 2007, p.m.

By the time we got back to Kathleen's there was a police cruiser sitting out front. I didn't figure we needed to invite the officers into an investigation about unsolved arsons and church riots. So we dropped Kathleen off and told her to call us when she was done with the law enforcement fellas.

Our friends in the Camaro were nowhere to be seen. The boys in blue gave Woodrow and me a close eyeballing when I opened the door and let Kathleen out of the truck. We just gave them a smile and a wave as we idled on down the street trying to do the speed limit and look respectable. We didn't act at all like we had contraband hid in Woodrow's cubby hole.

I guess their investigation was pretty thorough, as they had to run through the list of potential cranks who had reason to be pissed off at Kathleen. You know, you can drive a truck for thirty years and count on one hand the number of people that might have a grudge. But work a miracle or two and let the media put a spot light on your ass, or put out a religious blog for a couple of years and watch the weirdoes crawl out of the gol' dang woodwork.

Barnes and Noble didn't have Dr. Soames' book in stock. We could have gone over to the library to have a look. But, instead, we decided this would be a good time for a massage. Teddy's sister's massage business is in a house in a private residence. When we pulled up, Teddy was pulling a trash can out to the curb. We drove up the driveway, and by the time Teddy boy recognized me, the Dodge was between him and the house. He put his hand in his pocket and walked up to us grinning.

"Well, well. If it isn't Leon Butane. Glad you're here buddy. Saves me the trouble of looking you up. I heard about your visit to ditzy little Tonya." He stopped about six feet away from us. "Who's your friend, Leon?"

"This here's Woodrow. You don't need to worry about him. He's just here to call you an ambulance if you need one." Teddy laughed. "Tell me why I'd need an ambulance, Leon. You're not suggesting you're here to do me some harm, are you? Surely you're not dumb enough to give me an excuse to blow your fuckin' head off." He laughed again.

Well, it's like this, Teddy. If you mind your manners and do as you're told, I won't pull that pretty ear stud of yours through your goddamn ear lobe after I knock out a couple of your teeth."

He got a snarly look on his face. "Well Woodrow, you better put some distance between you and your friend Leon, 'cause he's liable to get shot any second."

Woodrow put his hand in the pocket of his overalls. Teddy pulled a revolver half-way out of his pocket. I was sure things were headed to a bad place and I decided to give Teddy one last chance to do the right thing.

"Look, Teddy. Maybe you can't help it that you're a chickenshit liar. You was probably raised bad. Maybe you don't know no better than to bully women and little girls. Lucky for you, I'm the kind of guy who will give a fella the benefit of the doubt. So here's the deal. First, I want you to call up Channel Nine and tell them what you said about me praying to the devil is bullshit. Then, I want you to promise that if you ever bully Tonya or Iris again, I have permission to look you up and stomp a mud hole in the middle of your dumb ass.

He got real red in the face. "You got to the count of five to get your ass out of here or you won't be needing a fucking ambulance, you'll be needing a Hearse. And you, Woodrow, let me see your hands."

Woodrow came out of his pocket with another keychain with a crystal on it—like the one he gave Iris. Teddy snorted.

"You got to five. One…"

"So I guess you're gonna be stubborn and not take the way out I offered you."

"Two…"

"Well, I guess we better go Woodrow." Woodrow stayed put and I took a couple of steps toward the Dodge. Teddy hadn't thought of that. With one moving and the other standing still, he had to be looking at one of us or the other. Woodrow timed his throw perfect. The crystal caught Teddy just under his right eye. His reflexes got the best of him. Both hands shot up to cover the hurt spot. Before he could get back to his revolver, Woodrow had him on the ground and disarmed. Woodrow stood up and stepped back out of the way. Teddy got up looking at Woodrow real hateful. "You dumb fuck. You could have put my eye out."

"Yeah. I missed. Now, you want to say something to Buzz Butane man to man?"

"You bet. I'd like to tell him …" He shot a short amateur-looking jab that glanced off my shoulder. I answered with a bona fide Oklahoma haymaker, and Teddy landed on the seat of his pants with both hands covering his mouth. Blood was dripping through his fingers. "Goddamn it, you made me swallow one of my teeth."

"Only one? I guess I'm getting old." I reached down and took hold of his earring. He tried to fight but I gave the ring a yank. He yowled like a baby and I was disappointed the earring didn't pull through. I guess his ear lobe is the toughest thing about old Teddy. He started trying to crawl away, but I caught him.

This time, I got his earring all the way out. He rolled around on the ground sputtering and bleeding.

"You still owe me a tooth, Teddy. I'm warning you. Do what's right or I'll come back and collect. Ask Woodrow here. I don't make threats."

He made a kind of whimpery sounding threat. "Next time I see you son-of-a-bitches, you won't have a chance. I'll just start shooting."

"Fine, dipshit. Then you won't see us 'til we've already taken your pop gun away from you."

Woodrow took the bullets out of Teddy's revolver and put them in his overalls. He dropped the revolver in the trash can.

As we walked back to the Dodge, I stopped to watch Teddy stumble up to his feet, one hand over his bleeding mouth and one over his bleeding ear. "Hey Teddy. You can keep the keychain. It's good luck. Woodrow's always got several of 'em on him to pass out to folks who need some luck. So long." Teddy was heading back into the Nirvana Massage house as we drove away.

When Kathleen got done with her law enforcement buddies, she called us. There was another post from Pinocchio on her blog.

Personally, I was about sick of hearing from Pinocchio. "Okay. What does the little freak have to say this time?"

"He says to follow the money."

"What money?"

"That's all I know. He's says to follow the money." I looked at Woodrow and he shrugged.

"Well, that sounds like the best advice he's given us so far. It's hard to go wrong if you follow the money." I figured we'd just have to get to the bottom of that one later.

We headed to Kathleen's house. On the way, I was looking out for that Camaro. I was hoping they had lost interest.

By the time we got to her house, it was getting dark. We decided we'd have supper at the Weloka Diner and talk over what we were going to do next. But first we needed gas. So we filled up at the Love's Country Store on Choctaw Road.

While Woodrow was pumping the gas, I went in to pay for the fuel and get Kathleen some water. I came out of the truck stop and got into the Dodge on the passenger side like always. As soon as I got in, I saw this guy with his hand up in the crack between Woodrow's headrest and the seat. I looked real quick and I saw this skin-headed dude sitting there with a hog-leg stuck against Woodrow's neck. The skinhead's arm had dragon tattoos all over it, like painted pictures crawling up his neck. He was grinning at me with a

mouth full of bad teeth. His voice was high and scratchy and was a good fit
for his shrimpy little body.

He said, "Get on in miracle worker. We're going to take us a little drive."
Then he jammed the barrel of his Glock into the back of Woodrow's neck
and said, "Follow that Camaro." As Woodrow was backing out, I checked
to see how Kathleen was. She was sitting in the dark backseat with her
hands in her lap chewing on her lower lip.

I asked tattoo boy, "What the hell is all this about?"

"Well hell. There's no Monday night football on, so I thought maybe
you'd like to come over to the house and show us some of your magic
tricks. Then, I got a trick or two of my own that I'd like to show you
guys." He started petting Kathleen's leg with his right hand that had a
Jolly Roger tattoo on the back of it. "How about it sister? You seen all the
miracle worker's tricks? You seen him raise the dead? By the time you seen
some of the tricks I can do, you'll forget all about these two old-timers
here."

The Camaro left the parking lot just ahead of us. Woodrow fell in
behind. All we could make out about the driver of that Camaro was some
stringy blond hair.

So we were back on I-40 headed east. I said, "Okay skinhead, what is
it you want?"

He gave me that snaggle-toothed grin again. "Well, the first thing I
want is to shave all y'all's heads. Just because of that 'skinhead' remark.
Maybe then you'll be a little more careful about your tone and your choice
of words when you talk to me. See, when you first got into the truck, I
hadn't decided for sure what to do with you all. I just figured to be led by
the spirit, don't you know. So here you up and call me a skinhead—which is
true—and I get me an idea where to start." He laughed a kind of snickering
"snee-hee" laugh and poked Woodrow's neck again while he kept rubbing
Kathleen's leg.

He went on talking. "Of course this head-shaving deal ain't no burden
on your dumb ass, because somebody else done beat me to it. But old
bushy-head here and this little darlin' of yours, I reckon they'll be asking
you to watch your mouth, because, hell, who knows where the Spirit will
move me next?" He leered over it Kathleen and reached up to slide his
fingers through her hair.

She pulled away and said, "Your nails are filthy." And they was. His
whole hands was filthy, like he'd just finished working on his car and didn't

want to waste any energy washing up. His eyes got real big. Like he was acting surprised.

"Did the lady say my nails is filthy? Well you know by God she's right. And what's this here? Is the spirit moving me again? Fuckin' A! The Spirit's telling me the lady's nails is too long and one of 'em's got to go. And the Spirit says if she shoots her smart-ass mouth off again, she might lose some more." He took one of his dirty paws and pulled the hair back from Kathleen's ear and whispered loud enough for Woodrow and me to hear. "After I shave your head, darlin', I'll probably have to do an inspection to see if there's anything else needs trimmin'."

Well that was all I could stand. I just had to shoot my mouth off again. "Let me tell you something you skinny little coloring-book–looking freak. You do anything to hurt this lady—or even offend her with another foul-mouthed insult, I'll cut your dick off if I got to come back from the dead to do it."

His eyes got real big again. "Amputated dicks and death? Is that what the spirit's telling me?" He gave us another dose of his little faggot sounding laugh. "Keep talking Mr. Big-Shot Butane, because the Spirit's damn sure speaking through your dumb shit pie hole tonight."

Then Woodrow spoke up. "Now let's calm down and see if we can figure how to get everybody what they want so our friend here in the backseat don't have to do no head shavin' or nail pullin' or stuff like that." Woodrow looked into his rearview mirror to eyeball the tattoo guy. "You got the gun mister, which says you get to do the talking. So tell us what it is you want."

Tattoo man sat back in his seat smiling. "That's good, Wooley. Let's get ass hole Butane calmed down so we can have an intelligent conversation. Looks to me like he's the only one here that's getting emotional. You and the lady and me are calm. It's our miracle-working turd in the front seat that's all bent out of shape. So you're right, Wooley. Let's get him calmed down so we can talk like grown-ups" Then he did that "snee-hee" laugh again. "Let's start with you. What do you want, Wooley?"

I was wondering how far we were going to have to follow that Camaro. It looked to me like it was weaving a little bit, and I was hoping it might rouse the curiosity of a highway patrolman. Something encouraging might happen if there was cops on the scene. But there wasn't any troopers right there at that moment. We was just going to have to find a way to deal with this on our own—maneuver according to circumstances.

So Woodrow said, "Well, the first thing I want is to know what to call you."

"Okay, Wooley. I don't give a shit what your name is. I'm going to call you Wooley. And you can call me Carl. And this lady here, I'm going to call her Angel. And you…"—he pointed the Glock at my head—"I'm going to call you Butthole. What do you think about that, Butthole?" I didn't say anything. "That's a good, Butthole. Learned to keep your fucking mouth shut. Now, the slut in front of us in the Camaro, when we're all together, we'll call her Queenie. Now that Wooley here has got his first wish, what else you want?"

Woodrow checked him out in the rearview mirror again. "Well, Carl, I'd like to know what you want from us so we can help you get it and everybody can get on down the road."

"Well I got to tell you, Wooley. The only thing I love more than torture and fucking is money. So I guess what we're looking for is a trifecta here. By the time this is all over with, I'm going to be a real happy camper." He bolted forward in his seat. "Watch it, Wooley. She's going to turn off up here if she don't have her head up her ass."

The Camaro's right signal light came on, and we got off I-40 on Anderson Road. Carl kept up a solid line of bullshit as we drove south across Highway Nine and out into the boonies. I remember doing some speed, maybe a lot of speed, back in my hippie days. So I know what a speed freak looks and sounds like. And our boy Carl here was looking, walking, and quacking like a speed freak.

So I thought I'd ask. "How long has it been since you had any sleep, Carl?" He snarled like a pissed-off house cat with asthma.

"Shut the fuck up, Butthole. I've decided that every time you open your mouth you dig yourself deeper into a hole. So do us both a favor and don't interrupt while I'm trying to have an intelligent conversation with Angel and Wooley here."

I couldn't help it. "Hey Carl. You know what an oxymoron is?"

"Huh? What the fuck you talking about?"

"An oxymoron. You were talking about having an intelligent conversation, and I just wondered if you knew what an oxymoron is?" It seemed like a bomb went off, but it was only Carl cracking me upside the head with the butt of his Glock. My ears was ringing so I couldn't hear what he was saying. But whatever it was, it was loud. I could feel Kathleen passing something soft up to me. A Kleenex. I put it against the side of my head to soak up the little bit of blood that Carl knocked out of me. The tissue felt good. Smelled good too.

The ringing in my ears was slacking off and I could hear Carl snarling something about "Who's the fucking moron now, moron?"

You probably figured out by now that my language is pretty salty. Bad manners. And, hell, I was pissed off at that little tattooed speed freak, because he was hiding behind an automatic weapon so he could talk tough to better men than he was. But what was really sending me over the edge was him treating Kathleen the way he was. I could see Woodrow working his jaw, so I knew he was pissed off same as me. I don't know if Carl knew it or not, but he was sitting in the club cab of a Dodge full of war heroes. I had my mind made up that before the night was over, me and Woodrow was going to kick Carl's scrawny little inked-up ass. Kick it good.

The Camaro made a right onto a muddy little road that turned out to be a driveway leading to a trailer house. There was a half-starved–looking pit bull that hit the end of a chain locked around a tree. He was barking and snapping like something out of a nightmare. When we got out, Carl, pointed his weapon at Kathleen and had us all standing out there in the moonlight while Queenie unlocked the trailer door.

When we stepped into the trailer, we got our first good look at Queenie. She was a bony little gal wearing jeans that came down below her pointy hip joints. Her tube top left her middle exposed. She damn sure didn't look dressed for winter weather. I'd guess this is the kind of shit she wears all the time. She had ear studs up and down both ears and silver BBs in her nose, a tiny barbell in her eyebrow, a butterfly tattoo on her flat little chest, and I'm guessing there were piercings and tattoos in places we couldn't see and didn't want to.

Queenie lined up three vinyl chairs in the ratty tobacco-smelling living room. Empty beer cans and Doritos sacks was all over the place. There must've been twenty ashtrays in that dump, and they was all full. Carl handed Queenie the Glock. "Keep this pointed at Wooley's eyeball while I get Butthole ready for surgery. If he puts a hand in his pocket, plug him." He shoved me into one of the vinyl chairs that had stuffing coming out of it and started going all over me with a roll of duct tape. After he finished with me, he started on Woodrow. When it was Kathleen's turn, she spoke up for the first time since she commented on Carl's hygiene . "I need to use the lady's room."

Carl laughed. "Lady's room! Get that. In this dump. This shit hole never saw any part of a lady until you showed up in here." He stood up grinning. "Why sure, Angel. I'd be glad to show you to the lady's room. Let me just make sure the rest of our company's entertained."

He reached behind a splintered bar that separated the ratty little kitchen from the ratty little living room and came up with a sawed off shotgun, twelve-gauge it looked like. He racked one into the chamber and clicked the safety off. He handed it to Queenie. So far, she hadn't said a word.

"Here you go, Queenie. Keep an eye on Wooley and Butthole here. Don't touch the trigger now, 'cause she'll damn sure go off. Hell, if I was you, I wouldn't even breathe on it. If their asses get blowed off, I sure as hell don't want it to be no accident. Now if they start wiggling or something, well you just go ahead and bust 'em. I'll just go on back to the lady's room with Angel here and make sure everything comes out all right." He gave that creepy little laugh of his again. Queenie spoke up for the first time.

"What are you going to do with her back there?" Her voice was more like a man's than his was.

"Don't worry, Queenie, darlin'. I'm not going to do nothing with her but look. You know there won't be no party 'til you can be there."

Kathleen sat in the third chair. "I've changed my mind. I don't need to go after all."

Carl grinned. "Are you sure? Once you get seated with your seatbelt on, you got to stay seated 'til I say it's safe to get up and move about the cabin." He really enjoyed his own jokes. "I'd be glad to escort your pretty little ass back to the facilities." Kathleen shook her head. "Okay, darlin'. Shoot yourself." He was the only one that thought he was funny.

After he had all three of us trussed up, he took the shotgun from Queenie and stepped to the trailer door. He touched the trigger and the gun went off. If you never heard a shotgun fired indoors, you got no idea how loud it is. Poor Kathleen jumped so hard her chair about fell over backwards. We could hear the dog whimpering outside. Carl racked another shell and fired another blast.

There was no more sound out of that dog. Kathleen bowed her head, and there were tears rolling down her cheeks. Carl put the shotgun back where it came from and knelt down in front of her.

"Tenderhearted, huh?" He started rubbing her knee. "Well that old dog's better off. Hell, nobody was ever around enough to take care of him. He was probably about starved to death anyway. At least this was quick. But look here, Queenie. She never even got a good look at that mutt and she's crying because she feels sorry for him. That's real sweet, ain't it?"

He reached a dirty finger up and touched Kathleen's cheek where a tear was. She pulled away. Carl sounded real bitter, like his feelings was hurt. "Well, well. She'll grieve over a good-for-nothing dog and won't let a real live man touch her." He gave us all a kind of cold grin and said, "Okay. Down to business."

He pulled an empty crate of some kind over in front of me and sat dangling the Glock between his knees. I was hoping that while Queenie and Carl were concentrating on me, Woodrow was finding a way to get unwrapped.

Carl started twirling the Glock like it was a toy. "What's all this horse-shit about you seeing visions? Puppets, wasn't it? And working miracles? It is all horseshit, ain't it? A con job of some kind."

"Hell yeah, I have visions and work miracles. Before the night's over, I'm going to work a miracle and get out of this tape. And I had a vision of me kicking what's left of your shitty teeth in."

He got real red in the face and said, "Queenie, go get me some scissors. The time has come for this loud mouth to see what he's in for tonight. He's going to get to watch me do some styling on his sweetheart here." Queenie walked out of the room. Carl kicked his crate out of the way and walked over where he could stand behind Kathleen. He took the barrette things out of her hair. I couldn't stand it.

"Hold on a minute here Carl. I'm sorry if I pissed you off. But I'll bet you're the kind of guy who'd get a little bit cranky if somebody hauled him off at gunpoint and started telling him what to do. So cut me a little slack here. Don't do nothing to hurt this lady. She hasn't done anything to you. If you're pissed off at me, let's me and you work it out between us. No need to let our business spill over on these other folks."

"Oh. So the big talker's got him a case of the polites now that his big mouth is going to get his girlfriend skinned." Queenie came in with a pair of scissors, and Carl, the chickenshit grease-ball, was grinning over at me when he started in on Kathleen's hair.

Woodrow and I started going ape shit trying to get out of them chairs. I was calling Carl everything I could think of, and I guess I hit a nerve when I called him a limp-dick-crack-headed-faggot, because when I said that, he jerked up, ran over in front of me and stuck them scissors in my right thigh. I guess old Carl was a lefty. Anyway, Kathleen was screaming and crying.

Woodrow was growling. Queenie was standing there with her big, hollow, stoned-looking eyes all over the red spot forming on the leg of my Levis. I figured I was a goner, so I decided I'd go out putting up the only fight I could.

So I laughed and said, "Only a sissy sticks a tied up guy with a pair of lady's scissors, so you just might as well suck my dick now that you got me all hogtied so I can't stop you." Thinking back, I'm sort of sorry I talked so crude like that in front of Kathleen. Anyway, since I couldn't reach old Carl, I hauled up as much spit as I could and let him have it right in the eye.

What I didn't know at that minute was that Carl had a heart problem. And, I didn't know that Queenie had a weak bladder. You'll see what I mean in a minute. Carl reared back and busted me on the right side of my head. Like I said, Carl was a lefty. And I'll be damned if he didn't knock my cryolite eyeball clean out of my head. At first he gagged, then he screamed, like Faye Wray in *King Kong,* when that eyeball hit the floor and started rolling toward his feet. He was making little noises that sounded like "eep, eep" and started hopping backwards away from that rolling eyeball. He backed plumb into the wall and was trying to back up some more. The closer that eyeball got to his feet, the louder he was hollering stuff like, "Augh! Augh!" And that's when his heart problem showed up. He dropped to the floor. He squirmed and kicked a little bit still watching my eyeball rolling toward his face. He was working his mouth like he was trying to say something. Sounded like "Pinocchio." Come to think of it, there aren't really many words that sound like Pinocchio. Anyway, he was dead as Hiram's door nail. The last thing old Carl saw was my eyeball closing in on him.

That's when Queenie's weak bladder showed up. She was standing there with her mouth wide open looking terrified at dead Carl and my glass eye. Then she peed on herself.

Kathleen, Woodrow, and I was sitting there hog-tied and stunned, looking at dead Carl, my cryolite eye, and wet Queenie. She started shivering all over like she was going to go spastic any second and faint. Then Woodrow spoke up.

"Queenie! Get them scissors out of Buzz's leg and cut us loose or you're going to be the next one to get dead."

Her mouth slammed shut and she started whipping her head back and forth between me and dead Carl. Then in a real whiney voice she asked, "Did you do this to him? Did you kill Carl?"

Woodrow spoke up again, real commanding like. "Damn right. He struck Carl's stupid ass dead. Carl shouldn't have stuck those scissors in Buzz's leg. He hates shit like that. Now cut us loose or you're next."

Queenie looked over at me all pleading like and said in her whiney, soggy voice, "Oh please don't. Please don't kill me. It was Carl's idea to kidnap you all and torture you. I tried to talk him out of it."

Then Woodrow thundered out real loud. "Goddammit, don't lie to him Queenie. He hates getting lied to about as much as he hates getting stuck with scissors. He's going to bust out of that chair in a minute anyway, so you might as well try to get on his good side and cut us loose"

She started bawling like an orphan calf and came tiptoeing over to the chair I was tied up in. I fixed her with my best fire and brimstone frown like I was going to strike her with holy lightning any second. She started touching around those scissors like they might be hot or something. She just stood there bawling and touching them. "Well, pull them out of there girl!" Woodrow hollered. She jumped, pulled the scissors out of my leg and started cutting away at that duct tape. She was in such a hurry to cut me loose before I smote her that she cut my shirt to ribbons.

Soon as I was loose enough, I grabbed the scissors away from her and took over to keep her from cutting my britches off. Kathleen was still crying when I got her out of that tape. I told her to call 911 while I tended to Woodrow. She made the call while I made sure Woodrow and I had control of the Glock and the shotgun. Then we made certain there wasn't any more firearms or blood thirsty freaks passed out in the trailer. Kathleen hung up the phone and said the sheriff and an ambulance was on the way.

I guess the county sheriff had a hard time finding the place, because it took quite a while for him to get there. We had time to wash some cups and brew up some coffee while we waited. When the sheriff and his deputy showed up, we about had Kathleen settled down, and it was Queenie sitting on a broken-down couch sobbing like she was the one that had all the trauma done to her.

The sheriff had a .357 in his hand and stood in the doorway for a minute looking at us sitting at that little Formica table having coffee. Then he looked over at dead Carl. Then he looked at my glass eyeball. Then he looked at the pee puddle in the floor. He looked at me sitting there in my shredded up shirt with scissor nicks all over me and a hole in my face where my eye belonged. Then he started his investigation.

"What the hell kind of fucked up party was this supposed to be, anyhow?"

TAPE 15

Well, Queenie spilled her guts and told Sheriff Bostwick the whole story. Somebody—she didn't know who—hired Carl to grab us, squeeze us for everything he could get out of us, and get rid of us. She didn't know him real good, and she was so dumb that she never figured out that old Carl, or whatever his name was, just needed her to drive the car, and he was sure as hell going to get rid of her too. No witnesses. Of course, the Camaro was stolen. It turned out the trailer belonged to a biker who got killed in a crack-up coming over the Sylvan Pass in Yellowstone a few months back.

We was lucky. Sheriff Bostwick has a soft spot for Vietnam vets since he did a couple of tours himself hauling around a "Prick 77" radio for the 23rd Infantry. We painted the big picture for the sheriff while the deputy searched the Dodge. We was just finishing the story when the deputy came into the trailer with Woodrow's stash and his magic pipe. He wagged them back and forth in front of Woodrow and me and said, "Which one of you soldier boys wants to explain this?"

Now the last thing I needed was to waste a bunch of time cooling off in the Shawnee County jail, but I spoke up without thinking. "That there is my marijuana and that there's my pipe too and these two didn't know nothing about it."

Woodrow had a better idea. "Well, see it's like this sheriff. Sergeant Butane here was in a bad wreck back in January."

Sheriff Bostwick nodded, "Yeah, I heard something about it."

"And they had to operate on his head—his brain actually. Poor son of a bitch was in a coma for over a month. Anyway, he's been talking out of his head since he discharged himself from the hospital. He's been saying all kinds of crazy shit. That isn't his marijuana. Hell, that belongs to that dead guy over there." I love that guy.

The deputy gave him a kind of narrow-eyed look and said, "So the dead guy put this marijuana in the glove compartment of your Dodge?"

"Yep."

Then the deputy looked at me and said, "That's bullshit, ain't it? This here's your marijuana, ain't it?" Woodrow was looking all calm and unphased, just sitting there fingering around on the stump where his left foot used to be. Kathleen stared hard into her coffee cup, like there might be a tiny dolphin swimming in it.

I gave the deputy my biggest good-ole-boy grin and said, "Yes sir. That there's my pot. It's a gift from Stan Laurel himself. You know who that is, don't you? Laurel and Ollie? We were all hanging with Anna Nicole having tea just before she croaked."

The deputy got all red-faced and waved the magic pipe in front of Woodrow's face. "So this belongs to the dead guy too?"

Once I started singing, I couldn't stop. "Nope. That's mine too. Got that off Jack Nicholson. He's a damn pot head, you know."

Then Woodrow took his turn again. "No deputy. That there pipe is mine."

The deputy leaned back on his heels smiling and said, "Well this is drug paraphernalia under the statutes of the State of Oklahoma, and we're going to have to run you in."

That's when the sheriff took a seat in the fourth chair at the Formica table and said to Woodrow. "Are you sure, Sergeant Mulholland? Are you sure this drug paraphernalia is yours? Because Deputy Fife here has got a duty to arrest you if that's true. I sure don't want you to go to jail for something that this here dead feller done."

The deputy's face got even redder. "It's Fite! Fite goddammit, and you know it. It's Deputy Fite, and after the next election it's going to be Sheriff Fite! And this guy may be a war buddy or something, but he's admitted to being the owner of drug paraphernalia, and I'm taking him in."

He started reciting Woodrow's right to remain silent and working the cuffs off the back of his belt. Sheriff Bostwick said, "Now just hold up a minute, deputy. We got some more investigating to do." He looked over at Woodrow all serious like and said, "Why would you admit to a crime? Why don't you wait to talk to a lawyer?"

Woodrow poured some sugar on the table and started making circles with his finger. "Well Sheriff, this here pipe is made from mammoth tusk. After I got back from Nam, I moved up to Alaska to try to get my shit together. Spent about a year up there thinking about what I'd done and why I'd done it. Thinking about what I was going to do next. I didn't see anybody for a whole year. One day, I was sitting on a boulder when a storm rolled in off the mountains and lightning hit a dead tree high up on a cliff above my cabin. First thing I thought was *'incoming!'* Hell, I even felt my foot get blown off all over again. Well, that tree fell several hundred feet and hit a boulder and busted it loose. So the tree and the boulder were crashing toward my cabin. There was all kinds of shit flying off both of them. Tree bark, branches, dust, chips. Everything was crashing toward that cabin in slow motion. There wasn't anything I could do but stand there and watch.

"I don't know how, but they missed the cabin and plowed into another tree that wasn't far from the place I was standing. Knocked it clean over. When the dust settled, I went over to take a look. There was the end of this tusk sticking out of the hillside where part of the old tree roots got pulled up.

"So I spent the next few days digging out what I could find. There was all kinds of busted up bones and this one tusk about five feet long. Hell, I never knew there was any mammoths up in Alaska but I guess at one time, they were all over the place. Anyway, the tusk was in pretty bad shape, and I had to take it out of there in pieces. They tell me it's over 12,000 years old.

"Well, I can't explain it, but I spent several days thinking about the whole episode—and it made me decide to pack up the tusk and come on home to Oklahoma and get on with living. So I made this little whatnot out of mammoth ivory, and I just carry it around for good luck."

Woodrow and the sheriff looked each other real close for a long time.

Deputy Fite was sniffing the magic pipe and said, "Okay, soldier boy. If this is just a good luck trinket, how come there's marijuana residue in the bowl that was burned recently?"

Woodrow put on a way overdone innocent look and said, "Oh, he done that." pointing over at old dead Carl—or whatever his name was. "The son of a bitch found my good luck charm and was smoking pot out of it. Can you believe that? Pretty damn disrespectful if you ask me."

Deputy Fite reached for his cuffs again. Sheriff Bostwick gave

Woodrow and me a wink. He hauled his big old self out of his chair, "Put the cuffs on Queenie here Calvin. We don't have nothing on these three. Hell, they were all just innocent victims is what they were. We're letting them go."

Deputy Fite was walking toward Woodrow and said, "Like hell. This guy here admitted to being the owner of drug paraphernalia, and he can go when he makes whatever the judge sets for bail. It'll be for the D.A. to decide on the charges and a jury will decide whether he's telling the truth or not. That's not our job."

Sheriff Bostwick stepped in front of his deputy. He tightened up like a coiled spring. A really, really, big, fat coiled spring. "Son, there may come a time when you're wearing the big badge in this county. But not today. See, today, I'm wearing it and as far as the high sheriff of this county is concerned, these boys here have already paid their bail on this deal. They was paying their bail in advance when they done their duty in Vietnam while your daddy was hiding out in Canada. Now you can go crying to the D.A. and the press if you want to. The fact is, I wish you would. I'd like to see you find a jury in this county that would convict these boys if I take the stand and say they ain't guilty. Believe me son, you're a lot better off swelling up and pouting than you would be if you take another step toward Sergeant Mulholland here."

They stood there looking at each other for a minute then the Sheriff said, "What are you waiting for son? You got a felony arrest to make. Take this girl to the jailhouse and book her on a kidnapping complaint and whatever other charges you think you can make stick. I'll take care of the questioning of these here innocent victims." I love that guy.

Well, Deputy Fite was grumbling and growling under his breath and started handling Queenie a little rougher than necessary to get the cuffs on her. Sheriff Bostwick spoke up again. "Aren't you forgetting something Deputy Fife?" The deputy stood there with clenched teeth and clenched fists. "Hell boy this here's a felony arrest. Take the girl outside and read her rights. It's probably too late. But do it anyway."

Fite, still grumbling, pulled her toward the door. "Barney, it don't make you no bigger to shove the little girl around. So try to rein in your natural inclinations to be a bully and be a little bit gentler with her. Okay? Or I just might have to uncuff her and let her whip your ass." The door slammed behind them and we could hear the deputy hollering outside about her right to remain silent.

Sheriff Bostwick gave Woodrow back his pipe. Then he looked over my way. "That leg wound doesn't look too bad Sergeant Butane. But I could arrange to get you to a hospital if you think it's necessary."

'No thanks sheriff. This here's only a flesh wound."

He pulled a pack of cigarettes out of his shirt pocket and lit one up. "I know a little something about your case, Sergeant Butane. Some of it was on the news, and I got some of it through official channels. The Oklahoma County sheriff wants to talk to you about some unsolved arson out in Jones, and the Edmond police want to talk to you about a riot in church or something. Now that I know you're in my jurisdiction, I really ought to let them know you're over here."

I was starting to ask whether we could get Kathleen out of there, when he acted like he didn't hear me and started talking again.

"Yeah, I reckon I'll have to notify Edmond and Oklahoma County as soon as I've arranged to get you some medical care. Of course, none of you are in actual custody right this minute." He winked. "So you wouldn't technically be doing anything wrong if you just walked out while I'm investigating and doing paperwork out in the cruiser." He winked gain. "Like I said. You aren't officially in custody." He pitched the baggie of marijuana over into Woodrow's lap. "Now where did Deputy Fite put the dead guy's marijuana? That's evidence. I sure hope the deputy followed procedures in case there are questions about chain of custody and stuff." Woodrow put the baggie in his overalls.

Just then the ambulance rolled up to haul off Carl's body. The EMT's asked Sheriff Bostwick if he needed to keep my government issue eyeball for evidence. Sheriff Bostwick flipped his cigarette out the trailer door. "Naw. Just sterilize the hell out of it and hand it back to Sergeant Butane there." We were making room for the EMTs to get their stretcher over to load Carl up when the sheriff motioned for us to step outside. "I don't suppose you all would testify that Queenie was cooperating with Carl out of fear for her life? Maybe we could keep her out of the pen and get her some rehab help."

We told him, "Of course." We shook hands, and, while he was in the cruiser doing paper work, we eased on back into the Dodge and drove off. We checked in at the nearest Holiday Inn Express to try to get some sleep, as we was all really tired.

Wednesday, February 28, 2007, a.m.

I couldn't sleep. I kept seeing Carl's bad teeth and tattoos and Queenie's hollow expression every time I closed my eyes. I guess the throbbing from that scissors hole in my leg didn't help any. I hadn't been in a mind-swamp like this since I was in Nam. Once the adrenaline charge wears off and you get time to roll it over, you get the sweats thinking about how close things came to turning out different. What if we hadn't got out? What if Carl done some real harm to Kathleen and Woodrow? What if…? Well, some of the pictures popping up in my head caused me to run into the bathroom and puke. It's kind of embarrassing for a fighting man like me to admit something like that.

Here's something else that's hard for me to admit. See, Woodrow and me have been friends since we was kids. The only reason he was tied up in that shitty rat hole of a trailer was because he was standing by me when the chips was down. He was a gnat's eyelash away from getting tortured and killed on my account. If that would have happened, if old Woodrow would have gone through that kind of hell on my account, I'm not sure I could have lived with it if I survived. But here's the hard part. I hardly even knew Kathleen. Hell, I just met her a few days ago. But if I would have had to make a choice; if it was between Woodrow and Kathleen, deep in my heart, I know I would have saved Kathleen and given Woodrow up. You can't know how shitty that made me feel. I really wanted to lie to myself and say I'd never give up a friend. But I'd already settled on the facts, and lying about it really wouldn't make me feel any better.

Naturally, then, I was asking myself, *Why? Why should I give up my oldest and best friend to save a woman I barely knew?* Hell, I hadn't even seen her naked or anything. I can't count the number of times Woodrow saved my ass. And here she was leading me from hot spot to hot spot, stirring up a hornets' nest of Evangelicals. It's probably her goddamn blog that got my house burned down. If anything, I really ought to kick her ass myself. So see, it just didn't figure. The thought of her getting killed, or even bruised, hurt me deep down in ways I can't understand and damn sure can't explain to this machine.

This may sound plumb overboard, but I was afraid if she asked me to, I'd spend the rest of my life, however much that was, trying to make up for the locks of her hair that dumb dead Carl cut off.

Continental breakfast started at six o'clock, so I just laid there turning all this over until then. It was dark and cold when I went down to the lobby. I was acting like I was reading the paper, which I really wasn't. My concentration skills was in the shitter, when Woodrow came down. He pointed to the TV. "We got to move again, Buzz."

There was a news gal named Stella standing outside the biker's trailer talking about the "bizarre story that unfolded in this rural Oklahoma mobile home last night."

There was yellow police tape blowing in the wind behind her. She went on with her report. "Apparently there was a multiple kidnapping with a possible murder plot that was avoided at the last minute by what has been referred to as a 'miraculous' interruption of the scheme." Next thing you know, there's a mug shot of Carl up on the screen. I guess they identified him by his fingerprints. He was a Texas ex-con named Ned Noonan, last known to be living in Dallas.

Anyway, the screen flashed to an interview with the EMT that pronounced old Carl dead and hauled him off. The printing on the screen said *Stan Watkins Shawnee County EMT.* He was saying "When we arrived at the trailer, we found one fella laying on the floor dead. At this point, we can't speculate as to the cause of death."

Stella asked, "Is there anything else you can tell us about the events that occurred on the scene before you arrived?"

"Well, Sheriff Bostwick and Deputy Fite were here investigating. The deputy took an unidentified female off in handcuffs. She must have either been a suspect or a material witness. Could have been a victim I guess." Stan enjoyed being a celebrity. "She was incoherent and kept muttering something about Carl, which I guess was the dead fella's name. Anyway, she kept saying he got struck down by an evil-eye curse or something like that. There was an eye on the scene. But it was a prosthetic and we returned it to its rightful owner."

Naturally, Stella wanted more on the curse angle, but Stan said, "That's all I can say for now."

Then Stella said, "We're switching to Doug Mayweather, who's live at the Shawnee County Courthouse. Are you there, Doug?"

There was a reporter on the screen all bundled up with a microphone sticking in Sheriff Bostwick's face. "Sheriff Bostwick, can you shed any light on the mysterious goings-on in that trailer last night?"

The sheriff ignored the cameras as he hauled his big old body from the courthouse to his cruiser. "I don't have any comment at this time, as this in an ongoing investigation." He got in his cruiser and backed out.

Then Doug had a microphone in the deputy's face. "Is there anything you can tell us deputy?"

"Yes, my name's deputy Calvin Fite—that's F-i-t-e—and I can tell you that there were things that occurred in that trailer that will sure raise the eyebrows of the voters in this county when the truth comes out. I can guarantee there will be a full-fledged by-the-book investigation, or my name's not Calvin Fite, F-i-t-e."

Then the camera switched to Queenie getting took out of the cruiser and walked up to the jail. There was a voice-over saying, "… whose identity remains the subject of speculation." Somebody off camera was trying to get her to answer questions about the curse deal and what happened and blah, blah, blah. Queenie didn't say anything. She just walked along with her head down all stringy headed and strung-out looking.

Right at that moment, I nearly puked, because there was that picture of me in the hospital bed with them turban looking bandages on my head and Irene's Bible lying open on my chest. The sons o' bitches got it off Kathleen's blog and plastered it all over the goddamn TV. Stella was saying "the official police report lists Leon Butane, Woodrow Mulholland, and Kathleen Wister as witnesses. Mr. Butane has been the center of numerous controversies since he emerged from a coma last week. He is being sought for questioning by law enforcement officials in Edmond and Oklahoma County."

There were four hotel guests having continental breakfast in there with Woodrow and me and every one of them was looking from the TV to me and back again. I could see the guy at the front desk on the phone. I didn't know who he was calling, but me and Woodrow had the same paranoia. So we decided to get a move on.

We didn't know if Kathleen was up yet, so Woodrow called her cell. As usual, he put her on speaker so we could all be in on the conversation. He started to tell her what was going on, but she interrupted him. "I've seen it already."

Woodrow said, "We've got to go."

She stopped him. "It's too late. I'm gone already. I checked out and took a taxi as soon as I saw those awful images on the TV earlier this morning."

We was stunned.

Woodrow tried to talk to her, but she was really sounding hysterical.

"Just shut up and listen! Since I met Leon at the hospital, I've been accused of being in league with the devil. I've been harassed by people who are supposed to be good Christians. I've been ridiculed by Christian writers all over the world. My life has been threatened. My home has been vandalized. My name was associated with an act of violence carried out within the very walls of a church house. I've been kidnapped and disfigured and now my name is being connected with this set of sordid sensational facts."

All this came between sobs and sniffles. After she caught her breath, she carried on some more. "For the first time, I'm glad my parents are not here to see the tar-pit their daughter is sliding into. I've stood all I can and I have to get away and clear my head. I can't think. I need some space and time to figure out what to do next."

Woodrow asked, "Just out of curiosity, Kathleen, where are you planning to go anyway?"

"I don't know. I just don't know."

"Well where are you now?"

"I'm in the parking lot of the Sunny Lane Baptist Church waiting for someone to get here and open the door so I can go inside and pray. I need to get my spiritual bearings and ask for forgiveness."

I decided to put in my two cents worth. "Kathleen, you can't just sit in a parking lot somewhere. You'll freeze. Let's get logical here." As soon as I said that, she exploded.

"LOGICAL? LOGICAL?!! How in the world can you possibly find the nerve to speak to me about logic in light of everything that's happened in the last few days?" She went on like that for a while, and I got impatient.

"Now hold on just a minute here. It was your goddamn blog that snow-balled and got all of us in this in the first place. You're the one that started honking all over the world about me working miracles and shit. So the least you could do is stick with us until this Pinocchio deal can work itself out. Then, I don't give a shit what you do."

She hung up.

Woodrow and I sat in the Dodge there in the Holiday Inn parking lot listening to Chuck Berry singing *Havana Moon*. That was the first time it really dawned on me that my time might be running out. It was like something really heavy settled on my chest. That happens sometimes when you've been up most of the night. We sat there listening to Chuck sing his sad song about missing the boat.

I guess lots of people have tried to get their minds around what happens the second after you die. A lot of people are cocksure they're getting whisked right up to heaven. But every time I've tried to get a bead on what heaven's supposed to be like, to tell you the truth, I didn't get much. I know it's just supposed to be wonderful and all. But really, I think you'd get used to streets of gold and pearly gates and angel choirs after a couple of hundred years. Then what? I really don't think I know anybody that believes they're going to hell. I know there's a big difference of opinion on that.

Then there're millions of people all over the world who think you can come back as somebody or something else—dogs and skunks even. And, of course, there are people that don't think anything happens. I was sitting there in the cab of that Dodge not knowing what I believed about it and feeling like that Jimi Hendrix song "Born Under a Bad Sign."

There's a kind of dark that most people, Americans anyway, don't know about. On some stretches of road in the western United States, you can pull over on a cloudy night and get out of your truck and you can't see anything. No stars, no house lights. No car lights or towns or anything. Just dark. And there's no noise neither. Not a cricket or hoot owl. Nothing. It's high country up there, so it's really cold in winter. For a second there, I got all-over scared that death might be like that. No light, no sound, and cold. I was starting to feel a little bit panicky.

I guess Woodrow picked up on it, because he put his big hand on my shoulder and said, "Well, partner. We got work to do."

I didn't know what kind of work he was talking about, but just making up my mind that I had to do something made me feel better. Even if it turned out that what I done was wrong, I'd rather go down fighting than whining.

There was something weighing on my mind, so I said, "Woodrow, I got to tell you something. And I'm not sure how to put it together."

"English buddy. Try it in English and spit it out."

"Okay. It's like this. After we checked in here, I really didn't sleep a wink, because I was feeling guilty. See, I'm not sure what I would have done if I had to make a choice between saving you and saving Kathleen. I know it ought to be automatic. I know I should never give up a friend. But I don't know man. I don't know what I would have done."

I didn't expect him to laugh—which is what he did.

"Well I'm glad you brought that up, Buzz. See, I was going to try to find a way to talk to you about that same thing later. But let me ask you this question. If it was my choice to make, you or Kathleen, what would you want me to do?"

"You know damn well what I'd want you to do Woodrow. I couldn't stand it if my living cost Kathleen her life. I'd never forgive you if you put me in that position."

He laughed again "It's unanimous. We both knew it without talking about it. We owe it to each other as friends to save that woman if it should come to that." He slapped me on the shoulder "Right?" I love that guy.

So I said, "Let's go to the Diner and see our friends." He put the Dodge in drive and we headed for Weloka.

Just as we were pulling out of the motel parking lot, Woodrow's cell phone rang. It was Kathleen. She was still sobbing and we could barely make out what she was saying. "I'm sorry. And you're right. This is all my fault. I'm just so—confused and every step I take is wrong on so many levels. And I don't know who I can ask for help—not real help anyway. Everything just got so ugly so fast."

Of course, Woodrow and I did what we always do when a woman starts crying. We started apologizing. We was stumbling all over each other about how this really wasn't anybody's fault, and it's just how the cards got dealt. Stuff like that. Then I had an idea about how to put together a temporary fix.

"Listen, Kathleen, me and Woodrow decided to go over to the Diner for some pancakes. There ain't anything to help clear up your thinking like pancakes made with genuine Weloka pecans in the batter. It's a sort of all-purpose remedy for what ails you. Pecan pancakes from the Weloka diner. What do you say?"

She sniffled a little bit and said, 'Okay." So we told her to stay warm as she could and we would be right over there to pick her up. When we got there, she was really pitiful looking. She was shaking from the cold. Her eyes were all red from crying all night. Her hair was all done up in a lady's bandana of some kind so no one could see the shitty hair cut Carl gave her.   Woodrow and I piled out of the Dodge, and as natural as can be, we all fell into a three-way hug. I got to tell you, I got all-over washed by a whopping big case of gratitude. We were all okay—except for my flesh wound and Kathleen's hair cut. I didn't have to make a choice between my friend Woodrow and my—well—Kathleen. Bygones was going to be bygones, and the Midnight Rider and his gang was back on the move.

It was cold when we left out of the church parking lot—thirty-two degrees according to the Dodge thermometer. Maybe it was my imagination, but the world just got calmer and clearer as we got near Weloka. The sun was shining, and it was already close to forty by the time we got there. Of course, everybody in the Diner saw the news and knew that me and Woodrow were caught up in bigger mischief than usual. Betsy told us that reporters, law enforcement investigators and process servers popped in from time to time fishing for information about two fugitives named Butane and Mulholland. Of course nobody in the diner had ever heard of them. After we said our hellos and filled everybody in on the highlights of what was going on, we settled down to have pancakes and some heart-to-heart with Kathleen on what to do next.

When things settled down in the diner so we could talk, I looked at her real close, and when I was sure the decks were clear and I had her attention, I laid out what I was thinking.

"Kathleen, I spent a lot of time thinking last night, and while I was doing that, something crazy popped into my head. I feel funny even saying it. I've not even mentioned this to Woodrow yet. But what if all this shit don't have nothing to do with me really. What if the puppet had you for a target all along? Maybe I was just a tool that was supposed to get you started on something. You know, like the jackass Balaam was riding." At first, she looked gut shot. Then she frowned and shook her head. Woodrow was nodding like he might know what I was talking about. Kathleen started digging in her purse looking for a Kleenex.

She blew her nose real lady-like and looked at me with her sad little girl look. "Would you explain what you mean?"

"Well, it's like this. This here is a pretty tough deal, but it ain't the toughest deal me and Woodrow have been through. You should've seen how stuff was in Nam. But you're going through something like you never have been through before, right?" She sniffed and nodded.

"See, in a way, I already had my test in Vietnam. I don't know about Woodrow, but I flunked. See I been thinking about something the puppet told me. I was bargaining with God while I was over there. I promised that if I could get out of there alive and get home, I'd damn sure clean up my act and turn righteous. Well, as soon as I got back, I forgot all about that bargain and never thought about it again until the puppet told me my time was running out. I wanted to pray last night, but I was ashamed. The Lord got me out of Nam alive like I asked and then I let him down. I don't figure I got the right to go back to the well again."

She was rubbing her nose with that Kleenex and looking at me like I was speaking Mongolian or something. "I'm not following, Leon. How does this make a link between me and the job Pinocchio gave you to do?"

"Well, like I was saying. I've already been tested and flunked. I think this is your test. Me and Woodrow don't have the option of pulling out, so there's no act of faith that would make us stay in this mess. I'm stuck, and Woodrow's my friend, so he's stuck too. But you've got a choice to stay or go. Looks to me like the puppet had this very minute in mind all along. Looks to me like the puppet's real aim was to get you to figure out where you stand in your life."

There were tears running out of her eyes, and she took a drink of her orange juice. "I'd like to hear what Woodrow has to say."

"I really don't know, Kathleen. None of this makes sense to me. I personally don't think our tiny little lives are important enough for God—whatever that is—to waste a lot of care and effort playing head games with us one at a time. All I really know about this deal is that my friend needs my help. How and why it happened doesn't make a shit. He says he needs it. I believe him. That means I'm here to the end. Whether there's some holy shell game going on where the real pea is getting shuffled around, I can't say.

"But I will say this. Buzz is right about one thing. Where you're sitting right now is a turning point in your life. Whatever happens in the next few minutes, you can't unmake the decision you're about to make—even if you change your mind." I don't know if Kathleen understood that last point. But I damn sure didn't. Whatever.

I decided to finish making my point and let it go. The chips would have to stay wherever they fell. "If you hang in there with us, I really don't know how much more you might have to go through. But I'm hoping you'll hang in there with us, no matter how it turns out. I just believe you'll be better off if you do."

She leaned over and put one arm around my neck and one around Woodrow's. Her face was pressed against the rough leather of my coat. I wanted her to hold onto me like that for a long time. The way she smelled like jasmine and the way her hair felt so silky on my chin put impossible thoughts into my dumbass head. Wouldn't it be great if I could come out of this okay and spend more time—lots of time—with Kathleen like this? Well, there was no use getting all sappy and wasting time dreaming about stuff that's out of reach.

She put the palm of her hand on the back of my neck and it made shivers all over me. "Thank you Leon. I don't know if you're right or wrong. But I know I've been weak and cowardly. I can see that, in a way, this is all my fault. I guess I was trying to prove something for the sake of my own injured ego. I'm sorry. I know what I have to do."

TAPE 16

Woodrow looked okay, but me and Kathleen were a mess. I had a bruised up face and a fat lip, and she had big patches of hair cut out of her head.

When Betsy brought the coffee pot over, I popped the question. "Hey Betsy. I hate to ask, but we're running out of places to hide out. Could you put up with some refugees for a few days?"

She never missed a beat. "Of course you can stay at my place. Way too much room for just me. I won't be in your way as I work here days and then at The Gold at night."

She stood holding her coffee pot, watching Kathleen fooling with her bandana trying to keep her hair covered. "You know, my sister-in-law Cheryl runs the beauty shop here in Weloka. I could have her come to the house and see if she can help with your hair." Kathleen blushed and nodded without looking up.

I'm no expert, but I didn't see how the mess Carl made could get undone to the point where Kathleen's hair would look nice. I guess we were a freak show trio, I with my shaved head and that big red scar, Woodrow stumping around on his mammoth tusk foot, and Kathleen with—well—what Carl done.

When we finished our pancakes, Betsy gave us a key and told us to make ourselves at home. Our call to Dr. Soames was supposed to be at noon. It was about 8:30 when we got to Betsy's. We figured if we could sleep until about 10:30. That would give us plenty of time to clear the cobwebs, get showers, and hopefully be sharp enough to get answers if Dr. Soames had some to offer.

But now, let me tell you something funny. Even with that rotten haircut Carl gave her, as I watched Kathleen taking off her bandana and her coat at Betsy's house, I thought she was the prettiest woman I ever saw. And you know what else? It seemed to me she got prettier every day. Of course that had to be my imagination. Right?

It didn't seem like I was asleep more than a minute when Woodrow had a hold of my foot shaking it real gentle like.

"Come on, Buzz. We're going to be making our call in about an hour, and you probably better get cleaned up and shaved and have yourself some coffee. This deal probably won't amount to shit any more than the Dallas fella did. But let's be ready just in case."

I took a little extra time stretching and enjoying the sunlight coming in through Betsy's checkered curtains. I was breathing in the smell of coffee that was coming up from the kitchen. I was even enjoying the mumbles I could hear coming from the TV downstairs. It was like the whole nightmare deal with Carl and Queenie was just that, a nightmare that drifts off like fog when the sun shines on it.

As soon as I stepped out of the shower, Kathleen was standing in the hall with a cup of coffee. Luckily, I had a towel around me, but I almost dropped it when I slapped my hand over my face to cover up the knothole where my eye is supposed to be. It was just reflex of course, because she'd already seen me without my eyeball. Still, at that moment, I couldn't tell whether I was more embarrassed for Kathleen to see me naked or eyeless.

She looked down real quick and blushed. "I brought you some coffee. Black. Right?"

I gulped real hard and said, "Yeah, fine. Black's fine." I didn't know what to do. She was standing there looking down with a cup and saucer in her hand. I was standing there holding a towel around me with my left hand and covering my face with my right. It wouldn't make any sense for me to walk over to her. Which hand would I use to take the coffee?

I guess I could have backed into the bedroom. But it was like my feet turned into roots so I couldn't go back or forth. She's the one that had to move. And she did.

She walked by me and into the bedroom without looking and put the coffee on the dresser. She was wearing fuzzy puppy-looking house shoes and a pair of jeans with the cuffs rolled to her calves. Calves. Boy. It didn't seem like that word could have anything to with any part of a woman like her. The white shirt she was wearing looked like a man's shirt with the sleeves rolled up. The top two buttons was undone and I tried not to look. But I couldn't help it. When she bent down to set the cup and saucer on the dresser, I could tell she wasn't wearing anything under that shirt.

She stood there just for a second looking over her shoulder. I know I should have looked away, but I couldn't. It seemed like we stood there looking at each other for a long time. Probably it wasn't, though. Anyway, she blushed again and said she'd see me downstairs. Then she was gone. But there was something wonderful left in the room behind her. I could try to explain it, but it probably wouldn't make any sense.

I will say this. It never occurred to me until that moment that I might be able to get away with talking to her about how I was feeling.

Well, I had to put that behind me for now. I wasn't even sure I'd be around this time next week. So I took a deep breath and got focused. I was dressed, showered, and shaved, and stuck my eyeball in where it was supposed to be. I looked in the mirror and cringed. Oh well.

I trotted downstairs with my empty coffee cup to see what was going to turn up today.

Betsy has a high tech wireless phone set up in her house, so we could get clear sound and volume control. That would be handy when we made our call to that Soames fella.

Nobody had much to say. We sat around in Betsy's kitchen letting the TV news do our talking for us. There was a report about the special that was about to air on that mystery tomb of Jesus deal. Kathleen occupied herself by working on her blog.

Wednesday, February 28, 2007, p.m.

When noon rolled around, me and Kathleen was at the kitchen table with our papers and pencils all primed to take notes. I don't know how Kathleen was feeling, but I wasn't expecting much. Woodrow had his feet propped up on Betsy's window sill, and he was carving up a Fuji apple.

At twelve o'clock sharp, Kathleen dialed Dr. Soames' number. At first, we was afraid that he had forgotten about us as the phone rang and rang and nobody answered. Finally, all out of breath a fella answered. "Soames here."

"Dr. Soames, this is Kathleen Wister. I have you on the speaker phone with Leon Butane and Woodrow Mulholland. Is it okay with you if I tape this conversation?"

"Sure. I don't care. Kathleen, I'm familiar with you, and I've heard of Mr. Butane. Mr. Mulholland, what brings you to this ice cream social?"

"Since Mr. Butane, here, can't drive anymore, I've turned into his chauffeur."

"Seriously?"

"Yep."

"Fine. Well, now that we're all acquainted, let's get started. Kathleen, I've done some checking into the question you posed and I have to say it's a lot more intriguing than it appears at first glance. I'm somewhat disappointed I didn't think to investigate this myself. If you wouldn't consider that I'm poaching on your ground, I'm toying with the idea of writing an article on the subject myself. Hope you don't object."

"Of course not, Dr. Soames. I'm frankly surprised and happy that you've taken an interest. This is very important to us."

"Yes. I've checked your blog. You'll forgive me if I'm somewhat dubious concerning your, um, remarkable story. No offense, hyperdeveloped scholarly skepticism, you know. Just the same, no matter how you arrived at it, you've exposed an interesting historical mystery that has gone surprisingly unexamined. So how do you want to proceed?"

"Well, first off, do you have any idea who these men were?"

"In short, yes, I think so. But even if I'm right, I'm not sure that solves your problem."

"I don't understand. If our assignment is to find out who they were, and we know who they were, why wouldn't that satisfy the requirements?"

I was all geared up to hear another load of worthless shit. Woodrow sprinkled salt on an apple slice.

Dr. Soames picked up again. "Mr. Butane. You're first name is Leon, I believe?"

"That's right."

"Do you have a nickname?"

"My friends call me Buzz. But what's that got to do with anything?"

"You were in the army. Am I right?"

"Yeah I was in the army."

"Now, if I were to ask your friends if they know Buzz Butane, they would know who I'm talking about. Correct?"

"Sure they would."

"Now, suppose I were to ask the army for records on Buzz Butane. Nothing would show up. See what I mean? The army just doesn't know you as Buzz Butane. You exist as a service number. Are you starting to see our problem?"

"I think I'm following up to a point. But line it out to the guys crucified with Jesus."

"Okay. Stay with me. If you had gone to Nazareth when Jesus was a young man and asked to speak with Jesus, chances are, even his friends and family wouldn't know who you were talking about. They knew him as Yeshua. The name *Jesus* is an English rendering of a Greek translation for a Jewish name. See the problem? It's highly unlikely that anyone in his inner circle knew him as Jesus. And yet that's how he's identified in the English translations of the Bible. Will you excuse me for a second? I was running late and didn't have time to get some hot water for tea. Hold on."

Kathleen asked, "Do you want us to call you back?"

"No. No, it'll just take a second." He came back on the line right quick. "Are you still there?"

"We're here Dr. Soames."

"Okay. Suppose the men crucified with Jesus were known to their friends as Dexter and Lefty, but their names were Tom and Jerry. If your assignment is to discover their names, you're not there—even if you know they're Dexter and Lefty. See?"

"Dr. Soames. Are you saying that the names we have for the people in the Bible aren't really their names?"

"Exactly. In most New Testament cases, what we have are English renderings of Greek adaptations. So you see, you're actually dealing with a riddle within a riddle. Even if they were identified in the New Testament, we still might not have their names."

I dropped my pencil. "Well we don't have them identified and we don't have their names. So how in the world would we find out?"

"Let's make some assumptions. They may or may not be identified, but at this point, this is what you have to go on. Assume the witnesses in Jerusalem at the time of the crucifixion knew the names of the men who were executed with Yeshua. Assume the first oral transmissions of the crucifixion story—the pre-Marcan passion narrative we scholars call it—identified these men. Assume the identities are preserved somewhere in the New Testament. How would we find them?"

"I don't know Doc. You're going to have to give us a hint."

"Okay. In my opinion, these men played a more important role in the original story than they do in the stories as related in the New Testament.

I believe their importance has been downplayed, but in my opinion, their identities are preserved somewhere in the Gospel accounts of the passion narratives. For reasons we can only speculate about, these men have been marginalized for 2,000 years. They were important figures at the time of the execution, but their role was downplayed almost from the beginning. But their identities were too tightly interwoven with the passion narrative to be completely written out. Now we may not have their names, but I'm confident we have some form of identification. In order to get a step closer to the solution to your problem, you have to examine all the people identified in connection with the passion narratives."

"You mean there may be some kind of shell game going on? Their names are hidden there somewhere?"

"Not necessarily their names, but some form of identification. Understand, a lot of the New Testament is written in code. Jesus' parables are all coded messages. At Matthew 11:7, Jesus makes comparisons between John the Baptist and 'a reed swayed by the wind and a man dressed in fine clothes living in a king's palace.' There is very good scholarship suggesting that this logion is a specific reference to Herod Antipas and the people of the time would know the identity of the target."

"Well, hell Dr. Soames. If we were supposed to identify Herod from that deal about reeds, it's hopeless because unless Kathleen gets it, it's over our head."

"Don't despair, Mr. Butane. Don't despair. So far as I know, you all may be approaching the passion narrative from a perspective no one else has. I know I'm going to look into it and I'll tell you my preliminary ideas about method.

"First, separate the passion narrative from the rest of the text. For my purposes, I'm beginning my examination a little earlier than most. The passion narrative usually starts with what's called 'The Triumphal Entry.' I think it starts with the events in Bethany immediately prior to the entry. There..."

Kathleen interrupted. "Just a minute, Dr. Soames. I'm trying to keep up with you here. Why do you think the passion narrative starts in Bethany?"

"Mainly because of the Gospel of John. John links the condemnation of the Jewish authorities directly to the events in Bethany. The connection is definite and immediate. The sojourn in Bethany is dealt with in all four gospels. But on this point, it's my opinion that John relies on a source that has close contacts with the original oral tradition.

"To continue, the passion narrative usually concludes with the discovery of the empty tomb. I would extend it somewhat. The reason is this. I think the first chapter of Acts has important information that may, perhaps, be read back to events preceding the empty tomb phenomenon."

"Can you explain what you mean, Dr. Soames?"

"Yes. There are two facts that point us backward. First, the death of Judas Iscariot. Matthew positions this before the crucifixion. Luke is vague. I am adopting the working hypothesis that Judas died before or immediately after Jesus. Next, the candidates put forward to replace Judas—Matthias and Barsabbas—seem to be linked to the events surrounding Judas' death. I think they have to be considered as possibly playing some role in the passion narrative in its original form." When he mentioned Matthias you can understand how I started getting the feeling like a circle was closing. After all, Dr. Ryland had Matthias on the brain from the start.

"Now, one final word about names. I have before me a very ancient Christian document that is not part of the canon. It's called *The Pseudo-Clementine Recognitions*. This is a fourth century document that purports to relate the conversion of Clement of Rome and his travels with Peter the Apostle. Its late date precludes its authenticity, but many scholars agree that this document is based on earlier works that may go back to first-century Christian sources. Now bear with me. This may be a little complicated. The document was originally written in Greek—like the gospels. But the original Greek is lost. We have two extant versions: one in Latin and one in Syriac. They disagree on some important points. I'll mention one in a moment. Until fairly recently, there was no reliable way to determine, in cases of disagreement, which was nearer the original Greek. Follow so far?"

I was trying to diagram it out. "Okay. Lost Greek. Two copies supposedly of the original Greek, but they don't always agree and we don't know who's right. Is that it?"

"Right. Not long ago, a partial copy of the *Pseudo-Clementine Recognitions* was discovered. This newly discovered version was written in Armenian. These fragments could possibly be another version not copied from either the Syriac or the Latin, meaning they appear to go back to the original Greek. If you compare all three, the Syriac and the Armenian agree more often, which suggests that, when they agree, the Syriac is closer to the original Greek. By extension, where the Syriac and Latin disagree, it's likely, not conclusive, that the Syriac is nearer the original."

"You said this is important. Cut to the chase and tell me why."

"Let me read something from the Syriac. 'After this, one Barabbas, who had become an apostle in the stead of Judas the traitor...' did you catch that? The Syriac says the disciple who took Judas' place was called Barabbas. Now, here's the same verse in the Latin. 'After him, Barnabas, also called Matthias, who was elected apostle in the place of Judas.'" There was a long pause on the other end of the line.

"So one says Barabbas and one says Barnabas called Mathias. What's the point?"

"Don't you see? This notice has profound implications to the question you're pursuing."

"I'm sorry Dr. Soames. You're going to have to spell it out."

"Well, you're just going to have to spend some time unraveling some things for yourselves. I'm not going to spoon feed you. It's there for you to see if you work at it. Now I will give you one more puzzle piece that's not in the gospels. Listen carefully. Take good notes. Are you ready?"

I was sort of getting offended by his attitude, but Kathleen looked really excited. Like she was seeing his meaning a lot better than I was.

She said, "We're all ears, Dr. Soames."

I wanted to say "Speak for yourself." But I figured, offended or not, I better be all ears too.

"At the end of the *Recognitions,* there's a pericope of how about 5,000 Christians fled Jerusalem and went to Jericho. They heard *'the enemy'* or *'hostile person'* in Latin, was on his way to Damascus with letters that would lead to the destruction of early believers. Does that sound familiar?"

I said, "No."

At the same time, Kathleen said, "Of course."

Dr. Soames went on. "Okay. Write this down exactly. If you need me to fax it to you later, I will. Ready? This is the Syriac, 'We buried two brothers in that place at night. Each year their graves are suddenly white. They quenched the fury of many because they knew that they are members of our faith and that they were worthy of divine remembrance.' Now the Latin, 'We had gone out to the graves of two of the brethren which would be whitened of themselves each year. By this miracle the anger of many against us has been suppressed for they see that our people are held in remembrance with God.' Did you get all that?"

"Yes. Let me read it back to be sure." I had it written the same way she did and Dr. Soames said it was right.

"Now. When you go back through the various versions of the passion narrative with the additional material from the *Recognitions*, I think you'll discover some very interesting facts. Call me later and we'll compare notes. Oh, there's one more thing. If we include the death of Judas in the passion narrative, I need to tell you something or you won't catch it otherwise. Every popular English translation of the New Testament says Judas fell. Look at Acts 1:18. Then look at the Greek. There's not a word about him falling. That's a blatant interpolation."

"Meaning?"

"It never happened. He never fell."

"Meaning?"

"Figure it out. Talk to you soon. Bye." He hung up.

Kathleen and I sat there looking at our notes. Woodrow finished his apple and walked to the trash can to drop in the core.

Kathleen spoke up first. "Let's start at the end. The Judas thing."

We got all our books out and went to the right place. Acts 1:18. Sure enough. Every single translation we have says, in one way or the other that Judas fell. The Greek doesn't say that. The Greek word just means he was on the ground in the prone position.

Kathleen was making question marks on her paper. "Well, if he didn't fall, how did this happen?"

Woodrow was looking out the window. "Somebody cut him open. That's how."

"Well, if that's what happened, why doesn't the Bible say that?"

"You tell me. What are the possibilities?"

"Maybe they didn't know."

"That doesn't explain why the translators put in a bullshit explanation about falling when it didn't happen. I don't mean to be crude here, but I've seen a lot of people with their guts out, and none of them got that way from falling. I've seen people who got dropped out of helicopters without their bodies busting open and their insides spilling out. Ask Buzz."

She looked over at me and I agreed with Woodrow.

"Nope. They left it vague on purpose. But if his insides were spilled out like the Bible says, it's because somebody cut him open. We don't know who, but we've got a pretty good idea why?"

"The betrayal? You think this could be a revenge killing?"

"Well, that makes more sense than him falling. Correct me if I'm wrong. But there are two possible reasons somebody would want to kill him. Right?

One is revenge. The other is money. Doesn't the Bible say he got cash for turning Jesus in?"

"Thirty pieces of silver."

"Do we know what became of the money?"

Kathleen got real excited. "Oh my goodness! Remember that odd posting I got from Pinocchio? Remember? He told us to follow the money? Maybe this is what he was talking about. Maybe there's some clue connected to the money Judas received for betraying Jesus."

She did some flipping around in some of the books. "Matthew says he gave it back to the priests and they used it to buy a field. Acts says he used it to buy a field himself."

Woodrow was looking over her shoulder. "So no matter who did the buying, the money winds up in someone's hands in connection with a land sale."

Kathleen was looking at him sideways. "You think where the money wound up is important?"

"If this is the money Pinocchio was talking about, it might. Write it down."

She made some notes and underlined something in red. "Just to follow your line of thinking, if he was murdered, there could have been a dual motive couldn't there? I mean, revenge for the betrayal, but why not take the money too if he had it on him?"

"Makes sense."

"So how does this bring us closer to the identities of the men crucified with Jesus?"

Then it hit me like a sledge hammer. "What if it was revenge, but what if the revenge was for what happened to the other guys? What if Judas had something to do with the other crucifixions too? And what if the guy or guys that killed him were friends or relatives of the men that died with Jesus?"

Woodrow grinned. "Hey, Buzz. You may have hit it right on the head. This whole deal makes sense if this was a revenge killing because somebody blamed Judas for the deaths of all three men."

Kathleen shook her head again. "I don't see anything that would indicate that Judas had anything to do with the deaths of these other two. The Bible is very specific. He betrayed Jesus." Nobody said anything for a while. "What are you thinking Woodrow?"

"I'm convinced this Judas guy was murdered, and it wasn't a random robbery because the money didn't disappear. Somebody came up with it in connection with a land sale. I'm convinced the Bible is vague about all this for a reason. I think we should take a look at this passion narrative and see what we can piece together between the lines on exactly what Judas did. I think there's more to it than you all learned in Sunday School."

Kathleen took a manila folder out of her brief case and wrote "Judas Iscariot" on it. Then we dug back into the books. Woodrow said, "Let's start with the basics. What does the Bible say Judas did that amounted to betrayal?"

It sounded like Kathleen was reciting. "He led the arresting party to the place where Jesus and the disciples were that night and then pointed out who Jesus was with a kiss."

Woodrow nodded. "Meaning that, without his help, the authorities wouldn't know where Jesus could be found, and if they could find his hideout, they wouldn't know which one was Jesus? I mean that has to be right doesn't it? Otherwise, why give him any money?"

"Okay. I guess so."

"Okay. Well it doesn't add up. How could they not know who he was? Hell, look at the fuss he made in Jerusalem. He shows up with a crowd. He starts a fracas in the temple. Unless they were just stupid, they didn't need anybody to identify him."

Kathleen said, "Well, that may be true, but the Bible says many times they wanted to arrest him someplace where there were no crowds. Judas showed them where they could take him with no one around."

Woodrow was scratching his jaw. "Still doesn't add up. Look here. At Luke 20:20, it says the authorities put spies on him right off the bat. Seems to me that's exactly what they would have done. Right?"

"That's what it says."

"So unless the spies were dumbshits, they were following him around. Right?"

"Well, you'd think so."

"Luke 23:39 says the place where they arrested him was the place he usually went. See that? If that was his usual hang-out, how come the spies didn't know it?"

"Maybe the verse means he went out as usual but not necessarily to a usual place."

"What about this, then? John 18:2 says Judas knew where they were because he often met there with his disciples. Look Kathleen. You've got to face it. They had spies that knew Jesus by sight, and if they were following him, they knew where he hung out. They didn't need to pay Judas to tell them where he'd be or who he was. If they gave Judas money, it was for some other kind of services."

I was bouncing back and forth between them like I was watching a ping pong match. Kathleen kept it going.

"Okay, Woodrow, suppose you tell us what happened?"

"Judas betrayed Jesus all right. But it didn't have anything to do with location or identification. Judas made their case for them. He gave the Jews the testimony they needed to condemn Jesus under Jewish law, and the Jews gave Jesus up to the Romans. The Jews fingered him as a revolutionary. So the Romans would have an excuse to execute him under Roman law."

My turn. "So you're thinking that Judas fingered the other guys too?"

"Yep. They got caught at the same time Jesus was arrested. The Jews tried them all together. They were condemned together. They were delivered to Pilate together, sentenced together, and crucified together."

Kathleen walked over to the kitchen window and looked at the horses grazing in the pasture behind Betsy's house. "Suppose you're right, Woodrow. What does that tell us about the identities of those men?"

He grinned. "If I'm right, we'll learn more if we follow the money. This must be what the puppet meant when he dropped his other love note to Kathleen. There's more there, and we just have to find it." He slapped me on the shoulder. "It's a murder mystery, Buzz. We figure out who did in Judas, and it'll point us to the identities of the guys crucified with Jesus. Elementary my dear Butane. Elementary."

Woodrow is handier working his way around the books so he started coming up with answers before I did. "Look here Buzz. I'm listing out all land sales I can find in the general time frame we're looking at. Either Judas or the priests purchased this 'field of blood.'"

"So who was the seller?"

"We can't say. But we do have two possible buyers identified." I looked over his shoulder as he navigated back and forth between books.

"Now look here Buzz." He pointed to Acts 4:36.

"Here's a guy named Joseph. Says here the apostles called him Barnabas."

"Say, isn't that one of the guys that was supposed to take Judas' place?"

"No, the guy you're talking about wasn't Joseph Barnabas , it was Justus Barsabbus."

"But wait a minute. Didn't Dr. Soames say that other document says it was a guy named Barnabus that took Judas' place?"

"This name deal would give me a headache even if I didn't have brain trauma. Okay, what about this Joseph Barnabas?"

"Well, he sold a field and the money wound up in the apostles' pocket—or at their feet it says here."

"So who was the buyer?"

"Doesn't say."

"So we don't know who the seller was in transaction number one, and we don't know who the buyer was in transaction number two. You suppose these two deals are really the same deal? You suppose the money that started off in Judas' pocket wound up in the apostles' pocket—or at their feet or whatever?"

"Well what do you think, Buzz? Would that look and feel like justice to an ancient Palestinian? Judas betrays Jesus and possibly others for money. He winds up dead with his guts spilled out. Jesus' followers wind up with the money Judas got for his treachery. Looks awful tidy doesn't it?"

"I don't see any flies on your thinking here, Woodrow. Do you see anything else that might open the crack a little further?"

"Well, well, what do we have here? Looks like another land sale. And guess what. People wind up dead because of it. Look." He pointed to Acts 5:1. "This happens right after the Joseph Barnabas deal. A man named Ananias and his wife Sapphira sold some property. Doesn't say who the buyer was. But they're both guilty of some treachery and they wind up dead. At least part of the money turns up at the apostles' feet. If you string all this together, we got dead buyers and dead sellers and money that winds up with the apostles and a field that gets identified as *The Field of Blood*. Sure seems to me there's a much darker story just out of sight. I just can't piece it all together right now."

It was getting dark when the "Tomb" show came on, and I wasn't feeling too good. But I wanted to be alert for the show because you never know if there might be a clue or something I needed to catch. I figured if I didn't get high, I'd just be distracted by the pain. And if I did get high, I might be distracted by the pot. So I decided to get high. Betsy and Woodrow decided to join me. But Kathleen sat there real attentive with her pen and notebook on her knees. She was getting real relaxed being around folks getting high for any reason they liked. I figured that was good for her blood pressure. She was so all-fired focused on that TV that you would've thought she was a racehorse waiting for the starting bell. And then they were off.

You probably saw the show, so I'll just hit the high points. Back in 1980, some guys found a tomb in the holy land somewhere near Jerusalem. There were three skulls and ten bone boxes in there. Back in Jesus' time, people used to put dead folks in these tombs and leave them for a year to decompose, and then the family or whoever would go back and collect up the bones and put them in a box. Then they'd put the bone box back in the tomb and leave it. Sometimes they'd carve the dead person's name on the box. There were names on some of the boxes they found in this 1980 tomb. The name on one of the boxes was "Jesus son of Joseph." Well naturally, you know, what's the first thing that would come to mind? Then there was a box in there for "Jose," which I guess was the name of one of Jesus' brothers. There was a bone box in there for a woman named Mary and a guy named Matthias. And then there was a box for a little boy named "Judah son of Jesus." There was some oddball stuff about some Greek writing on a box for a woman named "Marilyn" or something. I got lost on that deal.

Anyway, after they got all the boxes out of the tomb, one of the boxes disappeared. They was all catalogued and put in storage, except for the one that got lost. Years later, this archaeologist guy with a hell of a long name got interested in all this stuff and started scratching around. Turns out the tomb got resealed after the bone boxes got taken out, and catalogued and nobody could remember where that sealed-up tomb was.

All the names on them boxes was common back in Jesus' day. But some statistics fellas done the work and figured out that this bunch of names altogether couldn't be just happenstance. So, according to their figures, this was probably the tomb of Jesus and his family. Meaning, I guess, that if he did rise up from the dead, he came back later and died again leaving his bones behind to put in this bone box.

I didn't read *The DaVinci Code*, and I didn't see the movie. But I did read about it in the newspapers, and I guess the story is that Jesus Christ was married to Mary Magdalene, and they had normal relations like any other married folks and they had a baby. Anyway, the guys on this TV show were guessing that Jesus, his wife, Mary and their little boy, Judah were all buried in this tomb.

So, after the show, there was a panel of experts arguing and being real cocky and insulting to these guys that made the film. I guess I went deaf in a way, because all I could hear was "blah, blah, blah" coming out of the set.

My thinking flew off to a whole different place. What the hell happened to the bodies of those other two guys? Where did their bones wind up?

I left the experts arguing about DNA and stuff and marched off into the kitchen to get the books and do some checking. Kathleen stayed with the TV taking notes. Betsy answered the telephone and was talking to somebody. Woodrow got himself another beer and came with me.

We spread the books out in the kitchen, dug in, and here's what we found. Okay, all three of the crucified men were dead. There's a guy named Joseph of Arimathea. The gospels aren't in total agreement about just exactly who he was. But, after Pilate made sure Jesus was dead, he said Joseph could have the body. So Joseph took Jesus down and saw that he got buried. The Bible doesn't say nary a word about the other two bodies. So what are our choices?

I asked Woodrow "What do you think?"

He took a drink of his beer. "Well, one thing we can be pretty sure of is that they didn't leave them hanging. It's for sure if they took one down, they took them all down and they took 'em down together."

"Makes sense."

"Does the Bible say these two guys were buried someplace different from Jesus?"

I flipped from gospel to gospel checking. "It doesn't say anything about what happened to them. It only talks about Jesus getting buried." We sat there high looking back and forth at the books.

Then Woodrow said, "Well, look here. John says Jesus got buried in that particular tomb because it was nearby. What does that tell us?"

I was pretty sure I followed his drift. "The number of choices is pretty small, right? Could be there was a closer tomb where they buried the other two. Could be they buried Jesus in the closest tomb and carried these other fellas somewhere further off. Or..."

"Or all three of them were buried together." We looked up at the same time.

Woodrow grinned and said, "Well, that's awkward, ain't it?"

Of course I caught his meaning right quick. "You suppose we ought to run this by Kathleen?"

"Well, let's just lay the problem out there about where these other guys got buried and see what she says." We sat there comparing the stories about the empty tomb until the TV show was over and Kathleen came into the kitchen for some tea.

By now, of course, we were getting used to that puzzled look on her face. "I just really don't know what to think."

Woodrow said, all calm like, "Let's change directions for a minute. Was that show on the level about how dead bodies were handled in Jesus' time?"

"I believe so. I read about the process before."

"Okay. What happened to the bodies of the other two?"

She said quickly, without thinking, "I don't know. The Bible doesn't say."

"Well, whether the Bible says or not, something happened to them. What do you suppose it was?"

"I'm not sure what you're after."

"Never mind about that. Just tell me what you think."

"Well, they were taken somewhere and buried of course."

Woodrow took her step by step. "Were they taken off their crosses at the same time?"

"Probably."

"By the same people?"

"Probably." And so on. When she actually started rolling over in her mind the possible places where they could be buried, you could see a shadow drift across her eyes.

"I guess what you're suggesting is they may have been buried in the same tomb as Jesus."

"Yep. And if that happened, we've got a sort of complication at the empty tomb, don't we?"

"Well, I see where you're coming from, Woodrow. But the Bible doesn't say anything that would suggest that they were buried together."

"And that proves what? The Bible's pretty quiet about who was present with Jesus at the temple. But I thought we agreed somebody had to be there. And it's just like I have been saying, we can't read too much into what the Bible doesn't say."

"Okay. Suppose they were buried together. What happened at the tomb?"

"We just have to take a look and see if there're some hints for us."

So, we started looking at how the different gospels spell out what the women found when they showed up on Easter morning. The stories are just too far apart to say they're all seeing the same thing and just seeing it different. Jesus disappears from the tomb and if they were all buried together, either these guys are left behind, or they're gone too. Mark says there was a young man inside the tomb, but he was alive. Matthew says there was someone there. But it was an angel, and he wasn't in the tomb. This angel came down from heaven and was sitting on the stone that got rolled away from the door. Luke says there were two men in fancy clothes inside the tomb, but they were alive. John said there were two angels dressed in white inside the tomb. So see, in three of the gospels, the tomb wasn't empty at all. There was somebody in there. Only they were alive—at least according to the story as it was finally written down. See that's another deal I've heard my whole life—the empty tomb. It wasn't empty at all. There was somebody in there.

It was getting late. We decided to call it a day. Woodrow said. "Listen. Let me just raise this as a possibility. What if the original story—the story before the gospel writers got hold of it—had three resurrections? What if all three of the guys buried in the tomb were gone the morning those women showed up? Remember what Dr. Soames had you two write out of that thing he read today? There were two guys buried at night in Jericho. Who were they, and why bury them at night? And why did they deserve this divine remembrance he talked about?"

Kathleen wanted to argue but Woodrow cut her off. "Look. We can take it up again in the morning. I've got to get some rest. I just want you to think about it and see what you come up with." I agreed that was a good idea. So we all went off to bed.

I couldn't sleep. It was getting impossible for me to keep everything straight. Here's the scenario I was working out. Judas is at the trial. He testifies against Jesus and some of his followers. It works, and Jesus is condemned. Judas gets paid for his treachery and skulks off, but a couple of guys are following him. They catch up with him and cut him open, take the money and leave him dead. Somehow or other there are other people involved and they wind up dead too. The killers take the money they got off Judas and give it to the Apostles. Jesus and the other two get crucified. The Jewish authorities don't want the bodies left on crosses overnight, so they get Pilate to let them take the dead men down. They're all buried together. Two of the bodies are removed from the tomb and hustled up to Jericho and buried by night. After that all was lost.

I don't know how they teach all this in Sunday School, but revenge killings, thefts, and underhanded land sales sure seemed to complicate the picture of Jesus' followers.

That night I went back to Jerusalem. But this time I was put down in front of three men hanging on crosses. I tried to look away but I couldn't. All three of the men were bloody and naked. Their faces was all purple and black. Their eyes was all swollen shut. They were so beat up they didn't even look like people anymore. From a distance, unless one of them had a big damn birthmark or tattoo or something, nobody could tell them apart. Hell, I mean one of them could've been Woodrow, and I wouldn't know which one. I didn't realize before that minute, on a crucifixion deal, when the Romans get through with you, you look like a piece of meat with arms and legs. The only way I knew which one of them was supposed to be Jesus was because he was the one in the middle. All three of them had signs nailed over their heads, but I couldn't read them.

People were busy taking them down off those crosses. It was a real messy business, and believe me, I've seen messy jobs in my life. Once they got the three of them on the ground, there wasn't any way to tell which was which. They all had long, dark hair and beards. I guess the Romans cut off big clumps of their hair or pulled it out because all of them had bald spots on their heads. I didn't see any thorny crowns, but they all had bloody head wounds.

It looked like maybe eight or nine guys were on the burial detail. When they got the dead men down, the detail put them on stretcher-looking things. There were two men to a body, and they started stumbling their way down the hill. I tried to follow, but I couldn't. I wanted real bad to know what happened. But I was back in the bubble deal again couldn't get it to move. But I could damn sure tell you one thing. The way they was stumbling and rolling over them rocks, they wouldn't want to carry them dead fellas any further than they had to.

Now here's something that started a chill running through me. The wind started blowing real hard and kicking up lots of dust. The sky was dark, all full of stormy-looking clouds. Two of the guys on the burial detail shaded their eyes and squinted up like they were trying to see the sun through the clouds. They was dressed a lot better than the rest of the detail and they wasn't working, so I figured they was the fellas in charge. They said something to each other, turned around and started hurrying the guys carrying the bodies.

Then the whole scene changed, and I wasn't in Jerusalem any more. I was a kid riding on a merry-go-round in a playground with another kid. A black kid. He looked familiar, but I couldn't call his name. He talked to me in a man's voice. "Why you crying, Sarge?"

"I just got Jerusalem dust in my eyes." He grinned and I knew who it was. It was Son, my army buddy who jumped on the grenade and saved my ass.

"It's okay, Sarge. It's just me and you. You can cry if you want. I won't tell nobody." Normally I wouldn't admit this, but hell it was only a dream and I was a kid and I started bawling like a lost lamb. I was bawling over the crucifixion, over him and his family, over Kathleen. I was even bawling for myself. I kept bawling and bawling and the merry-go-round kept turning around and around. Son kept smiling at me like the little son of a bitch couldn't have been happier.

I put my foot out and started slowing the merry-go-round down. By the time it stopped moving, I had my crying out. Me and the merry-go-round stopped spinning at the same time. I looked at Son who was still sitting there just grinning. "It's you, isn't it, Son?" He smiled and nodded. "I just want to tell you how sorry I am about you dying and me carrying on like this. About me losing track of your kinfolks. I'm sorry about everything."

He said, "No need to be sorry Sarge. You've only seen a little part of the picture. It's like a sort of coin that's got two sides to it and you can't see both sides at once with your naked eye" Then he used his foot to start the merry-go-round again. "What you got in your pocket, Sarge?"

I didn't know, so I reached in my jeans to find out. It was a marble. Tiger eye. They were always my favorites. I felt like I ought to do something for him, so I said, "Son, this here tiger eye is the only thing I've got in my pocket. You can have it if you want."

The merry-go-round was going faster and faster, I was getting dizzy, and we were whipping up a lot of dust. I started having a hard time seeing again. I heard Son saying, "Hold on to it, Sarge. I'll get it from you later." Then everything was cool and quiet and sanitary.

This is a good time to tell you about my dreams. If you're listening to these tapes, you probably think I've got a real active imagination and I dream all the time. Well that ain't the case. I remember having some dreams when I was a kid, but they was always about being stuck up on a roof or a cliff or something and I couldn't get down. Maybe I dreamed about other stuff, but I don't remember.

When I got back from Nam, I stopped dreaming altogether like my dreaming mechanism got unplugged or something. Well maybe that ain't exactly right. See, sometimes I'd wake up all covered with sweat and wore plumb out. So maybe I was dreaming but just didn't remember any of it.

What I'm saying is, for what it's worth, this was the first time I came up with any recall about a dream that had anything to do with me trying to somehow square up with Son for me not jumping on that grenade like I knew I should. I just thought I'd throw that in.

TAPE 17

Betsy was downstairs making pancakes, scrambling eggs, and frying bacon. I love the way a kitchen smells when bacon's frying and coffee's brewing. I'm not going to dwell on this much, but there's something extra special if you're stretched out in the morning sun thinking this may be the last time in your life you get to experience it. Betsy was humming a song as I stopped into her kitchen.

"Hey, nightingale, what's the name of the song you're singing?"

"Well, I'll tell you Buzz. This week will mark the anniversary of the day Patsy Cline, Hawkshaw Hawkins, and Cowboy Copas got killed in a plane crash. That was in 1963. It'll also be the anniversary of the day John Belushi turned up dead. So I've been singing all their songs every day this whole week. Patsy Cline, Hawkshaw Hawkins, Cowboy Copas, and the Blue Brothers. That song I was humming was one of Cowboy Copas'. It's called 'My Filipino Baby.'"

Of course, everybody's heard Patsy Cline singing. And anybody that loves movies has seen *The Blues Brothers*. Hell, I've got several Blues Brothers albums that wasn't even part of the movie soundtrack. "I'm embarrassed to tell you, Betsy, but I've never heard Cowboy Copas singing, and I'm a country and western fan."

"Well, I'm just tickled to death to broaden your education." She put on an album called *Tennessee Waltz*. I forgot how cool it is to hear a good yodeler. You don't hear yodeling in music anymore, and it's too bad. It's hard to be sad and listen to a someone that's got respectable yodeling skills Try it sometime and you'll see what I mean. I decided to tell Woodrow

261

that if I didn't make it, I wanted the guys down at The Gold to add some yodeling to my memorial jamboree.

Me and Betsy occupied ourselves listening to music and talking lyrics while Cheryl, Betsy's sister-in-law, tried to do something with Kathleen's hair in the other room.

Rubber Biscuit was playing when Kathleen walked into the kitchen. She was wearing a stocking cap, so I couldn't tell nothin' about the way her hair looked after Cheryl got through with it. I was fixing to ask about it when Kathleen took the initiative and asked to borrow Betsy's little Dodge Neon. "I've got meetings all day with Ernest Bidding's people. We need to put the finishing touches on the plans for this—I don't know what to call it—showdown or whatever. The "event," let's call it, will be at Bidding's megachurch in Mustang, and there are details to work out, so if it's okay with you, I need to take off."

Without thinking I just blurted out, "No way. After that crazy Carl deal, I'm not letting you go anyplace by yourself." Kathleen gave me a look that said she didn't like the idea of me putting my nose in here. It looked like there was about to be a stand-off. But Betsy stepped in and took the pressure off.

"Don't worry Buzz. Maggie's going to look after the diner today because I expected to baby sit you all anyway. If Kathleen doesn't mind the company, I'll just ride along. Okay with you Kathleen?" I could see that Kathleen was relieved to have the company. It was probably a pretty good compromise, because Betsy's tough and smart and carries a .38 wherever she goes. That made me feel better. So everything worked out. They left together, and Woodrow and I sat looking at the TV.

The weatherman said it was going to get close to seventy degrees, so I said, "Hey, Woodrow. You know what I think I'd like to do today? I'd like to go to the zoo." I probably should have told him about the dream. The dead guys in Jerusalem, Son on the merry-go-round. You know, all the stuff I just got through telling this machine. But I guess I just didn't feel like it right then. So I didn't. He sort of scratched at his beard, then he shrugged and off we went.

On the way over there, we were listening to Sam Cooke singing *Further Along* on the iPod. "Look here, Woodrow. This isn't the most pleasant subject, but I have to tell you how I want things lined out if this deal turns out bad."

He squinted over at me all disgusted looking. "How about if you just keep that kind of thinking to yourself. Don't get all negative on me here. And even if it does turn out bad, why can't you let Wanda line shit out?"

"Come on, Woodrow. We can't be ostriches. We have to face the fact that it's out of our control, and Wanda couldn't cope if I were to call her and start talking to her like this. I have to tell you, because I trust you and you can handle it."

Woodrow's no dummy. He could see the good sense of what I was saying. "Okay. I'll hear you out on this. But only on one condition."

"Okay. Shoot."

"I get to tell you how I want things if this fire drill gets mixed up and I'm the one that ends up getting dead. Deal?"

"Deal. I'll go first. I don't want a funeral, Woodrow. I want to get cremated. Wanda may kick a little bit. But I'll write her a note and give it to her. She'll be okay. Then, tell Billy and Stu and the boys down at the Gold to pick out some really good blues, you know, Watermelon Slim, R. L. Burnside, Junior Kimbrough. I couldn't ask for a better send-off. I want some yodeling too, like Roy Rogers or Cowboy Copas. Yodeling's cool. Then I want my ashes carried up to Cottonwood Pass in Colorado on June 20 and scattered up there."

"Don't want much do you? Why June 20?"

"That's the anniversary of the day I got discharged from the army. In a way, that's more of a birthday than my birthday."

He nodded. I could tell he understood. "Okay. Here's what I want. I want to get cremated too. I want the boys at the Gold to have a pool tournament. Billy's disqualified because it needs to be a fair game. The winner of the tournament gets to decide what to do with my ashes. I just hope whoever wins has some class along with a sense of humor." You've got to admit. Woodrow's got style.

Thursday, March 1, 2007, p.m.

When we rolled up in front of the zoo, I said, "Woodrow, I don't want to hurt your feelings or nothing, but I need a little time to myself."

He put a big old hand on my shoulder and said, "Of course. I understand. And, to tell the truth, I'd sure like to get away from you for awhile too as you're starting to wear on my nerves with all this talk about cremation and shit. How much time do you think you'll need?"

"Pick me up in a couple of hours." He gave me a real good once over.

"You going to be okay in there by yourself? I mean this is the first time since you been awake from your coma that you didn't have a babysitter."

"Don't worry about a thing Woodrow. I'll be fine." He started to say something else, but didn't. Instead, he gave me a nod. I got out, and he drove away. I watched the Dodge turn north on Eastern and disappear. I stood there wondering for a minute how many people have a really good friend? I mean the kind of guy who would drop everything when the chips are down and stick with you to the end, good or bad. I knew I could count on Woodrow no matter what. And I'll tell you something. He knows if the shoe was on the other foot, I'd damn sure do the same.

I guess there's several ways to figure it, so there's no way to get an accurate count, but we both saved each other's bacon several times. It's never come up which one of us owed the other the most. Even if you was to think in those terms, which I never did, friends don't ever mention who owes who the most. Like I said, it never came up between us.

Don't get me wrong. I wouldn't say I was ready to go. But if my time was up, it was worth living to have a friend like Woodrow Mulholland.

The Oklahoma City Zoo is a really cool place, especially in the winter when the kids are all in school and you got it pretty much to yourself. Some of the animals are indoors because they can't stand the cold. But there're plenty of others to see. Even if looking at caged-up critters isn't your thing, the plants and stuff out there are really nice. Peaceful feeling.

It's an easy place to think about your life. When I was driving for a living, I saw a whole lot of scenery zooming by my cab windows. Some of it was beautiful. Most of it I grabbed on the move. I could get a good sense of the big changes. Like from the desert to the mountains in California. And I got a good sense of how it is when the seasons change. I mean it can be green in Oklahoma and at the same time it can be crazy colorful going over the Green River Gorge in Tennessee. Believe me, I love seeing this country that way, and it would break my heart if things worked out that I never saw it that way again.

But that day at the zoo, I was feeling like I needed something else. I couldn't tell you what.

Of course, it would be crazy of me to expect to walk up on that picnic table and find that gol' darn puppet just sitting there waiting for me to drop by so we could have a nice chat about how I'm doing. No matter what, I knew it would be quiet and the birds that would be there are the ones that stick it out all winter. I couldn't tell you why, that just made me feel good somehow.

I strolled down the sidewalk in the oldest part of the zoo where they used to keep the bears and lions. I don't know what's there now, because I wasn't looking. I was just walking and thinking. I was almost up to the picnic table before I looked up, and I'm telling you, I had to do a double and triple take. There was somebody sitting there, and I swear to God I thought for a second it was that damn Pinocchio. Of course it wasn't. But I was having a hard time handling the shock. Wouldn't that have been a crazy wind-up to this freak show? For him to show up early and me without an answer ready? Lucky for me I didn't keel over with a heart attack right there.

It was an old guy sitting there wearing a faded field jacket with a 1st Cav patch on the shoulder. The jacket had oil stains all over it like he wore it to work on cars. He had long stringy brown hair and a beard that looked like it had cereal in it. He was just sitting there talking to himself.

The concession stand there is closed this time of year, or I'd have bought us both a cup of coffee. I walked over and stood there waiting for him to look up. He didn't. So I said, "Mind if I have a seat?"

When he did look up, I could see his eyes were all bloodshot, like he hadn't had any sleep for days. "Sure. Go ahead and sit, because I'd like to have a word with you."

I sat there and listened to him mumble. I couldn't understand a word he was saying, and I didn't say anything. I just waited there.

Finally, he looked over at me and said, "This isn't my coat you know. I'm not 1st Cav. I'm 25th Infantry."

"I know your outfit. The Tropic Lightning. Good bunch."

He nodded. "What's yours?"

"I was in the 196th Armored."

He nodded again. "What are you doing out here so far from your unit?"

"I'm not sure what I'm doing here. I got separated from the service more than 30 years ago. Maybe I'm looking for somebody."

"Well you found somebody."

"So tell me what you're doing out here?"

"I'm looking for somebody too." Then he went back to mumbling.

Maybe it was wishful thinking, but I got the feeling this meeting was set up for a reason. "This is going to sound strange fella, but have you got anything to tell me?"

"Maybe. What do you want to know?"

So I just up and asked him, "Do you know the names of the men who were crucified with Jesus?"

He gave me a cough-sounding laugh and said, "Of course I do. Remember the song? The Sam Cooke song?" Then he started singing.

Were you there when they crucified my Lord?
Were you there when they crucified my Lord?
Sometimes it causes me to tremble, tremble, tremble.
Were you there when they crucified my Lord?

You wouldn't judge by looking at him, but he was a pretty good singer. That song made me get all excited for some reason. "Sure I know that song. I know all the gospel songs Sam Cooke did."

Then he looked at me with a twinkle in his bloodshot eyes and said, "Well. Were you there?"

I told him, "Buddy, you may not believe this. But I was there last night."

He nodded and said, "Me too. I'm there every night." Then quick as a wink, he was crying. He pulled a frayed old bandana out of the pocket of that field jacket and covered his eyes with it. Then he started singing again. *Were you there when they nailed him to the tree?*" Then he looked at me again and said, "You were there last night. Did you see me?"

"There were several folks there. Maybe I did see you. I don't know."

What he said next caused me to start trembling, like I was falling in slow motion. Spinning.

"I saw you there. You was in the bubble." Everything was getting unreal and I knew I was passing out. But I needed to hang on. I tried to focus on the name on the pocket of the field jacket. "Elder" it said. I was holding on to the daylight and trying to talk.

I don't know if I said it with my voice or just with my mind. I was talking to him through a wide fall. "I don't have long Elder. Who was it? Who were they? The guys crucified with Jesus?"

Then he said in a voice so sad it would have broken your heart. "It was me. It was me and my son. We were the ones crucified with him. You know my son." It looked like the guy was pointing to the name on the field jacket. He spoke to me from way down deep in a well. "This isn't my name. This is just what they called me."

He was winking out like starlight. The last thing I remember was asking, "Come on man. I got to know. Who was it got crucified with Jesus?"

His finger was pointing to the name Elder on that jacket. "I told you soldier." Then the curtain came down.

I must have bit the inside of my mouth because I was bleeding when I started coming around. Believe me I was turned plumb upside down about my psycho-chat with that burned out old GI. Of course, he was gone when I started getting able to focus. I was laying under the picnic table and had no clue how long I'd been curled up on the dirt.

When I was able to roll out from under there and pull myself up on the bench, you know what I was thinking? *I wished I had a cherry snow cone like I did the first time I met the puppet here.* Only I needed one that wasn't so lethal in the brain freeze department.

I was sitting there with my head in my hands when a guy rolled up in a golf cart. "Are you okay man?"

"Yeah, I think so."

"Some old-timer lady in a dirty green field jacket said there was a guy passed out drunk under this picnic table. You're not drunk or stoned or anything, are you?"

"No, I'm fine."

But I was thinking, *I'm really not too sure.*

"Well, you can't pass out under my picnic table. If you're going to pass out or sleep, you need to do it someplace else." He sat in his golf cart watching me for a few minutes. "You're bleeding man. I can call you an ambulance if you need one. I got a radio."

"No need, pal. I'm getting up here." The golf cart guy shrugged and drove off, and I sat there on that hard bench wondering whether a brain injury could really change what's happening on the outside world or whether the outside was just like it always was only the transmission got scrambled in the way stuff got processed.

I don't know, and I'm not whining or worrying about it. I guess all you can do is figure out what you can and hang on if the ride gets too rough.

When I managed to get myself hauled into the passenger seat of the Dodge, Woodrow was looking over at me with a worried expression. "Jesus, Buzz. What the hell happened? There's blood on your tee shirt. Dude, you look sick." So I spun out the whole weird deal.

Now get this. The second I got to the part where the old vet pointed to his name "Elder" on the jacket, Woodrow's phone rang. It was Kathleen. She was real excited.

"Listen you two. I got an email from Pinocchio. He says we're on the right track. He says one reason Judas died was because of the role he played in the death of Simon the Elder. Does that name mean anything to you? Simon the Elder? I've never heard of him—that I know of anyway."

I felt my jaws lock like I was about to have another seizure. This had to be it. This Elder guy says he and his son were crucified with Jesus and now this Simon the Elder deal comes up. To tell you the truth, I wasn't in much shape to talk, so Woodrow brought Kathleen up to date on my zoo adventure.

"Hey, Kathleen, Buzz's a little out of it right now, but he just met a guy at the zoo who had a name tag on that said 'Elder'! And, for what it's worth, he says he and his son were crucified with Jesus. Did this Pinocchio message say that this Simon guy got crucified? Kathleen, are you there?"

"Yes. I'm here. I was just thinking. He didn't say anything about Simon being crucified. He just said one reason for Judas' death was revenge for Simon the Elder."

"Where are you now?"

"Betsy and I are on our way back to her house. In addition to getting this Pinocchio message just now, I've had quite an interesting afternoon with Bidding's assistants. I'll tell you all about it when I see you."

"Well, it looks like this Simon deal is a hot lead, so I think we better dig into the books again as soon as we can and see if we can uncover a trail."

"Okay. See you at Betsy's."

After we all were back at Betsy's, we got all set up on her kitchen table and spread our stuff out again while Betsy put on a Hawkshaw Hawkins album. It seemed like we'd been over and over the same old shit so many times, I could almost start quoting chapters and verses. I know we saw the name Simon a bunch of times. I just couldn't remember Simon the Elder. So we started combing the books again trying to find out who he was. Like usual, we started in the order Dr. Ryland gave us. I had Mark. Woodrow had Matthew. Since Kathleen was the faster reader and knew her way around the books, she had Luke and John.

Then we did like Dr. Soames said and concentrated on the passion narrative starting with the events that happened just before Jesus got to Jerusalem and made his celebration entry.

So I started. "Okay. The first Simon that shows up in Mark's passion narrative is in Bethany where that woman pours oil over Jesus' head. This all happens in the house of a guy named *'Simon the Leper.'*"

The next Simon is the disciple. He's sleeping when he's supposed to be on watch. That's at Mark 14:37." I turned a few pages. "Now here's a guy named Simon at 15:21. He got drafted to carry Jesus' cross to the crucifixion. Says here he had two sons named Alexander and Rufus. Looks like he was just walking by, coming from the country it says and..."

"Hold it." Kathleen was making some notes. "Two of these translations, the Amplified Bible and the New Century say he was coming from the 'field' or 'fields.'"

Woodrow asked, "What difference do you think that makes?"

"I don't know. Probably none. I just want to be sure we have everything in case we need to put something under a microscope later. Go ahead Leon."

"Well, before we go on, let's just take a look at that Interlinear Greek deal. What does that say Woodrow?"

He looked up Mark 15:21. "Says 'field,' not 'country.' Far as I'm concerned, they aren't necessarily the same thing."

Kathleen said, "Noted."

"That looks like it. Simon the leper, Simon the disciple, and Simon the Cyrenian. Nothing about Simon the elder. What's Matthew got to say?"

Woodrow was running his finger down the pages. "Same three Simons. Except Peter isn't called Simon in Matthew's version. He's just Peter. Same Simon the leper and the Cyrenian. In Matthew, they don't say where he was coming from. It just says they found him. Inconvenient for him that he just happened to be walking by a crucifixion when they needed a mule."

Of course, I knew how the poor sombitch felt. I just happened to be driving the wrong rig when it jackknifed, and look at the jam I landed in. Then I just blurted out. "Unless there was more to it than just coincidence."

"What makes you think there might be more than just coincidence here, Buzz?"

"I don't know. Just seems funny."

"This is odd." Kathleen was looking back and forth at her two Bibles. "Luke doesn't mention Simon the leper."

"He doesn't mention him anywhere?"

"Well, I'm just looking at the passion narrative right now. I'll go back and check to see if he's mentioned earlier. But for now let's just focus on the events surrounding the crucifixion." She made some notes then went back to her books. "Here's Simon Peter at 22:31 and the Cyrenian at 23:26. Nothing about his sons. These sons, are they mentioned in Matthew?"

Woodrow checked. "Nope. Nothing about any Cyrenian sons. Is that important?"

"I don't know. We'll keep our eye open for possible connections."

Kathleen started flipping pages. "Okay, let's look at John. Nothing about Simon the leper. But here's another curiosity. In Mark and Matthew didn't you say that the anointing in Bethany happened at the home of Simon the leper?"

I checked my Bible again. "It did in Mark."

"Matthew too."

"Well, in John, there's an anointing in Bethany, but here it looks like it's at Lazarus's house. You remember Lazarus was the man Jesus raised from the dead."

"So you figure there's some connection between Simon the Leper and Lazarus? Like maybe father, son? Brothers? Maybe the same guy? What?"

"I don't know. It'll take some time to look into it. Let's just finish this first." She had her eyes real close to the pages and she was studying hard. "Another Simon turns up at John 13:2. This is John's version of the Last Supper. He's telling about the devil coming into the heart of Judas Iscariot. But here it gives the name of Judas' father. It's Simon."

Woodrow was rubbing the back of his neck. "Hell, it looks like there were tons of Simons. But no Simon the Elder."

Kathleen got real excited. "Hold on! Hold on here! There are lots of references in John to Simon Peter. But guess what. Not a word about the Cyrenian. In fact, at 19:17, John says Jesus was carrying his own cross." Woodrow and I both turned to John 19:17. By now we could find it real easy. Sure enough. Nothing about the Cyrenian. Nothing about his sons. And, sure enough, according to John, Jesus was carrying his own cross.

Woodrow sat back in his chair and Kathleen was going on with her hard examination of those pages. "Well which one was it Kathleen? Do you reckon the Cyrenian carried that cross or did Jesus do it by himself?"

She didn't look up. "They both could have carried it. Jesus could have begun the ordeal and collapsed. Then, the Romans could have forced Simon to help. That could explain the difference."

"Maybe so. But I don't buy it. If that's the way it was, it's real easy to say it just the way it was done. Then there's no confusion. John was the last gospel written. Right? Looks to me like he was trying to rule out any suggestion that the Cyrenian carried Jesus' cross for him."

You could tell Kathleen was tired of Woodrow calling every little thing into question. "Okay. Woodrow. Give me one good reason why it would be an issue important enough that John or anyone else would lie about it. What difference does it make whether Jesus carried his own cross or whether Simon did?"

"Here's why it makes a difference. We're trying to find out who got crucified with Jesus. You get a spooky email that says one reason Judas Iscariot got killed was because of the role he played in the death of Simon the Elder. Maybe this Simon the Elder is one of the men who died with Jesus. Now we got a guy named Simon carrying a cross to execution, but the guys who tell us about it say it isn't Simon's cross. It's Jesus' cross. What if John's right? What if Jesus carried his own and Simon the Cyrenian carried his own. What if the Cyrenian and Simon the Elder are the same guy?"

"But why, Woodrow? Why would they gloss over the fact that Simon was a condemned man? What do they accomplish by distorting these particular facts?"

"I don't know Kathleen. It just seems like from the very beginning somebody wanted to blur some of the facts. Obviously, from the beginning people telling and writing the crucifixion story knew he was there—the Cyrene—but over time his role gets shrunk until in John he disappears completely. Doesn't it make more sense that the Romans would make all the condemned men carry their own crosses?"

"If the condemned man was capable, of course."

I had a question. "If the Romans beat a guy so bad he couldn't carry his cross, wouldn't that mean they botched the job? They went too far? I mean wasn't they supposed to be experts at this?"

"Well, for now, I'm assuming that Simon the Cyrenian and Simon the Elder are the same guy. And Simon the Elder was one of the crucified men."

"How do you account for the fact that there's no Simon the Elder mentioned anywhere in the Bible?"

"I can't explain that any more than I can explain why you and Buzz have creepy experiences that have the name 'Elder' in common on the same day—practically the same minute. My insides tell me I'm right. Simon the Cyrenian was known to be carrying a cross to the execution. I think he got nailed to the cross he carried. Just like John says, Jesus got nailed to the one he carried."

Kathleen mumbled something I couldn't understand. I had an idea. "Well, let's call Dr. Soames and see if he's ever heard of this Simon the Elder guy." Kathleen was dialing the phone before I even stopped talking. Dr. Soames wasn't in, so she left a message.

"Dr. Soames, this is Kathleen Wister. Someone has suggested that Judas may have been murdered, partly, because of the role he played in the death of a man named Simon the Elder. We can't find any references to such a man. Also, Woodrow thinks Simon the Cyrenian and Simon the Elder may be the same man and that the Cyrenian was actually crucified. Would you call us back so we can talk about this?" She left Betsy's phone number and her own cell number.

It was about time to get into our afternoon antiheadache ritual. We were just starting when the phone rang. It was Dr. Soames.

"Simon the Elder. I have to say you've roused my curiosity. What put you on the trail of this Simon the Elder fellow? "

"It's a long story Dr. Soames."

"I've made time. Really, I'm interested. Tell me about it." So Kathleen unrolled the whole deal. Simon the leper. The Cyrenian coming from the country or the field or whatever. His two sons. Which gospel writer dropped what. Blah, blah, blah. She didn't say anything about my creepy zoo deal.

After she finished, the phone was quiet and we was afraid we got cut off and would have to get Dr. Soames back on the line and run the whole deal again. But he was there. "Remarkable. Simon the Cyrenian is also known as Simon the Elder. He is crucified with Jesus. The fact is too well known to be completely written out of the passion narrative, so his role is altered to that of an innocent bystander who is carrying a cross to Golgotha by pure happenstance. He disappears from John altogether. Judas is, of course, blamed not only for the death of Jesus, but also Simon. Some friend or family member of Simon's takes revenge and Judas is murdered. The two candidates for his position are Matthias and Barsabbas. Remarkable. Wonderful."

"What are you thinking Dr. Soames?"

"Is your recorder still on?"

"Yes."

"Well turn it off."

"Okay. It's off. What are you thinking?"

"Now I don't want to be quoted on any of this because I truly am just thinking out loud. What I'm about to say may have no scholarly merit at all. I need to give it a good deal more thought, and I damn sure need to verify with some research before I take a position. I probably shouldn't even say anything until I mull this over for awhile. But, with your word that you won't repeat what I'm about to say, I'll offer a partial working hypothesis. Deal?"

Woodrow laughed. "Hell doc. You make it sound like you're about to spill the beans on the secret formula for Coca-Cola. You've got our curiosity index through the roof. I think we can all keep a secret."

"Mr. Butane, Miss Wister, can you keep a secret?"

"Of course."

"Yes."

"Okay. There is no Simon the Elder that I know of. But your scenario offers some appealing explanations for a number of puzzling historical mysteries. I won't go into all of them until we get together face to face…"

I interrupted. "Look Dr. Soames. We don't have time…"

"Yes, yes I know. But I'll be in Kansas City tomorrow night on business and I know it's not too far from where you are. I'm hoping you can meet me there. I'll be with someone that I really think you'll want to meet. Can you come to Kansas City tomorrow night?"

Kathleen didn't bother to wait for Woodrow and me to say anything. Guess she didn't need to. "Yes. We can be there. But what do you have to tell us tonight?"

"Maybe this will whet your appetite and hold you until tomorrow. First, I should tell you that you're not the first to put Simon the Cyrene on the cross at Golgotha. The Muslims have been saying that for hundreds of years." Kathleen and I were writing as fast as we could, and Woodrow was staring at the phone. "Now, let's talk about this revenge angle. Assume that one of the men crucified with Jesus was Simon the Elder. Judas is murdered. One of the candidates for his place is Barsabbas. Do you know what Barsabbas means in Aramaic? It means the son of Saba. One possible translation of *saba* is 'the elder.' One of the applicants for Judas's position may have been known as 'the son of the Elder'."

I felt like a bolt of electricity went through me. For a second, I was afraid I was feeling some preseizure quakes. I guess everyone was trying to say something, but nothing was coming out.

Dr. Soames went on. "You see where this might lead. If Judas' betrayal, whatever that was, led to the deaths of Jesus and others, the son of one of those others may be responsible for Judas's death and thus his claim to that office. If you're right. If the Cyrenian is, in fact, Simon the Elder, then Barsabbas could very well be his son."

Kathleen was on it quick. "And the other applicant? Matthias? What were his qualifications for the job?"

"Okay, try this on. Remember what I read to you yesterday? The verse in the Pseudo-Clementine *Recognitions* where the names Barabbas and Barnabas were interchanged? Follow me here. In that verse, another name for Matthias is either Barabbas or Barnabas. See? They may be the same man. So what happens? Barabbas is identified as a man who committed murder. Barnabas was a man who sold property and gave the money to the early church fathers. Look at Acts 4:36. This has always been something of a puzzle to Bible scholars as Barnabas is identified as a Levite. Under Mosaic law, Levites were forbidden to own property. Either he was not very observant for a Levite, or the property sale was a convenient explanation for where the money came from.

"If we string everything together, here's what we have. Judas is found murdered after he betrays Jesus and others. Matthias as Barabbas is known to be guilty of murder but he is not punished. Matthias as Barnabas comes up with a sum of money he got from a land sale. A land sale is somehow connected to Judas' death. Matthias is chosen to take Judas' place. You have to read between the lines, but it fits."

Kathleen was trying to come up with something to say, but she was overwhelmed. Dr. Soames sounded out of breath.

We were all peppering him with questions, but he said to hold everything until tomorrow.

"I'll be at the Fairmont on the Plaza about 3:00. Meet me at the hotel bar at 5:00. I think we'll have some exciting ideas to exchange. Oh, by the way, if you should hear any more from Pinocchio, call me right away. Good night." We spent some time kicking everything around but Woodrow was the only one that had his heart in it. Kathleen was writing names and drawing lines and circles; Barabbas, Barnabas, Barsabus, Jesus, Jospeh, Justus, Simon, Simon, Simon....

I was thinking about a guy I saw in Nam. He got hit in the belly by some ricochet shrapnel. The medics carried him away on a stretcher. He wasn't making a sound. He was just looking straight up using his hands to hold his insides in. The medics was running to get him on a chopper telling him to hang in there. He was gonna be okay, they said. I wondered how long you could live with your insides on the outside. I wondered if the men who cut Judas open made sure he knew who done it and why. I wonder if Judas said somebody's name before he died.

I guess I had a glassy look in my eye 'cause Woodrow knuckled my shoulder a little bit. "Hey, Buzz, you okay? You look like you been eating too many green apples."

"It's just this headache Woodrow. Too much happened today I guess. I need some weed therapy and a good night's sleep."

He nodded. Me and him stepped out on Betsy's back porch and enjoyed the remedy.

That night, I dreamed I was back at the Hotel Coloniale in Saigon. I was in the lobby again smelling strawberries and honeysuckle. Only it was different this time.

There was this lady walking toward me like before. But this time it was Kathleen. She had this parasol deal covering half her face. I couldn't see her eyes. I stood watching her because there was something I wanted to say, but I didn't know what. She walked right up to me and stood there smiling.

As soon as I said, "Kathleen ..." she put her finger up to my lips to stop me. Then she raised the parasol up so I could see her eyes, and it made me stumble backward. There was a hole where her right eye should be. I stood there being so shocked and broken hearted I couldn't stand it. I felt like her losing her eye must be my fault. But the smile on her face was so sweet. Like nothing happened or whatever it was, she didn't mind. Then she reached down and got a hold of my hand and raised it up. She looked down, and I couldn't see the hole anymore. She was beautiful like always. She put a lacy little handkerchief deal in my hand. Then she covered her face with the parasol—except for her smile—and walked past me out into the sunlight on the Saigon street.

I woke up not knowing exactly how to feel about that damn dream. Part of me was happy about having a little part of Kathleen in a picture of Vietnam. Then there was a part of me that felt guilty about her lost eye, even though, I knew it was just a dream and her eyes was fine. Then there was a part of me that was thrilled that she put that lacy little handkerchief in my hand. Then there was ... well, this isn't going anywhere, is it?

TAPE 18

Friday, March 2, 2007, a.m.

Yesterday morning at breakfast, Kathleen gave us the low down on how this whole deal was supposed to play out. Bidding's church was a new kind of set-up called a megachurch. I guess thousands of people show up there every week and then thousands more watch on TV. On top of that, there was going to be even more people tuning in for a pay-per-view special service where I was going to be the main attraction. It was going to be an honest-to-goodness, bona fide religious smackdown. The whole deal was being played so you'd think God himself was going to show up for a cage fight against the underworld heavyweight champ and all his buddies.

Bidding and The Forces of Good wanted me and my "entourage" to show up in a limousine. I don't know what sort of entourage they was expecting, but I was figuring to show up in a Dodge with a peg-legged dude and a Christian lady. Some of Bidding's helpers was supposed to be there to protect me from the faithful if things got out of hand. I wasn't worried. Me and Woodrow had whipped a houseful of the faithful before.

We showed up at the tabernacle about nine that morning. The mega-church was already buzzing like a Shawnee County bee hive. There was sound people and video people climbing around in the rafters like monkeys. There was people on stage tuning up guitars and testing microphones like they was expecting Pink Floyd to show up.

I stood there looking around and being amazed at the size of the whole gol' darn production. Woodrow tapped on my shoulder and pointed. I saw this movie-star-looking woman gliding toward me. She had these fellas trailing along behind her and both of 'em was sporting Conway Twitty hairdos. She stared right at my face and smiled like a new bride. The closer she got, the weaker my knees was getting. I never in my life saw such a beautiful woman moving that fast and coming my way on purpose.

By the time she got up in front of me and stopped with her hand sticking out, I was about to keel over. "So this is the famous Leon Butane. I'm Debra. I can't tell you how much I've been looking forward to meeting you, Leon. It's okay to call you Leon isn't it?" I made sure my eyeball was in place and stuttered that she could call me whatever she pleased.

I reached out and took the warm little hand she was offering under them batting eyelashes. Now over the years, I've looked at a *Playboy* magazine or two. I didn't think women living in the real world could be dolled up like that. *Playboy* women, if they was real, was all corralled up in movie star mansions and penthouses and stuff like that. But you know, when you look at them blurry, soft-lighted pictures, you can't help but imagine what it would feel like to reach out and touch one of them. They had to feel different from other women. They had to feel to your hand like butternut ice cream tastes to your tongue. Does that make sense? Anyway, while I was standing there melting into Debra's blue eyes, I was thinking *This here is what it feels like. This here is what it feels like to touch the hand of a gol' darn* Playboy *bunny.*

She acted like she could barely stand to tear her eyes away from my face, but she looked over my shoulder. Sounded to me like there was a sort of chill in her voice, "Hello Kathleen. Interesting hair style. It's new isn't it?" She didn't stick her hand out.

Kathleen had a chill of her own, "Debra, this is Woodrow Mulholland." Debra looked at Woodrow for the first time. He was standing there all bushy-headed and grinning in his Weloka-made overalls. He stuck that bear paw of his out. Debra looked him up and down like he was a car door that needed closing.

"Yes." She said it like she'd say to somebody who asked, *May I put your luggage in the trunk, ma'am?* She put four of her little fingers against his palm then pulled them away.

I was glad when the subject came back to me. She slipped her arm inside mine like we was on a date or something and started guiding me toward a couple of tall carved office doors.

As we walked, she was pointing and explaining how everything was going to be in the broadcast. "I'll be waiting for you at the back door at 10:45. There will be cameras to catch everything from various angles."

She pointed up to a giant sheet hanging from the ceiling. "Everything will be broadcast onto that screen so everyone can get a good look at all that happens. I'll escort you to the stage, and then Reverend Bidding will set you free."

We was all breezing toward those tall wooden doors that had angels and globes carved all over them. I let her guide me through them doors like a calf following mama. There was a big desk with a couple of high dollar leather chairs in front of it. Debra sat in one and patted the seat on the other one. That's where she wanted me to sit. So I did with a grin. I looked back at Kathleen and Woodrow. The Conway Twitty twins herded them over to a couch at the back of the room. For some reason it looked like Kathleen was giving me the evil eye. After we all got settled in it got real quiet in there like there was some agreement none of us would talk again until we got the go-ahead.

It reminded me of the kind of quiet you hear in an examination room while you're waiting for the doctor to show up. I was thinking I ought to tell or joke or something when I felt a cool breeze start up. Then I heard soft music coming from someplace. A book case behind the desk flew open. Hell, it was a door. And in stepped Ernest Bidding himself. He blew in there holding his hand out and smiling at me like I was his long lost brother. I just automatically got to my feet. At that moment I forgot how mad I was about how shitty he treated Kathleen. Looking back, I'm ashamed how easy it was for me to get plumb suckered into the hype.

Anyway, it was like Bidding didn't see anybody in that room but me. He came striding over and took hold of my right hand. He held onto it with both his hands and looked me in the eye. His expression looked like he understood everything I was going through and he felt sorry for me.

I thought I could feel a tingling running from his hands into mine, and I was damn sure tongue tied. I plumb forgot about telling any jokes. He stood there putting that *I-feel-your-pain* stare on me for a second, or two. Nobody in the room made a sound.

When he finally spoke up, it was like Vaseline on a sunburn. "Hello, Leon. I've been looking forward to this meeting." You'd have thought a magic spell got broken. Seemed like everybody in the room breathed at once—myself included. "Please sit down, Leon. We have a lot to discuss before Sunday." I sat down like he told me. I shot a look over at Debra. She was looking at my hands like she was measuring them or something.

Reverend Bidding sat on the edge of his desk like he was posing for a picture. He's a lot bigger in person than he looks on TV. You can see how he could be a linebacker on a pro football team.

"Leon, believe me. I know everything you've been going through. I know about the confusion, the worry, the disappointment. I know about the guilt and sorrow. I know about the regret. I've experienced all this and more myself. You believe me when I say I know these things, don't you, Leon?"

I gulped "Yeah. I mean, I guess so."

"Of course you do. You feel you're caught up in a struggle that you don't understand, and you've been asking yourself, '*Why me?*' haven't you?"

"Well, yeah."

"Of course. Leon, do you sense that there are unseen forces at work around you? Forces that you are not able to explain or comprehend?"

"Uh, yeah, sure."

Then he leaned real close to me and put his hand on my shoulder. I was feeling that tingling everywhere he touched me. He looked at me real hard with them pale blue eyes and said, "Leon, do you believe in the power of God Almighty?"

What was I supposed to say to that? "Sure."

"God bless you, Leon." The way he said it made me feel relieved. Like a traffic cop letting me off with a warning. Then he said, "Do you want God to free you from this demon's control?"

And I said, "If this here puppet is a demon, you're damn straight. I want to get free." I felt my face redden a little bit. "Pardon my French Debra."

Reverend Bidding gave me a movie-star smile, shook my hand real hard and looked up toward heaven. He still had his hand on my shoulder when he spoke sounding like Moses hisself. "Open your eyes, Leon! Can't you see this demon has sent you on a mission to slander the son of God himself? Can't you see that this demon has endangered you and your friends? Haven't you been in a state of fear for your very life since this demon has troubled you?" He took his hand away and gave me a hard stare. "Leon! How can there be any doubt? How can you not see that the very controller of this demon puppet is Satan himself? Open your eyes, Leon! These evils that have plagued you are all the product of the devil's plot to discredit Jesus Christ and confuse the faithful. Amen?" Everybody in the room except Kathleen and Woodrow said "Amen!" Hell, I might have even mumbled it myself.

Then Reverend Bidding stood up and put his big old hands together like he was praying. He was still looking up and said, "Leon, if it were up to me, I'd free you from this spirit right now. But, in order for God's glory to be more fully revealed, he has commanded me to wait until his triumph can be witnessed by the multitudes—by all the multitudes—both believers and unbelievers."

He reached down and pulled me to my feet like I was a kid. He put both hands on my shoulders and looked at me real hard again and said, "Leon, we can't understand the ways of God. We can't divine his reasons. We don't know why you were chosen to be a battleground between the plots of the devil and the revelation of the Holy Spirit. But we do know that God has chosen to transform this stumbling block to your soul into a blessing for you and the world. So rejoice, Leon. Your deliverance is at hand." He nodded to the Conway Twitty twins.

They swooped down on me and started moving me toward the door with Debra cooing about my courage and what a blessing I was to all of them. Stuff like that. To tell the truth, I felt like a load was lifted off me. I thought, *Leon, old hoss, your troubles are just about over. You're going to get free of the puppet. You'll be back on the road before you know it. Then watch me. I'll start going to church every Sunday no matter where I am.* I was about to make my mind up about tithing too; but I'd have to think about that one little bit more.

As I was being hustled out, I looked over my shoulder to say goodbye. I saw Reverend Bidding smiling at me. The only other time a guy looked at me with a expression like that was in a high school football game. I was playing defensive end and a halfback from Thunderbird High got a step on me and caught a pass for a touchdown. I stood there in the end zone with him feeling my whole team's eyes on me. This halfback took off his helmet and smiled at me just like Bidding was smiling at me then. Bidding gave me a little wave as he strolled toward his bookcase door. I thought I saw him look in a mirror and give himself a little wink. Then he was gone. It all happened so quick, I thought it might be my imagination. Maybe the devil got a hold of me the minute Reverend Bidding turned me loose and started putting doubt in my mind.

I didn't have time to think it through, because the Twitty twins and Debra had me sitting at a table and were putting papers in front of me to sign. I was going to do as I was told. But Woodrow said "Hold on there, Buzz. You ought to read this stuff before you sign it."

As soon as he said that, it was like Kathleen snapped out of a trance or something. She barked "What are these?"

Debra spoke up with that purry kitten voice of hers. "These are just some details that Ernest would like to have Leon approve. Strictly routine." She was smiling a glittery, quiet smile and pointing to a line for me to sign. She was wearing a low-cut white dress with pearls hanging into her cleavage. She leaned down to help me sign. My eyes couldn't help but follow them pearls as they rolled out and dangled near my shoulder. Then there was that lace just dying to be admired and me just dying to admire it.

She got so close her perfume about took me over. She was almost whispering in my ear. "It's okay, Leon, dear. Just sign here." Woodrow stepped over to the table and took the pen out of my hand.

Kathleen gathered up the papers real business like. "We'll get back to you."

Debra put her hand on mine and I got the same sort of tingling I got from Reverend Bidding's touch. She talked to me like there was nobody else in the room. "Leon. You have to trust Reverend Bidding. He's the only one that can help you. You're so close to deliverance now and it's important to us—to me that nothing interferes with what Reverend Bidding is trying to do for you." She dropped her eyes and my heart fluttered like a little bird. She squeezed my hand and right then I would've done anything to please her.

But Woodrow broke the spell. He pulled my chair back from the table. He and Kathleen got me to my feet and ushered me out the door. I looked back over my shoulder at Debra. I was probably smiling like a jackanapes. I was thinking, *You know, if the puppet demon gets driven out and I survive, I think Debra likes me. Maybe I should ask her out.*

That sweet smile vanished from Debra's face and she looked daggers at the back of Kathleen's head. I thought, *Isn't that sweet. She's jealous.* When we stepped outside, Kathleen and Woodrow hurried me to the Dodge. I inhaled all the cool air and sunshine I could get. I was walking along on a cloud thinking, *Well that was damn sure special, wasn't it? I'm going to get the puppet off my back. I'll be back to driving before you know it. And who knows? Maybe Debra would like to see America from the cab of a semi.*

Just like that, I started getting dizzy and having trouble breathing. I could hear that puppet voice in my head saying, *Careful, Mr. Butane. If you abandon the quest prematurely our arrangements and your life come to an end. Careful.* I leaned against the Dodge to try to steady myself and catch my breath. Woodrow and Kathleen helped me into the pickup.

Woodrow asked "You need to go to the hospital, Buzz?"

"No. We just need to go someplace where I can think. I need to sort through what just happened."

Kathleen was reading over those routine forms and mumbling to herself as I leaned back against the head rest.

We pulled into the Skyline parking lot before the lunch crowd started showing up. The Skyline is one of the best truck stops in the whole world. There are not so many truckers in there now as there used to be because the Transcon truck yard next door closed down. But it's still full of blue-collar guys and gals, and you don't have to wait to be seated. You just sit down wherever you see an empty spot. And best of all, the food is great.

By the way Kathleen was looking around like a lost lamb, you could tell she'd never been inside an honest-to-goodness truck stop before. She didn't ask, but I could tell she wondered if the food was safe to eat. Woodrow and I both got homemade beef stew with onion and cornbread. Kathleen got hot tea.

After we got settled in, I asked "What the hell happened back there?"

Kathleen said, "Well, for one thing, you let that floozy Debra sweep you off your silly feet. Really, Leon. I gave you more credit than that."

"I don't know what to say Kathleen. It's like the minute I stepped in there, all my will power got sucked plumb out of me. Hell, it was like I turned into a sheep or something. I'm okay now though. Believe me, I'll be ready for their magic tricks next time."

Kathleen took a deep breath and shook her head. "It's really not your fault, Leon. I've seen this many times before. That's what big-time televangelists do. They specialize in catching people up in a whirlwind. That's their profession. They are experts at taking crowds and sweeping them toward a trance. The closer they can move groups of people toward a communal mind-set, the more successful they are. And it's not just groups. They practice one-on-one techniques too; create the atmosphere of faith that makes people believe in miracles. The next step is to make people believe they're actually seeing and experiencing miracles."

Kathleen leaned across the table and slid me the papers Debra was trying to get me to sign. She had some of the printing circled. At the top of the first page she circled the word *"Novation."*

"So what the hell does 'novation' mean?"

"That means everybody is backing out of the contract we first signed, and they're substituting a new deal. So this is not just a routine formality. They've redrawn the whole agreement." I wasn't really up on what our deal actually was in the first place, so I wouldn't know how this one would change stuff.

She had a $10,000 figure circled. "This is the consideration for the novation. They'll give you this amount when you sign the new contract." Well, hell, that sounded great to me because I didn't get shit when I signed the last one.

So I asked "What's wrong with that?"

She said, "If you take the $10,000, you're giving up almost everything else."

"Like what?"

"Well, as things now stand, you get twenty-five percent of any and all revenues realized as result of your appearance at this event. They're selling tickets to it; like a rock concert."

I couldn't believe It. "You mean they're selling tickets to a church service?"

She nodded "They bought time on a cable network and the Ernest Bidding Ministries is buying advertising time from the Tabernacle. They're using that advertising to sell Bidding's books, tapes, and so on. So you'd be entitled to twenty percent of the net advertising revenues." I was stunned some more.

She kept talking. "Then, this novation would give them sole ownership of all audio and video recordings of the event. In the beginning they were willing to pay you a straight up $20,000 if you'd give up all rights. I told them 'No'. I said we'd negotiate for the rights to the recordings after the event. We'd have a better idea then what they might be worth. So, not counting all the other revenues, your share of 'the gate' at the Tabernacle should be around $6,000. The rest of it could be in the tens—even hundreds—of thousands of dollars. I don't think you realize what a tremendous amount of interest you're generating here. This is being packaged and sold like a major media event. The Tabernacle and Bidding Ministries stand to make a fortune, and they didn't want to share it with you." I couldn't believe that sweet-looking Debra was trying to take advantage of me. Right then I changed my mind about asking her out. She'd just have to find somebody else to see America with. And I was glad I hadn't committed to no tithes.

Woodrow said "Hell, Buzz. You're old enough to know any time somebody tries to stampede you into signing something, there's sure to be a snake in the sleeping bag." So I sat there feeling real fickle and foolish. A half-hour ago, I felt like Bidding was going to pull me out of this. Now I felt like he was just taking me in like a rube at the carnival. I wasn't sure where that left me, but I decided to enjoy my beef stew.

Friday, March 2, 2007, p.m.

Okay. I just took another break to stretch my legs clear my head for a second so I'm ready to finish this deal up. Okay. Where was I? Oh yeah. Dr. Soames and Kansas City.

After we finished lunch, it was time to head to Kansas City. We couldn't have asked for a nicer day for a drive. It was clear and the temperature got up to about seventy degrees. Perfect. We got there a little early so we decided to walk around the Plaza. I was there once in 2002 when I came up for the Big Twelve basketball championship. While we walked around looking in the shop windows, I got sort of overwhelmed by the desire to buy something nice for Kathleen. But I really didn't know what she liked, and I'm terrible at buying that kind of stuff for women. I decided to think positive. I made my mind up I was going to survive this nightmare and make a bunch of money to boot. Then I'd get some help from Betsy and buy Kathleen something real pretty.

Anyway, there is an Eddie Bauer store on the Plaza, and Kathleen bought me a hat. All my life, the only hats I ever wore was cowboy hats and ball caps. The one she bought me was sort of like an Indiana Jones job. Know what? If I say so myself, it looked pretty good on me.

At 4:50, we walked across the street to the Fairmont. We looked in the bar, and saw our people sitting by a window. Kathleen spotted Dr. Soames, because she'd seen his picture on the back cover of his book. We walked over to where they were sitting, and Kathleen put her hand out.

"Dr. Soames. I'm Kathleen Wister. I'm very glad to meet you in person. This is Leon Butane and Woodrow Mulholland."

Dr. Soames gave us a big charming smile. "It really is a pleasure to meet you all. I have to say that I've lost a good deal of sleep because of you, and I've let myself get into quite a state of excitement. Let me introduce Dr. Freda Bloom. She's a much respected New Testament scholar. Her modesty won't allow me to extol all her virtues—scholastic and otherwise." He gave her a wink. You could tell she didn't like his manners right at that minute.

When she talked it was real cold and business-like. "Miss Wister, Mr. Butane, Mr. Mulholland. I've been told a good deal about your—problem. Let me be frank. I'm very skeptical about this entire affair. I don't mean to offend, but this sudden sophomoric frenzy over newly found biblical evidence is an embarrassment to legitimate scholars. I'm ..."

I interrupted. "Well, all due respect Miss Bloom ..."

"It's Dr. Bloom."

"Dynamite. With all due respect Dr. Bloom, we didn't come up here to get lectured. I don't really care what you think about my problem. I'm looking for answers, and Dr. Soames here says you may have some. I hope he's right."

It was Kathleen's turn to interrupt. "Dr. Bloom. Of course we appreciate your skepticism. I assure you, we're not interested in interfering in any way with the progress of legitimate New Testament scholarship."

"So would you be willing to agree to sign a document promising not to use our names or any information we might share for any commercial purposes?"

That's when Dr. Soames spoke up. "Come on. Relax Freda. Who cares what they do with it if our names aren't connected. I'm telling you, they're onto something. They can probably do us more good than we can do them." He looked me right in the eye. "We can trust these people. If they promise they won't mention our names in connection with any spectacular disclosures, they'll keep their word. There's no need for signatures on legal documents. Right, Mr. Butane?"

"We won't say where we get the information unless you say it's okay."

"Fine."

In case, you're wondering, their real names ain't Soames and Bloom. I don't want you to think I'd blab my mouth once I promised I wouldn't.

It was Woodrow's turn. "And then you all agree not to use our names on anything we give you unless you ask us first. Right?"

Dr. Soames busted out laughing. "What do you say Freda? Dr. Bloom? You promise not to use anything we learn from these people for commercial purposes without their permission? I mean what's fair is fair. Right? Sauce for the goose, and all that."

"This is ridiculous."

"I agree. Let's start all over again so we can sit down together and play doctor." He winked at me. "What do you drink, Leon?"

"Coors."

"Woodrow?"

"If you're buying, Doc, I'll have scotch on the rocks."

"Precisely my beverage of choice. Miss Wister?"

"Hot tea."

Dr. Bloom started to light up a cigarette. "Sorry Freda. No smoking allowed."

"But this is a hotel lobby bar for Christ's sake."

"We're not in Jerusalem. This is Kansas City." She mumbled as she replaced the cigarettes and lighter in her purse. "Now Freda. Would you like to tell them what you know about the Cyrenian, or would you rather I teach your class for you?"

"You're such a putz, Barry." She took a deep breath and reached into a beat up briefcase and pulled out a folder. We took a seat. Kathleen and I took out our papers. Dr. Bloom put on a pair of glasses. After the waitress brought our drinks, we got down to business.

She showed us a black and white photo. "This is a photograph of an ossuary found in the Kidron Valley by Eleazar Sukenik in 1941. I assume you know the function of an ossuary."

Kathleen answered. "Yes. We have a decent understanding of how it worked."

"Fine. Then I won't go into detail. I'll just summarize. For a period of time leading up to the destruction of Jerusalem in 70 CE, the Jewish dead were placed in rock cut tombs and left to decompose. Approximately a year later, the bones were retrieved and placed in these ossuaries and reburied.

"This particular box was found in the valley that separates Jerusalem from the Mount of Olives. The inscription reads," she wrote it out in English "*Alexandros (son of) Simon.*' On the top of this ossuary is a Hebrew word. The meaning is unclear, but there are other indications in this tomb that the occupants had Cyrenian contacts, which would lead us to believe that there is a simple error carved on the box. If that error is corrected, the inscription would be rendered '*Cyrenian.*' If this is true, we have the ossuary of Alexander, son of Simon who had Cyrenian contacts. This could be and probably is the man mentioned in Mark."

Woodrow was scratching his jaw. "So, help me here. What's this add to the solution to our problem?"

Dr. Soames sat back and crossed his legs. "Well, Mr. Mulholland, it was that spelling error on the top of the box and your suggestion that Simon the Cyrenian might also be known as Simon the Elder that started us thinking. In just a minute, I'll yield the floor back to Dr. Bloom, but let me contribute a little more background. Freda and I have been collaborating on a treatise on the most recent archeology and scholarship concerning the trial, crucifixion, and resurrection of Jesus. I'm embarrassed to say there are a number of obvious problems that have simply been overlooked by scholars for centuries. Indeed, Freda and I overlooked them ourselves until we happened on Miss Wister's blog. Thanks to you all, a number of important threads are drawing together." He had a happy expression on his face and took a man-sized gulp of scotch. "Take it away, Freda."

"Well, to start with, no one has heard of Simon the Elder in connection with New Testament scholarship. We know of Simon, Jesus' brother; Simon Peter; Simon, Judas Iscariot's father; Simon the Leper; Simon the Cyrenian, and others who are not really central to the passion narrative.

"One of the problems of New Testament scholarship has to do with Simon the Leper. Why would Jesus and his disciples have close contact with a leper when they were on their way to Jerusalem where their purity was of critical importance?" She frowned and stared at the spoon in her teacup.

"None of it made sense. One suggestion was that Simon, himself, wasn't there when Jesus and his disciples gathered in his house in Bethany. But the Luke description of the anointing occurs earlier in his gospel and he has Jesus speaking directly to Simon though he's not described as a leper on that occasion. He's called the Pharisee. Look at Luke 7:40. The evidence weighs in favor of this Simon the Pharisee being the same man they're calling Simon the Leper in Matthew and Mark, and he was present.

"Another possible explanation is that Simon was a leper that had been cured or recovered. Possible, but not convincing. It would be too simple to say that. Another hypothesis is that there was an error in transmission from the Aramaic to the Greek and the original rendering was Simon the Potter. We considered that, but the scholarship making the connection didn't hold up.

"This would however, lead to some interesting speculations about some potential connection between Simon the Potter and Judas's 'Field of Blood' which was also, apparently known as 'Potter's Field.' We'll just have to leave that unexamined for now.

"The last suggestion that has scholarly support is this. Jesus simply didn't care about strict compliance with the purity laws. Maybe so. But it's unlikely his disciples would, in a group, be so cavalier. Again, not convincing.

"But here's what we never considered until you raised the possibility. Maybe he wasn't a leper at all. Maybe a linguistic error is, in fact, the more plausible explanation. Look here. Let me show you." She took a piece of paper and wrote some blocky looking letters. "This is the word 'leper' as it is written in Aramaic. In English it would look like *sara* or *tsara*. Now here's one of the Hebrew words for elder." She wrote another blocky looking word. "This could be pronounced *saba* or *tsaba*. A scribal error that could easily be made by an unskillful copyist could produce a significant error in transmission. The lower horizontal on the letter *beth* is accidentally dropped it then becomes the letter *resh*, in this way, *tsaba* becomes *tsara*. Simon the Elder becomes mistakenly identified as Simon the Leper. We looked at her writing and we could see what she was talking about. She sat back looking pleased with herself. This is a very plausible explanation which would hold up to a careful scholarly analysis." Her point was starting to sink in.

I looked over my notes for a minute. "So Simon the Elder, Simon the Leper, and the Cyrenian might all be the same person?"

"Let me caution you. I think it's unlikely. But it is possible."

Dr. Soames was smiling. "See the scenario? A less than capable Aramaic scribe does his best to relate the story in his own language. A translator is copying the Aramaic to Greek and makes an error in translation or, for some reason injects an intentional corruption. Simon the Elder becomes Simon the Leper years after those who related the oral tradition are unavailable to correct the error, and it winds up corrupting the Mark and Matthew traditions we have today."

Kathleen was on the edge of her seat. "Dr. Soames. If this Simon the Leper is really Simon the Elder; if he's one of those that got crucified with Jesus, how did it happen and who was the other man?"

Dr. Bloom signaled the waitress. "I think I'm ready for something a little stronger. I'll have the same thing as Mr. Mulholland here."

Dr. Soames was still smiling, playful looking. "Looks like we're in for an interesting evening. What do you think Freda? Who was the other one?"

"You know what I'm thinking, Barry. It could have been Lazarus."

Kathleen's eyes were big as saucers. "You mean after Jesus raised him from the dead, he might have been crucified?"

"Miss Wister. I don't believe in the resurrection story. I believe the name Lazarus was known to the early Christian community. I believe his story was somehow intertwined with that of Jesus and became distorted as the tradition evolved. The puzzle pieces unmistakably link Lazarus and the mysterious Simon. They clearly occupied the same house. They were probably father and son if you want my opinion."

Kathleen shook her head. "There's too much of this for me to process. Please break it down in pieces."

"Okay. Start with this. John says the Jewish authorities condemned Lazarus right along with Jesus."

"Excuse me Dr. Bloom. Where does it say that?"

"In John 12:10, immediately after the story of the anointing in Bethany, we're told the chief priests made plans to kill Lazarus too. Take a moment to look it up. My drink's here."

Kathleen thumbed to the verse in John while Dr. Bloom took a ladylike sip and sat back to wait. Kathleen ran her finger along the page and nodded.

"Now, if you'll look at verse seventeen, Lazarus is mentioned for the last time. It follows immediately on the heels of Jesus' messianic entry into Jerusalem and Lazarus is at the core of the excitement surrounding Jesus of Nazareth. Nothing more is said about the plot to kill Lazarus. Now we have the name of a man other than Jesus who was targeted for death by the Jewish authorities. We have the name of one man other than Jesus who was carrying a cross to crucifixion. I have to say—even before all this—if pressed to name viable possibilities for the identities of the cocrucifieds, these two are high on the list."

"But why? Why be so vague? Why not say that these are the men who died with Jesus? What's to be gained by this—deception?"

Dr. Soames leaned forward and put his elbows on the table. "That's where I come in. Remember that passage I read from the *Pseudo-Clementine Recognitions*? The two brothers buried at night in Jericho? I've been haunted by that passage for years and this may explain it." He waited smiling for someone to ask. I couldn't stand it.

"Okay, Doc. You've got the floor. Spill it."

"I never connected that to the crucifixion until your call. See, I've believed for years that the early Christians felt awkward about the facts surrounding the resurrection. Why? Now I think I know. If the men crucified with Jesus were close associates, they were most probably buried with him."

"Well they were buried with him, Doc. I saw it."

He blinked with his mouth open for a second. "I beg your pardon?"

"Never mind. Go ahead."

"Yes. Well. If they were buried together and the tomb was found empty, the other two bodies had to disappear as well. Luke and John show some sensitivity to this as they both emphasize that no one else was in the tomb. Look at Luke 23:53 and John 19:41. Coincidentally, they are also the only gospel writers to mention Lazarus. But something was happening when the gospels of Luke and John were being completed that caused those writers to counter the implication that there were others in the tomb. I think the original tradition had three resurrections. Some scholars have been saying for years that the so-called transfiguration pericope was originally intended to be a resurrection story that became reordered earlier in the narrative. What we have now is a reworking to smooth over an awkward branch of the tradition and emphasize the uniqueness of Jesus' resurrection."

Kathleen laughed. It was phony. "Don't you think that's a reach?"

"So tell me Miss Wister. Where do you think the others were buried?"

"I don't know. Somewhere else."

"Who was the young man Mark says was in the tomb?"

"An angel I guess."

"Take a look at Mark 12:25 and 13:27. If it was an angel, Mark knows how to tell us it was an angel. In fact, Matthew says it was an angel. In Luke, who were the two men in the so-called empty tomb? Don't say angels, because Luke tells us there were angels announcing Jesus' birth. In the tomb, he says they were men. John says they were angels. You have to admit. There are difficulties."

"Well, I think they were angels."

"So you don't detect any awkwardness about just who was there in that tomb?"

"Not really."

"Okay. Then tell me about the other people Matthew says were resurrected."

"What other people? I don't remember Matthew saying anybody else was resurrected."

"Take a look at Matthew 27:52" She didn't try to look anything up. She just sat there looking at him. "Go ahead. Take a look."

She opened her Bible. "It's a little dark in here."

"It says, according to the NIV, 'The tombs broke open and the bodies of many holy people who had died were raised to life. They came out of the tombs, and after Jesus' resurrection, they went into the holy city and appeared to many people.' So who were these 'holy people' and who saw them?"

"I don't know and I don't see how it relates to the subject at hand."

"Matthew is trying to reconcile conflicting beliefs and conflicting facts. There were early reports of multiple resurrections. Matthew had to account for them."

"If that's true, why don't Luke and John have the same problem?"

"They do. They both insert a Lazarus story to illustrate their point. In Luke, it's a parable, the point being that the resurrection of Lazarus wouldn't be important. The real point is it's only the resurrection of Jesus that has the power to lead people to belief. In John, the resurrection of Lazarus is repositioned to the days before Jesus arrives in Jerusalem. They can't be raised together in John because Jesus has to have center stage at the pivotal point in history. John adjusted the time frame just like he did in the temple cleansing event. "Okay. Bottom line is this—"

Well naturally I had to clear that up. "Wait a minute, Dr. Soames. I don't remember seeing a temple cleansing talked about in John. Did I miss something?"

"You didn't go back far enough. John positions it as far from the crucifixion as he can. He places it at the beginning of Jesus' ministry. Take a look at John 2:13. Since the event was too firmly grounded in the Jesus story to be omitted, John simply *repositions* it to counter the suggestion that this disturbance was directly linked to the crucifixion."

Woodrow sat his empty glass on the table. "Okay doc. I'm not sure we're on track here but if this is going to take some time, I could use another scotch." Dr. Soames smiled and signaled the waitress. He cleared his throat and went on.

"The earliest reports likely said all three of these men were raised. This version got watered down to the point it wasn't recognizable but it was so firmly grounded that it couldn't be written out completely."

Kathleen snorted. "So you're saying God raised all three of them from the dead?"

"No. I'm saying I don't know what happened. But whatever it was, it involved the three men who were crucified together, and there's an early church document that says two brothers were unaccountably buried in Jericho at night. And I know that Matthew wants to counter the claim that Jesus' body was stolen at night."

Kathleen turned to Dr. Bloom. "What do you think about all this?"

"I'm afraid I can't help you Miss Wister. I'm Jewish. In our traditions, Jesus is not portrayed well. According to our version of the facts, he was held for forty days to give ample of opportunity for some supporters to come forward and testify in his behalf and no one came. I don't believe that version any more than I believe that he was raised from the dead. I believe he was executed by crucifixion and something mysterious happened to his remains. There's an early tradition, as Barry points out, that there was a mysterious night-time burial of two early Christians—probably martyrs—in Jericho. This could be where the bodies of the other men were interred after they were carried away from Jerusalem. At this point, it's rank speculation of course. Barring the discovery of some remarkable documents, I don't think we'll ever know."

Kathleen sat back in her chair and looked out the window. It was dark so she couldn't see anything out there but lights on the patio. I couldn't see any reason to stare at them, but that's just what she did. Dr. Soames tried to make small talk. But it really went nowhere. It looked like we were done, but it was too late to drive back to Oklahoma. So I decided, what the hell. Let's splurge. I'd never stayed at a really nice hotel. So we checked into the Fairmont. Woodrow and I shared a room and Kathleen got the room next door.

After Kathleen mumbled goodnight, Woodrow and I bundled up and went for a walk so I could take my headache therapy. We hunkered down in the cold watching our breath disappear in the Plaza lights.

"Well, what do you think, Buzz? Are we at the end of the line? Do you know who those other two guys were?"

"I know what our best guess is. I know my chances would be better if this were a multiple choice question. Anyway, however it pans out, I guess we'll know by Sunday midnight."

Out of nowhere Woodrow threw his big head back and laughed loud enough to be heard in Denver. "What the hell's got into you, you maniac?"

"Well, Buzz, it just occurred to me why the puppet sent you to see Augie in the first place."

"You got me in suspense Woodrow. I'm all ears. I'm sure as hell wondering about that since we started this road show."

Woodrow pulled his collar up over his ears and laughed again. "Didn't Augie tell us that our old man was crucified with Christ?"

"Yeah, and…"

"Ain't another way to say *old man*, 'elder?'"

Naturally I was took plumb off guard. Old Augie had pointed us in the right direction for the totally wrong reason. We dismissed the clue he gave us without giving it a second thought. You might know that had me and

Woodrow both laughing at Augie's accidental wisdom all the way back to the hotel.

We finished our walk without saying too much more. That night, I was back in Jerusalem. But I wasn't in the bubble. I was free to walk around the outside of the city. So I stumbled around all night long. I didn't see anybody, and nothing happened.

Saturday, March 3, 2007, a.m.

After breakfast this morning, we waited in the lobby while the hotel guy drove the Dodge around. When we stepped out to mount up, there was a heavy snow falling. Woodrow shaded his eyes and looked up. "If it's shitty like this all the way to Oklahoma, it will take us the whole damn day to get home, if we make it at all." Since I couldn't see the weather getting any better just because we stood there looking at it, I helped Kathleen into the cab and we headed south.

I-35 was in so-so shape, so Woodrow was able to do about fifty-five and still be pretty safe. Kathleen was all settled into the backseat with Bibles and stuff spread all around her, and I was fiddling with the radio trying to find a station that would give us some idea about road conditions between Kansas City and Weloka.

When I finally got some information, the news was good. A cold front was blowing through and it was cold as hell in Oklahoma, but the snow stopped somewhere between Emporia and Wichita. If Woodrow drives careful and the weather holds, we'll be at Betsy's by early evening.

Saturday, March 3, 2007, p.m.

It was on the way back that Woodrow got the idea that I should get everything down in my own words. So I been filling up these tapes and handing them off to Kathleen and she's been feeding me fresh ones. We're pulling into Betsy's now, so I'm going to break for a little bit. I'll get settled in and bring everything up to date.

Sunday, March 4, 2007, early a.m.

It's the last day on the countdown, so I guess it's the jitters, but I can't sleep. So I'm dictating here in Betsy's kitchen, trying to keep it quiet so everybody else can sleep; I'm a little tipsy and sentimental now, so if this comes out a little mushy, I'm sorry. When we got to the house, Betsy had left a note on the door. "Come on down to the Gold. Everyone wants to see you, B."

Well, after all the morbid shit I'd been thinking about and all the facts I'd been trying to reconstruct, and all the throat-drying dictation I've been doing, going down to "The Gold" sounded like a great idea. I mean that sounded like one of the greatest ideas I ever heard. I'd been trying not to focus on the possibility that I might be down to my last night on earth. I was playing around with "mind over matter" trick, you know? Every time that "fatality" deal would slip into my mind, I'd try to think about some-thing else, something pleasant like an all-night stop-over in Santa Fe when you can still see snow on the mountains and you feel good because you know you're driving the other way. That's funny isn't it? How whether you love the look of snowy mountains depends on which way you are driving. But you know how it is. If I tell you not to think about hubcaps for thirty seconds, how many times will a hubcap pop into your head?

But there it was, looking me square in the eye, so I asked myself, *Buzz, if this is it; if tomorrow is your last day on earth, what would you like to do tonight? Hell, I'd like to go down to the Gold and see my buddies.* Woodrow didn't need any persuading. Kathleen said she'd wait for us at Betsy's.

Even though Betsy's sister Cheryl done a good job of making Kathleen's hair look cute—she looked a lot younger, because Cheryl gave her a sort of pixie look—she still felt like she was ugly. When I heard her say that, it made me wish that Carl wasn't dead so I could kick the shit out of him for making her feel so bad. She was being too sensitive, though, because I thought she looked great no matter what. I decided I wasn't going to let her get out of it.

"Look here Kathleen, this may be hitting below the belt I know. But you really ought to come with. I mean, after all, tomorrow might be the end of Leon Butane. Could be I'm running out of time here. I'd like you to come to the Gold with me, and I don't have time to wait for your hair to grow back." I was serious when I told her that if I was running out of time, I'd like to spend as much of it with her as I could. That hit her guilt button dead center. She got teary eyed and said she'd come down to the Gold with us.

"What should I wear?"

"You can wear anything but a cocktail dress or a can-can and you'll fit in. I'm wearing just what I got on." My jeans was reasonably clean and so was the work shirt. They was both faded, though. I guess that's the style now anyway. Woodrow was wearing his overalls, a red flannel shirt, and Wolverines—those are boots if you don't know.

Kathleen took a few minutes to fix herself up, so Woodrow and I took a peek at the news. The snow storm we drove out of that morning was slamming the dog shit out of the whole Midwest. We was lucky to be getting away with just the cold.

When Kathleen came downstairs, I was thunderstruck. She was wearing tight jeans with the cuffs rolled up over her Laplander looking boots. She had a creamy colored sweater on. The way she usually dresses, you could tell she has a pretty face, but it's hard to really appreciate what a great figure she has.

She had one of those ski bunny stocking caps that covered up her pixie hair cut. I guess the way I stared embarrassed her because she blushed. Her embarrassment didn't hurry her none. She glided down Besty's stairs real slow, which gave me the opportunity to take a nice long look. And I did.

Woodrow went out to warm up the Dodge so Kathleen wouldn't have to get into a cold vehicle. While we waited, she came and sat next to me on the couch. She could have sat on the end, but there she was, right by my side. I was surprised and embarrassed to find I was tongue tied. After I cleared my throat, I was able to get some words out.

"Well, I've just got to say, Kathleen, that you look wonderful."

She smiled. "Can I ask you something?"

"Anything." I meant that.

"Would it be okay if I call you Buzz? I mean just for tonight. That's what everyone at the Gold will be calling you, isn't it?"

It seemed like the most natural thing in the world for me to reach out and touch her hand. I'd touched her before, of course. But that night she felt warmer and softer than any woman I ever touched, even warmer and softer than Debra. She didn't pull away like I thought she might. Right that minute I was kicking myself in the ass. What was I waiting for? Why didn't I give myself a chance? Maybe if I tried a little bit I could have got closer to her when I still had some time. But as it was, everyway I figured it was a dead end. "Kathleen, I'd love for you to call me Buzz all the time, not just tonight."

She took her other hand and put it on top of mine and we sat there looking at each other. I've got to be honest here. I'd been admiring Kathleen since the first time I met her. But that minute we were sitting there holding hands, I got real stirred up in a manly way. You know what I mean? Well if you're waiting for me to draw you a picture, forget it.

I could have sat there with her all night just like that. It would have been okay with me if the feelings of that second went on forever. This is going to sound hokey to you, but it was at that minute that I made my mind up. I wanted to go to heaven. If it was anything like being someplace with someone you wanted to be with, to talk to and, you know, to touch. If you could just have that feeling for eternity—well, that would be a heaven I could look forward to.

The Dodge horn honked, and we knew Woodrow was letting us know the cab was warm. She jerked her hands away like she got caught doing something wrong. I started to say something, but I figured she was right. Things was the way they was supposed to be. We didn't say nothing to each other. I held the door open for her and we stepped out into the cold.

When we got to the Gold, we could see that those hoodlums had it all decorated up for me. There was a big *'Welcome Back, Buzz'* banner stapled across the front of the place. When we stepped inside, everybody hollered "Boo-yah, boo-yah, boo-yah!" and clapped their hands like I was a rock star or something. I was plumb bowled over.

The lights was dim in there, and I was glad, because I'm pretty sure I was blushing, and I know damn well my eye was watering. Billy brought over my mammoth ivory eye. I tucked my cryolite eyeball into my coat pocket and I slipped the other one in place. There was another "Boo-yah," louder than the others. Everybody started slapping me on the back and complimenting me on being famous and having a new hairstyle and all.

I wanted to be sure Kathleen didn't get lost, so I kept her right there with me. Everybody was asking her name. I was saying over and again "Kathleen Wister, Kathleen Wister." I guess Billy was the first one to start calling her Kate, because, before long, that's what everyone was calling her.

I liked that. Kate.

We got the VIP table. Billy and Stu save it for special occasions. That night, they'd saved it for Woodrow and me—and Kate.

Saturday nights are always crowded at the Gold, but tonight it was packed and most of the crowd in there were vets and wives of vets and grown sons and daughters of vets and a few widows of vets.

Anyway, Billy went up to the mic and made an announcement. "Okay, you freaks, quiet down for a minute because I need to say something. You all know tonight we're here to honor a hell of a fighting man and a damn good guy. Let's everybody raise up a glass to our friend, Buzz Butane." There was another loud "Boo-yah." Then Billy went on "Tonight we're making it official. From now on, as long as the doors are open at the Tolosa Gold, March 3, is going to be Buzz Butane day." That brought the house down, and I got a man-sized lump in my throat. There's no way you could know what an honor that is. If you get a day named in your honor at the Gold, you aren't allowed to buy your own drinks that whole day. If nobody else buys them, they're on the house. There are only about twenty guys that have a day named after them. Five or six of them didn't get their day until after they died. Stu and Billy decide, and nobody knows for sure what your qualifications have to be.

Poor Kate had to sit there for about a half hour and listen while different people went to the mic to razz me or praise me or something. All this was supposed to welcome me back out of my coma, but I was feeling like it might be a sort of going away party in case things didn't work out.

After all the nonsense, Billy asked Woodrow and me to play something. Now I'm not a bad hand with a guitar, but I got a pretty good singing voice if I say so myself. Did you ever hear Tim Hardin? Well I sort of sound like him. Now Woodrow's a damn fine musician, but his singing is, well, kind of iffy, if you know what I mean.

But all that being said, we aren't afraid to perform and we're a pretty good team. So up we went. Now this sort of music thing ain't unusual. It happens every Saturday night at the Gold. You'd be surprised how many of us vets can play and sing a little.

Billy was sitting with Kate to be sure everybody watched his manners. She was looking up at me like she was seeing me for the first time. I guess she'd never seen anybody play the blues in person. Well, the first number we did was "Who Do You Love?" Everybody in the house knew that song, so they were all singing. Kathleen was looking all around her at everybody having a good time. She was smiling like a kid at Christmas. It looked to me like she was having a blast. Seeing her enjoying the crowd and the music was more than I could hope for.

Now and again, Betsy would come over and say something in Kate's ear, but Kate would just shake her head. I guess she was drinking Diet Cokes. While we were doing *Howling for my Baby*, I looked down and saw Kate with a glass of milk in front of her. At least I thought it was milk. What I found out later was that Betsy talked her into trying a White Russian. If you don't know, that's Kahlúa, vodka, milk, and ice. That was the first liquor Kate had in her whole life. She must have liked it, because she had two or three of them. Maybe more. I don't know.

After about four songs, Woodrow and I turned the guitars over to Tommy and Red a couple of our 1st Cav buddies. Everybody was shaking our hand and slapping us on the back as we made our way back to our seats at the VIP table with Kate. Just as natural as can be, she put her hand on mine. "This is wonderful! I mean it really is. I've never experienced anything quite like this. I'm glad I came."

I guess those White Russians loosened her up a bunch, because before the night was over, I had Kate on the dance floor. To be honest, she was pretty stiff and awkward at first. But after a little while, she let the music get into her and she let herself go.

Now here's a mystery for you. That woman had never danced a lick, But she took to it like a dove fledgling takes to the air. I mean she was doing things with her legs, hips, shoulders, and arms that looked like she must have been practicing in her head for her whole life.

You probably already know this, but when things are just right, the music's good, you've had just enough lubrication, the people around you are putting out good vibes, and you got a good dance partner, something magic happens. You sort of feel this happy connection with everybody in the place. And not just that. You feel sort of hooked up to every human being that ever lived who let himself dance in hard times.

The second that crossed my mind, Kate stopped dancing and just put her arms around my neck. She put her face on my chest and started crying. I knew it was time to go. Woodrow said to go ahead and take the Dodge. He'd ride home with Betsy.

TAPE 19

I naturally had to let Kate drive. I tried to make conversation, because I was dying to know what she was thinking. I mean up to that point I was getting stronger and stronger signals that maybe there was more to what we were doing than just chasing down a religious question. She wasn't saying much, though. She just drove.

Finally, she looked at me and said, "Leon, I need to ask you something."

"What happened to 'Buzz'?"

"I need to ask you something."

I didn't like the way this was sounding. But I was along for the ride. "Sure Kate—Kathleen. You can ask me anything."

"Will you be honest?"

"Well hell, Kathleen. What kind of question is that? We're friends ain't we? Of course I'll be honest."

She reached up in the dark like she was brushing something off her cheek. "I'm not your friend, Leon."

I was on full stun. "How can you say that? Look at all you've done for me? You didn't need to get yourself all mixed up in my nightmare, but you did. Sure you got faint-hearted there for a minute. But that's how friendships get tested. If they're still working after they get stressed real hard, you know they're for real." I could hear her sniffling.

"I've been using you."

"Well that's okay Kate—Kathleen. If that's true, we been using each other. I mean I been using you for a guide and interpreter and stuff like that. But that don't mean we're not friends."

"But I've been wrong, Leon. I've been using you for spiteful reasons."

I felt something breaking in my insides. "What kind of spiteful reasons?"

"Let's just drop it. I'm sorry I brought it up."

"Not on your life sister. You did bring it up and if there's something I need to know, now's the time for you to spill it."

She pulled the Dodge over on the shoulder and covered her face with her hands. Something told me I was in for a heartache. I sat there quiet and let her cry it out.

Finally, she got where she could talk. "I've been using you as a tool to embarrass Ernest Bidding. He's trying to discredit you to get even with me."

I was trying to add up the figures in my head and no matter how I did it, everything was coming out wrong. "You're just going to have to walk me through it, Kathleen, because I'm not following."

She grabbed the Dodge's wheel and shook it like it was all the wheel's fault. She had her another good cry. Then she settled down, took some Kleenex out of her purse, blew her nose and turned her back to the door so she was looking at me. She took a deep breath and reached out to take my hand. I let her. "Leon, I told you about my husband being gay. Well, it was Ernest Bidding that told me."

"So?"

"So, Ernest could have ruined him. He could have exposed him and fired him. But he didn't. He said he would look the other way to protect me. At first I didn't believe it, about Wendell being gay. When I confronted Wendell, he broke down. He admitted everything. He begged me to understand. He told me he couldn't help it. I couldn't believe what I heard."

She took her hand away and blew her nose again. I sat there waiting to see how all this was coming around to me. "I told Wendell to get out and he did. He kept his job with Bidding's ministry, but he was tiptoeing around like he was walking on egg shells. I couldn't stand being around him—or even seeing him. I didn't know until later that Ernest was holding it over his head like the sword of Damocles." I didn't have a clue what that sword deal was, but I didn't figure it was important to the plot, so I let it go.

"Ernest started sending Wendell on mission trips. I was glad for him to be gone. Then it seemed like more and more occasions came up where

Ernest and I had to be alone together. I thought he was doing all this for my good and out of kindness for Wendell. Then we had to go to a meeting in California, and I found out after we arrived there, that Ernest and I were the only ones there. I won't—I can't go into all the details, but Ernest was—he wanted ..." She couldn't say anymore, but I got the picture. I started to say something, but she stopped me.

"Let me finish, Leon. I need to tell you. I was so sorry about the way things were turning out; I told Ernest I couldn't continue working for him. He tried to stop me, but I insisted on leaving. When he saw that my mind was made up, he threatened Wendell. He told me how sorry he would be to expose Wendell, and he hoped it wouldn't come to that. I didn't know what to do, Leon. So I called Wendell and told him everything. He beat Ernest to the punch. He went public himself and resigned. He was ruined, but he did it to keep Ernest from having a hold over me. So I quit, and, God forgive me, I've been trying ever since to find a way to expose Ernest for the hypocrite he is."

She was tearing that Kleenex into little tiny pieces. "From the very beginning, I saw you as an opportunity to—get even I guess. I tried with Denise, but that backfired when Ernest was able to conspire with Denise's husband. So I've been fueling this conflict between him and you hoping he'd get his payback."

Well, you might know that when I heard all this, I was one pissed off son-of-a-bitch. I couldn't wait to get my hands on that hypocritical asshole of a Ernest damn Bidding. I was going to kick his lecherous butt from Mustang to kingdom come.

She sniffled a little bit and went on. "I took a gamble. If you were legitimate and could help Denise where Ernest had failed, I thought it might help take a step toward exposing him for the fraud he is. I really played it up Leon. I exaggerated everything. I ridiculed Ernest for failing where a humble trucker was able to produce a miracle. It was all from malice. I didn't spend any time at all thinking about how you might be hurt. Then everything snowballed. He accused you of doing the devil's work. That's when I got the idea of forcing him into a face-to-face meeting. He's always escalating things, so the meeting is being turned into a media circus. Everything's just out of hand and I don't know how to stop it now."

"Well hell, I'll tell you how to get it to stop. Tell him we quit. Tell him to forget it. Tell him we changed our mind. Tell him we're not playing anymore. He wins. Game over."

"It's not that simple, Leon. If we don't go through with it, you're ruined, I'm ruined. Bidding will trumpet it from the rooftops as proof that he has power over the devil. There's just no way to calculate how much spiritual harm he may do."

"That isn't really my problem, is it? Doesn't the book say to let the blind lead the blind? If folks want to follow a fella like that, more power to 'em. It's none of my business."

"But, in a way, it would be your problem, Leon. You'd be agreeing to let him use you for a tool. You'd be a knowing party to his misrepresentation."

"But whose tool am I if I go through with it? Tell me that. No matter what happens, I'm getting to be somebody's gol' dang tool. And who do I have to thank for that? It's you, isn't it Kathleen? All this time I thought we were partners—friends. Hell I even thought you were maybe developing—you know—feelings. Now I find out I wasn't nothing much more to you than a goddamn puppet you were jerking around for your own secret reasons. Great. Thanks Miss Wister."

Well, that did it. The flood gates really opened up then. Of course, I felt like a heel for making her cry more than she already was. Hell, I admit. I'm a pushover. I melted.

"Now come on Kathleen. It isn't your fault, really. None of us would be in this spot if that little puppet freak didn't take a interest in the only accident I ever had. It's okay. Really. Everything's going to be fine."

That's when she threw her arms around my neck. I just sat there and let her cry it out. When she was done, she looked up at me. It was real dark so I couldn't see her face.

"Can I ask you something, Leon?"

"Every time you ask me that, I always say 'yes.' Call me Buzz."

"Alright, Buzz. Do you think I'm pretty?"

I didn't even have to think about it. A second ago I was ready to black her eye, and now I'd die before I'd hurt her feelings. "I sure do Kathleen. You're about the prettiest woman I ever knew. If you won't laugh, I'll tell you something. Even if this deal doesn't work out and I don't make it, I'd do it all again just for the pleasure of knowing you for the last two weeks." She didn't laugh. Those words just hung around in the cab like steam, sounding and feeling real mushy like.

Then, like a flash, her arms were around my neck again. "Oh, Leon—Buzz. Everything's going to be fine just like you said. I can feel it."

"Well sure it is darlin'. Woodrow and I have been in lots tougher scrapes than this." I felt a lump coming in my throat. "Yeah, it's going to be fine. This time next week, you'll be back to your blogging stuff full time Ernest Bidding will be nursing his bumps and when you remember all this, it will be just like a funny movie or something. You'll forget all about me and old Woodrow before you know it."

She accidentally laughed and it came out like a little snort. Then we both laughed at that. "I don't think so, Buzz. If I ever have a decent hairstyle again, I'll think of you every time I get it fixed."

It was good for us to get out of the heavy stuff. It doesn't do any good to roll around in it.

We didn't say nothing else 'til we got to Betsy's house. We didn't say nothing when we got there neither. A couple of times she looked at me like there was something on the tip of her tongue. But nothing came out. There was lots of stuff on my mind too. But, I didn't see no point.

When we got to the head of the stairs, we mumbled goodnight to each other. I got undressed and laid in bed. I didn't have no interest at all in sleep. I didn't want to be in the light; so I turned it off. Then, I was feeling lonely in the dark so I turned the light back on. I just couldn't get settled. A time or two I got as far as my bedroom door. I stood there listening for noises from somewhere in the house. Nothing.

It occurred to me this might be a good time to pray. I felt like I'd done pretty much the best I could and it wasn't enough. But I couldn't. I figured God bent over backwards several times to keep me from getting killed or crippled in Nam while I was there. I kept saying over and over again *if you'll just get me out of this Lord, I'll be a new man, when I get back to Oklahoma. I'll quit cussin' and fornicatin'. I'll live by the Golden Rule. I'll make you proud if you'll just save my ass.* Course I didn't do none of it. Fact is, I was probably worse when I got home than I was when I left. So I figured it would be real low class for me to come crying back now. I figured the Lord would appreciate it if I'd not embarrass both of us and just take my medicine like a man. What I'm saying is, I wanted to pray. But I couldn't.

I heard Betsy and Woodrow drive up and I thought I'd talk to Woodrow when he came up. He didn't. Well, at least Woodrow and Betsy was putting a sweet touch to the evening. There damn sure wasn't nothing happening upstairs.

TAPE 20

Sunday, March 4, 2007, a.m.

I guess Kate had an undiscovered knack for drinking because she woke up Sunday moving around like nothing happened last night. Me and Woodrow was a little worse for the wear and tear.

From time to time we'd look at the TV, which was always tuned to CNN. Gasoline hit three dollars a gallon in California. The murder rate in big cities had jumped ten percent since 2004. And in Colorado Springs, a lady came out of a six-year coma three days ago. She talked to her family for three days, then she slipped back.

That was my wake-up call. I had to face the fact that we were down to the lick log here. You know where that saying comes from? "Down to the lick log?" Well I'll tell you. The lick log was the last stop a steer made on his way to the slaughterhouse. A log would be hollowed out and filled with salt. The steer would be allowed to lick up as much salt as he wanted. This naturally made him thirsty. He would then be allowed to drink all he wanted. This naturally increased his weight. This naturally allowed the rancher to get a few more dollars for that steer. So that's what I meant when I said we were down to the lick log. Last stop before the final destination.

Well, that's it. Everything's up to date now and I've laid out all the facts as best I can.

At a time like this, a fella' might get tempted to get sentimental. But, all in all I've had about as good a life as anybody. So, I guess that's it. Let's wrap it up and get the last of these finished. Over and out.

TAPE 21

Sunday, March 4, 2007, a.m.

I guess this would count as a debriefing about what happened after I finished dictating—when was that? Guess it would have been early on Sunday the fourth. Well, here's what happened after that.

I don't know how much of this you seen on TV, or if you seen any of it. But I guarantee you didn't see all of it because somebody monkeyed with some of the videos, and some of them just plain disappeared. So I will use this last tape to fill in the gaps.

It was raining like hell on Sunday morning, March 4, 2007. I'd been out of my coma for two weeks and it sure seemed like a lot longer. A lot of shit happened in those two weeks what with my escape from the hospital, my being on the run, my house getting burned, the riot at the church house, all those miracles, our chat with Teddy, our discovery of Carl's weak heart and Queenie's weak bladder, all the driving, all the pouring over all those books, all the surprises and weirdness, and now we were getting close to the end. Pretty soon I'd be standing in front of thousands of people to see if Reverend Bidding could chase the devil out of me.

I'd be the first to say that I didn't know what the hell was going on. But whatever it was, I didn't feel like I had any devil in me. But maybe that's how you're supposed to feel when you do have a devil. Maybe that's how Satan gets away with it. I mean there you are walking around telling people there ain't a devil in you while all the time it's not you but the devil doing the walking and talking and you don't even know.

I read a magazine once about a parasite that gets into a rat's brain and makes the rat believe he can kick shit out of an alley cat. So the rat squares off with the first cat he can find. No matter what the rat might think it ain't a fair fight and the rat always gets eat up. And it all happens because the parasite needs to be in the cat's gut to reproduce. So all the time the rat's looking for a alley cat thinking he's going to teach the cat a lesson, he's really being driven by a parasite that actually wants the dumbass rat to get eat up.

If there is a devil, maybe that's how he works. He gets you to do stuff because you think it's what you want. But really, the stuff you're doing is deadly to you and good for the devil.

Well it makes me dizzy thinking about it, because if that's the deal, we think we're at the wheel driving someplace of our own choosing when we really have no choice where we're going at all. So, hell, maybe there was a devil driving me and I didn't know it. I'd have to wait and see what stuff looked like when Bidding got through with me.

There wasn't much talking at breakfast that Sunday morning. On the way to Mustang, there wasn't any talking at all.

Woodrow pulled up behind the Tabernacle right on time and let me and Kate out in the rain. I held my jacket over Kate's head so she wouldn't get wet. It wasn't too bad for us because Woodrow got us pretty close to the back door. The parking lot was so full that Woodrow had to park a long way off. When I saw him running across the parking lot, I couldn't help but laugh. He looked like a drowned rat in a hurry to get to the showdown with a killer cat.

When Woodrow got inside the tabernacle, I laughed and he laughed. I wanted to say something, but I couldn't. He gave me a big old wet Woodrow bear hug "Don't worry about nothing Buzz. I'll see you when it's over."

We could hear loud singing and rock music playing in the auditorium. Debra the Twitty boys and some others swarmed over me and started putting make-up and shit all over my face. I brushed them away and told them I didn't need or want that crap.

Debra didn't look near as gorgeous this time. There wasn't no school girl smiles and fluttering eyelashes. There wasn't no invitations for me to peek down the front of her dress. She was all business, and I could see the muscles working in her jaws as we was getting close to show time.

Woodrow and Kate was following behind as I got rushed up toward the music and singing. We got to a curtain, and Debra stepped in front of me and put her hand on my chest while she peeked through the curtain. I could see over her shoulder. There were thousands of people with their hands up in the air waving them back and forth while they was singing.

The biggest group of people I ever stood up in front of, if you don't count graduation, was when Treena and I got married. There must've been sixty or so in the church, and on a scale of one to ten, my anxiety level was about six and a half. I wasn't panicky but I was nervous enough that it was uncomfortable.

While I was standing backstage there at the Tabernacle, my anxiety level suddenly hit around a nineteen. My palms got sweaty, and my old heart got to pounding like a M-60 firing ninety to nothing. It came crashing back on my brain that I didn't have a clue about what was about to happen. I really don't know what I was thinking up to that point. I guess I thought it would be like graduation when I'd walk across the stage, smile, shake hands, and then get the hell out of there. But I could see it wasn't going to happen that way at all.

Then a memory popped into my head about r-and-r at China Beach in Vietnam. Me and some buddies were out fooling around like we knew how to surf. We was ridiculous, though, because surfing beaches are rare in Oklahoma so there's no place to practice. I remember getting picked up by a big wave and tumbling like I was underpants in the rinse cycle. I was rolling around in that wave so long I ran out of air. I panicked. I started trying to swim. But it wasn't any use. For all I knew, I was trying to swim upside down and backward. It didn't matter though. I was going whichever way and however fast that wave wanted me to. At the end of that ride, that gol' darn wave smashed me face first on the beach and then flipped me over so hard I thought my neck broke for sure. When I was able to get up, all the hide was rubbed off my nose and my shoulder felt like it was busted.

Well, standing backstage there trying to get my breath. It seemed like I was back in that wave again. Hell, the voices out there even sounded like a wave. I just hoped I still had some working parts when the ride was over.

The noise started backing off and I could hear Reverend Bidding leading the congregation in prayer. I figured everybody in the place could hear my heart thumping. He was praying in that movie announcer voice of his. "Lord, let the Holy Spirit descend on this gathering and let the collective faith of this body of believers be sufficient to deliver a sinner from the grips of the evil that possesses him." There must've been twenty video cameras shooting me, him, the crowd. Everything. It got real quiet. I mean nobody even coughed.

Bidding raised up his hands and started speaking in tongues. I never heard that before but it's amazing how his holy speech sounded like gibberish to a sinner like me. Anyway, a breeze started blowing through the auditorium and almost everybody in the place turned into murmuring tongue speakers.

Debra took a hold of my hand and led me out on to the stage. I almost couldn't walk. Way back somewhere in the auditorium, somebody started singing "Amazing Grace," and that song spread like a wave at a football game. In a few seconds everybody, including Reverend Bidding, was singing along. It caused me to shiver all over.

Debra led me over to Bidding. He put his arm around me, and the singing got drowned out by cheers. I didn't feel tingly this time. I felt like I ought to be keeping one hand on my pocket. People was crying and hollering, "Praise God!" I was glad of the noise, 'cause my knees was knocking together real hard.

I sure hoped that hollering would go on a long time and give me time to get a hold of myself. I was still sweating and shaking when the singing and cheering stopped.

Bidding had his arm around me and said "By now everybody in America has heard about Leon Butane. Leon has been called everything from false prophet to Devil's disciple. But Leon himself has never claimed to be any of these things. Have you Leon?"

I cleared my throat, looked at my shoes and said, "No. I never claimed any of that."

"So why has Leon Butane generated so much media attention, so much excitement? Why have so many in this country and around the world been focused on the comings and goings of this man? Why are the passions of believers and nonbelievers alike aroused by the media's coverage of this man? Leon himself is crying out to know the reason why. He himself is powerless to explain why he, of all men, was chosen to be the center of so much contention and distress and—yes—even violence.

"Many of God's faithful have been brought to confusion trying to answer the questions that, by God's mighty arm, have brought Leon to this tabernacle. Brothers and sisters, what's going on? The Lord will reveal the answer to that question to all who have eyes to see and ears to hear, and this revelation will come before the passing of one more hour." He stood there letting that sink in and there was a murmuring from the congregation. Then he picked it back up.

"I tell you that before we leave here, the Holy Spirit will descend on this place like a mighty rushing wind and all those who are with us here in this sanctuary and all those who are joining us by television and all those who are with us in spirit will witness the healing power of God, and all who pray to receive it will experience the miracle of spiritual cleansing." There was some more murmuring. I couldn't tell if it was coming from inside my head or somewhere else.

There was a chair on the stage. Bidding led me over there and real gentle-like put me in it. He went on talking.

"Did the Lord not tell us that the good Shepherd will leave the ninety-nine and go seek the one lamb that is gone astray? What happens if the Shepherd stays home? Would the devil not use that one wayward lamb to sing a song of false freedom in order to lead the others into the wilderness? Does anyone think the devil lacks initiative? Does anyone think the devil lacks ingenuity?

"Brothers and sisters, the anger, sorrow, the envy, the confusion, and the hatred surrounding the recent life of Leon Butane are works of the devil. Our God gives a spirit of peace, security, fairness, steadfastness, humility, and most precious of all, Love. It is to exalt the devil that the spirit of negativity has been allowed to surround this man." He was standing behind me with his big hands on my shoulders. I saw cameras in people's hands and on cables moving. It was like I was hypnotized and couldn't keep my eye on any of them.

Bidding kept right on rolling like him and the crowd was feeding energy to each other. "Brothers and sisters. I speak a truth to you that has already been impressed on your hearts. The tree is judged by its fruit. Amen?" Everybody hummed "Amen" right back to him. He left me sitting in that chair and started roaming around the stage. Some of the cameras followed him and some stayed on me.

"Is healing the fruit of the Lord if that healing poisons the minds and hearts of the faithful? Is healing the fruit of the Lord if that healing results in the exaltation of the devil? Brothers and sisters I say to you that only those healings done in humility and done in the name of the mighty God are the true fruit of the Lord Jesus Christ.

"Now, behold the power of our mighty God. In his name I am commanded to release Leon Butane from the grasp of this demon. All this is done so that the world may know that there is one God who is the master of all creation, and all power for good is given by the grace of our God." He nodded to Debra backstage and she came out with three good-sized fellas I hadn't seen before. Bidding walked over to me, and I couldn't have been more nervous if I had been going to the electric chair. The place was quiet as a cemetery at midnight on Christmas Eve.

Bidding took my arm, and I got up on my shaky legs. Then those three guys took up positions behind me. Cameras was circling over our heads like buzzards. I knew everybody in the world was looking at me, and I noticed that Debra was making signs to the video guys. Reverend Bidding put his hand on my shoulder and looked me in the eye real hard. When he spoke, his voice was soft, but a battalion of mic's sent it all through the auditorium. "Leon, do you believe that Jesus Christ is the only son of God?" I've seen the tape and I'll tell you that what came over the loudspeaker ain't what I said. I don't know what my answer was going to be, because at that moment, I wasn't sure what I believed. But the fact is, I didn't answer him. Just the same, I heard a man's voice over the loud speaker say:

"Yes. I believe." If you watch that tape real close, you'll see I'm just standing there with my mouth open when them words come over the speaker. Reverend Bidding went on.

"Leon, do you believe that Jesus Christ was crucified for our sins and was raised from the dead so that we might have life everlasting?" Same deal. I'm standing there trying to figure out what to say. My lips never moved, but a man's voice from somewhere said:

"Yes." I could feel those guys behind me getting closer, and I felt a camera guy closing in on me.

Bidding went on. "Leon, do you believe with all your heart that God can deliver you from the spirit of wickedness that possesses you now?" Same thing. I didn't say nothing, but somebody did.

Then Bidding hollered, "In the name of the Lord God Almighty, I command all unclean spirits that are troubling the peace of our brother Leon to depart. DEMONS OUT!" And he thumped me on the forehead with the heel of his hand and it sent me stumbling backwards a little bit. That's when I got smacked by about 1000 volts of electricity that nearly jolted me off my feet. I didn't fall, because them three guys stepped up to hold on to me. I don't know why I didn't get spastic, but I didn't.

By the look on Reverend Bidding's face, you'd have thought he got shocked too. But only for a second. The three stooges pushed me back in front of him and he stepped forward real quick and commanded all unclean spirits to leave me alone. He hollered again, louder this time. "DEMONS OUT, I SAY!" and he smacked me on the head again. I fell back into the guys behind me and one of them grunted, snorted, and started making gargling noises. He fell on the floor kicking like he was having a fit or something. I almost tripped over him, but I got some cooperation out of my wobbly legs, so I was able to vault over the guy squirming all over the stage.

Bidding stood there with his mouth open watching his pal kicking there. By his expression, you'd have thought he was watching a snake in his oatmeal. When I looked at them other two guys on the stage there, you know what I seen? One of them son of a bitches was standing there with a gol' darn Taser! No shit! I guess he was fixing to tase me again when I tripped backward and he wound up accidentally tasing his buddy.

Anyway, there was all kind of feedback coming out of the PA system and I just stood there like a dummy looking from the guy on the floor twitching to Bidding and Debra, then to that other fella still holding that Taser. The camera guys were shooting pictures of me, Debra, Bidding, and each other. Debra hissed "Keep the cameras on Reverend Bidding, you idiots." There was a low roar starting up from the auditorium. It was like the microphone feedback and the crowd was trying to outgrowl each other. Debra stepped up to the guy with the Taser and took it out of his hand. Then she and Bidding started stepping toward me, and Reverend Bidding was stuttering and trying to say something that would get the demons out of me once and for all. When Debra reached out to touch me with the Taser, I jumped to the side to try to get out of the way of that thing, and one of the guys still standing on the stage threw a arm around me. Then, I'll be a son of a bitch if Debra didn't accidentally tase his ass. Down he went. Then there were two of them twitching on the stage floor.

That's when somebody screamed and the tabernacle bunch stampeded. People were pushing, shoving and squalling everywhere. Some of them were trying to get to the exits. Some of them were trying to get to the stage. Bidding and me just stood there looking at each other. I guess Debra got the Taser knocked out of her hand when that second fella went down, because she was on her hands and knees trying to get it out from under him.

I can't describe the look on Bidding's face. I guess it's the expression a guy has the instant after he realizes his parachute ain't going to open. Anyway, everything turned into real slow motion.

With a camera right there in his face a tiny drop of blood oozed out of Bidding's right nostril. It turned into a red line running down to his lip. His right hand took a long time to get up to his nose and his fingers left the red smear.

The way his eyelids started fluttering reminded me of the puppet's, and he said in a voice that sounded like one of those disguiser devices you sometimes hear witness use on TV: "Killll thh caammerraas!! Killl tthh caaammeeraaas!!" Then a little drop of blood showed up under his left nostril. About that time, Woodrow showed up and broke the spell.

"Come on Buzz. We've got to get the hell out of here before these Christians tear you to pieces." Then I realized that's what some of them had in mind. The one guy that didn't get tased got a hold of my arm and tried to stop me from leaving the stage. Debra came up with the Taser and reached out to try one more time to zap my ass. Woodrow pulled that last guy between me and Debra and down he went in a snorting, quivering heap.

We dodged around everybody and ran off the stage, while people swarmed all over Bidding with tissues and stuff trying to get control of his nosebleed. It looked like a pretty good one.

We hotfooted out of there and picked up Kate on our way to the back door. We ran through the rain following Woodrow to the Dodge. We jumped in wet as a whale's butt and headed east. Kate started to chuckle a little bit. Then her chuckle turned into a real grown-up laugh. Me and Woodrow was happy to join right in. Steve Winwood's "Freedom Overspill" was playing on the iPod. We decided that the best way to wind up a busy morning at the Tabernacle was to get some homemade meatloaf at the Weloka Diner.

Sunday, March 4, 2007, p.m.

Okay, here's how things wound up between me and the puppet.

After we made our getaway from Bidding's tabernacle, we headed straight for Weloka and hit the diner about the same time as the church crowd. We called Betsy on the way and she had us a table reserved by the front window.

We had a blast. We told everybody about them multiple Taser mishaps and Bidding's inconvenient nose bleed. I was pretty sure the Taser deal wouldn't ever make it to the video, but Kate, who was laughing right along with the rest of us, got the whole thing on her cell phone. We got copies. I can show you if you like. Ain't modern technology a wonderful thing?

Anyway, we had a celebration lunch with homemade meatloaf, buttermilk biscuits, mashed potatoes, candied carrots, and fresh-brewed tea. To top it all off, Betsy had apple cobbler and hand churned ice cream. The whole place was jammed, and every damn body got in on the celebration. I can't remember a time in my life when I was so happy. I mean, what a night I had last night. What a morning. What a lunch.

The way everybody was carrying on, you'd have thought the whole deal was over. But I knew it wasn't. Some time before midnight, I was going to have to settle accounts with the puppet.

We went back to Betsy's house to wait.

Kate sat on the couch with her hands clasped in her lap. Woodrow paced around looking out every downstairs window Betsy had.

"So how's this going to happen, Buzz? Will it be a dream? Will he show up here in the flesh—or wood—or whatever? What are we supposed to be expecting?"

I had a deck of Betsy's cards and was playing solitaire on the kitchen table. "I don't know Woodrow. I'm hoping the puppet gets occupied with some other poor, brain-damaged sombitch and forgets all about me."

Woodrow was looking at the horses through Betsy's kitchen window. "You sure you've got the count right? Today's the day?"

"I woke up on Saturday. He said it would be two weeks from Sunday. This is Sunday. He said time would be up at midnight tonight."

Kate spoke up. "Is there something else we need to look at? I just feel like we've overlooked something."

I wasn't having any luck at solitaire, and I was hoping that wasn't a bad sign. "I'm afraid if there's something to catch and we haven't caught it by now, it's going to stay uncaught."

So that's how we passed the afternoon. Kate sitting on the couch staring at a blank TV, Woodrow going from window to window looking out, and me losing hand after hand of solitaire.

When it started getting dark, everybody's nervous level went up. We could feel time closing in on us. I got tired of losing, so I threw the cards on the table. "I'm going up to my room to lay down a little bit."

Woodrow stopped pacing and looked at me all big-eyed with an expression I never saw on his face before. "I think we ought to stay together, Buzz. I don't want you passing out again when nobody's watching."

"It really don't make any difference whether anybody's watching or not. I've crashed by myself, and I've crashed with people around. When the call comes, I've got to go, and even if you're standing right there, it won't make any difference. But I might be able to rest a little bit if I'm not distracted by all your pacing around."

I could feel him and Kate watching me as I went upstairs. When I got into my room, I got all washed over by a desire to pray again. I really didn't want to die or slip back into that big dark zero of a coma. But I reminded myself I'd give up my right to pray when I didn't hold up my end of the bargain.

I laid down on the bed and sure enough, before you could say "Howdy Dooty" I was either passed out or asleep. I don't know which. But there I was sitting on the merry-go-round with Son again. He was grinning at me just like he did last time.

"Hey, Sarge, you still got that tiger eye on you?"

I reached in my pocket and pulled out the marble. "Sure, Son. I got it right here." I held it up so he could see it.

"Want to trade?"

"You don't need to trade nothing for it Son. You can have it."

"But I want to give you something for it, Sarge. Toss it on over." So I did. He caught it real easy and held it up to his eye. "Know what this really is, Sarge?"

"It's a tiger eye, ain't it?"

"No, that's just what people call it. It's really something else. Know what?"

"I don't know Son. What is it really?"

"It's asbestos, Sarge. The deadliest kind of asbestos there is. If it could get out of this glass and down inside your lungs, well, there's no telling how much damage it would do."

"I don't get it. How could that pretty little marble be dangerous? What are you trying to say, Son?"

He was still holding it up to his eye. "It's beautiful, ain't it, Sarge?"

"Yeah, it's beautiful, Son, but I'm not following. What's going on here?"

He stopped smiling for the first time and put the marble in his pocket. "I'm not taking this from you because it's beautiful, Sarge. I'm taking it from you because it's dangerous."

"I'm lost here, Son. I need you to explain."

"You've been carrying this around because you think it's pretty, but that's only because you don't know what it really is. That's all I'm saying, Sarge."

"Come on, Son, if you got something to tell me, spit it out. I'm running out of time."

"I don't think I'll be seeing you again, Sarge.

"But I said I got something for you—and I do. Here's what I'm trading you for this tiger eye, Sarge. I'm giving you forgiveness. I'm telling you everything is square between you and the Lord. I'm telling you he's waiting to hear from you. He wants you to know you can still pray if you want to. You always could."

When he said that, that soft yellow light started shining all over him and me both. I tried to reach out and touch him, but he disappeared.

I sat bolt upright there in the bed thinking *Holy Christ, I've fucked up royally!* It was dark and I switched on the lamp there on the table so I could see my watch. My heart sunk. It was after eleven. I didn't know how much time it would take to straighten stuff out. I charged downstairs and Kate and Woodrow both started my way looking anxious.

Kate was the first one to talk. "Is it over? Were we right?"

"No it's not over yet, and we screwed up. Their names ain't Simon and Lazarus."

Woodrow frowned. "Well, if they ain't Simon and Lazarus, who are they?"

"We got the right guys. We just got the names wrong. Remember that Jesus-Yeshua deal?"

Woodrow smacked his forehead. "Holy shit!" You're right Buzz. What we got is a Greek version of something else." He looked over at Kate. "How do we figure this out? How much time do we have?"

"If time's up at midnight, we have just under forty minutes. We have no time to waste. If you'll start the computer up, I'll try to reach Dr. Soames."

Those two turned into a blur of activity, and all I could do was stand there and watch. Dr. Soames didn't answer. Kate left a message and charged over to punch her password into the computer. She went to banging on the keys and right quick she said. "You're right Buzz. Look here."

I looked over her shoulder and saw that Lazarus is an adaptation of Eleazar. Kate was reading ahead of me. "Oh my. Look at this. Eleazar was the chief of the tribe of Levi. It may not mean anything, but remember Dr. Soames said the Barnabas who came up with the money from that unusual land sale was a Levite.

"And look here, when Moses died, Joshua was his successor. Remember, the Jesus-Yeshua-Joshua connection? But Yeshua was subject to the supervision of Eleazar. They ruled Israel together. Could it be that the Yeshua–Eleazar connection was being reestablished in the Yeshua–Eleazar partnership in

Jerusalem that Passover? Wouldn't that have been a powerful combination in the eyes of the Jews of Jesus' day if they were looking for a reestablishment of a godly Israel? And if that's true, if Jesus and Lazarus were supposed to be joint rulers, then wouldn't the Jewish authorities want Lazarus to die along with Jesus? Wouldn't that put an end to the movement?"

I could feel my teeth clenching. "Hurry. Get me a name for Simon." I could tell she wanted to slow down and make notes, but I was feeling time running out. "Hurry Kate." Woodrow crowded in so he could see too.

Kate gasped. "This Simon is a little unclear. It could be Simeon or something like Shimon. I just don't know. One of the Simons is the youngest son of a man named Mattathias. Looks like he was a war leader of the Jews during the Maccabean revolt."

I felt myself falling. I heard Kate saying my name. I felt Woodrow's hand on my arm. Then everything was black.

When I started coming around the room was dark. I knew there was somebody else in there. "Who's in here? Woodrow? Is it you, Son?"

"No Mr. Butane. It's me."

"Well, you're a punctual little bastard, aren't you?"

He put his little wooden hand out. He was holding the keys to Woodrow's Dodge. "Let's go for a ride. You're driving."

"I thought I wasn't supposed to drive no more."

"This is your last time. Come along." He clacked out through the front door and I followed him. I don't know where everybody was, but there were no lights and no sounds.

I didn't hear the other door open, but he was already sitting in the cab by the time I got in. "Where to?"

"Just find a highway and go." I backed out of Betsy's drive and headed toward the moon. It felt great to be driving. I never thought I'd have that experience again. There was something real pure about it. Like a cool drink of water when you're real thirsty.

Credence was singing "I Put a Spell on You" on Woodrow's iPod, the perfect song for the situation. There wasn't anybody else on the road, and I was happy, because I'd hate it if the last thing I did was bust up Woodrow's truck in a wreck with some innocent passerby.

We turned on Highway 99 and headed south. "Okay Buster. It's your show. Where do we go from here?"

"Just keep following this road, Mr. Butane. Do you know the names of the men crucified with Jesus?"

"No, I don't. I got some ideas. But I don't know for sure." We started picking up speed even though I wasn't pushing down on the gas.

"So, who do you think they were?"

"I think they were Jewish patriots, like some of the guys we met in Nam. I think they were willing to risk their lives to be part of what Jesus was doing. I think they were involved in rebellion and bloodshed, and I believe that's why the Romans executed them."

"Is that all?"

"No. I believe they was probably decent men who loved their families. I believe they were trying to do what they thought was right. And I think somebody sacrificed their good names because they were inconvenient to the people telling the crucifixion story."

"Anything else?"

"I think it's a damn shame the way they've been treated all these years. I believe they were good friends of Jesus' and he'd be real disappointed at what happened to their memory. I think they died for him and he wouldn't want them to be forgotten."

"Mr. Butane, you've allowed yourself to get quite emotional about two unknown men who died 2,000 years ago. Do you think you're projecting some private resentments of your own?"

"Well, excuse me, but I've been getting real emotional about a lot of stuff lately. That might happen if you come to the place where I'm at and can't get clear answers when you know the answers are out there somewhere." We was going faster and faster, and I was thinking, *This is the set-up to the crash that will end my last drive.*

The puppet didn't seem to notice we was flying way too fast for the road. "Those crucified men would be glad to know, Mr. Butane, that, after all this time, somebody is finally speaking out on their behalf."

"Yeah, well, me caring about it right now don't do them or me any good. Are you going to slow this thing down?"

"Just the same, they would appreciate the fact that you regard them as men of honor even though, to others, they're nothing more than thieves and robbers. Very well. The names. Give me the names." We must have been doing over a hundred, and I was sorry I was going to take Woodrow's Dodge with me here at the end.

"Okay, pine nut. Here's what I got. Jesus started the ball rolling in Bethany at the house of Simon the Leper who was really known to Jesus' followers as Simon the Elder. Some people called him "Simon the Cyrene" because that was his hometown. They could have called him Simeon or Shimon. He had a son named Lazarus who was important enough to Jesus' plans that the Jewish authorities wanted him dead right along with Jesus. Jesus-Yeshua called him Eleazar.

"They got their death warrants sealed either at the temple deal or the arrest. But Jesus, Simon the Cyrene, and Simon's son Eleazer were tried, condemned, crucified, and buried together. As for what happened after they was buried, your guess is good as mine, and that wasn't part of my assignment was it?"

"Hardly, Mr. Butane. Hardly. My compliments on unraveling some complex riddles. But I'm afraid you've fallen short. I'm sorry."

That soft yellow light was shining on the puppet. I figured it was the end of me and Woodrow's Dodge.

"Good bye, Mr. Butane." The truck left the road at Nehi Knob and sailed through the air. I thought, *Well, this is about as good a way for a driving man to go as any.* I thought I saw three crosses reflecting off the water as the truck crashed into the lake.

From somewhere way far off, I heard Kate crying. I felt Woodrow pushing on my chest hard off and on. I heard him say "Kathleen, call 911."

"No. Please don't do that. And lay off my chest Woodrow goddammit. You're crushing me."

He jerked me up like I was a doll, and Kate dropped beside me on the floor. They were both crying, and I did the only thing a guy could do under those circumstances. I hugged them both. I guess that's what you call a real redneck threesome.

"Help me outside will you. I'm burning up and I need some air." I leaned on Woodrow while Kate opened the door and we stepped out in the cold.

That's the minute I got reborn. I looked up at the stars there, and they were never more beautiful to my eye. While I stood there looking up, there were two shooting stars overhead. Woodrow and Kate didn't see them. But I did. You can judge for yourself whether it was somebody saying "thanks."

I promised right there that things were going to be different from now on. I was going to be a better man for the rest of the time I had left. I was going to do everything I could to let Kate know how I felt about her, and I was going to be better about looking after Wanda. I was going to be a better friend of Woodrow and the other guys, and I would work at being a better guitar player. I wasn't ever going to be ashamed to pray again, and I was going to think about tithing to some church—but I didn't want to do anything hasty there.

I gave a wave to the tails of those two shooting stars as they disappeared in the dark. I slept like a baby that night. No headache at all. The next morning, Kate got another email from Pinocchio. Not the real Pinocchio, but Wendell her ex-husband. I guess he was doing what he could to help us behind the scenes. So I figured I was obliged even if he was a fag—or a homosexual. Whatever.

We decided to celebrate me getting another chance to turn myself into a righteous man. We all drove over to the zoo together. We was sitting there at the picnic table when a lady went by with a baby stroller for twins. She had a boom box playing gospel music—to help the babies sleep I guess.

Anyway, as she walked by, the song playing on the boom box was "Give Me That Old Time Religion."

Okay. That's the end of these tapes. Thanks for listening. Buzz Butane signing off.

LaVergne, TN USA
11 August 2010
192906LV00003B/49/P